Blackcountrywoman

To Jackie

with love and best

wishes

Pete Ablaster

DEC 2010

Blackcountrywoman

Peter Arblaster

Matador
5 Weir Road
Kibworth Beauchamp
Leicester LE8 0LQ, UK
Tel: (+44) 116 279 2299
Fax: (+44) 116 279 2277
Email: books@troubador.co.uk
Web: www.troubador.co.uk/matador

ISBN 978 1848765 191

British Library Cataloguing in Publication Data.
A catalogue record for this book is available from the British Library.

Typeset in 11pt Palatino by Troubador Publishing Ltd, Leicester, UK
Printed in the UK by TJ International Ltd, Padstow, Cornwall

Matador is an imprint of Troubador Publishing Ltd

Mixed Sources
Product group from well-managed
forests and other controlled sources
www.fsc.org   Cert no. SGS-COC-2482
© 1996 Forest Stewardship Council

Acknowledgements

I wish to acknowledge my debt of time to my wife Hazel who has encouraged me for six years in my apprenticeship, the Bromyard Local History Society for their help, to Ann Richards for her impressive editing, and all the others who have put up with my cries for help.

Chapter 1

'The damned, rotten thing! That's the third time I've scraiged me shin this morning!' Elsie Stretton looked up at the tall man who had saved her from falling. 'I'm sorry, Dad. I know I shouldn't swear, but me shin 'urts!'

James Stretton looked down at his seventeen-year old daughter, a mock reproof on his face. The tall, lanky man loved the way she expressed herself.

'Let's sit down for a minute. There's plenty of time to get to Wednesbury. We can be there in not much more than an hour. Stand on this rock and you'll be able to see it. It's down there, see, where all the smoke's coming from?'

James lifted her gently onto the rock. They were standing on top of the heath that ran across the top of Hill Top, halfway between West Bromwich and Wednesbury. Elsie clapped her hands.

'Oh yes; I see it. It looks a dirty hole, Dad, don't it?' She stood on tiptoe. 'It'll be dark here soon, won't it?' Elsie held onto his hand lightly and jumped down. 'Look, there's a flower!'

Elsie reached down and picked the small buttercup, holding it up to show him. He took it gently from her and held it under her chin.

'You like butter; I can see that, Elsie.'

James's face became serious again and Elsie became anxious about the time. She knew that they had little chance of getting a bed and meal for the night if they didn't make swifter progress. Their journey had started in Birmingham at seven o'clock, this April morning of 1904. James was looking for work, any sort of work but preferably work in engineering, where he could use his skills.

Everything had seemed to get worse since they had lost Evelyn, her mother, to consumption, last year. Now James had a daughter to support and no one to look after her while he was working, if he found work. Evelyn had been the light of her father's life, the one who had put on a smile to cover any tribulation, who had made the dark in the sky turn to sunshine. That was the way he saw it, anyway.

Evelyn had lost weight in a few months, and her strength as well. Now she was gone. Elsie felt the tears well up in her eyes as she watched her father struggle with the grief that was ever-present on his face.

James turned his back to his daughter and started to stride out, easily leaving Elsie behind. He obviously needed a little time away from her, to think things out. He was losing weight. Was he worrying that he was going to be the next victim of the wasting disease? What would happen to her if he died? What action could she take to ensure her survival? Her hurrying steps made him look down at Elsie's anxious face.

She looked up at him and felt that she knew what he was thinking. He was always thinking of her and how to make things better. He had been the same with her mother. When he had come in, late at night, from the giant Soho works in Handsworth; his first thought had always been for the comfort of his Sweetheart as he had always called Evelyn. He had been a millwright, looking after the shafts, belting and machines that produced the products for a thousand trades. He had always called himself an engineer.

Now, after an argument with a gaffer, he was out of work. His pride had cost him his job but he still retained his experience. Many men fell out with employers but were still taken on at other factories. James had high expectations that he would be able to fit in somewhere but maybe nowhere near Handsworth.

He reached and took Elsie's hand as they started down the long sloping road that led towards Wednesbury. The air seemed to take on a different taste as they descended, becoming more acrid due to the waste gases that were expelled during the various production processes. It was also starting to get darker, the sun hiding behind great clouds. Elsie walked closer to him, as if by so doing she would be more secure.

James was aware that his young daughter was growing to maturity and it was another thing that frightened him for the future. She was as tall as his shoulder now and her legs and bosom were taking on the shape of adulthood. She was impetuous at times, like her mother. He loved her for it and sympathised with anyone who argued with her opinions.

They came to the bottom of the long incline and started to climb again. There were more buildings now and a railway to their left; they could hear the locomotives noisily shunting. If only he had bought two tickets from Birmingham. They would have had less money in their pockets, but they might have had an earlier start to their search for somewhere to stay. There was no sign of anywhere to eat. Was everything hopeless? They were almost at the top of the rise. James stepped to one side as a woman came past them. An impulse made him speak.

'Excuse me.' The woman stopped and turned back to look at him and he spoke hurriedly, speed showing his nervousness. 'I wonder if you know anywhere a decent man and his daughter can find somewhere reasonable to eat and sleep while I look for work?'

He was amazed he had been able to speak as well. The petite woman turned further to him, her full attention on him.

'Are you the decent man?' She asked him the question with a small smile on her lips. 'I can put you up for a night or two at a reasonable rate, if you don't mind that it's not posh, just very ordinary. The good Lord tells us to take in strangers; they may be Angels in disguise; we'll see! Come with me, child.'

The woman reached for Elsie's hand and started marching back along the way they had come. James followed, a bemused look moving across his features. She was a strange woman! Nevertheless he followed her, feeling that neither he nor his daughter were at risk. Somehow, the strange woman seemed to exude a quality of trustworthiness and compassion.

They turned off to the right and he could just see in the darkening light that it was Union Street. She turned off again, up a narrow alley that led to a small yard where a number of tiny dwellings faced onto it. During the few minutes they had been accompanying the woman, she had not spoken. She moved across the yard where some small boys were playing, and opened the door of a small house. The woman turned and spoke.

'Come along in, straight through the front room, into the back kitchen. What's your name, young girl? Have you come far, today? Are you from Birmingham?'

The woman turned again without waiting for an answer and led the way through. The tiny room at the back of the house contained everything she needed to survive. James stood, his cap in his hand, not knowing what was expected of him. He was weary, as weary as he had ever felt. If this strange, eccentric woman had not offered them food and lodgings on the spur of the moment he would have been at a loss to find food. He had seen a few shops along the main road, Upper High Street it was called, but it was Sunday; none of them were open. The woman spoke again.

'Sit yourselves down, if you please.'

James sat precariously on the edge of the slightly rickety settee and relaxed. He was exhausted. This day seemed to have been one of the longest he could remember. He leaned back against the cushion; the temptation to close his eyes too much. His breathing became slower.

'Will you get me some water from the pump, young woman?' Elsie jumped. 'It's just in the yard. Can you do that? What's your name? What's your father's name?'

Elsie was amazed that the quiet woman had suddenly come to life. Four questions, all at once.

'Elsie,' she replied, 'and my Dad's name is James Stretton. He's an engineer.' He had always told her that. 'I'll get the water.'

Elsie reached for the large cast-iron kettle and carried it out into the yard. The boys were still playing there. She reached to lift the kettle up to the spout but couldn't make it; it was too heavy, no matter how hard she tried. She was just too weary.

''Ere y'are, cock; I'll do it,' a voice said, suddenly. The kettle was taken gently from her hand and she saw the boy lift it with ease and smile at her. 'See?'

He held it up as another boy swung on the long handle, sending large spurts of water into the kettle. Inevitably some of it splashed onto her dress, wetting it. Still, it was filled, that was the main thing. Elsie spluttered her thanks to the laughing boys and carried the kettle into the house where her father, seeing the way she was struggling, relieved her of the weight and hung it on the large, forged hook over the fire. Then he settled back into the cushions on the settee and Elsie did the same, her eyes closing almost immediately.

There was a lovely aroma in the air when Elsie awoke; a lovely smell of bacon and eggs. She looked at the clock. She had been asleep for over half an hour. The strange woman was standing over her with a large sandwich in her hand.

'Here you are, young lady. Get this down your neck. There's more if you want it but it looks as if you need rest more than food.' She put the sandwich on a page from a newspaper and placed it onto Elsie's lap. 'Wake your Dad up. I'm coming back in a minute with his.'

The woman disappeared into the back kitchen. Elsie sat up and pulled at her father's sleeve, gradually waking him. As he awoke he sat up and looked around. 'Where's the lady? Has she given you that sandwich?'

'There's one coming for you, as well, Dad,' Elsie told him and, as she spoke, the woman came in. She smiled and placed the sandwich into his hand and disappeared, only to return with two large mugs of tea. A moment later the woman was sitting by her father on the settee with a cup in her hand. She didn't seem to talk much, until she had questions to ask, Elsie noticed. The time went by until the food and drink had all gone and then the woman turned to Elsie.

'Now, young lady, you should be feeling better, now. How about you, Mister Stretton? You're a quiet man, aren't you? Still, I suppose you've had your mouth busy with other things! You must have been hungry! In case you are wondering, my name is Mary, Mary Bowyer. I am a spinster of this parish, you might say. This is the first time I have taken in a couple of vagrants. Still, it is Sunday and we should try to do good works on a Sunday, shouldn't we?'

Mary looked at the pair of vagrants and they all started laughing. James replied,

'I've never been called a vagrant before, Missus Bowyer. This is a new experience for me, and for Elsie. We've always been in work until a week ago, when I told a gaffer that he was doing a job in the wrong way. He knew I was right but he couldn't bring himself to admit it. Still, it was just as much my fault as his. I should have kept my mouth shut but I didn't want to see him make a fool of himself. I don't suppose he thought of that when he gave me the sack.'

James lapsed into silence, drinking the last of his tea, while Mary bustled about, putting the plates away, watched by Elsie.

'Please Missus Bowyer, can I wash up? It's the least I can do to help.'

'Look, child; you don't have to call me Missus Bowyer. The good Lord gave me the simple name of Mary when I was baptised and I shall be happy if you use it; that applies to you as well, young man! I don't believe in privilege and I'm not going to condone it in my own house.' She turned back to Elsie. 'Yes, you can give a hand in the house if you want to. It would be a help. You don't mind, do you, Mister Stretton?'

The woman turned to face James but he was dozing again. She touched him gently on the shoulder and he started.

'What? I'm sorry; what did you say?' James stopped and Mary repeated her words. 'No, I don't mind. She's a good girl, my Elsie, but what I really need is some work for myself and Elsie as quickly as possible. My pockets are really getting quite low now. Do you know of any chances of a job, Mary?'

Mary sat and looked him in the face. She could see from his expression that he was speaking in earnest. Her reply was in line with what they had come to expect, direct, thoughtful and to the point.

'Yes, I do know of a chance, not a guarantee, you understand, but a chance.' The man and his daughter gave her their full attention as she spoke. 'Fred Stone at the High Bullen has got what he calls a rectification job to be done on some iron bars. If you go and see him and tell him that Mary sent you, he might give you a start, for a day or two.' She paused for breath and then went on. 'If you go back to where we first met and then carry on up Upper High Street, you will come to the High Bullen. Look for the name, Fred Stone, over the door. If I know Fred, he's probably still working. He asked for the work but he's not at all sure he will be able to put them right in a reasonable time.' Mary closed her mouth, evidently having said all she wanted to on the subject. Then she found a last thing to say. 'Whether or not he gives you work, there'll be a bed for the night for you. The door won't be locked. I'll see you later, Elsie; Mister Stretton.'

They were dismissed. All they had to do was find their way in a strange town, impress a stranger with their abilities and they would have work for a few days. James put on his large coat and helped Elsie with hers. So far, it seemed that fate was finally on their side. It was dark in the small yard and they felt that unseen eyes were watching as they passed through the court, up the alley and turned up the incline towards Upper High Street. In a few minutes they were at the High Bullen, looking for Fred Stone.

A light shone from behind a large door and over the top was the name, F. Stone, Smith. Noises of activity came from within. Elsie pushed the door gently and it opened with a small screech. She moved forward into the dark space inside, where there was a forge with a man working at it. He was pumping the bellows to bring heat and life to a small area of coke. He picked up a long bar which lay at the side of the heated area of cokes and plunged it into the small, bright yellow flaming mass. The man, Elsie noticed that he was exceptionally broad, carried on pumping to heat the bar. She could see that it was going to be hard work. The man had to work on the red hot bar and keep the pump pushing hot air into the fire at the same time.

Impulsively, Elsie moved forward and took the bellows handle from his hands. Stone stood amazed as she moved the long handle up and down and his mouth moved as if to say something and then stopped when he saw James step forward out of the shadows to pick up the seven-pound sledge hammer. Quick to take advantage, Fred Stone snatched the bar from the fire and put it on top of the anvil.

Clang! The hammer came down and bent the length of bar. Clang! Down it came again. The man picked up a punch and placed it carefully on the heated mass of iron. James stepped forward and down came the hammer again, creating a hole in the bar. Fred Stone picked up a bolt and tried it through the punched hole. It was tight, too tight. He placed the punch back into the hole and gave a quick nod to James. Crash again. The metal was cooling fast but the blow had done its work. Stone put the bolt back into the hole; it was a good fit. He finally spoke.

'Good man. Thanks; and you, young woman. What are you doing, walking into a man's forge and taking on work that has nothing to do with you?'

Stone was working as he was talking, doing everything in carefully measured movements. Putting another bar into the fire, he nodded at Elsie. She slowly started to move the bellows handle up and down. Fred Stone was not looking at her; he was looking at her father. James started to try to explain.

'We're staying the night at Mary Bowyer's and she said there might be a chance of some work for a day or two if we came to see you. It does look as if you could do with a bit of an 'and, don't it?'

James smiled. There were about two hundred of the long bars lying in a pile on the floor. They had all been made without the joggle, the small double bend near the end of the bar. Nor was there a hole in the end for a hinge pin. Stone smiled back at James.

'Well, you do seem to know your way round a forge and

I could, as you say, do with a bit of an 'and. You look as if you've got a bit of a story to tell. Come on. Let's knock off now. I don't need to work until the early hours, not now I've got an 'elping 'and. Mary is my friend and she's forever doing good works. It certainly looks as if you were Heaven sent this time. I'll see you at seven in the morning Mister…?' Stone hesitated.

'Stretton, James Stretton. Thank you for the chance, Mister Stone. I'll be here. Can you find something for Elsie to do, do you think? Missus Bowyer has said she can help her in the house but she won't be working there all the time.'

He felt suddenly weary again. What a day. After a long, harrowing day they seemed to have landed on their feet! Stone was speaking again.

'If you get here before me, James, the key will be under the brick outside the door. I think we can find something for your young girl to do, if it's only pumping the bellows. She seemed to know what she was doing, anyway.'

He turned away, slightly dismissive; he the employer, they the workpeople. James looked round the forge with its pattern of tools hung around the walls, hot and cold sets, fullers, hammers and tongs of all sizes and shapes. A place where things in iron were created, not just made; a place where he knew he could be happy to work.

James, too, turned his back, to face his daughter. It seemed to him that the grace of God had lightened their path today. He had heard of people who took seriously the Bible stories of helping neighbours before, but he had never met one who took the message so literally.

He reached out his hand to Elsie and they went out of the door. There was still the rate of pay to be discussed but he knew that whatever he got, it would be better than the nothing they would have received if he hadn't spoken to Mary. The night was dark in Wednesbury as they made their way back to Union Street. The idea came to him that if anything happened to him, Mary Bowyer might be the person to look after Elsie. It was a comforting, disturbing thought.

Elsie was happy to have her hand secure in her father's. Her mind had been constantly worried by thoughts of starvation, sleeping rough and her father's apparently failing health. The thought of coming home from the forge to a cooked meal delighted her but also made her feel she would suffer more from the lack, when it came to an end. She was suddenly grateful for the luck that had landed them on Mary Bowyer's doorstep.

Their short sojourn with Mary was like a foretaste of Heaven. Mary Bowyer had lived on her own for many years and having Elsie to stay revitalised her sense of motherly feeling. Within a few days, the woman and the young girl developed an affection close to love.

Sometimes, Mary would demand from her brother that Elsie be given time off to help with her housework because Elsie loved to clean the house when Mary was out, on business, as she called it. The house came to life as Elsie polished the hand-made furniture and scrubbed the pine kitchen table. Always scrub with the grain, her mother had taught her. The table seemed to become new as it dried and the grain was revealed in long, white, narrow stripes. The brass ornaments round the fireplace gleamed after the polishing she gave them and the cast-iron fireplace itself became a gleaming blackness that reflected the little sparkles from the other polished odds and ends in the room.

The work dragged on at the forge. The additional work from Fred's brother, Albert, had put Fred Stone behind with his normal activities and the two men were kept busy trying to catch up all the time. A week passed before most of the long bars had been bent and punched to the original specification.

There were about two tons of iron there, James Stretton estimated; just about a decent load for a good horse. What would they do now the job was finished? He could see that, although Fred might be busy by himself, there would not be sufficient work to support two men. James was enjoying the exercise and feeling fitter. It wouldn't last. What new obstacle would be put in their way? He shook himself, trying to lift the mood of depression that seemed to surround him lately.

Chapter 2

A Little Rest
April 1904

It was Good Friday and the work was almost finished. Elsie and James now had a long weekend to relax before they had to load the cart and drive to Willenhall. There was a market on Saturday and Mary was describing it.

'There's always the chance of finding a real bargain. I love market day. Perhaps, Elsie, you would like to come with me?'

Elsie agreed so the following day Mary and Elsie visited the market which was laid out along a quarter of a mile stretch of the High Street. There seemed to be hundreds of people there, almost as many as Elsie had seen at the Bull Ring Market in Birmingham. She linked her arm possessively into Mary's and they set off up the slope. Mary had given Elsie a shilling's worth of coppers to spend and, so that she wouldn't have too much cash in one place, Elsie hid the coins around herself, some in her little cotton, string-necked bag and the rest spread into different pockets for safety.

The sun was shining as a prelude to the Easter festival which would take place in the local churches and chapels and there was a genuine holiday atmosphere. The stalls were selling brightly coloured hair-ribbons and hats for the better off and imitation gold and silver jewellery to tempt the ladies, while for the men there was hairdressing oil, ties, scarves and hats of all sorts; stovepipes and bowlers; straw hats and caps. There were crocks and tools, clothes and shoes, a wonderful display that all had to be packed away if not sold by the end of the day.

Elsie was entranced by the colour of the displays and wanted to spend her shilling as fast as she could, just for the pleasure and feeling of being able to spend. She eventually settled, after consultation with Mary, for a pair of sparkling green earrings. Mary said they matched her eyes. They had a glass of lemonade at about three o'clock.

There was a juggler who could throw five balls into the air at a time and a stripped-to-the-waist, muscular man who you could tie up with chains and would get out of them in seconds. There was another man who, amazingly, could make money appear and disappear before your eyes.

Three o'clock came and went and they found themselves still there at four o'clock. It was time to call an end to a wonderful day. They bought a bag of pork scratchings each and chewed into them on the way home. When they got there, James was asleep in the armchair. They shushed each other until the sound of their shushing woke him up.

'What time is it?' he asked noisily. 'Where have you been?'

He put his head back on the cushion, asleep again. Mary and Elsie stared at each other and then burst out laughing. Saturday had been a wonderful day for fun. Tomorrow was Easter Sunday, full of pomp, ceremony and doing the right thing.

They made tea between them and woke James to eat it. He was a bit grumpy but the day of rest had done him good and tomorrow would do him more. He was looking more relaxed, with fewer lines showing on his face now, as if the world wasn't such bad a place to live in.

Sunday was a sunny day and James agreed to come with them to church. They were among the early arrivals and sat with other people who knew Mary. The vicar made a long sermon about the graciousness of giving. When he finished, the organ was supposed to strike up a strong hymn but the young boy who had the job of pumping the organ had gone to sleep and had to be woken to bring the organ to life with the long pumping movements of the handle. That started them giggling and the mood seemed to take half of the congregation, with the other half looking on, disapproving.

Lunch was served on a help-yourself basis, as Mary called it, and they each took turns at helping the others. Fred Stone came back with them from the church and stayed with them until the evening. He had a bagful of beer-bottles which he seemed anxious to share with James. It looked as if he had been pleased with the work that had been turned out by the small team.

Everyone seemed to have benefited from the day's rest from work and there was still another day off to come. Easter Monday was a day spent slowly, in church, but they all attended with good grace. There was a lot to be grateful for. Tuesday was different again, back to work. Elsie was up and about early with her father. Fred was at the forge when they turned in, and had brewed tea in a bucket, with a stick of wood floating on the top, to keep the taste of the smoke out of the tea.

'Come on, me little darling,' he said. 'I hope you've recovered your full strength now you've had a holiday!' He looked across his anvil at her and placed his fuller onto a red hot bar. 'When I nod my head, hit it!'

Elsie smiled at the old joke and pretended to heft something heavy to hit the fuller.

'I can do it, Mister Stone; just don't move, that's all!'

They all laughed at the posture she struck, with an imaginary hammer in mid-air. It was time to buckle to again but they were still able to get a laugh from life. James was looking better for the rest, Elsie thought, even if he was yet a bit skinny. Elsie still had fears about whether he would return to full health or be brought down by the consumption.

The forge was cold from the few days' disuse. Fred had arrived early to get the fire burning but there was little urgent work to be done so they moved the long flat cart outside ready to be harnessed up to the Shire horse that Fred Stone's brother, Albert, would send. It took them half the morning to load the cart and when it was done they sat down for tea and a sandwich.

'Mary said these were your favourites, Mister Stone.' Elsie spoke up to fill the silence that sometimes descended on them. 'She got the pork from the market on Saturday and made the stuffing out of her own head, she said to tell you.' Elsie suddenly realised the mistake she had made and tried to rescue her words with a joke. 'I don't know if it was the head you wanted hitting when you nodded!'

The two men burst into laughter at her strange gaffe, and she joined in. She looked up a moment later to the sound of hooves from outside and the sound of a low voice talking to the horse and then a young, red-faced youth entered the smithy.

'Good morning, Uncle Fred.' He spoke without looking round as he walked in. 'Father wants to know if the bars have been done, and if they are, how I'm going to get them home.' The youth walked looked round and saw the strangers. 'Hello,' he said. 'Who are you two? Where's Mister Stone? Have you got permission to be in here?'

Fred Stone walked out of the shadows and took the youth by the hand.

'Hello, Stephen. These two good people are the ones responsible for putting right the mistakes that your father has asked me to rectify. Have you brought the horse? Good. There's still a few bars to be put right so you can give us an 'and with 'em, can't you?' He took three bars from where they had been leaning against the wall and plunged them into the cokes, sparks flying across the forge. Then he stood and waited patiently as the metal heated to a dull red. 'Come on, off with your jacket. You'll soon get warm when we put these three bars right!'

There was something about the way he said the words that made Elsie wonder if it was Stephen who was responsible for the mistakes in the bar. At first she thought Stephen might refuse to strike for his uncle; then he picked up a five pound hammer and stood ready. Elsie moved over to the long bellows handle to be ready to pump it and get a better look at the nephew. James had his hand on a seven pound hammer, just to be ready. The nephew was tall, broad and well-dressed. Elsie thought he might think he was too good for such physical activity, as if it were beneath him. The bars were bright red now and Fred pulled one out and held the fuller on it to give it its shape. He looked at the two facing him.

'I'll use both on ya! Are you ready?'

Fred didn't wait for an answer, he just put the end of the bar on the anvil and placed the fuller in position and nodded at James. Crash! There was a shower of sparks as hammer met fuller and fuller met metal. As the heavy hammer moved back into the next swing, Fred nodded at Stephen. Crash! The five-pounder came down with a splash of sparks. A few repetitions of this and then the bar was put back into the glowing cokes and the next one taken from the fire. In an hour the whole job was complete.

The two strikers stood sweating, looking at each other, James with the heavier hammer looking as if he had just put a pen down; Stephen breathing heavily.

'How do you do that?' Stephen's breath was still ragged in action. 'You're older than me and yet you seem to be able to do it easily.'

James replied quietly. 'The trick is to use your arms for lifting the hammer, not for forcing it down, you know. It's easy to wear yourself out, lifting up and banging down; doing twice as much work as you need to. Let the hammer do the work; that's the trick.'

Elsie had moved herself into a position where she could get a better view of Stephen. The fire flared as Fred tidied it up and then she saw the young man's face as he saw hers. He was tall and would fill out as he matured; that was plain. He smiled at her and his smile seemed to capture her. Elsie gasped and felt an irresistible weakness, as if she had never seen a young man before.

Stephen too, was held enraptured by the shadows and light from the forge playing across Elsie's features. He knew he would have to possess her one way or another.

The moment passed and the fire died down, leaving Elsie with a strange sense that it had all happened before, like renewing an affair with a lover from the past. The horse neighed outside, calling for attention. The work was waiting to be moved to Willenhall. The two older men looked at the young man and woman and smiled at each other; they had seen it all before; the look, the sharp intake of breath; the slightly bewildered, smiling expression. Fred determined to interrupt them before impossibilities became possibilities and then probabilities.

'Come on, you two. Mary will have some snap ready before we start out. That'll make the journey go easier. Stephen, James, get the horses harnessed up. Elsie, go and tell my sister that we're on the way down to her. I'll lock up and come and join you. I shan't be using the forge again today.'

Elsie turned and ran along Upper High Street towards Mary Bowyer's, followed by the eyes of both her father and Stephen Stone. They each wondered about her future with some hope and some trepidation.

Mary was expecting the small work force's arrival and had prepared a good lunch. It was soon consumed and they started to get ready for the journey to Willenhall. There were not many items to taken with them, just a few clothes.

'I'm going to miss you both,' Mary said to Elsie. 'I feel as if I've known you forever.'

James looked across at them and took his courage in his hands.

'Yes, I'll miss you too, Mary. Who's going to cook us the sort of meals we've had here?'

He blushed, not being used to small conversations.

'Aunt Mary,' said Stephen, 'father would like to know when you're going to make a visit to us. You could come with us! It'd save the fare if you did, then you could come back when you felt like it. Mother'd be pleased to see you as well.'

Fred looked at his sister, wondering what was going on in her mind.

'You wouldn't have to worry about me,' he said. 'I'm sure I can manage for a few days.' He looked at her again and could see the want in her face. 'There, that's that settled then. Bring yourself a few clothes; if you run short you can pick something up out of the pile.'

'I will! I will come. It'll do me the power of good to see your mother and father! I do miss seeing them, you know. Just give me five minutes and I'll be ready.'

Elsie watched her dash to the house and wondered how much influence on her decision had been supplied by herself and her father? Whichever, it would be good to have her along. She had learned to love the older woman in the few days they'd had to get to know each other. She suspected that her father too, was captivated by her. Soon it would be time to part again. What 'pile' was Mister Stone talking about?

As she stood, Mary came dashing out of her small house. She turned and locked the front door, then hurried along the dark alley to join them.

'Come on then. Let's go!'

The enthusiasm of the little woman was infectious and they all stepped out to the forge where the horse, harnessed to the cart, was standing patiently, eating from his nosebag. It was a pleasant start to the journey, just a slight incline and then onto the flat road that led from Wednesbury to Willenhall. The horse seemed to be enjoying the journey too, walking along at a leisurely pace.

Two hours later they were there, passing through the market area of the small Black Country town. The Stone's home was only a quarter of a mile on and they turned in to the yard at the back of the shop with great relief. As they pulled to a halt, a man came to the back door and watched them. It was obvious that he was the owner, Albert Stone. He shouted out as he saw them.

'Hello Mary; what the devil are you doing weighing that cart down with all that extra weight?'

He stood there laughing as Mary climbed down from the high seat.

'Let me tell you, Albert Rotten Stone, you take up more room on the scales than I do, so there!'

Albert held out his arms and helped her down from the step. It was obvious that they were good friends. The day was a happy one and everyone seemed intent on making the most of it. James sighed with relief. A chubby woman came out of the back door of the shop then, and squealed.

'Mary! Mary Bowyer, as I live; have you come to stop with us? What a lovely thing to do. I never thought you would trust yourself to my little Stephen to drive you here. I hope our horse is all right.' She looked round for her son and saw him removing the harness from the horse. 'That's a good lad. I like to see a man who looks after his horse before he looks after himself. Don't you think he's good, our Mary?' Another quick look brought James and Elsie to her attention. 'Who have you brought with you? They look like a pair of vagrants.'

A look from Mary silenced her.

'Mildred! As if I would bring vagrants to you! This is Miss Elsie Stretton and her father, Mister James Stretton. Mister Stretton helped Fred to put right those bars you sent us. Elsie helped in the forge, pumping you know, and helped me in the house with the housework. James, Mister Stretton, has worked in the great workshops at Soho, in Birmingham.' She went quiet, realising that she was giving away the depth of her friendship for the pair. Then she went on. 'He certainly knows what to do with a hammer anyway. Fred told me he must be a smith in his own right!'

Elsie caught the expression on Mister Stone's face. He seemed to be wondering about her and her father – wondering why they were there. It was obvious, really. He put the question to James.

'Are you looking for work, Mister Stretton? If you are, I might be able to accommodate you for a short while – if you can do the sort of work that's needed. I need a man who can use a file and a hammer and chisel one minute and swing the arm of a press the next. Is that you?'

He stood awaiting an answer, looking James in the eye and James met him eye for eye.

'Mister Stone, I can use a hammer and chisel, a scraper and file. I can scrape for a shaft bearing or a machine bed. I can use a lathe, a milling machine and a planer or a shaper. I can strike for a smith or work on my own, welding or riveting. My daughter Elsie is also very handy, having to take care of our house before my wife died. If you want us, we're free; if not we'll move on.'

He stood still, tall and proud; a Midland journeyman able to turn his hand to a dozen trades and Albert Stone did not hesitate.

'You can find yourself somewhere in the factory to get your head down then, and start in the morning. Your daughter can find herself something to do in the house. Mildred will soon put her right.' He turned back to Mary who was trying to attract his attention. 'Yes, Mary. What is it now? I've given your friends work for some time and I'll find you work as well, if you want it. You can help Mildred. Our daughters are too idle or too young to be of much use. Stephen is still learning. He's still got some way to go before he presents me with a lock.'

Mary knew that when an apprentice locksmith finishes his time he has to make a lock that is the combination of his skills; it speaks for him to any prospective employer. So, apparently, Stephen was still playing games with the other trainees, playing tricks on his elders and running errands to give him a change from standing filing at the bench. She turned to Mildred.

'It's really nice to see you, Millie. You don't know how much I miss the times we used to have together. I'm sure you'll find Elsie a great help in the house. We'll be able to have more time to spend together.'

Mary reached, put her arms around her sister-in-law and felt Millie's arms around her. They had shared a lot of their youth together and each had great affection for the other.

'Come in, Mary. You must tell me how you have been getting on in that tiny house in Wednesbury. I bet none of your neighbours know you own the yard, do they?'

Elsie listened with interest to that. Fancy Mary owning all those houses! There must be at least half a dozen! The rent collector came round every week; she had seen him. He had called on Mary and taken the rent from her but no one even knew that she was the owner. There was more to Mary than met the eye! Elsie became conscious that Stephen was watching her and she found herself blushing.

'Stephen.' Albert Stone's voice rang out. 'Go and see if you can find a sleeping berth for Mister Stretton, James, did you say?' He looked James in the eye and then turned back to Stephen. 'Go on then, son! Don't just stand there looking moonstruck!'

Albert Stone smiled and turned away. He had seen the way his son was looking at Elsie. She wasn't old enough for all that messing around and his son was bound for more suitable relationships. He had spoken to Mabel Elkins and found her to be just the sort of girl he wanted for his son. Her father was owner of a coming firm so they might be a force to be reckoned with if they were joined together by marriage. Still, he felt that the arrival of the Stretton family was going to make a difference in some still undefined way and it made him feel uneasy.

Elsie, too, felt that she had arrived somewhere. The Stone family was going to change her life, she knew. The young woman had seen the way that Stephen Stone had looked at her and she had felt the birthing of a new emotion; the first youthful pangs of love. Somehow Elsie felt that their lives would be bound together, not necessarily by a marriage certificate but by something unwritten. It was an impracticable idea, but it stayed there in her heart and mind.

Stephen beckoned James in the direction of the small factory and led him in through the door. The light quickly reduced, making the atmosphere seem suddenly cool. James had been in many places like this, having been brought up in a similar factory. There were hundreds of rivets all over the floor which had been shaped on a heading machine and cut to length in the same operation, ready to be pressed into a padlock. He bent and picked some up.

'That's waste; there's enough on this floor to pay a man's wages; you wouldn't throw that on the floor, would you?' He turned and looked the young man in the face. 'It's right, isn't it? Every time you allow waste like this, it's money being poured down the drain. You let your father down by allowing it. Try to remember that.'

Neither of them realised at the time that because he didn't speak loudly or brashly, the message got through to Stephen. He watched as James picked up a broom and pan. The strange man could be useful to him; he was the father of Elsie, after all, and Elsie was the one he had just fallen in love with. James might end up as his father-in-law! The youth would learn to listen to James simply because he was Elsie's father. How would their future connect them?

Chapter 3

James was feeling extremely lucky. He had been feeling like that since they had first arrived in Wednesbury and had been inspired to talk to Mary Bowyer. He was always warm, and he could cook on the forge fire without having to spend money for fuel. There was a tap for water and he was able to keep himself reasonably clean.

Stephen too loved the factory. In a way it was as if it were miles away from his home, at the back of the haberdashery shop which was on the front of the property. The girls who came in to work there were entirely different to his sisters. They chatted to each other about men and boys; he had heard them as he had worked, never letting them know, of course. They entered in bright clothes and changed them for the overalls that they left hanging in the changing room.

They seemed to exchange their personalities then, turning into lithe production machines. Annie Summers had taught him a thing or two. He had watched her as she had entered and left the changing room. She was a few years older than him and her body had a shape that could not be hidden by the overall she wore. Blue when new, the overall had been burnished to a shiny pewter sheen by contact between her body and the oily metal components she handled as she worked the long, swinging arm of the hand press. As he worked at his vice, he had watched her body moving beneath the overall.

He had been aroused for hours at a stretch by his filing movements at the bench and seeing the sliding movement of Annie's breasts as she pulled back and forth. Sometimes he felt sure that she knew. He had tried to work it out and had come to the conclusion that one of the characteristic differences between men and women was that while men looked, women were looked at.

Women seemed to arrange themselves in different postures, he thought, to best show off their bodies. Men never seemed to do that, not consciously at any rate. The shine of the sun through the window as it glanced off the shape of Annie's body beneath her dirty, burnished overall seemed to give it a life of its own. She had offered to teach him the best way to work when he had been given a job to do on a hand press. One of the mill-hands had showed him what to do, demonstrating to him how to push the long metal strip against the 'stop' of the press. Then, keeping the strip in position, he had swung the arm and the tool had come down, cutting a measured length from the strip.

The first time Stephen had tried it, the press tool had not cut all the way through the metal and he had had to repeat the action, to the amusement of some of the girls who were watching. He had struggled for an hour and then Annie had come to him and offered to give him a few tips.

'Can I show you a better way to do it, Mister Stephen?'

All the girls called him Mister Stephen. It was recognition of his position as son of the owner of the firm. He had nodded and she had pushed herself in front of him.

'Look at the way I move; you have to do it the easy way, as if you are enjoying it, so to speak, not as if it's a great struggle.'

Annie had slipped the length of strip metal into the jaw of the press with her left hand as she leaned forward to grasp the handle. Then she had just leaned back and the arm had moved as if it was part of her. She reached behind her and felt his hands. Then she had put them onto her waist and had repeated her movement.

'Can you feel how it works, Mister Stephen?'

She moved back a little and he felt himself become erect against her. She did not comment but put the strip of metal into the press tool again. As she leaned forward, he could feel her buttocks almost take hold of him.

'Can you feel how to put it in now, Mister Stephen?'

His hands slipped from her waist to her breasts completely involuntarily and he felt her pull herself backward, giving an even closer sensation of intimacy. His breath came from him in a great gasp and he pulled quickly away, knowing that orgasm was only a heartbeat away. Her voice whispered in his ear.

'Do you think you know how to do it, Mister Stephen? I think you've got the idea now, ain't you?'

She turned around in his arms and took hold of his hands, replacing them on her breasts but he moved away from her, knowing by instinct that there was danger in association with her. It hadn't stopped him wanting her though, and he found himself up against her as they passed each other in doorways. She had mocked him in those situations.

'Can you put it in now, Mister Stephen?'

She whispered in his ear as they passed and he reached for her buttocks, pulling her against his rising manhood. Stephen moved his mouth to the mound of her breast and she pulled the overall back to give him easier access to her large brown nipple. She breathed heavily then, her hands reaching to guide him to her. They each knew what the other wanted until finally, in the small packing room of the factory, he found her lying down on a pile of bags during the lunch break.

'Oh Mister Stephen, you've found me out. I always hide away here for a little lie down. You don't mind do you, Mister Stephen? Will you help me up?'

Stephen reached to help her and she pulled him down to her, laughing, her overall falling away to reveal her body. Without further thought he slipped his trousers down and placed himself on top of her body. Annie reached and guided him into her and a few moments later he felt the mounting pleasure and pain of uncontrolled orgasm. In the days following, she taught him how to control his passion until he could time things right to suit the feelings of each of them.

After a few weeks she left the firm. He noticed that she was not coming in to work and thought she might be ill. He enquired about her among her friends but they knew nothing. He asked his mother and she told him that a better position had been found for her, at a firm in Bilston. It was two years later when he found that she had claimed that she was pregnant and had been paid off. She had been to see his father in an apparently distressed condition. His father had just handed her a few sovereigns and told her to get out.

*

Elsie was shown one of the small bedrooms in the roof of the old shop. It was small but still twice the size of any room she had known before. The young woman was maturing quickly due to the fast changing circumstances in her life and she felt a little sorry for her father who was going to have to sleep in the factory but he was used to making do for himself. When she had settled in, she went down the stairs to find Mildred waiting for her.

'Please, Mrs Stone, have you got any work for me to do?'

Elsie felt nervous, speaking to the strange woman, but if

she was a sister-in-law to Mary Bowyer, she might be a nice person. The room was quite nice, she noticed, as she awaited an answer. Mildred Stone was a great believer in paying your way. 'Yes, there's plenty to do. You don't need to start this evening but if you see me in the mornings I shall tell you what I want you to do for the day. If there is nothing to do in the house or the shop, you may have to work in the factory. Either way, there will always be a way for you to pay for your bed and board.' She smiled at Elsie, softening the factual words she had used to instruct her in her duties. 'Never you mind me, my dear. I'm sure we shall get on like a house on fire – like my own daughters.'

Her own daughters, it turned out, were in the shop, cleaning, and Elsie would not be needed there today. Instead, Elsie was given the task of black-leading the fireplace, a job she enjoyed because she liked the result; a shining, black brilliance that made every flame give of its best to the light in the room. She had always loved bright black for its sparkling, sanitised look.

Mary Bowyer was sitting by the side of the fire as she started and she looked up as Elsie started cleaning.

'You don't have to start tonight, Elsie. I'm sure I heard Mildred say that, didn't I?'

Elsie knew she was right; she had just started work because she did not wish to be obliged to anyone.

'Yes, Mary. I'd forgotten; I just feel like working, I suppose.'

'The others will be in soon,' Mary replied, 'and you'll have the chance to meet some girls of nearer your own age. They're both friendly girls and you'll soon get to know them. They're at work now, in the shop at the front of the house.'

Mary was knitting and she turned back to it as she stopped talking. She looked up again as she felt Elsie's eyes upon her.

'What's the matter, child? Why are you looking at me like that? Have you never seen anyone knitting before?'

Mary put down her pins impatiently as she waited for an answer. Elsie let out a small sob as she spoke.

'My mother used to knit and I haven't seen anyone knitting since. She was going to teach me to knit but she died before she had the chance.'

Mary leaned across to wipe her eyes and Elsie allowed herself to be comforted by the warm, motherly presence of the older woman and she listened as Mary spoke to her in soft, motherly tones.

'You've suffered a cruel loss, my girl, but many young women, yes women, not just young girls have been through the same ordeal. You've landed on your feet. Many have lost both parents and died themselves because of the flu and one disease or another. Here you are with a room of your own, in the middle of a family of girls when it could have been boys. You're getting three meals every day. You've also got the chance to learn a trade, maybe two. So don't look so sorry for yourself. I don't like to say this but you may just be better off than if your mother had lived!'

Elsie had stopped sobbing by now and was listening to what Mary was saying. She knew that she would never recover from the loss of her mother but the rest of it was true; she was lucky to be in such a situation. She should be showing gratitude, not self-pity. She smiled at the older woman.

'I'm sorry, Mary. I know you're right and I'll do my best to make things right. I'll work hard and be grateful for whatever I get. I've had my little grumble; now is the time to start on the rest of my life!'

Elsie moved from Mary's side and restarted the black-leading, rubbing the cast iron until it was shining almost like black silver. Suddenly more mature, the young woman seemed to have taken on a new idea of life, moving quickly through her self-imposed tasks.

The door from the shop opened and a pretty blonde framed face showed itself.

'Hello,' the blonde said, 'I'm Victoria. We heard you'd come. You must be Elsie. Why are you black-leading the grate? I suppose you must feel as if you have to do your share of the work. You don't need to worry about that. Mother will soon put you right, you know. She decides who does what.'

Victoria advanced into the room and held out her hand. Mary looked at Elsie in a significant sort of way and Elsie responded to Victoria by holding out her hand. They each smiled and the air seemed to clear.

'You're right of course, Victoria. Perhaps I should wait to be told what to do. It's just that if I see that something needs doing, I do it. That's not a bad way to do things, is it? Anyway, I had been given the job, the black-leading I mean. It was more a matter of when I did it – not what I had to do.'

Although Victoria had been friendly towards her, Elsie still knew that she had been given the job and she wasn't going to allow anyone, no matter how nice, to decide when she did her work. Just as she finished speaking, Mildred Stone walked into the room.

'My goodness, Elsie, you're keen aren't you? We usually do the black-leading in the morning, when the fire has just been made. That way, everything's free from lumps of coal and ash. D'you see what I mean? Leave it for now, there's a good girl. There's nothing you need to do tonight. Just slow down a bit. We all do our share here. You don't have to work hard at doing more than your share.'

Elsie blushed. She could have worked all that out for herself, if she had had the confidence. She wouldn't make the same mistake again. What a lot she had to learn! The door opened and another young woman came into the room. She introduced herself as Agnes. She was younger than Victoria but a little older than Elsie, and, like them, was in her growing years. Elsie began to realise the fortunate position she was in, with friendly young people around her.

Stephen walked in then. She'd almost forgotten him. She was still attracted to him but he hardly seemed to see her. Mildred Stone seemed to notice the way Elsie looked at Stephen and introduced them, although they had spent most of the day in each other's company.

'This is our son, Stephen, Elsie. We've got great plans for him. We think the future of the firm may depend on him and we intend that everything shall work out for him. Mabel will make him a very able wife.' She changed the subject quickly. 'We have another son, Bert, but he is staying with friends at the moment.'

Mildred became silent and Elsie got the feeling that more was being said than just the words she had used. Who was Mabel? Elsie suddenly realised that Mildred was telling her not to get any ideas about a future for her with Stephen. What an idea! All that she had thought on the subject was that he was nice. What would happen if this unwritten rule that had just been laid down for her was broken? There was too much at stake for her to try to impose her own will upon this powerful woman. Anyway, there might be other, more attractive prospects in Willenhall. Who knows? The idea brought her thoughts back to the present.

There was the sound of plates being rattled in the kitchen. There was a creak as the door opened and Agnes, the Stone's younger daughter called to Elsie, 'Elsie, would you take this to your father, please? Oh, I suppose you don't know where he is. Stephen will show you. We heard you were coming to stay with us for a while.'

Agnes smiled an introduction. She had a Billy-can in one

hand and a bowl filled with stew in the other. Stephen took the bowl from her. Agnes handed the Billy-can to Elsie, nodding her head to indicate that she should follow Stephen. Elsie turned and Stephen was waiting for her at the door. She looked round and saw that Mildred was looking in a disapproving way at the situation.

Elsie quickly moved to follow him. She had been told to, after all. It was dark in the factory and it took her all her time to follow him through the darkness so she was surprised when they reached the light of the forge, to find her father reading. Elsie knew that he loved to read philosophical books and she looked at the book in his hand. It was by Samuel Smiles and was called 'Self Help'. He turned his head at their approach and held out his hands eagerly for the Billy-can of tea and bowl of stew. He smiled at them.

'Hello Elsie, Mister Stephen. That smells good. Who do I say thank you to, for this?'

'Well, Agnes handed it to me so I suppose she must have cooked it.'

'Who's Agnes? Does she work here, then?'

James looked at them both and they looked at each other. They started to smile and then held it in. Stephen answered.

'Agnes is my younger sister, Mister Stretton. It was her turn to cook tonight, so she prepared a meal for all of us. I hope it's all right for you.'

James lifted the bowl up to his nose and drew a deep breath. His lips were being licked with enthusiasm.

'This is brilliant cooking. Please convey my compliments and thanks to Miss Agnes.'

The older man sat and poured from the Billy-can into its lid and then lifted it to his lips. He took a deep draught and put it down. Then he lifted the bowl to his lips and allowed the stew to slide over his lips, into his mouth. Elsie smiled at him. He was looking healthier already and she suddenly realised that her worries about him had probably been for nothing. He was looking fitter than she had seen him look for ages.

Her father sat there, chewing on the pieces of meat he was finding in the bowl, smiling all the time. He was as much at home here as in the Stones' home, more so, in fact. Elsie found she was discovering her father, finding facets of his personality that she hadn't known about before. He was content at the side of a forge. It wasn't that he was less intelligent; it was that, like an animal, he was able to settle down wherever he was. If he was getting paid, well that was good. If he wasn't, it didn't matter much. He also had the freedom to settle down with an inspiring, informative book and she knew he enjoyed philosophical works.

A cough disturbed her, turning her thought to the sound. It was Stephen. She blushed; she had been holding him up.

'I'm sorry, Stephen. I suppose you want your own dinner, don't you?'

He caught her eye and smiled.

'I suppose I do. How about you, Miss Stretton? Aren't you hungry?'

Stephen's eyes held a query but Elsie wasn't sure whether the question in his eyes was the same as the one on his lips. Nevertheless, there didn't seem to be any harm in them. There was a twinkle; a definite twinkle. Well, why shouldn't he have a twinkle? It wasn't a sin or a crime to have a twinkle in your eye, was it?

'Yes, thank you, Mister Stephen. I'm definitely ready for something to eat.' Elsie turned to her father. 'I'll probably see you in the morning, Dad. Are you sure you'll be all right there? There might be mice or rats running around, you know.'

Elsie didn't wait for an answer. She knew her father could survive a few rats. He had worked in dirty industrial jobs since he was twelve. With a nod to Stephen she stepped out towards the darkness of the factory. She had better watch out for him, this would be an opportunity for him to get to know her better! Elsie could hear his shoes treading along behind her. They came to a darker place and she could not make out which way to go. The hairs suddenly stood up on the back of her neck.

Elsie turned to Stephen but he was not there. Suddenly she felt nervous. Her eyes looked round, seeking a way out in the dim light. Suddenly, there was a touch on her cheek. Elsie started and raised her fists in defence. There was a chuckle in the dim light and Stephen was moving to enclose her in his arms. As he moved closer, she lashed out with her fist and felt it strike home with a crack. She heard him cry out and then curse.

'Christ! I was only trying to have a bit of fun with you. Don't you like fun?'

He moved towards her again and she felt sorry for him, and felt like laughing, at the same time.

'I like to be consulted about my idea of fun, not crept up on in the dark. How do you like my idea of fun, Mister Stephen?' Elsie could see him better now. He was holding his hand over his face, nursing it, making her feel suddenly remorseful.

'Come here; let's have a look at it, you big babby.'

Elsie reached for his face and turned it towards her so that she could see it better. His arm went round her and she felt his lips on hers. Suddenly she didn't feel like hitting him. Her arms found a way to hold him close and her body felt things she hadn't felt before. It was nice, very nice.

'You've got a good punch, you know.' He spoke as his hands started to explore her body. 'I thought I'd been hit by a steam roller!'

Elsie wriggled out of his grasp and stood; arms akimbo, glaring in the dark. He could see that her face was red. She was angry. Was she angry at him for doing what he had done, or was she angry at herself for letting him? It seemed that neither of them knew the answer. At last the anger in her exploded into speech.

'Anyway, you should keep your fun for your promised, Mabel the Able!'

Elsie didn't know what to say then. Somehow, what she had said seemed so ridiculous and stupid and silly. She found her lips starting to curl up and saw that his face too, was beginning to smile. Suddenly he burst into laughter and she found herself doing the same. Their laughter seemed to bounce off the machines in the darkened factory. He took her hands.

'You do like fun. I knew it! I knew it when I first met you, in Wednesbury, last week. Christ! Was it only last week that we met? It seems like I've known you forever.'

He moved to put his arms round her again but Elsie was in full possession of her wits now. How could she become just his plaything? There was too much to be done with life. For all the laughing, there might soon be no one to turn to, for her. She needed to be able to look after herself in all sorts of situations. The thought made her smile again.

'Come on, Stephen. Your mother and father will be worrying about where you are, with that new girl from Wednesbury!'

Elsie moved herself away from him, towards the door that led out towards the living part of the business. Would she ever let him take liberties with her, again? One thing was sure; she would never forget the young man who had taken her in his arms. She had enjoyed it, she confessed to herself but if she was caught out, it would be a quick way of getting thrown out of the only place that had given shelter to her father and she couldn't afford to risk that. There were a lot of risks here.

Chapter 4

Settling in
May/June 1904

'Get your hands off me, you bully!'

Elsie looked up from her work. At the far end of the workshop, the figures of Stephen and the new girl, Mabel Elkins, were entwined. The girl's cry of protest had more than a hint of falseness in its tone. Mabel was obviously enjoying the intimacy of his hands and so was Stephen.

Elsie knew she had nothing with which to compete against Mabel. Stephen's mother had told her so in no uncertain way and Elsie had decided to forget any romantic notions and had just got on with the business of surviving in her new environment. Elsie's desire for him still gave her a pain though, every time she saw him flirting with Mabel. It was jealousy and it hurt even more because Elsie had always regarded the emotion as useless.

The sheer variety of Elsie's work gave her a lot of pleasure. There were tasks in the shop, the house and the factory. Each place gave her fresh skills to learn and use and new people to meet. The young men in the factory all paid court to her, in their shy, polite ways; smiling and giving way as they moved around the crowded gangways of the factory. Stephen still spoke to her wherever they met but he had additional responsibilities on his horizon and couldn't offer himself to her in any other way but a friendly one.

One of the young men in the factory seemed more serious than the others. Dan Barr was always there to help her or show her a better way to do the job and she always seemed to have a good reason for smiling at him. Dan had been told to show Elsie how to do the job, the first time she had to work in the factory. Unless she wanted him for anything, he was always standing at his bench, filing lock parts, but if she needed help or advice, he was always available. Even Stephen's younger brother, Bert had made an advance to her but he was just too immature for her taste.

Elsie knew there was nothing like friendship between Dan Barr and Stephen. Stephen was the son of the gaffer and therefore a person to be avoided by working-class men. The gaffers were there just to exploit the workers; they had no right to expect friendship as well. One day, perhaps, it would all change, like it had in Russia. That was Dan's way of thinking.

'Do you fancy going to the theatre on Saturday, Elsie?'

Elsie started at Dan's words. He rarely spoke to her unless it was necessary so it was a shock for Elsie to hear his invitation. She thought about it for a moment and then decided that it might be a good night; a bit of a change.

'Yes, that'd be nice, Dan. I've heard it's a good show. Shall I see you there or will you call for me?'

So it was settled; they were a pair, much to the regret of the other young locksmiths who had been thinking about asking her but had not got round to it. In a way, Elsie was in a strange position, living in at the gaffer's house but still one of the workers. Her father had found lodgings just along the road from the factory now so she didn't see him as often. Elsie called on James to tell him that Dan Barr had asked her out and her father seemed pleased that she had found herself what he called a nice young man. James was also pleased that Elsie was discussing her circumstances, not exactly asking his permission but having the courtesy to see him about the situation. James approved of the possible match because of the potential security it offered.

'He seems a steady young man, to me, daughter. If you tie up with him, I don't think you'll come to any harm.'

Their evening out was pleasant but uninspiring. Dan seemed to be a dull sort of person but at least Elsie felt safe with him. The show was entertaining. Elsie was surprised when he asked her to go out with him again, on the following Sunday.

Dan took her to the Methodist Church at Wednesbury. It was a long way to go on a Sunday but there was enjoyment to be found in the journey and pleasure too, when they got to the church, for Mary Bowyer was at the service. Mary was delighted to see Elsie.

'You'll come back to the house for a cup of tea, won't you, Elsie? You can bring the young man of course.'

Elsie looked askance at Dan and he nodded acceptance of the invitation, although he looked as though he had reservations. Elsie wondered why but did not ask. All the time they were making their way back to the little house, Mary was asking her questions. They were going down Union Street, now almost at Mary's house but Mary was still asking questions.

'How is James, Elsie? I hope he's looking better than when he stayed with me.'

Elsie thought before answering. There had seemed to be the beginnings of a friendship between her father and Mary. Dan was paying a lot of attention to what was being said and Elsie felt that he might, in some way, make use of it. The thought sent a small shiver down her back.

'Yes, Mary, he's much improved.. He doesn't sleep at the back of the forge now; he has lodgings, just down the road.'

Mary seemed to pick up on what she was thinking and feeling so didn't ask her any more questions about James. Elsie had noticed that the older woman was very astute. Mary turned to Dan.

'What do you do, young man? Do you work at Stones'?'

She waited for an answer and Dan seemed hesitant about the way to give it.

'Yes, I'm a locksmith. I have been for about three years. I'm not married and have no particular prospects. I'd like a change, though, I think.' Elsie was surprised that he opened up so readily but he went on. 'I think I'd like to get away from there.'

He seemed surprised himself that he had admitted the feeling. Mary just looked at Elsie and smiled as she answered.

'All young men feel like that if they have any guts at all. The trick is to know when to respond to the feeling. You should become irreplaceable before you threaten or suggest that you might find your way in life at a different firm. Think on it young man. If you left now for instance, where would you go? Would you have enough money to last a month, or even a week?'

Mary turned to Elsie and Elsie got the feeling that the lesson being delivered was as much for her as for Dan. Elsie was learning to love this woman and would love to know more about her. Loyalty to her father must come first, though, through thick and thin.

Perhaps Mary was right and Dan was just a malcontent. Was it a stage he was going through or would he always be the same? Then the thought came to her; perhaps he was right. Time would show the answer to that question. He certainly didn't have the same ambition as Stephen Stone, for instance. Then, perhaps he didn't have the same opportunities. The evening was approaching and Elsie realised that they should be starting back for Willenhall. She turned to Dan, 'I think we should be starting back, don't you, Dan?'

He looked at his watch. He always seemed to do things by the time appointed.

'Yes, Elsie; I think you're right. Thank you for noticing. I might have got you into trouble.'

Mary looked at Elsie and smiled, doing her best to ignore the unintentional double entendre. It was the right answer, though. He wasn't just taking over the decision-making role. He was consulting her opinion. Elsie was quite surprised as most men wanted to wield the power. Elsie spoke to Mary,

'It's been lovely seeing you again, Mary.' She turned to Dan. 'I hope you bring me again, Dan.'

That set the tone of their goodbye. Mary smiled at Dan, the smile letting him know that he would be welcome. It seemed to make him grow in his shoes, as Elsie recalled the incident later.

Their courtship was not without hiccups. Dan was sometimes a bit too steady for Elsie. All he seemed to want to talk about was the International Situation, with the rise of the Communist Party in Russia as his first interest. He was scathing in his opinions of the 'bosses' as Dan called them. If he had his way, they would all be hung from the nearest lamp-post.

'If you feel like that, how can you carry on being exploited?' she asked him. 'Why don't you go and join the Revolution, when it happens?'

'I might just do that, but there are wrongs to be put right in this country, without travelling halfway round the world to do it. It's this country that counts for me; I believe in what the Russians are up to but I'm still an Englishman. I don't think it's necessary to get rid of the Royal Family to bring about better dealings for the workers.' Dan seemed to ponder on her question. 'I think the workers have to educate themselves to the point where they're ready to govern themselves, and the rest of England.'

Elsie was amazed that he thought so deeply about such large issues and started thinking he was quite clever. At least he was capable of thinking. Her father heard Dan speak and commented.

'He'll grow out of it. It's just a phase he's going through.'

Nevertheless she started to respect Dan's opinions and defended them when she heard him disagree with other workers. He was a member of the Fabian Society and occasionally he went to London to hear notable speakers. Edith Nesbit was one of them and Elsie had read most of her books, having become a member of the public library. Elsie was fascinated by the mixture of magic and adventures that the usually middle-class families she wrote about, endured.

Elsie didn't seem to see much of Stephen Stone now; he was engaged to Mabel and plans were being made for their wedding. When they met in the factory or the shop, Stephen acted as if he couldn't speak to her but just carried on as if she didn't exist. She believed that he ignored her too much for his ignoring to be real; she felt it was just a screen to hide his true feelings. But what were her feelings? Elsie asked herself the question but so far had not been able to come up with an answer.

Dan was a serious man but Stephen always seemed to be laughing. It was only when he was near to her that his face lost its happy expression. Occasionally Elsie saw him out with Mabel. It was at those times that he ignored her the most, fiercely, steering Mabel in another direction so that they would never meet face to face. Elsie smiled across the street when that happened and knew that Mabel had seen and heard all about her.

James was still weak from his illness and Elsie worried about his continuing with the hard physical work that he carried out. He seemed to have settled in at the workmens' lodging house along the road from Stones'. Occasionally, Elsie heard him coughing phlegm into the forge fire and cursing to himself as he did so but gradually, she noticed him settle down into a routine of work. Albert Stone never seemed to give him so much work that he could not cope with it and James turned the little lodging house he lived in, into a bright little home. It was strange, Elsie thought, that she had never moved back in with him but she was comfortable in the Stones' home. Part of the reason for this was that she had now made friends with the Stones' sisters, and it was almost as if she had become another sister.

Dan seemed more serious than ever now, and accompanied Elsie on her visits to Mary Bowyer. He liked Mary because she was knowledgeable about world affairs, and the fact that she was friends with Elsie enhanced her in his eyes.

They were betrothed when she was eighteen and James gave her permission to wed when she was ready. Sometimes though, it was as if she was at the mercy of other people's plans for her.

Chapter 5

First Love
August 1904

Elsie loved going to Willenhall market on Saturday mornings. It was her own time; she had to answer to no one. The traders all seemed to gather near the clock tower. They were a kaleidoscope of colours, with scarves, gloves, dresses, and food, all being sold in close proximity to one another. Occasionally she sometimes accidentally met Stephen as she walked round and Elsie came to understand that Stephen too, liked the atmosphere of the market. They smiled at each other on these occasions but hardly exchanged more than a few words, but their meetings seemed to have an importance that could not be measured by the time they spent in their short conversations and brushings of hands.

Market days were her favourite, when Elsie was shopping for meat in the market. She had been advised to wait until the last minute because the traders sold it off cheaply rather than take it away with them. As Elsie inspected the meat, she became conscious of being watched. It was Stephen and he was very close to her; she had noticed the familiar smell of his shaving soap. He stood close so that his body was pressed against her. Elsie moved away, trembling, and shopped at a different stall but she was sure that the feelings she had had were shared by Stephen.

She looked around for him. She knew he could not have just forgotten her and wandered off! It would not have been in line with either his character or his actions in the market place. It was a ten-minute walk to the Stones' house, where she lived and she found him, about halfway there, sitting on the trap that the Stones rented for small errands. She walked past the trap, ignoring him but he called to her.

'Elsie!' He called again. 'Elsie! It seems silly to walk when you can ride.'

When she again ignored him he snapped the reins and trotted forward until he was about twenty-five yards in front of her, then stopped again. He jumped down and waited for her to catch up. Her face was red when she came level with him and she suddenly felt helpless and angry at the same time. Her hands seemed to flutter as if she did not know whether to hit him, run for shelter or hold him. She took hold of his collar and shook it.

'What do you want with me? What is it?'

He put his arms round her and pulled her close to him.

'You know what I want, what I shall always want from you, what I shall always need. I couldn't live without you; do you know what I mean?'

She tugged ineffectually at his lapels, expressing her feelings by the pressure on his coat.

'I want as well as you, you fool. You must know that. What am I to do?'

Stephen removed his arms from her and beckoned her towards the trap, smiling at her. She stood for a moment, studiously, then climbed aboard and sat primly as if she was the owner. Stephen climbed and clicked his tongue at the pony and they moved off, silently. Their silence continued as they moved out of the small town into the countryside. Stephen turned into a lane and the pony trotted along as if enjoying the day. The sun shone and filled the silence they had around them, so that the silence was absent, and they warmed in its rays. Stephen leaned back on the reins, stopping their movement and then stepped down. He walked round the trap and reached for her hand and she found herself accepting it and the support it gave as she stepped down.

Stephen reached for her hand again and she accepted that and the step forward she was invited to take. They walked for a few steps and found a small hollow, just large enough to accommodate them so they sat in its shelter, still silent. Eventually, Elsie turned to Stephen.

'What is this? Why am I here? What do you want with me?'

Her eyes were suddenly damp with tears that showed the conflict she was undergoing. If her father or Mary could see her now she would be ashamed. She had never been so alone with a man. How alone could you get? It was inevitable even if it was shaming. There was nothing shaming in the way Stephen was smiling – as usual.

She smiled back at him and he took the whole of her face in his hands and pressed his lips onto hers. She could feel the touch of his fingers sliding across her cheeks and it was the most wonderfully caressing feeling. His hand moved from her cheek to her neck and his lips moved to hers again. Then the lips moved to her neck and the flutter of her being seemed to keep time with his.

They sat down in the hollow, in the shade of the rowan tree, with the sun's rays, dappled by the moving leaves, fluttering in time with her heart. She laid herself back, the possibility of shame forgotten, knowing there was more to come. She felt as if her body had a plan of its own, that would be soon revealed to her.

Her blouse had come undone, somehow. His lips moved from her neck to her breast and the delight of her senses mounted to a sudden fervour of inexpressible wanting. Her breasts pressed back against his hands and lips and she found her legs moving to avoid the restriction of her clothes.

Stephen moved to help her and suddenly she was almost naked, exposed to the air and the wonderful feeling of his hands touching her here - and there, gently and forcefully until she realised that he was part of her body and she was drenched with passion and the sun poured down unheeded on them.

Elsie gradually came back to herself from where she had been. Stephen was lying atop her body, obviously also spent. The sun seemed to have moved round in the sky but was still warm. She moved to look at him and he was smiling and she, surprised, found that so was she.

They lay quietly for some time, completely content with each other's closeness, a time disallowing of apprehension or care. They each realised, confirmed and accepted their unique relationship, aware of the consequences but, for this moment, making the most of their feelings. This time might never happen again but the fact that it had, was of monumental significance now.

Eventually Elsie moved to become more comfortable and looked at Stephen. His face was wreathed in smiles and it annoyed her. He was always smiling, the pig! She was contrite immediately and smiled herself. She reached and tickled him under his neck, causing him to sit up. He looked and she tried to emulate sleep.

'Come on, you little madam. I know you're awake.'

She sat up and stretched and he took advantage by putting his arms around her. She responded by holding him tightly and they sank back onto the grass again. Time slowed again and the sun was sinking when they became aware of the real world once more.

'What are we going to do?' Stephen spoke gently in her ear. 'Shall we get married and have twelve kids?'

'Ha, ha. Very funny, Mister Stone. I always thought a stone was hard but not you. Oh no. You are only hard where

I am concerned. You are soft as mallow where Mabel the Able is concerned!'

They lay silent for a minute or two and then she decided it was time to go.

'I've got to take this meat home for my Dan. He was expecting me half an hour ago. He'll be starving.'

They stood and walked back to the trap. It was time to return to reality.

Chapter 6

Back to Wednesbury
1905

Mabel Elkins and Stephen were married quietly, with no honeymoon. All the members of the firm attended though, to make the occasion more festive. They were a bunch of bright sparks, Elsie thought; not a dull day while they were around. She had expected to feel miserable as this meant there was never any likelihood of a wedding between her and Stephen but it didn't seem to affect her, almost as though the wedding could not touch the connection between them.

Mabel joined the firm then. She had a lot of experience and she pulled her weight as much as the men.

Elsie had to give her credit; Mabel sweated more than her husband. He was always tied up on more important tasks. The tasks had to be completed but why always him? Stephen was on her mind more often than she thought he ought to be, and he often smiled at her when there was no one else around.

He just smiled as he always seemed to do. It got her angry the way he did. Somehow, when she walked through the packing room, he was always there, making sure that the full quantities were always packed. He caught her alone one day in the darkened passageway.

'Hello, Else; how are you, Elsie?' He pulled her to one side and slipped his arms round her, his body alive and seeking hers. She could not bring herself to deny the way she felt and just responded to his touch as he was responding to hers. His next words shocked her. 'I love you!'

Elsie heard his words through a sort of daze as she found herself getting closer and closer to him. It seemed that more and more of her skin was touching and caressing more and more of his skin, and more and more of his skin was touching and caressing hers. Her overall gradually came off and his hands and lips seemed to be all over her body. Her breasts ached with longing, as if they knew that there was more but didn't know how to get more. She heard the words again. 'I love you!'

She realised the words were hers. All she was doing was confirming what she felt. Was he doing the same? If he felt anything like she did, he had to mean it. Her body was spreading itself on a soft pile of sacks, opening to him; receiving him; feeling him inside her; feeling a different, higher, more intense, painful, beautiful emotion that took in and took care of all her careful considerations.

Stephen moved inside her and Elsie found that she was moving into a higher emotional plane. The pair altered and re-altered positions, each moving to get the most out of the tactile sensations they were experiencing until the final, exhilarating thrill of culmination.

Elsie leaned on him, trying to find a trace of tenderness, and did. He moved his body to accommodate hers and they merged again, not just as loving friends but as lovers as well. The feeling that she had first known when they met at Wednesbury returned; the feeling that they would always be bonded together, regardless of their relationships with others. She looked up at him and he smiled at her; Stephen always smiled. She smiled back and felt that she had completed something, become part of a whole, as if their thoughts and feelings were combined into an unbreakably cemented attachment.

Stephen felt the same; they were two parts of a whole. The problem was the expectations of others. He knew that the future of his family was in his hands; that the destiny that had been dreamed of by his mother and father, by Mabel's mother and father was his responsibility to carry out; to achieve. He felt that he was carrying a load on his shoulders that had been placed there by other people, but he could not lay it down. What were Elsie's expectations? What were his responsibilities to his own feelings? Did he not have a right to his own emotional ambitions? He looked back at Elsie and it was as if she could read his thoughts as she spoke.

'Don't you worry, my love. I know the hopes of your parents are with you. I've got you and I'll always have you, regardless of what others think and feel. You'll always have me as well; never mind whether I am married, widowed or single. I'm yours.'

Elsie would never know what inspired her to make that little speech but she knew she meant it. Stephen leaned back against the pile of sacks and his eyes revealed that his feelings were the same as hers. He would always be hers!

'I love you, Elsie. I always will. You are right; my family rely on me to carry out their ambitions and I can't let them down. I've my duties and I've got my feelings. They're not the same thing and I can't let them conflict with each other.'

The young pair seemed to relax where they were, taking in the import of what had been said by each of them. Then Stephen smiled and Elsie got angry again as they ended the moment of combination.

'How the hell can you smile all the time, feeling as you do, Stephen? I feel as if you've taken advantage of me and now you are just going to cast me off.'

Elsie relented, knowing that neither of them had a choice but had to accept their situation; she smiled back at him and Stephen pulled her to him.

'Don't you see, Elsie, it's either smile or cry. You take your choice. I have to have you in my life, whether it works or not. The only trouble is I have to make the other things in my life work as well.'

Stephen pulled himself forward and buried his face in his hands. Elsie could see his chest heaving with the emotion that was affecting him and she knew how he was feeling because she felt the same. It was all right for a man, though. A man would get a bigger reputation as a bigger, better man if he was found out, while she would get the reputation of a slut. In spite of that Elsie still had the sense of a dilemma that was unsolvable. Perhaps they were not the only ones who had had the problem. Perhaps there were others who had had the problem and solved it.

Stephen smiled at her again in such a way that seemed to tell her that her engagement was of no importance to him, just to other people. Why was she always so certain of the link between them?

Perhaps Mary Bowyer would be able to give her sane advice. She would go to her, on Sunday and ask her. What if Dan should offer to take her? Elsie's mind wandered and then was brought back to the present by Stephen moving away from her. She knew what he was thinking; they couldn't stay away from everyone for long without being detected; she sat up.

'Come on, Stephen. We'd better go now. They'll hang us if we get caught like this.'

Elsie stood and he followed. He squeezed her hand and turning on his heel, strode away into the gloom of the factory. Elsie stood and looked at the shape of their bodies in the pile of sacks, swiftly smoothed them and then briskly walked away.

After that, she somehow managed to keep track of what was happening in his life and Stephen seemed to know what was happening in hers. He even congratulated her on her engagement to Dan.

'I'm sure he'll be a good husband to you, the same as I'll do my best for Mabel and, in between, you and I'll do our best for each other in spite of all the rules.'

Chapter 7

Willenhall Life
A death in the family
1906

The weekend seemed to arrive swiftly. Elsie hadn't been able to make up her mind how to approach Mary. She knew that Mary would have divided loyalties on the subject but hoped that her special kind of wisdom would mean that Mary would give her some good advice. Elsie hoped to speak to Mary during the weekend, after the week's work was out of the way.

She had been entrusted to carry out some of the accounts work for the shop. The Works Office was where all the bills and accounts were sorted and totalled and usually Victoria did the work but she was going to Wolverhampton with her mother.

Mildred had stayed with Elsie for a few minutes, checking that the work was being carried out in a satisfactory way. Then, after giving Elsie a quick wave of her hand, she went out of the door, pushing Victoria in front of her. Elsie bent to the figures in front of her and quickly added the line of figures to arrive at the total sales for yesterday. She could do this kind of work easily so she just bent to it. There was a sound from behind her.

'Would you like a cup of tea, Elsie?'

Elsie started and looked up with a jump as she heard Agnes at her elbow.

'Whew! You made me jump, then. Yes, I would really like a cup of tea.'

It was the first time they had really had anything to do with each other and Elsie hoped to get to know her a little better. She watched as Agnes poured the tea and topped it up with some milk.

Agnes blushed as she realised that Elsie was watching her and Elsie quickly explained. 'I didn't mean to embarrass you. It's just that I like watching people, don't you? It gives me an insight into what kind of person they are. People are so interesting, I find. What do you think?'

Elsie spoke quickly, trying to keep her tone light to let the other girl know that she hadn't meant anything unkindly by watching her. Agnes was swift to reply. 'Oh,' she said, 'I'm just the same. I love watching folk. I love to see the different expressions fly across their faces when something happens that they weren't expecting, or when someone tells them something that shocks them.'

Elsie turned so that she could see Agnes better in the poor light. She was quite what Elsie called a handsome girl. The girl was not above medium height but gave the impression that there was more of her than there actually was. Elsie smiled at her own thoughts. Agnes wore black and white all the time, she had noticed. Today she had a white cotton blouse and a long black skirt, along with black shoes.

The two girls stood appraising each other unashamedly and without rancour. Suddenly they burst out laughing. The difference between the girls was small; they were enough alike to be sisters. Agnes spoke,

'Here's your tea, Elsie. Don't let it go cold; it's on the way now. It's been stood while we've been inspecting each other.'

'Thank you, Agnes.'

Elsie thought; was this the one from whom she should seek advice? Then the thought occurred to her that because they were so alike, neither of them could deal with the other's problems or they would already have dealt with them!

She bent her head and returned to her work and when she looked up, Agnes was gone. She must be busy, Elsie thought. Her mind started to wander as it did when she was performing a task that was so easy that she could do it without thinking. There was a noise from outside the window and she craned her neck to see whatever it was that had disturbed her.

Outside was the yard between the back of the shop's living quarters and the lock manufactory at the rear of the premises. The paving of the area was made up of the dark blue bricks that were used where tough, knock- resistant flooring was needed. She could see Agnes and a youth; she had seen him before but didn't know his name. They were standing in the doorway of the factory room where the locks were black japanned, a paint process. The room wasn't a busy one and consequently the door was not often used. The youth had his arm around Agnes and his lips were close to hers.

Elsie knew that Agnes would be in trouble if Mildred came home early and caught them, but they didn't seem to care. The youth put his hand on Agnes's breast and she pushed him away as if making a half-hearted protest. He pulled her to him and she responded, kissing him on the lips. Elsie felt herself both respond to their feeling and cringe in fear at their unknown predicament. She turned her mind back to the accounts that she had been told to complete and finished them off. The sun had moved across the sky when she heard the front door open. It was Mildred and her elder daughter, Victoria!

What should she do? Elsie thought quickly and moved to the window that overlooked the yard. She opened it when she saw that Agnes was still there, talking to the youth. Elsie opened her mouth to shout and then realised that if she did so, Mildred would hear. She picked up a penny from the cash box that lay open on the large desk in front of her. Pulling her hand back, she tossed it in the direction of Agnes who instantly heard the distinctive sound of the coin dropping near her on the black setts and looked up. Elsie mouthed the words to her.

'Your mother! Your mother's here!'

She used her thumb to back up her words, motioning in a meaningful way. Agnes moved away from the young man who stood gaping as Agnes dashed across the yard and up the stairs, barely in front of Mildred and Victoria. She moved to the desk alongside Elsie and dipped her pen in the inkwell as Mildred walked in the room and surveyed them. Mildred strode to Elsie and looked at her work.

'Well done, Elsie. I like to see someone who sticks to her work.'

She turned on her heel and, ignoring Agnes, clip-clopped down the stairs towards the toilet. Victoria looked down at them.

'I hope you two have done something while mother and I have been out shopping. She's annoyed with the whole world, this morning. I couldn't get her to spend a penny. I don't know what's the matter with her.' Victoria turned to Elsie. 'You'd better help me with something for lunch before she goes berserk. She's always like this at this time of the month. Come on!'

Elsie stood and followed as Victoria led the way downstairs. Elsie turned and winked at Agnes as she went. Agnes flushed and bent her head to her books. She was saved from the wrath of her mother. Elsie smiled to herself. These posh people were no better than anyone else. She turned into the kitchen and picked up a butter knife.

'What would you like on these sandwiches, Victoria?'

Victoria turned on her heel. She too, seemed to be in the grip of a bout of annoyance. Was the whole family like this? Then Victoria seemed to soften.

'I'm sorry, Elsie; I shouldn't take it out on you. You are the only one who seems sane at times and yet your father must be a source of worry to you.'

Why had Victoria brought up the subject of her father? How was she supposed to answer that question? She decided to find out.

'What do you mean, Victoria? Why should my father be a source of worry to me? I know he was ill when we first came to work here but he's improved a lot since then.'

She looked to Victoria for an answer.

'Well, I saw him spitting blood up, the other day. Like you, I thought he was getting better but it seems to me that he is trying to hide his illness.' Victoria looked at Elsie with sympathy in her eyes. 'I know how you must feel but I think it's better to know than not know, don't you?'

Elsie felt herself go limp, and sat down. What Victoria was telling her was ringing true; she hadn't taken a lot of notice of her father lately and he always seemed to be in a good mood. She would have to pay more attention. Now was as good a time as any.

'Can you carry on with these sandwiches please, Victoria? I must go and have a look at him.'

Elsie didn't wait for an answer; she just walked, almost ran across the yard, startling the youth who had been with Agnes.

'Oh; go and find something useful to do, won't you!'

Elsie pushed past him and trotted along the darkened passageway towards the forge. Slowing down; Elsie moved quietly along the dark passageway; there was no need for her father to see the anxiety on her face. The dim glow of the forge glowed around the next bend in the passage. James was sitting at the side of the fire, his face in his hands, his sides rocking as he gave a low cough. He turned as he heard her approach, and smiled.

'Hello, Petal. What are you doing here? I would have thought you would have plenty to do, to fill up your time.'

He seems all right, she thought. Was Victoria deliberately trying to make her feel anxious? Then Elsie noticed that her father had a bright pink flush to his cheeks. He turned his back to her for a moment and she heard the hiss as his spit hit the cokes. He turned back and wiped his lips but not before Elsie had seen the small trickle of blood.

'Oh, Dad; look at you! You should be seeing a doctor and resting, not working on a Saturday afternoon. What's the matter with you?' She answered her own question. 'You've got consumption, haven't you? And all this time I thought you were getting better!'

Elsie looked at her father. James was obviously discomforted by her finding out his true condition. Perhaps she shouldn't have found him out in such an obvious way. When he spoke, he sounded angry,

'I suppose one of them Stones' girls has been dropping me in it!' He seemed very annoyed by it. 'All I wanted to do was to keep working as long as I could. I'm all right. I know I'm going through a bad patch at the moment but I know I'll get better soon; don't you fret yourself, Elsie. I've been like this before and got over it.'

James seemed suddenly to shrink in front of her, the strength clearly going from his limbs. Elsie felt terrible for finding him out; her father was doing his best to hide his illness from her. She moved towards him and put her arms around him.

'Oh, Dad; I really don't know what I'm going to do with you! You should try to rest more. I remember you saying the same to our Mom, and look what happened? She carried on as if there was nothing the matter with her, and then we lost her. I can't bear to think I might lose you, Dad.'

Elsie began to understand then, why he was acting in this way. Her father was just refusing to recognise that he was in the grip of the deadly scourge. It was all the man could do. James was not the sort to plead sympathy; he was just passing time until his time ran out; living the last of his life in the best way he could. There was just no other way for him to be. Elsie moved away from him, pretending to go along with his self-created fiction. Her words were meant to be a comfort.

'I suppose you'll soon be back on your feet, banging hell out of your bits of iron. I'll see you later, Dad.'

Elsie turned and walked away from him, back towards the house, where her chores were waiting. She muffled her sobs as she walked; gradually bringing herself to an appearance of normality. No one said anything to her as she walked in but she could feel their sympathy.

The days passed and she tried to put thoughts of her father's condition out of her mind. When she did see him, he always seemed cheerful, giving her a friendly wave as they passed each other.

Dan took her to see Mary again, the following Sunday. They met up in church and Elsie felt as if she just wanted to be held in her friend's arms and pour out all her troubles. There was no opportunity to do so, however, and before she knew it, it was time to start back, forcing a smile onto her face.

As she entered the Stones' house, Mildred called her. 'Come here, child. I want a word with you.' She waited until Elsie had taken off her hat and coat, and then sat by the fire. She turned to Elsie and said, 'There is no easy way to tell you this, Elsie. Your father has been very ill today. Mister Stone went to see him, to give him a job, and he was lying at the back of the forge. He was obviously very ill so Albert sent for the doctor, who had him removed immediately. Your father is now in the hospital, in an isolation ward. I'm sorry to have to tell you that the doctor has told us that he doesn't have long to live.'

Mildred Stone reached across the fireplace to Elsie who dropped down on her knees and buried her face in Mildred's lap, sobbing.

'I knew it would come to this; Mother went the same way. I've got to go and see him, Missus Stone. I've got to see him as soon as possible, before it's too late.'

Elsie stood and composed her appearance as well as she could. Mildred Stone looked down at her, sympathy and sadness showing on her face.

'Yes; of course. I'll ask Stephen to take you. Have a drink before you go.' She bustled out of the room and returned a moment later with her son. Stephen seemed to reach across the room to her and Elsie followed him blindly out of the house and watched as he harnessed the horse into the small trap.

Elsie hardly remembered the journey across the Black Country to the hospital in Walsall. A few minutes later, Stephen was steering her along the long corridors to the isolation ward. James was lying very still when she found him, near the door of the ward.

She took his hand and her father looked up and smiled.

'I knew you'd turn up, sooner or later, Petal. I'm sorry about this.' James spread his hands to indicate his apology for being ill. 'They're all very nice here. The food is nothing to write home about though.'

James smiled again and Elsie saw that he was near the end. His illness could not be denied and she felt as if she were missing him already. James looked up, saw Stephen standing there and spoke to him.

'Thank you for looking after my daughter, Mister Stephen. I am very grateful.'

James lay back and struggled with his breath; each succeeding one seeming slower and to drag on for minutes at a time. Then, as he seemed to gather his breath for a last intake of air, his eyes became fixed. James was gone.

The two people watching gathered each other in their arms and released the emotion that everyone feels at the loss of another. Elsie sat for a moment and then reached across to close her father's eyes. She bent to kiss him and then turned away, the loss hitting her again as she sat there. Her breast gulped air as she sobbed and Stephen put his arms around her, enclosing her in a sheltering cocoon of love. He lifted his arm and the Sister came across to them, beckoning a nurse to assist. Between them they managed to persuade the young people to leave the terrible scene of Elsie's great loss.

The journey back to Willenhall was slow, the trap stopping often so that Stephen could enfold her in his arms to give her some emotional support. When they arrived, Mildred was the next one to offer her the comfort of loving arms to hide in. A feeling came over Elsie that an important phase in her life had come to an end; another was about to begin.

The funeral was a poor one. The Stone family paid for it and Mary came to the service. Elsie found that she could face the world on her own but not at Willenhall. Mary offered a place in her home and Elsie accepted it with gratitude. Dan called on her and eventually he came to be accepted as her young man. Stephen called rarely and often was unable to do more than exchange greetings and pleasantries with her, but Elsie knew that she would never forget the secure feeling she had experienced in his arms as Stephen had comforted her at the time of her loss.

Then Dan asked Elsie to marry him. It was both expected and a shock. Elsie knew that there was no one to grant her permission at her young age, but would anyone be bothered? She thought not. In her mind, Elsie had always thought of Stephen as her lover in spite of his marriage to Mabel Elkins. On the night that she accepted Dan's proposal, she had cried herself to sleep for the loss of the lover she would never have the right to love. Dan, she knew, was a good man, willing to do anything for her but somehow there was always something missing.

Elsie accepted Dan's proposal knowing that she would be provided for and security was the first in her list of priorities. It was no good mooning around, she thought to herself; she had to survive and the harsh social environment of the Black Country was no place to get sentimental about her relationships.

'Yes, Dan, I'll take you if you'll take me,' she said, looking firmly at the young man, and conscious of her deception. 'We should be good for each other. I'll be as good a wife as I can and I know you'll be as good a husband as you can.'

Dan was on his knees when she replied to him and Elsie gently drew him up as she noticed the tears in his eyes, knowing that he had brought all his courage to bear to get him to this point.

'Come on, Dan. We're not a couple out of a penny novel, all lovey-dovey. We're a young, strong pair who'll stand by each other to do well and perhaps have something to leave our children.'

Dan rose and they walked into the front room of Mary's house and gave her the news. Elsie hadn't got round to telling her of her feelings for Stephen. Somehow, Elsie thought that Mary knew without being told but had let her seek her own destiny in her own way, as opportunities came along. Mary was full of congratulations.

'Well, here we are then. Where are you going to live? You've got to be practical, you know!'

Elsie was wondering how practical it was possible to be but Mary went on.

'There's a house just off Upper High Street that you might like to have a look at. I've asked the landlord to keep it empty for you. I wondered when some young man would take you away from me, and I had no intentions of letting him take you far. I think too much of you.' Mary turned to Dan. 'Just you be a good husband to her, Dan, and don't let me hear of you being cruel or violent to her. I know too many young men who would be willing to act as her protector. If you think that's a warning as well as a good turn, you are right. This young lady has been through the mill in the last few months, and I'd like to think that the bad part of her life is behind her, now.'

They managed to find a few pieces of furniture, and moved in on the day that they were married at Saint Mary's. The house was only a few yards from Fred Stone's small enterprise, and Fred offered Dan a job but he would not take it, saying, 'I've trained to be a locksmith and that's what I'll be.'

He bought a bicycle and cycled to Willenhall each day. He was a very proud man and would not think of changing his trade. At times, Elsie compared him to her father who had continued learning new trades almost until the day of his death. She had to admit to the determination of her young husband though, as she saw him off each day; although she couldn't help wondering if this was how her life was going to be from now on. Somehow there must be something for her to do, too.

Chapter 8

Another Sort of Work
1906

'You can work for me, any time, my girl,' Fred Stone had said. 'You are bright, fit and willing and you can't ask any more than that.'

Fred Stone had offered Elsie a job at his smithy for a short while, but she found the work too taxing and she was considering what other type of work she could do. She spoke to Mary, trying out some of her ideas.

'Mary, I think the work is going to be too heavy for me at Fred's. Do you know of anyone who might give me a position in office work? I learned a lot from Mildred Stone and I think it might be a good way for me to make a living. I've worked on a hand press as well, so that's another possibility. I can't afford to hang around, doing nothing.'

They were sitting in the front room of Mary's house as they did sometimes while Dan was at work. Elsie and Dan were struggling to find enough money to manage on. Although many Black Country men were too proud to have their wives go out to work, Elsie had seen the benefits that came from both partners working. All the Stone family worked, married or not, and this gave them an advantage over many others. Their girls had been brought up in the same way and they were all the more prosperous because of it. Mary seemed to consider for a moment and then she replied to Elsie's question.

'I wonder if you could look after some property. It'd

mean you learning a lot of new things but I think you might have the brain and mind for it.' She hesitated for a moment then spoke again. 'I know you've not been married long but why is it that you can't do the work now that you could do easily a month or two ago? Are you pregnant, my dear?' She looked closely into Elsie's eyes and read the truth that could not be held back. 'Come on, my dear; you can tell me all of it. You know that, don't you?'

Mary cried miserably as Elsie confessed how she had given her body to Stephen.

'Oh, Mary, I don't know how it happened; we just sort of wanted…,' Elsie hesitated and then seeing no disapproval in the older woman's eyes, went on. 'I know it sounds silly, but it didn't seem wrong at the time; it just seemed the most natural thing to do.' She paused for a moment. 'Mary, there's no way that we could get married or anything like that. I couldn't hurt Dan. I know he's not perfect but he's really tried to be a good husband, and Stephen's not free, either. He's got obligations that he can't avoid. Their two families expect him to carry on with the expansion of the firm, to make it bigger and better. They would all break their hearts if he let them down and, I know it sounds daft, it would break mine as well!'

Mary leaned forward, putting her arms around her young protégée.

'Listen, Elsie. I can't say I approve of what's happened between you but there's no way it can be changed. You'll have to live with it and the only way you can do that is to deceive your husband. You'll have to tell Dan that he's the father of your child. If I know him, he'll be delighted. He'll think it proves his manhood.'

Mary moved away and poured a cup of tea. There seemed to be two problems, the emotional one and the practical one. She had to keep Elsie's marriage off the rocks and she had to find a way for her to earn some real money.

'I think I can find you some light work. It will be different to anything you have done before but it will, if you work at it, show you a way to gain your independence.'

Elsie was confused as she knew that Mary had a little property and that she lived on the rent she gained from them. Surely there couldn't be enough work to supply the need for a full-time assistant? She waited for Mary to continue. What was going to be revealed now? Elsie had always felt that there was a greater depth to Mary than was apparent on a first appraisal.

Mary seemed to be considering, as if what she was about to say was very important. She bent over a slip of paper and then looked up.

'Look, Elsie,' Mary broke into her thoughts, making her start. 'Give this note to Fred. This is to ask him to give you Monday off; don't worry about losing the wages for the day; you will be paid. Then, go to Jenkins the solicitors; he's my old friend, at the bottom of the High Street. Tell them that you are enquiring about the vacancy in the rent office. They'll interview you and you'll be told the outcome later. Now, that's enough for today. It's time I was in bed. You had better go home now; your husband will be wondering where you are.'

The weekend seemed to pass slowly. Mary had mentioned the possibility to Dan that Elsie might work as a bookkeeper and he hadn't been all that impressed; probably, Elsie thought, because he knew nothing about that type of job. Still, neither did she, so she would have to wait until Monday to find out. On Sunday, after church, she pressed her black skirt and white cotton blouse, determined to look business-like at her interview.

Dan watched as she did so, a sardonic smile on his face. He's hoping I don't get this job, she thought. It might mean that I contribute as much to this household as he does. Black had been a fashionable colour ever since Queen Victoria died in 1901 and part of Elsie's mind wondered if she would ever wear it for Dan's funeral.

Elsie decided then that she would not reveal her income to Dan, even if it meant making out a false pay packet, if she got the job. She could always open an account at the bank to deposit the balance. She would be independent of him. She could not envisage when it would be of any use to her but she was sure she wanted to be able to hold her head up, and only she would know why!

Suddenly Elsie felt excited and nervous, all at the same time. There was no reason to think she would get a job offer, she had no experience of the sort of work they did in a solicitor's office.

Monday came and Dan went off to work in his usual way, harshly commenting on the interview Elsie was to have that morning.

'Don't you get worrying about working in a solicitor's office,' he said. 'We can live all right on my wages, the same as most folks. Locksmiths have always been able to keep their families; not like the Stones. They always make their women work; disgraceful I call it. I'll see you later. Tara.'

Elsie smiled to herself as he peddled up the street. Perhaps Dan was right! She closed the door behind her and sat to her breakfast. There was a pile of washing to do before she started out for the interview. Her office clothes were hanging on a coat hanger, ready to put on. The thought came to her; perhaps she was right! There was no reason why a man had to be right all the time. Perhaps, just perhaps, she might be offered something.

Elsie didn't even know what the job was, yet! Mary Bowyer had seemed quite mysterious when she had started to speak about the possibility of the position. Firstly, Mary had seemed to be offering the position herself and then she had changed what she was saying, to imply that the solicitor would be the one who had the job to offer. What was the truth behind it?

Elsie looked out of the window. The sun was shining; it was going to be a fine day. She picked up the dolly-maid and pounded down on the sheets in the barrel. There was a lot to do! Elsie looked round; there were other women carrying out the same, almost traditional task.

'Mornin', Mrs Barr. Nice day for it!'

It was Elsie's neighbour, Ruth Mallory. They were all close here. There was no choice really, living almost on top of each other. There was security and comfort in the closeness. They were all in the same boat. She felt her back stiffen at the thought. She had no intention of being in the same boat or any other vessel as them for the rest of her life. Elsie tried to keep her voice friendly as she answered, 'Morning, Mrs Mallory; yes, it's lovely this morning. This'll be done and dried before we know it. I might iron it later on, if I get time.'

Elsie turned her mind back to the washing, lifting it and twisting it in a tight, wringing action. She had better move herself. There was no point in standing canting to the neighbours, with so much to do. Perhaps Mrs Mallory would do her washing for her, if the job worked out! Elsie took a grip on herself; she mustn't get delusions of grandeur, as she had heard Mildred say to her daughters.

It was ten to nine; her appointment was at nine o'clock. Elsie sat in the narrow passage on the upstairs floor of the solicitor's office. The office was at the end of the commercial properties, as if it was trying to keep itself to itself. Elsie had never noticed it before.

An elderly man in dark clothes made his way past her, excusing himself as he did. He seemed to look keenly at her as he turned to go into the office. There was a name on the office, S. Jenkins. Well, that was a coincidence, or was it? Were S. Jenkins and Mary Bowyer related? There were a lot of knots in this piece of string! A few moments later the door opened and the same man looked through it and beckoned her.

'Mrs Barr? Would you like to come through, please?'

He stepped back to allow her room to walk into the office. It was larger than she had expected, and light too. The sun was pouring through the window. The man moved past her, to sit on the other side of the desk. He coughed and picked up a piece of paper. After perusing it for a moment he turned to her.

'I understand that you have some aspirations of working here? Have you ever worked in a legal office before?' He went on, after her reply. 'Do you know the difference between the work here and the work anywhere else?'

Elsie didn't know what to say. Work was work as far as she was concerned. Work could be carried out in any sort of premises. She looked back at him, feeling suddenly miserable. Then she had an inspiration. Everything Mary had said to her had seemed to be secret; perhaps that was it. Elsie spoke quietly.

'Please sir, I think it might be more confidential here, than in other offices. Is that what you mean?'

Elsie hesitated. Was that the right reply? The man was after all, the one who was asking the questions, not she. He was smiling at her now.

'Yes, that is the right answer. Well done. What is needed here, for now, is a sort of secretary. Do you know the meaning of the word, Mrs Barr?'

It was obvious, really, and Elsie told him so.

'Yes, it is a person who keeps secrets and records for a living; telling her employer's business to no one.'

Elsie was crossing her fingers in her lap, hoping he would

not see. The man was smiling again; he looked quite nice when he smiled. He spoke again, 'Tell me about the work you have done before, Mrs Barr, so that I can get an idea of whether we can use you in the position we are trying to fill.'

As she spoke, telling him of her early history, Elsie came to life with her vivid descriptions, spoken with a mixture of Black Country and Brummagem tongues, of the way she had started work. Helping her mother at first, in the nail trade, in Birmingham, working so fast that if she dropped a nail, there was not time to pick it up; you had just had to start making the next one from the length of wire you were already holding. Their life had revolved around the work that was made by them each day in their small cottage with an anvil to work on. There had always been something to do, cleaning, pumping the bellows, cooking, washing the few clothes they had. Life had not been easy in Deritend, formerly Dirty End, in Birmingham

As he listened to Elsie's life story, the solicitor took notes. When she ran out of things to tell him, he smiled at her.

'You've certainly had a busy life for one so young, Mrs Barr. How did you find working on the accounts books for the Stone family?'

Elsie told him of how she had had to use the mental arithmetical skills she had learned at school. How she had worked in the shop, the lock factory and the house, acting as a housemaid for them and become proficient at all of the tasks she was given. At length, Elsie became lost for words, feeling that he had dried her up. He smiled again.

'Well, I am really impressed with what you have accomplished at such an early age. Now I think you've got to start all over again. We are going to offer you a position where you will need some training, although the skills you have will certainly come in handy.' He reached to shake Elsie's hand. 'You will, as you have mentioned, have to keep secrets and if you ever give away any of our clients' business dealings, you will be dismissed immediately. How do you feel about that, Mrs Barr?'

How did she feel about it, indeed? She felt quite excited. Elsie knew that Mary had had something to do with this offer. It had, after all, been her idea in the first place. How should she put her feelings to this man? She decided to be as honest as she could.

'Well, sir, I feel frightened and pleased, all at once. I don't mind learning a new trade, if that's what you call it. I've spent most of my life learning new things, so I'm sure I can learn something else.

'As for the confidential side of the business, I can keep your secrets if you can keep mine. I intend to keep the details of my salary a secret from everyone, even my husband. You can rely on me, sir. I shall open a bank account to put a part of my pay into, and that will be my secret, sir. Yes, I would like the job, if you offer it to me, as you say you are going to. There is one more thing I must tell you, sir; I'm pregnant, four months. It shouldn't make any difference to how well I can carry out my duties but I thought I should tell you.'

Elsie closed her mouth, waiting for him to speak. This might be the most important day of her life, as far as work was concerned. She had said her piece and she was saying no more before he spoke. She placed her hands in her lap and smiled up at him; he did seem to be a tall man. What was he going to say? At length, he pressed a bell on his desk and a stocky man with a pleasant face walked in. Mr Jenkins introduced them.

'Hello, Luke. This is Mrs Elsie Barr. She is going to start work for us at her earliest convenience.' He swivelled in his chair so that he was facing her. 'Would next Monday morning at nine o'clock be convenient for you, Mrs Barr?' On receiving

Elsie's nod, he turned back the other man. 'Please make a note of her details. Elsie will be training to look after the Bowyer accounts. You can fill her in on what she has to do, after she starts.' He turned to her again. 'I hope you don't mind me calling you Elsie. We're all quite friendly here. If you'd like to go with Luke, he'll talk to you about the work you will be undertaking for us. It may be some time before we meet again. I hope you enjoy your work, Elsie. Good morning.'

The man named Luke ushered her out of the office as the tall man bent back to his work. It seemed to Elsie that she was just one of the parts of the day's work, nobody important. What had Mister Jenkins meant; the Bowyer accounts?

'Come through into here.' He moved her into the small room at the end of the passage. 'Sit down. Thank God someone is going to give a hand with these accounts. I've been working sixty hours a week, trying to get them all collected in. Now, name, address, date of birth, etc. etc., then you can go home until next Monday. I shall arrange a small desk so that you have somewhere you can call your own. You realise you'll be paid monthly, I suppose?'

Elsie hadn't known about that but it didn't matter. Her employer would simply be saving her pay for her, and that was the real purpose of her employment, whatever Dan thought. It was her second secret from Dan! She felt guilty in a small way but the secret had a pleasant side to it as well, as if she had a power that no one else knew about. She had the other secret too, her child, but there was no hurry to tell about that to her husband or her lover. The thought made her shudder and she eased herself back into the present.

It didn't seem to take long before Luke knew all about her and her relationship with Mary Bowyer. He looked at her when she gave her address as if he was realising something. Elsie explained how Mary had taken her and her father in when they first came into Wednesbury, and how they had moved to Willenhall on the recommendation of Fred Stone.

'Oh, I see,' Luke said, 'a nice lady.'

He offered no other comment, just seeming secretive. They parted an hour later and Elsie felt that he knew a lot more about her affairs than she did about his. Mary was in the house, waiting, when she went to see her. The look on Elsie's face told her how the interview had gone. Mary's face lit up as she greeted her.

'I am so pleased for you, Elsie. I knew Sam would give you a fair crack of the whip!'

'Who is Sam? What's he got to do with anything?'

'Oh, didn't he introduce himself? That's just like him; he thinks everything's a secret. He's my other brother, Sam Jenkins. He's worked for himself there, for years, since his father, Bernard Bowyer was the owner. My mother married twice, you know. I hope you don't think you got any favours from him. He's a stickler for doing things in what he calls the right way. If he gave you the position it's because he thought you are the right person for it; congratulations, my dear!' Mary put her arms around Elsie and hugged her. 'I suppose you want to get back to work, now. Fred is going to be disappointed when you give him the news. He was getting used to having you around the forge again. He'll have to find somebody else now.'

The rest of the week seemed to fly by. Fred was disappointed for himself but pleased for her when she told him she had been offered a position by Mister Jenkins. Dan hardly mentioned her new position, just asking her whether she had got the job.

'It can't be all that hard if they think a woman can do it.'

No word of congratulations, just reminding her of her

duties in the house. It almost seemed that he regarded her as a competitor for the breadwinner's role. It was as if any money she earned detracted from his position as head of their little family.

Elsie missed the intimacy of the Stones' girls and the occasional glimpse of Stephen; he would have found something encouraging to say, she felt sure. Was marriage going to be worth the trouble? Perhaps she would have been able to support herself without a husband.

Elsie had always wanted the sudden excitement that she felt could occur, even in a familial relationship. She still went to church with Mary but Dan seemed to have lost interest. Had his visits been just a cheap way of 'taking her out'? He was getting more interested in going down to the pub, now, and coming home drunk, demanding his rights and his share of her money. He never did find out how much she earned. He even called into the office for her salary on one occasion but was sent away with a flea in his ear.

Elsie heard about it from Luke who had sent him away. He had been most amused by the incident.

'Who gave anyone the right to pick up somebody else's wages, I'd like to know. I've never heard of such a thing!'

Elsie had been most embarrassed by the incident, but was glad that Luke had taken the action he did. She never mentioned it to Dan, leaving him wondering whether she knew what he had tried to do.

The work itself was a revelation to her. At first, all she did was keep the books, adding to the daily totals by the amount that had been paid into the accounts. The firm assisted a number of landlords to collect their rents and these were handed in by the rent collectors. Elsie gave a signature for each collector's book, after she had checked the amounts paid. Then she added the amounts into both a total book and a book containing the totals taken by each collector.

For much of the day she sat checking the totals from the day before, and then she started receiving the monies. She was given the responsibility for some of the firm's collector's takings and Luke handled the rest. Some of the rents were collected in quarterly and some, the tenants of the small, back to back houses, were called on weekly.

After a time she started getting finished early so would sit looking out of the window. She could see the high clock in the middle of the street and it was a nuisance, telling her the time, all the time. She had a good view of the town and saw the changes that were made each market day by the erection of the stalls, twice a week.

Elsie asked for more work so that she wouldn't be bored and each time she did, another collector was added to her list until she felt she was doing as much work as Luke. Then one day she was given the accounts that were collected by Henry Brown. She looked to see whose rents he collected, and it was Mary Bowyer's!

She added up the collection from Brown, and was amazed at the figure that was the total. He had collected twenty-five pounds, three and four pence! That was only one day's rent so she assumed it was the total for the week, but each day he came in with a comparable amount. Suddenly she realised; her friend Mary was a rich woman! This is a time for keeping a closed mouth, she thought. What she wanted to know was how she could do the same thing! Perhaps there would be other things that she would find out in time if she just kept her own counsel.

A month later, Henry Brown left. He had been offered some important administrative position in the South Wales Borderers, who were about to send some replacements to South Africa and Elsie was offered his position. The promotion, so soon in her new career, was a worry to her and she wondered if she would be able to manage the extra work, along with the new skills she had to learn. There always seemed to be something to learn in life. You just had to decide whether the challenge was for you. Where was this job leading her? There had been a lot to learn and now it seemed there was still more. Would she ever know enough to be proficient at it? Had Mary had to go through this much learning on the way to her wealth?

Chapter 9

A Friend in Debt
1906

Life became interesting for Elsie. The work was light and she could easily handle the figures involved. She was finding out more and more about the inhabitants of Wednesbury. All her neighbours were tenants of Mary Bowyer. Many of them were in arrears to a certain extent, but not to the point where they would be evicted. Some of the leading investors in property were people who she had had no idea were so prosperous.

Elsie's pregnancy was now beginning to show although Mr Jenkins didn't refer to it. Luke joked that no thief would suspect her of carrying large sums of cash around in her condition. Dan had to be told of her pregnancy and he seemed quite pleased to think he had brought his wife to this condition in such a short time, doubtless feeling that it reflected favourably on his masculinity. The Stone family were told; she went to make one of her occasional visits with Mary and there were promises of items for the infant.

Occasionally, someone would come into the solicitor's office to discuss business with one of the partners of the firm. Luke was not a partner but, he confided to Elsie, he hoped to be one day. He never mentioned Mary Bowyer but he never spoke about any of the other investors, either. Elsie worked closely with him and took the opportunity to look over his shoulder as he buried himself in his account books. Sometimes he was explosive in the way he spoke of tenants.

'I'm fed up of this one,' Luke said showing his irritation. 'She's had a dozen chances to pull her arrears back into control but just ignores anything I say on the subject. She'll have one more last warning, and I do mean a last warning. If she doesn't pay her way she will have to go!'

Elsie was surprised by Luke's words.

'Why do you speak like that, Luke? I know you are not a cruel sort of person and yet it seems you would see her out on the street.'

Luke looked at her questioningly but she just sat, waiting for his justification. His face softened and he explained,

'Well, it's like this, Elsie. Never mind what you are doing; come and look at her account; come on; you'll see what I mean.'

Luke slid along the long bench that he usually sat on, making space for her to sit beside him. The book in front of him was open and the name and address were open to the eye. Mrs Ruth Mallory, 4/48 Union Street, her neighbour! There was a small red mark every so often, by the payment column.

'See that?' said Luke. 'That's where I've asked her to try to pay a little off her arrears.' He counted the small red marks. 'Seven times! She's even offered to bed me if I could see my way to forgetting her arrears. I wouldn't mind but she's not all that pretty; I wouldn't bed her if she jumped into bed with me.'

Luke smiled at her but all Elsie could think of was that Ruth was going to get evicted – and she couldn't let her know. Her first instinct was to warn her neighbour in as quiet a way as possible but then she decided against it. She would see how it worked out. That way she would learn something. Would Ruth Mallory learn as well? She decided to tell Luke about her problem, but to her surprise he already knew.

'Yes, we wondered what your reaction would be. You could easily be too soft for this job. You see, Elsie; there are people you can help and others you can't. You could lend her the money to pay off her arrears, or I could give her three more last chances and it wouldn't make any difference. She'd find something that the money needed to be spent on, and she'd spend it. Then, when the owner finally gets sick of waiting for a return on their investment, we would be seen as cruel bastards, throwing a poor woman on the mercy of the street!

'I'm really pleased that you were honest enough to tell me about how you feel. How do you feel about the job, now? Do you think you have the strength of character to realise that some of our landlords are just working folk, the same as you and I? They've worked hard and sacrificed many things in order to help buy the house that people moan about but do not take the trouble to save for themselves.'

The exposure to the opposing point of view shook her for a moment or two, and then she recalled that she too, was doing the same thing, making sacrifices, saving part of her salary each month as an investment. She could have spent it on frivolities like Ruth, but she hadn't. She had kept her own counsel, even from her own husband. What would he think of her if he knew the secrets that she kept? It didn't matter, she thought. He didn't seem to think her opinion was worthy of any consideration, anyway. Elsie realised that she had developed and matured at a different rate and in different directions from her husband. He seemed an uncouth young man to her now, even if he did have ideas about the international situations of the time. She replied to Luke.

'Thank you for teaching me so much. It's all very well, though, but how can Mrs Mallory be helped from the consequences of her own lack of common sense, not just for her sake but for the sake of her three children and the other one on the way? You might be right in what you're saying but how will you feel when she is on the street because we could not find some way to help her? We can say that we are cleverer than her, but not clever enough to be able to make her just a little bit cleverer!'

Luke stared at her and burst into laughter.

'Yes,' he said. 'I know it's a great pity, but there's nothing you or I can do about it. It brings us back to the first point I made; there are people who can be helped and others you can't. With all the loving kindness, and all the best will in the world, you can't change that. All you can do is use the brain that God gave you to look after you and yours. That's what others must do as well; if they don't, it's a waste; that's that, and that's all I have to say on the subject.'

Luke turned his attention to the books again and she realised that she was being dismissed. If she could not understand the logic of his argument now, there was no point in continuing the discussion. Suddenly she had an inspiration and spoke sharply to him.

'Look, Luke, if you could find a way for her to get rid of her arrears, would you allow her to continue as a tenant?'

He turned his gaze back to her and thought for a moment.

'Yes, of course I would, but I can't think of a way, can you?'

'Yes, I'd like to try one more thing, if you agree to it, not if you don't. Listen to me.'

Elsie outlined her plan and he thought quietly, a grave look on his face.

'All right, Elsie, we'll give it a try your way. I don't think it will work but either way, we'll learn a lesson, won't we?'

Luke turned his back to her again and the rest of the day was spent in near silence. The next day would see if the plan was likely to work. The young always thought they knew it all. One thing about her, though; she had some pluck, arguing with him! The next morning, Elsie passed Mrs Mallory on her way out of the court where they lived.

'Morning, Mrs Barr!'

'Morning, Mrs Mallory! Nice day for it; too nice to go to work'

She continued along Union Street and turned downhill as she got to the top of the street. Luke was waiting for her in the office, his face looking grim.

'Come on; let's get this job done with.'

In a few minutes they were back at the court. Ruth Mallory was inside the house. Elsie knocked the door and the woman appeared.

'Hello, Mrs Barr, what can I do for you?' Ruth turned to Luke. 'Hello Mister Bryant, I thought I'd told you I was going to settle up with you, next week? I ain't got any cash in the house.' She turned back to Elsie. 'I'm sorry; it's a bit of business I have to sort out. I'll see you later.'

Elsie looked her right in the eye.

'Mister Bryant and I are together, Mrs Mallory. Can we come in, please?'

Elsie moved Ruth Mallory aside and walked in, to the woman's surprise. She sat down on the little couch and picked up the young girl who was playing there.

'Hello, Katey. What are you playing; house? I like your baby.' She held the doll for a moment then gave it back and turned her attention to Mrs Mallory. 'Look, Ruth. I'm working for Jenkins, the solicitors, and I've been asked to put you out in the street because you are so far behind with your rent. I've told them that I'm not willing to do that and they've told me I shall be dismissed if I don't! I've no other choices but to take the side of either my employer or you. You can see that I wouldn't easily find another position. After an argument I've been allowed to come and see you with your collector, Mister Bryant, to see if there's any way to sort this out. How can I go home to Dan to tell him that I've had the sack because I couldn't evict somebody who's been asked seven times to try to bring their arrears back? Why should I get the sack for you, Ruth?'

Elsie placed her hands in her lap and composed herself. She could say no more to help the woman. It was up to her, now. The two collectors remained silent while the import of what was being said seemed to sink into Ruth Mallory's mind. Elsie had told Luke that the only way to deal with Ruth was to be ruthlessly honest. Ruth would appreciate that, she hoped, and also see that she had to do something about it or lose her home. Her rent was two shillings and four pence per week. She was ten weeks in arrears, a total of one pound, three shillings and four pence. The three of them sat in silence, the clock on the mantelpiece noisily marking the passing of the seconds. Eventually, Ruth stood up and turned to face Elsie.

'I know how hard this must have been for you, Elsie, and I can see that you've tried on my side, to get me more time. It'd be nice if I could just go to a drawer and pull out the money to clear the rent but I can't. My husband is a boozer! I've only just found out that he's lost his job through it. He's been going out in the morning, as if he was going to work. He's been looking for a job but no one'd take him on. We've had to manage on what the Parish would give us, six bob a week! How could we afford two and four pence out of that?'

Ruth broke down and started sobbing and Luke and Elsie looked at each other, stunned. Neither of them had known of the problems that Ruth Mallory was facing. There was nothing the woman was able to offer, to pay her current rent, never mind the arrears. Luke stood and Elsie followed his lead.

'Look here, Mrs Mallory,' Luke said. 'I'm going to have to go back to the office to report what you've told me, to Mister Jenkins. I can't offer you anything; I can only come back to report what he says to me. Come along, Mrs Barr. I'm sorry you've had to face one of your neighbours with this problem to solve. I shall see you again, Mrs Mallory, very shortly, I expect.'

Surprisingly, Luke held out his hand to Mrs Mallory and she shook it, surprised at the respect with which she was being treated. Luke led Elsie out of the court and back up Union Street. As they walked, he seemed to be gathering his thoughts. He turned to her.

'Now, Elsie, this is a case where you must be very confidential in your dealings with the tenant. You must never let her know who her landlord is. Can you imagine what would happen if you did? All the neighbours would jump on the bandwagon and we'd never be able to collect a decent return on her investment. What we have to do now is to let Mister Jenkins know what has happened and let him take it from there. What he does then is not our business; if she asks you, you don't know; just tell the truth about that.'

They were back at the office, now, and they separated, she to return to her accounts books and he to knock on the door of Mister Jenkins. Elsie tried to keep herself busy, telling herself that it was all none of her business, but she kept getting a mental picture of her neighbour being put out by the bailiffs. Luke returned later, to carry on with his office work, hardly glancing in her direction.

Mister Jenkins did not call her into his office so she felt that she must have passed some sort of appraisal. The day passed without her being dismissed and she felt a little more confident and secure at work. She was in the house, having finished early, when Dan returned from work. He seemed to be in a good mood for a change.

'Mister Stone's has given me a rise, a penny an hour, that's a good rise. We should be able to go out now, occasionally, Elsie. When you're short of money, life can get a bit dreary, can't it?'

Elsie felt guilty as he spoke; knowing that half of her salary was going into a bank account as her own investment. She was tempted to confide in him but something made her keep silent. Instead, she congratulated him on the rise and asked him if he had had to take on any more responsibilities to earn the rise.

'No, not really; I've been looking after a small section, eight women and boys, for about six months now. I suppose he thought I should get paid for it. I would have done it for nothing, I suppose. He's made me a sort of charge-hand, that's an unpaid foreman who does the same sort of work as his mates but tells them which sorts of locks to work on, and makes sure the locks are all up to standard. It's a sort of first step towards a foreman's job.'

They spent the rest of the evening in a jovial mood, Elsie taking up from Dan, his small happiness. They chatted about the times when they had worked together at Willenhall and had come to Wednesbury to worship at Saint Mary's Church, just to save money. Dan complained that he had had to put tuppence on the collection plate.

'It might have been cheaper to go to the theatre.' He smiled wryly. 'Still, I suppose I got a good bargain when I got you. There ain't many married women who go to work to help with the household expenses. Do you think you might get a rise, soon? Things keep going up in the shops.'

What a cheek, she thought, replying immediately.

'How do you know, Dan? When was the last time you went short of food? For the matter of that, when was the last time you did the family shopping?'

Dan had the grace to blush a little, then. He had never assisted with anything to do with the family budget. What had brought that on, anyway? He seemed to anticipate her question as if he wanted to get the answer off his back.

'It's just that I hear the men at work moaning about the

cost of things. I suppose I'm lucky, ain't I? You've always been a good manager and you've never asked me for a rise, ever since we got wed. How do you manage it?'

Elsie was tempted to tell him how much she earned, nearly as much as him, but decided against it. Dan would want it from her, to take to the pub and buy drinks for his mates and then they would be no better off. She had started collecting some of the rents in, now, from some of the local traders, and when she called, she seemed to get things a little cheaper, as if she were part of a club or secret society.

Elsie was always welcome, becoming part of the well-known people of Wednesbury. 'Good morning, Mrs Barr', they would say, and slip an apple or two into her bag. Sometimes she went with Mary Bowyer. Mary was like an aunt to her, now, and she seemed to know how well she was doing at Jenkins'. Mary was also well known in the town, but no one knew she was an investor in their business!

'How are you getting along with Luke,' Mary asked Elsie, one morning, 'Is he treating you well?'

Elsie had not known that Mary and Luke knew each other, but it wasn't to be wondered at, as he accepted the rents from her properties. She just hadn't thought about it before. Elsie tried to tell Mary how thoughtful he was to her, guiding and explaining as he guided her. Since she had become obviously pregnant he had been very deferential to her, always helping where needed; always finding her a seat.

Elsie had never spoken to Mary about the incident with Ruth Mallory but felt that the older woman knew all about it. Ruth had altered the way she had been with her rent, gradually reducing her arrears until Luke came in one day and marked her as 'account clear'. Elsie had felt that she had contributed to that state of affairs, but no one had ever complimented her on the way Ruth had changed. Mary brought up the subject.

'I'd like you know that Mister Jenkins and I are very pleased with your progress. From just filling in the accounts, you've started collecting, yourself. I had my doubts about whether you'd be able to handle the task but you've been able to do it well, and got to be liked by the trades-people of the town. The way you were able to motivate Ruth Mallory was well done, too. Her account has changed beyond recognition. Did you know that Fred has given Mister Mallory a job at the forge?' She paused for a moment. 'Do you have any savings of your own, Elsie? Now that you are doing well, I think you might be asked to be an investor, but it's no good if you've nothing to invest.'

Elsie was shocked. She had had no idea that she was that well thought of. They must have discussed her abilities in her absence. She opened her handbag, pulled out her bankbook and passed it to Mary who inspected the entries and then handed it back to her.

'Well done, Elsie. I wouldn't have believed you could have saved as much, in the short space of time you've been working for Sam Jenkins.'

Elsie told her confidentially that half of her salary went into her savings account; that Dan had no idea of her worth and that she intended to go into business, one day, not that she knew of any sort of business she could go into.

'How do you see Dan fitting into this dream future?' Mary spoke quietly, trying to impress Elsie that her ideas for the future could be brought crashing down around her, if Dan got a whisper of what she was up to. 'You see, Elsie,' she went on, 'The law might take your husband's side if there was any question of whose property your bank balance was!'

Elsie started. She hadn't thought of what view Dan might take of her ambitions. He was, after all, putting all his earnings into the family, to pay their way. Where would she be if he decided to save half of his earnings? She could carry on doing what she was doing but it might all look very underhanded if she was found out. A woman might sympathise with her viewpoint, but not a man. What should she do? Anticipating the question, Mary continued with the advice she was giving her.

'Look here, Elsie. You can still have your savings and you can still be an investor.' She saw the look of surprise on Elsie's face. 'Yes, you can. All you have to do is to become an investment company, yourself. You can then buy shares in your own company, and all you will be is a shareholder, if that is what you want. I can be an officer in your company, the secretary, for instance. I would then decide on which investments to make, after consultation with you, of course, and return whatever per cent suited you, nothing, for instance, if the company decided that the best business strategy would be to invest any accrued profits in property instead of paying a dividend. Your husband couldn't interfere with the workings of a company, nor force the company to pay any money to him.'

Mary paused for breath and saw that the import of what she had been saying was being absorbed by the young woman. Yes, she had got it; Mary could see that. It was going to be all right. She continued, 'Perhaps the first thing you should do is to buy your own house. I'd be willing to sell it to you at a reasonable price. I would take what you have in the bank as a deposit and you could pay me the balance, interest free, as and when you could.'

Elsie's eyes opened wide. She knew she was being offered a good start in business. It would use up her savings but she would now be able to put her rent away, as well as half of her salary.

'Thank you, Aunt Mary. I'm so grateful.'

Mary was pleasantly surprised at the title Elsie gave her

but somehow it seemed natural and she gradually took on the role as the two women came to develop the bond between them. How can I help the girl, Mary thought, after I am gone? Sam has enough and will not need any of mine, even if I die before him, but this young woman has to be helped. How can I best do that?

Chapter 10

Moving Again
1906

It was silly to wait until you were dead, wasn't it? Why deny yourself the pleasure of seeing the recipient's face when the news of the gift was given to them! Over the months, Mary decided to hand over more of her property to Elsie..

Elsie went about her business in her usual way; gradually building up the portfolio of properties she partly owned along with Mary. She had withdrawn most of her savings from the bank and was investing it under the guidance of Mary Bowyer and Sam Jenkins. Her first purchase was her own home and it took her all her time to keep the knowledge from Dan. He was now paying the rent to her, on her own home! She was quite competent at her allocated tasks and was treated with respect in Wednesbury. Sometimes she was embarrassed when this respect was accorded to her in the presence of her husband, as occasionally he came with her to buy the last minute things from the market.

Dan commented on it. 'You do seem to be well thought of, our wench. Why's that, I wonder?' He looked at her quizzically and went on. 'Why is it that so many of the men take off their hats to you, Elsie? Do they know something about you that I don't?' He smiled, obviously feeling pleased with himself. 'It's a sort of respect for the husband, if the wife is respected, ain't it?'

Elsie explained that some of the local traders knew because she called on them to collect their rent. She had been collecting rents for months now, and he had never known. Dan was horrified. 'I'll not have it!' Dan was livid. 'I'll not have my wife risking her neck to collect rent for some bloated capitalist. You could be attacked and killed; don't you realise that?'

Elsie didn't answer his charge but instead asked him a question. 'How did you know I was collecting rent, Dan?'

She waited for his answer and was surprised at the anger in his voice when he answered.

'Well, I know because you've just told me; that's how I know!' He turned to her, his face grim. 'Why are you asking me silly questions?'

Elsie's reaction was as swift as his. 'Because, you silly thing, if you didn't know until I told you, who else do you think I would have told? I'm not stupid, you know. In fact, some people think I'm quite bright. I don't go around telling people that I've got a handbag full of money. Come here, quickly!'

Elsie pulled him into an alley and opened her handbag for him to see the contents. There were a number of envelopes in it. She put one into his hand so that Dan could feel the sovereigns inside it. 'I've collected this money while I've been shopping with you! Did you notice? No! I've been collecting rents from the shops for three months, now, and I've not had a shadow of an attack on me, and I'm the one you call silly. Come on.'

Elsie pulled him out of the alley, back into the bustle of the market, linking his arm with hers. Dan walked a little taller; it seemed to her, as if he was ready to protect her. He was silent and she saw that Dan was thinking over what she had been saying to him. He was a dour man, sometimes, very serious about life, she thought. If only she could find his sense of humour.

They were standing outside a gent's outfitters on the

corner of Union Street. Elsie turned and looked up at him.

'I think it would be a good idea if you came in with me, Dan. It's more sort of ordinary if the wife is accompanying the man into a gent's shop, rather than the other way round, don't you think?' She pointed to a jacket hanging in the window. 'Look, Dan. That'd suit you very nicely, wouldn't it?'

The jacket was a Lovat green with a check pattern. The mannequin in the window was wearing it with a trilby hat. Elsie pulled his arm, giggling. 'Come on, Dan. Let's see what you look like, all dolled up like dog's dinner.'

Elsie walked into the shop and nodded to the assistant. As she did so, the owner came from the rear of the shop to greet them.

'Good afternoon, Mrs Barr. Good afternoon, Mister Barr. I have something for you.' The tailor reached into his pocket and brought out an envelope. Elsie took it and handed him a written receipt. No one noticed except Dan. The proprietor turned to him. 'I saw you admiring the green jacket, Mister Barr. Would you like to try it for size?'

The tailor snapped his fingers at the assistant who seemed to almost fly across the shop with the jacket. Before Dan knew what was happening, his own jacket was off his back and the other one was on it. Then, his cap was whipped from his head and the trilby was placed upon it at a jaunty angle.

'There you are, Mister Barr; see for yourself!' The tailor turned Dan around so that he was facing the long, swinging mirror. 'Don't you think that suits you, as an up and coming young man? I do, anyway. I'll tell you what; I'll give you twenty per cent off the price and throw the hat in with it. How would that suit you? What do you think, Mrs Barr?'

Dan caught sight of himself in the mirror. He really did look like the man about town. He had never looked so smart in his life. The shopkeeper was looking at Elsie, awaiting her answer. Elsie looked up at him and said, 'Yes, thank you. We'll take it with us if you'll wrap it up. I'll settle your account at the end of the month, if that's all right by you?'

They stood waiting as the assistant wrapped the suit and hat into neat parcels. The proprietor had given his assent to her offer of payment by a nod of the head. Dan was sullen, looking as if he had been robbed.

When they got home, Elsie hung up the coat and put the hat with it in the back bedroom then walked down the stairs. Dan was still standing, looking displeased.

His wife spoke quite sharply to him. 'What's the matter with you, Dan? Have you never had anything given to you, before? It's the first thing I've given you since I started work with Jenkins. I thought I should take advantage of his offer of a fat discount on the hat and jacket. You wouldn't want me to have refused him, would you?' Elsie did not wait for his answer but just continued talking. 'It was a good offer. He's one of the best tailors in Wednesbury. You're quite lucky to get such an offer. Just take it and be happy, for God's sake. Merry Christmas, Dan! It's only a week away, you know. Why can't you just be happy for a change?'

Dan stood as if he did not know what to do; he was so used to being hard up that he felt as if something dishonest had taken place if he found that he was a little better-off. Suddenly he smiled.

'Yes, I know just what you mean, Elsie. I am happy. It's just that I'm not in the habit of being happy. It's a smashing jacket, and hat as well. When shall I wear it? That's what I ask myself. The blokes at work will ask me if I've robbed a bank.'

Dan sat down, the smile disappearing from his face. It was obvious that he was troubled. He was about to learn. Here comes the next surprise, Elsie thought.

'Dan, we're going by invitation to Willenhall, to see my friends, the Stones, for Christmas. They looked after me, and my father, until the day he died. Surely such friendship should be repaid by showing my face every so often? I remember when my father and I first came to Wednesbury. We were not much more than vagrants but Mary took us in when no one else would have done. Mary was a true Christian then, and she is, still. Her family was brought up the same way, and I'm sure they would make us most welcome.

'You might find that it does you a bit of good, as well, to be a friend as well as an employee. Albert Stone might see you in a different light if you were able to show him another side to your character.'

Elsie looked at Dan, meaningfully, forcing him to think. It couldn't do him any harm to mix with the gaffer, could it? He might get a preference when it came to getting promotion. It might seem to his mates that he was arse-licking but it didn't matter all that much what they thought, did it?

'Yes, I suppose you are right.' He felt a sigh of released tension leave his lungs. 'It might be nice to tell somebody else what to do for a change. When do you want to go to see them? If you let me know, I could tell Mildred what you've got in mind.'

Elsie too, found the tension leaving her; she had been frightened that Dan might resent being forced to mix with gaffers. 'It's Sunday tomorrow. We could go to church with them and then let them invite us back for lunch; what do you think about that?'

The crafty little minx, Dan thought, wangling an invitation like that. It'd save a bit on her food bill for the week. What was Elsie going to think of next? He was not left long in finding out. Before he had answered her question, she had come up with another idea.

'I might have a word in Mary's ear, you know, Dan, and

see if she wants to come with us. She could get us a lift in Fred's cart, then. That would save us the train fare, and we could put more on the church offertory plate.'

All so innocent, Dan thought, the way she had arranged things. Still, if she was that devious and clever, she might do him a bit of good in the long term. He decided to go along with her proposals.

'Yes, it seems as if it might be a good day out. Have a word with Mary; she might get us a ride. Tomorrow seems fine to me.'

Elsie looked in his direction with a crafty smile on her face. 'That's all settled, then. Will you bank up the fire before you come to bed? I'm going up; it's been a busy day. Goodnight, Dan.'

Her husband watched her go upstairs and sat down by the fire. He had found out more about his wife today than he had found out since they were married. He had known a little about her job but nothing about her abilities, and her presence; her air of confidence in the tailor's shop. Who had taught her to act like that?

Elsie was like a woman of real power and wealth, rather than the husband of a working man with no prospects. Dan recalled his first glance into the mirror in the tailor's shop. He had felt as if he were looking at a stranger. He had liked the look of the stranger, though. How had the tailor described him? An up and coming young man! Well, why not. On impulse he took off his waistcoat and mounted the stairs.

Elsie was lying half asleep but awoke fully as he entered the bedroom.

'Who's that?' She asked the question quietly in a mumbling voice. Dan turned her so that she was facing him and pulled down the top of her nightdress. He kissed the exposed breast then lifted the bottom up. He moved onto her.

'It's an up and coming young man!'

Dan pushed himself into her, feeling the warm damp softness of her. She pushed against him and he felt the climax begin. Suddenly her body was hot and wet and he was drowning in the heat that burned his body. The climax went through his body like a boiling waterfall and then it was over. The excitement went from him and he felt her hold him tight, asking for more.

'Dan! Oh, Dan!'

Elsie pulled at him as if willing him to begin again. Suddenly he felt tired. He slipped his hand into her to replace his member. Elsie pulled and pressed him, her body seeming to suck his hand in then she screamed in the darkness of the room and Dan felt her start to climax again. A few minutes later they were both lying completely relaxed. Elsie turned and whispered.

'Thank you, Dan; that was lovely.'

She lay back on the pillow and he felt the energy stream away from his body. He relaxed into the darkness of the room and then it was Sunday morning.

'Come on, Dan. Are you coming to Willenhall?'

It was Elsie shaking him. Slowly Dan awoke, adjusting his body position to see the time displayed by his hunter. It was nine o'clock.

'Mary's coming for us at ten; you'd better be ready. You know what she's like; she keeps everything to a timetable. Still, it seems to work for her; she does everything to a system. You would think she was Sam Smile's wife!'

Elsie smiled to herself. No wonder Mary was so prosperous, the way she did things. Yet, she recalled, Mary had taken two vagrants from the street, just at the request of one of them. Elsie had often wondered why the woman had been motivated to perform such a Christian act. She mentally examined her own character, an act which she seemed to do increasingly often; would she perform the same act, herself?

Dan bustled about, trying to catch up with his wife's progress. His breakfast had been ready for him to sit and eat when he had got up. He sat, still in a bit of a sullen mood, but better for the sexual act, last night. It had always surprised him that Elsie had so much passion in her. A touch seemed to light her fuse and when it was lit, an explosion followed, with gratitude afterwards.

How did Elsie know that Mary was coming at ten o'clock? A thought struck him; when had she made the arrangements with Mary? Had she made them before she'd cooked breakfast, or had she made them even before she'd suggested asking Mary for the lift? If so, his wife was even more devious than he thought. It was something to think about.

Dan looked up at her from the table and Elsie smiled at him in that certain way that she did after they had done it. It was as if her gratitude carried on for a few hours. Anyway, it wasn't a bad way to feel, was it? Elsie had always had the ability to surprise him. He knew she was a special woman. In a way, it was surprising that some handsome, rich young bounder hadn't won her heart.

Stephen Stone. That was the one who might have done it. He never had, though. Elsie had always been faithful, he knew. Dan always felt good after they did it, but he was never sure how she felt. He knew that he always fell asleep straightaway. Did Elsie do the same or did she lie wanting more? She had got more, last night, even if it had only been from his hand.

His breakfast finished, Dan stood and went to the small scullery at the top of the kitchen steps. A bowl of hot water awaited him and his shaving brush and razor were there. A few minutes later, as pulled his new hat into shape, he heard the clip-clop of the Shire horse approaching. It seemed strange to have such a large horse pulling the trap but if you only had one horse, that one had to do. Elsie was at the door waiting for him.

'Are you ready, Dan? Mary's here.'

Fred must have harnessed the horse into the trap. It had taken a bit of organising, to get everything ready. It had taken him all his time to be ready, after all the work had been done by everyone else! Dan smiled and gathered himself together.

'Good morning, Mrs Bowyer. How are you today? It's a lovely morning, don't you think?'

Dan surprised himself with his own affability. His feeling of sullenness seemed to have risen from him, leaving him feeling good. Mary was an exciting woman; he had noticed before that she made him feel ready. Not that he minded feeling ready; it was just embarrassing at times, when he thought it showed. Dan had caught Mary looking down at him sometimes, as if she was wondering why he had such a lump in his trousers.

'Good morning, Mister Barr. You are looking smart today. Yes, it's a lovely day. I think I'm going to let you be in charge today. Have you ever driven a trap being pulled by a Shire horse, Mister Barr? It's a bit of a strain on the arms. Fred, Mister Stone, that is, harnessed Henry up for me, but it's a bit too much for me. You come on up here, and Elsie and I'll sit in the back. That way, you won't have to listen to a lot of women's chatter. I'm sure Henry'll provide enough interest for you.'

Mary turned and stepped around the seat, to sit in the back. Elsie placed her foot on the step and swung herself up expertly. Dan picked his foot onto the step and helped himself up. He picked up the reins with a flourish and growled at Henry.

'Walk on; walk on.'

Dan clicked his tongue and Henry seemed to understand,

moving off up the gentle incline of the hill. Dan settled back with what seemed to the women to be a sigh of relief. He took his hat off and placed it at the side of him. It was too good a hat to lose in a gust of wind, even if he had got it for nothing.

The journey through the Black Country took them less than an hour. Being in the trap reminded Elsie of the day she had ridden with Stephen, out into the country. They turned into the Stone's factory at half past ten. The church, a hundred yards away, was holding Holy Communion at eleven o'clock.

The family members were just starting out, to be sure of a place in their own family pew. There were greetings all round, and Albert Stone shook Dan's hand for the first time ever. They were in the church in a few minutes. The group made a noisy entrance, the local working class people looking up as they entered. Elsie was sandwiched by Stephen and Dan. Stephen was with Mabel, who was all smiles to Elsie and Mary, whispering of how happy she was as a married woman.

Elsie felt sick. Although she was married to Dan, she had always felt somehow, that Stephen was her own. She still felt like that but Mabel was an uncomfortable intrusion. Silly, she had no right to feel like that.

Elsie felt Stephen's hand touch hers and, as he looked the other way, he opened her hand and stroked the palm, sending shivers of an imagined anticipation through her body. Dan was helping Mary into her seat in the pew. Mary knelt and was silent for a moment or two, and then she smiled as if she had had happy thoughts in her prayer.

Elsie felt her heart beating furiously. Stephen was really playing her up! She lifted her foot and placed her heel on the top of his instep then pressed down with as much force as she could apply.

'Hell!'

Stephen moved his foot quickly from under hers and looked at her. She was busy trying to find the hymn from the number posted near the pulpit. She looked at him and he was smiling. It was one of the things she had first noticed about him; he was always smiling, no matter what occurred. He looked at her and his face was strangely full of pain and smiling at the same time. It was as if he were saying 'you've hurt me but not enough to stop my smile'.

Elsie had a moment of remorse; he had not tried to hurt her; he had been flirting with her! She put her hand back in his without thinking and saw his face beam. Past him, Mabel was singing, her voice clear in the church, her hand holding Stephen's left. He was being pulled both ways! Nothing changes, Elsie thought; why can't I just be content?

The vicar was giving his sermon now. It was some time since she had listened to him so she tried to catch the import of his words. He had always been one to concentrate on the simple messages that the Bible delivered. The text today was from Saint John and told the story of the thief who got into the sheep-pen by climbing over the fence. The shepherd, the one who should be there, goes in by the gate without having to sneak in by devious means. Saint John went on to say that Jesus had said that the truth will set you free. Stephen bent to whisper in her ear, 'Does that mean I'm a thief, holding your hand, which should be mine? Or does it mean that we don't face the simple truth but are bent from it by our commitments to family and such?'

The question shook her, forcing her to face how she felt about everything in her life. If she was asked who the person she most loved in life was, how would she reply? Would it be Dan or Stephen? What was her truth, the truth that would set her free? Was she seeing life through the same perspective as the children of Abraham, unable to see truth?

The question puzzled her and she was glad when the

time came to kneel in prayer so that she could ask for help. All she could get into her mind was that she should give to Dan what was his, and give to Stephen what was his! This was not the answer that she had been seeking and yet it made a sort of illogical sense. Was this the answer? Should she live two separate lives, dividing herself to get the most from her feelings? It was attractive to think about making that choice but would not even the knowledge of having made that choice make her a hypocrite?

The service was nearly over and Mabel was looking strangely at her. She didn't speak but just grabbed hold of Stephen's arm and manoeuvred him away from Elsie and Dan.

'What's the matter with her?' Elsie asked. 'She's like a cat on hot bricks.'

She looked back at Stephen; he was grinning as if the whole thing was seriously funny and she suddenly realised that it was. For all their antics, they were like clowns in a circus. Her lips turned up and a smile appeared on her face. Mary, who was standing by Dan, suddenly got a smile on her face too. Albert Stone turned to Dan.

'Are you coming back to lunch, lad? I think you and your wife are expected, you know.' He turned to Elsie. 'Mary has been telling me about your little job with Jenkins. You must have impressed him to give you a job like that!' He waited for an answer from Dan and when it wasn't forthcoming, he turned his attention back to Elsie.

'Eh? What?'

'Well, yes, Mister Stone,' she said. 'I've enjoyed working for him. I hope to do even better when I know more of what I am doing. I might even become an investor.'

Elsie shut up, realising that she was close to giving the game away to Dan. He looked at her strangely again, but said nothing. Perhaps he didn't know what they were talking about. They moved faster now, to get away from the press of people leaving the church doorway. Mary was waiting for them in the churchyard and Elsie moved to her side. 'What did you tell Mister Stone about me and my little job for, Mary? He was just asking me about it, in front of Dan, who knows nothing.'

She felt quite annoyed; Mary was usually quite close-mouthed about such things. She looked shocked. 'I thought I had made it quite clear to Albert that anything I told him was to remain confidential. I'm so sorry my dear. I shall let him know what I think of him, and make sure that I don't take him into my confidence again. However, you did let him know that you were hoping to get more responsibilities from Mister Jenkins, didn't you? If you want something kept secret, you shouldn't talk about it.'

They fell silent and Elsie wondered if she was being too hard on her friend.

'I'm sorry, Mary; I can't fall out with you. You're right: I should be as careful as you, if not more so, when it comes to minding my own business. I shall have to let this be a lesson to me.'

Dan was standing with his mouth open. It was obvious that he had no idea what they had been talking about. He seemed to be speculating about her job again as he often seemed to. Elsie tried to give him an explanation.

'Albert seems to know more about our business than is his right, just because he employs you, Dan. It seems that Mary accidentally told him that I was working for Jenkins and he thought it above my station, apparently. I've asked Mary to be more circumspect in what details of our life she gives to Mister Stone!'

For a moment she thought she had presented what she wanted to say to Dan with too much aggression, and he might swing in her defence to confront the older Stone.

Elsie placed a hand on his arm, gently. 'Don't worry, my love; it's all a storm in a teacup.'

Dan mumbled something then and seemed to quieten, turning his back on Stone. The small gathering merged again and Elsie mixed with the sisters whom she had got to know so well. Although Dan worked in the Stone factory, he hadn't really got to know Victoria or Agnes, and he was charmed by the extent to which they gave their hospitality to the young couple. Stephen and Mabel came across the room and Mabel was formally introduced to Elsie and Dan.

'I'm pleased to hear you are enjoying married life,' said Elsie.

'Yes,' said Mabel. 'We are very happy and I must say a wedding does send out a message to some people to accept that I am the woman for Stephen. She laughed. 'When we were courting, some of the girls seemed to have the idea that he is available.'

There was an uneasy silence between the two couples. Elsie flushed and Dan looked closely at her again. There were more secrets coming out at this little gathering to worship, than he had thought possible. What did she mean?

Mabel couldn't have meant that there was something going on between Stephen Stone and Elsie, could she? He put the thought out of his head. Elsie didn't have the time, let alone anything else! He suddenly felt very uncomfortable among this crowd of old gossips. Dan turned to go, almost angrily, but Mary Bowyer caught his eye.

'Dan, I think we'll have to be leaving in about half an hour. If you go out to the yard, you'll find a man looking after Henry. Would you please ask him to harness up for us in half an hour's time? Thank you very much, Dan. I've been watching you today. You are, I must say, a model of self-restraint in the middle of so much chatter. It's surprising how much nonsense is spoken at a gathering like this, and how easy it would be to cause mischief, to the loss of the innocent!'

All at once, things became clear to him. Someone was stirring things up; trying to get rid of him! Who could that be? Dan looked round. Could it be that he was the target, or Elsie? Old Stone had seemed genuinely friendly, as had his daughters. His wife, Mildred, was as good as gold, he knew. Who did that leave? His eyes alighted on Mabel. He had his doubts about her. Why should she have anything against him – or Elsie? He looked across at Stephen who was talking to his father but his eyes kept straying to Elsie. Was that it?

Dan decided to talk to Elsie about it when they got home but Mary came in with them and stayed until eleven o'clock. They were in bed before he could raise the subject.

'Look here, Elsie, I've an idea about who might be spreading trouble for you.' He looked at her shocked face and went on. 'I was looking around the room, the other day, when we were at Stone's. That Stephen was looking at you. Oh, he was talking to his father, at the time, but his eyes were on you. That Mabel was watching as well and I'm sure she saw him. How do you get on with her?'

Dan gently watched the way she replied. Perhaps he was going to get the truth, now. For a moment Elsie lay looking at her husband. What would be the outcome if she just told him the truth, that she had loved Stephen Stone since the first day she had met him, at Uncle Fred's? Elsie stared at him, apparently in amazement. Dan felt stung by the look on her face.

'Dan Barr, what are you thinking of? Don't you know that all men of any worth are always looking at young women? Didn't you look? Don't tell me you don't! I've seen you. If I'd just asked you how you got on with Mabel, you wouldn't reply. I saw you looking at Mabel yourself. It's only to be expected, isn't it? There's no chance of Stephen

Stone making a pass at me! Mabel is too sharp to allow that. Not that the men, including Mister bloody Stone, haven't tried it on with me. It would surprise me if you hadn't tried it on with a girl or two at Spire's. For all I know, you still do!'

Elsie stood and Dan realised for the first time what a formidable woman she was. She seemed to gather her strength to say something else.

'If I'd wanted to bed with some other man, I could have done it months ago. Don't you think so, Dan Barr? Don't you think I could have managed that? Don't you think I'm attractive enough to manage that?'

Elsie was the essence of all the things that Dan admired in a woman. He did not know how to reply to her. He stood quiet, like a fawn under the gaze of a predator. Eventually the look in her eye softened.

'Oh, Dan, you are so gullible sometimes. Perhaps that's one of the things I admire about you. I'm your wife; no one else's and that's that!'

Dan usually went to the public house on Sunday evenings on the pretext that he was taking a constitutional walk, for his health. She had wondered if there was some other attraction there, but no rumour had come to her ears so she had assumed that he was just having a drink in the company of men of his own class. It might be a good idea if she kept her ear to the ground but when she suggested that she accompany him, he replied to her quite forcefully. 'No, thank you, Elsie; I might drop in and have a glass or two, that's all. Sometimes it does a man good to talk over the situation in the country.'

Elsie smiled to herself. Dan always thought he had an expertise about the country's affairs. She questioned him again,

'How do you get to know so much about the country's affairs, Dan? You always have an opinion about the Government, and what they are doing.'

'Well, it's just a matter of reading the papers and trying to read between the lines. I enjoy reading about what's happening in the town, as well. The local papers keep you in touch with that. I don't buy one because I can always read the paper in the library, on the way home from work.' He turned to her. 'Goodnight, Elsie. It's back to work tomorrow; I've got to get my sleep.'

He turned away and a few minutes later she heard him snoring gently. He was a strange mixture of attributes, she thought. He took the trouble to cycle to the library on the way home so that he could read about local, national and international news!

Christmas came and went without fuss. Dan had already had his presents and wore them as often as was possible without seeming to be showing off. He bought her a watch, to be worn on her wrist. She treasured it as she knew it must have cost him more than money. It had cost him; just to think of buying a present! Anyone who was mean had to be secretive, she knew from her dealings as secretary to Jenkins. What secrets was Dan keeping from her?

Chapter 11

Power, Tom's Birth
1907

The New Year also came and went. Elsie was acquiring more expertise in the way she dealt with the various rent accounts. As she walked the town, the traders always showed their courtesy by offering her a seat as she entered their premises. The winter seemed long and hard and she found it difficult, walking through the snow. Mister Jenkins seemed to keep an eye on her too and she had heard him asking Luke how she was coping. She was determined to carry on as long as she could. The spring came and she felt better in some ways and worse in others. Her back often ached with the effort of getting around.

A showery day in April came and Elsie was at Mary Bowyer's, resting, as she often needed to be. She was relaxing, listening to Mary.

'Some day, I will tell you how I started as an investor,' said Mary. 'You know more about me than anyone except Sam Jenkins. He's guided me for as long as I can remember. I haven't always been prosperous, you know. I started from very small beginnings.'

Elsie expected Mary to say more but she just changed the subject.

'When is your little one expected, Elsie? I know you've told me once but I seem to forget things nowadays.'

'May, I think, Aunt; in about three weeks. I'm sure I must have told you once, if not twice or three times.' She smiled at the older woman. 'I know just what you're doing, Aunt, you're trying to take my mind off what you were tempted to tell me. Don't worry, Aunt. I shan't pester you for all your secrets. I've learned that much from Luke Bryant. I've never known anyone as close-mouthed as him.' She picked up her cup and noticed it was empty. 'Would you like another cup of tea, Aunt?'

Elsie picked up the teapot and carried it into the small kitchen. This little chat they were having could yet turn into a revelation of Mary's life. Not that it was any of her business but it just sounded so intriguing! She carried the teapot back into the small parlour.

As she poured the tea, Mary said, 'You remember that I suggested a few weeks ago, that you might buy your own house, Elsie?' At a nod from Elsie, she carried on. 'I've been thinking about it. I've had another idea. What about if you bought a house in Willenhall for investment? I can arrange it for you. Then, when the time seems right, and the property is empty, you could move into it, making it easier for Dan to get to work. I know it would make it harder for you to get to work, but you could travel on the train. The amount you would be earning would easily cover that small expense. It would be comical really if you were paying yourself the rent that Dan would be giving you. There's a nice house, better than this one, you could have, and you could charge yourself little more than I am charging you for this one! The other thing is; you could pay someone else to collect your rents in for you.'

Elsie smiled, seeing what the older woman was getting at. She knew that Mary would really be paying most of it for it for her.

'That sounds like a complicated bit of manoeuvring but it might be fun, Aunt. Thanks for the opportunity.'

They carried on talking about the possibility and suddenly everything became clear to Elsie. She would also be closer to Stephen! The thought excited her but then she realised that it would also leave her exposed to temptation. Would she be able to resist? Would it matter, if she had some love in her life? She had to decide. A thought came to her; perhaps she could find a way of buying a pony and trap for herself. Then she would be able to take her baby with her when she went to collect her rents!

'Yes, I think I will go along with your suggestion, Aunt. It would be very convenient for Dan and I'm sure he'd think he had a little more status from a better house, not like you, eh, Aunt?'

They both laughed at the little joke. No one could ever tell the state of Mary's wealth from where she lived! Then it was time to go. Dan would be home, expecting his dinner. He was miserable when he came home. He had been told off for allowing his people to go home two minutes early. Albert Stone had had him in the office and told him that if it happened again he would be put back on the shop floor.

Elsie smiled to herself; he hadn't left the shop floor! Albert Stone was just keeping him under his thumb. Dan had no chance of losing that job; he was too good at it. Still, it might do him good to feel a little less secure.

A fortnight later her labour pains began. She had been dolly-maiding the washing when it came on. The sudden back pain caught her unawares and she was unable to move for a while. She finished her washing and hung it, and then she went to see Mary Bowyer.

'Mary, I think I'm going into labour,' she said. 'The pain I had an hour ago was dreadful and I think it must have been the first of my pains. I don't think I shall be able to collect the rent today. Whatever shall I do?'

Mary was organised, as usual. Her eyes swept over Elsie, then she said, 'Well, the first thing to do is to get a doctor to look at you. Just sit back and relax while I arrange that. The rent will keep; no one is going to run off with it, you know. Do you think it hasn't been organised for weeks? Sam Jenkins knew you were pregnant and if he knew that, he knew that someone else was going to have to collect it. Luke is going to collect it, my dear. I can't. I shall be too busy looking after you!'

As they were speaking the second pain came, not as bad as the first but bad enough, Elsie thought. Mary sat while the pain subsided and then she said, 'I'm just going to go to see Ruth; she'll make the arrangements while I stay with you.'

Mary bustled out of the door and was back in what seemed to be a few minutes.

'That's that settled, then. Ruth has gone to see the midwife and she'll call here. If she thinks you need the doctor, she'll send for him.'

Elsie went outside with a large kettle and came back with it full of water. Carefully she poured it into the large pot hanging over the fire and put some small coals on. She went back outside and came back with more water.

'That's enough for now,' Mary said. 'All we can do now is to wait for the midwife and your child. It'll be strange, having a child here. That hasn't happened for years.'

Her eyes seemed to be in another world and Elsie could sense that there was another story to be told there. She was tempted to ask but decided that sometimes it was better to guess and surmise than to know all of it; it was more exciting. She was learning more and more about Aunt Mary!

Elsie's pains were coming more frequently now, and the strain was beginning to tire her. The midwife arrived and examined her, announcing that everything was normal enough to carry on without the doctor. It was late afternoon when the baby started to make itself known, making her scream. The midwife timed it well, walking through the door just as she was needed.

'Lie yourself back and push when I tell you, Lovey. It looks as if it's going to be an easy birth.'

Easy birth, thought Elsie. I'm in agony and she says it's an easy birth! She sat up again and drank another cup of tea, her hand shaking. I should be having this child at home, she thought. What a mess I shall be making of Mary's house. She made to get up and spoke to Mary.

'I've got to get home. I've got everything ready at home. How can I have this child anywhere but at home?'

As she spoke, another pain came and she felt the gush of water between her legs. There was a sharp pain and the midwife spoke sharply to her.

'Push now, Mrs Barr. Push! It's coming! Here it is! He's a boy!'

It happened so quickly that Elsie could never say that she had had a bad time in her labour. The small bundle was put in her arms after a few minutes, crying noisily. She looked at him, wrapped in a sheet. He was her son, Tom! Tentatively she unwrapped him and looked him over, mentally tallying all his parts. He was perfect; complete right down to his big blue eyes. The midwife was talking to her.

'What are you going to call him, Mrs Barr?'

'Tom, Tom Barr; that's who he is, Thomas Daniel James Barr, after his father and grandfather. That's who you are, ain't it, Tom?'

Elsie looked adoringly into his blue eyes and relaxed. The worst was over. All she had to do now was to rear him until he was grown up! The thought filled her with a sort of dreaded anticipation for all the difficulties this, her child, would have to face in a lifetime. She made up her mind that he would go short of nothing; he was far too valuable to allow him to take risks.

She was thinking in a silly fashion, she realised. He would

make up his own mind about what risks to take, if he was anything like his father. His father! She looked deep into his eyes and saw Stephen looking back out of them! It was not possible! She looked again, trying to be as objective as possible. It was not possible to find anything that could easily be construed as a similarity to either Dan or Stephen. She relaxed.

'He looks like his Dad, don't he?'

It was the midwife speaking. Elsie looked from her to her Aunt.

'Yes, he does, don't he? He's a proper little chip off the old block. What do you think, Aunt?'

You've got to keep your sense of humour, Mary thought. At least Elsie's got a sense of humour. Perhaps that was what had attracted Stephen to her. He was always laughing.

'Yes, my dear. He's the spitting image of his Dad. That reminds me, girl. Your husband will be home soon, wondering where you are. Do you think you could get back home, now? If you can, I'll put Tom into his own little cot and get something ready for Dan to eat. It's a long ride on a bike from Willenhall, you know. Mind you, when he sees his son, he won't be thinking about food; he'll want to go and wet the babby's head down the pub, won't he?'

Mary sighed. Elsie knew that Mary was completely against drink, having seen how it had affected her tenants. There was a noise from the door.

'Hello, Ruth, come in,' said Mary as the red face appeared at the top of the stairs. 'She's quite all right, and so is Tom. Tom is her first-born. Come and have a look.'

The two women were occupied for the next few minutes discussing the attributes of the infant. Elsie started to feel quite jealous at the amount of time that was being devoted to him, at her expense. Then she wanted to be with them, showing him off. He was lovely, after all - and he was hers! She slipped on her coat.

'I'm taking him home, now, Aunt. He'll sleep better in his own little cot.'

She reached for him and Mary reluctantly handed him over. He seemed to settle down in his mother's arms and the small group of women stepped across the small court. In a matter of moments the infant was installed in his own cot, moving around as if he were hungry already.

Dan was surprised and not all that pleased to find three women and a baby in the front room. His dinner was on the top of the fireplace, though, ready for him to eat. He looked at the small child and moved over to be close to him, looking at him every few seconds. After a while he started to enjoy having the company of the little child. He was also shocked to find that he had been named. It wasn't every day you came home from work to a new babby!

After Ruth had gone, Elsie explained that a house might be available in Willenhall for them, a larger house. They just had to wait for it to become empty. Dan looked as if he didn't know whether to be pleased or not.

'What's the catch?' he asked. 'It just seems too good to be true. You know what they say. If it seems too good to be true, it's because it is. Let's think on it. You seem all right in this little court and you get on with the neighbours. You must do, or they wouldn't be round so often!'

Dan doesn't like people liking me! The thought came to her that she was doing better for them than he was, even if he didn't know about her income from Jenkins. He was jealous! That was the only explanation. Somehow she had managed to get them the chance of a better place to live, not he. She had better start being a lot better at deception than she was now. How could she manage to get him to accept the better things in life that she was going to achieve?

Perhaps women had always had to function like this; trying to pass the credit to their husbands for the achievements they had worked for. It wasn't fair. Dan certainly didn't have any flair for business; perhaps she would have to learn to arrange things so that he got the credit, even if he hadn't actually done anything towards things.

Elsie decided to put the whole thing to the back of her mind. Very often this seemed to help, as if her mind functioned without her trying, then coming up with an answer just when she needed it. Perhaps if she spoke to Aunt Mary about it, she could think of something.

There was a crying noise. It was Tom. It was his first hungry cry! She picked him up and snuggled him down to her breast. This was a moment to be cherished. Perhaps he would turn out to have more of a brain than his father. There was a very good chance of that, she thought.

*

'Why don't you ask him to be put on an agent's list, or I'll do it if you like?'

Elsie and Mary were talking over ways and means of getting Dan's agreement to move into the house in Willenhall. At the moment he didn't even know where the house was that Mary owned in Willenhall and neither did Elsie. Mary spoke.

'If you like, I could get one of the Stone's girls to mention that it's a very good prospect. He might make his own enquiries and make an offer. The agent would be in on the act, so to speak, so his offer could be accepted without any fuss.

So, it was settled. A few days later Dan just happened to be in the Works Office when he overheard Victoria and Agnes talking about this house that was about to come on the market.

'We can't really afford anything as grand as that but Herbert says it's just the place for a coming man and his family. It's quite reasonable as well, considering what you're getting for your money. It's got three bedrooms and a parlour. There's even a space where you could keep a horse and trap, not that we would need one. It's so close to work. The house is not even on the market yet so keep your mouth shut. I'm hoping to have another go at Herbert, my husband, to make an offer for it.'

Dan felt himself get excited. Here was a chance, perhaps, to get a better home for Elsie and Tom and himself! How could he take advantage of this information? How could he ever afford it? When would he be able to afford a horse? It was silly, really, but he couldn't get the place out of his mind. There was nothing to stop him having a horse, if he did some more overtime! After all, when it was paid for, all you had to do was to put hay down its throat!

'I might have a look at the agent's, to see if we could live closer to work. I'm having to cycle to work at the moment; it's a long way. I couldn't afford anything grand, just something for the three of us. Where's the agent's office, Agnes? I never have chance to look round Willenhall; I'm always too busy for just admiring the view, so to speak.'

Agnes turned and looked at him as if she had only just noticed he was in the office. This was a good chance to get him going!

'Oh, hello; Dan; I hadn't noticed you were there. Well, there are two agent's offices. The one we were talking about is at the end of the High Street. They don't seem to have much to offer in the class that you might be interested in, but you never know, they might have something in.'

Dan was livid; the cheeky young madam! How dare she make assumptions about what he could or could not afford?

He would show them, and his missus! He kept a straight face as he thanked Agnes for her help.

The thought came to him that this bit of information that had just been given to him could be one of the biggest things to happen in his life! Could he afford it? He would have to and so would Elsie. She tried to present herself as an ambitious woman so perhaps she might contribute something towards the cost of a bigger house. He still didn't know what her earnings were; how could he find out?

Chapter 12

Moving to Willenhall
1907

The man in the office didn't seem to be impressed by Dan.

'Yes, what can I do for you? We don't have any vacancies for labourers at the moment; just keep in touch.'

He turned his back and looked down at the ledger he was filling in. Dan coughed to attract his attention and the man looked up.

'Was there something else?'

'As a matter of fact, yes there is. I'm interested in renting a nice house in Willenhall; something with two or three bedrooms and maybe somewhere to stable a horse. I can't pay the earth but I'm willing to pay a sensible rent.'

The man stopped what he was doing and looked more closely at Dan. It just goes to show; you can't judge a book by the cover! Who would have thought that this scruffy man would be in a position to rent a decent property? Then he realised who this scruffy person must be!

He fiddled with his files, pulled two out and coughed as he replied. 'We have two houses of a similar nature on the market at the moment, sir. One is six pounds a month and the other is four pounds a month. Neither of them is available until the first of March, next year. Would you like to have the details, sir?'

The agent handed over two files. Dan couldn't believe his eyes at the price of the two properties. The one priced at four pounds a month looked as good, if not better, than the more expensive one. The man looked at him and smiled.

'If you decide to make an offer for this one,' he indicated the cheaper property, 'it has to be accompanied by two months' rent as deposit.'

Dan's face fell. He hadn't bargained for finding large sums of money. What should he do? He must play for time.

'Has there been any interest in these properties?' Dan asked the man tentatively. 'I might need a day or two to get the bank to release the funds.'

He felt foolish about saying a bank would need time to release eight pounds! The deal sounded good, he thought, but still he felt hopeless. What could he do? He walked back to work; full of bad temper as he thought he had probably lost the chance and wished there was someone who could give him some advice.

He felt no better when he arrived home as Elsie's Aunt Mary was ensconced in his chair in front of the fire with Tom on her lap. They were talking about money. He couldn't help listening to Mary.

'Do you know, Elsie, most people in business when they want to get on, use other people's money to finance their projects? It saves them having to use their own cash, especially if they don't have it.' Mary turned to him. 'Come and sit here, Dan. I know it's quite chilly out, and I've been too close to the fire for my own good. I shall be getting red-legs. What sort of day have you had today, young man?'

Mary moved onto a smaller chair, making way for him to sit closer to the fire. He suddenly felt of more importance; someone had deferred to him! Perhaps Mary could help him. Dan didn't want to ask in front of Elsie. He chatted until Mary was going, and then offered to see her across the court, to her own place. She seemed quite pleased that he should do so.

As they walked along, side by side, he said, 'Aunt Mary; there's something I'd like to ask you about.'

She answered, 'Well, if there is anything I can help you with, Daniel, I will. What's the problem? Are you in debt? Have you been gambling?'

'No, of course not! I've never been in debt, and I've never gambled.' He took a deep breath. 'It's just that I've found a much nicer house that we could live in. It's not yet on the market. I've made enquiries about it and it's a three bed-roomed house with room for stabling. It's in Willenhall. I know it seems grand for us but I think I could afford it if I did some occasional overtime. The only thing is; they want two months' rent in advance from anyone who wants to make an offer. I don't have eight pounds for the deposit. I wondered if you could see your way clear to lend us the money for the deposit until we are on our feet?' He stopped and looked Mary in the eye. 'It would be very important to us, you know, Auntie Mary.'

What was she going to say? Perhaps it had been too much to hope for. Perhaps she didn't have that much money herself! He was just beginning to regret asking her when he saw that she was smiling.

'Of course I'll lend it to you, Dan. Just come into the house and I'll get it for you.'

Mary led the way into her house and disappeared into the other room. She came back with a small money bag. She smiled as she handed the bag to him.

'There is ten pounds there, Dan. You can pay me back at ten shilling a week, starting when you've been in the house a month. Will that suit you? I know you won't let me down. I won't say anything about this to Elsie, if you don't want me to.'

Dan felt that he was growing again. He had achieved something! His tone was respectful as he replied. 'Thank you so much, Aunt. As you say, I won't let you down, and this will make such a difference to our lives. Little Tom will never know what it's like to scrimp and scrape.' He put the small moneybag in his pocket and kissed her on the cheek. 'Thank you again, Aunt.'

He let himself out of the house and made his way home, whistling He was bursting to tell someone. He couldn't. It could still go wrong. Tomorrow would tell. He walked into his own house and did his best to act as if there were nothing out of the ordinary going on.

The next day seemed to take forever. As soon as Dan had let his workers go, he slipped his overalls off and trotted up the road, followed by the eyes of Victoria and Agnes Stone.

The agent had been pre-warned by them and was acting hard to please. 'We don't have any other properties that I think would suit you, sir; sorry.'

Dan was pleased to be able to put the man in his place. 'I don't want another place. I've had a look at this one,' he said holding the details in the air, 'and this one'll do nicely. Here's the deposit.'

He dropped the small bag on the counter, having taken the extra money out. The man recovered quickly enough, pulling out a receipt and filling it in for Dan.

'There you are sir; a receipt for eight pounds; if you'll just sign the contract. It's for twelve months with an option to take it on again for another twelve months.' The agent handed Dan a pen and signed it himself as witness, then reached under the counter. 'Thank you very much. I hope you will be very happy in the house, sir. There's a certain amount of work to be done there, but your tenancy will start no later than the first of March.'

Dan walked out of the office on clouds. He had a posh house, now! I'll keep it to myself for a bit, he thought. No one, not even Elsie is going to find out about this for a day or two. It was just the right size for bringing up a family, he thought. He had two pounds left in his pocket. He could buy a few sticks of furniture with it or he could put it away, to help to pay Mary off. Perhaps he should tell Elsie about it as soon as possible. The cycle ride home passed in daydreams.

Elsie kept her face as straight as possible as Dan came into the house, his face animated with excitement. He's done it! She could tell by his expression. She had to ask.

'Hello, Dan. Is everything all right?'

Elsie couldn't trust herself to enquire too closely. She would have burst into laughter. Anyway, he seemed pleased enough. She watched him closely out of the corner of her eye as he sat down at his usual place at the table in preparation for his dinner. She bustled round cooking and serving his meal onto his plate. Tom started crying in his pram so Dan picked him up and started comforting him. Elsie put the meal in front of Dan and sat down with him. He was taciturn; speaking as necessary.

'Nice bit o' beef, Elsie.'

'Thank you.'

So the meal went, with little conversation, each just cutting up food and transferring it to the mouth. Elsie was beginning to get frustrated at the way the conversation was going. She got her frustration under control with difficulty, realising that he might think she was controlling what was happening, Dan was still the one who might have thoughts of his own. After they had finished, Dan asked, 'Do you ever wish we had a bigger house, Elsie?'

His wife looked up at him and said, 'I suppose it would be nicer if we had a bedroom to call our own but there'll always be something you want and can't afford. I'm learning to be content with what I've got, you know. Why, when my father and I first came to Wednesbury, we had nowhere to live. My father just happened to ask Mary Bowyer if she knew where we could find something to eat and work, to pay for it. I've never forgotten that day; it changed our lives completely. What made you ask that, Dan? Would you like a bigger house?'

Now was the moment when he could reveal what he had done. Dan suddenly realised that he had not consulted her at all. Never mind; it was a big thing, to have acquired a bigger house and he wanted the feeling of power that it was going to give him.

'Yes, I'd like a bigger place for you and little Tom.' He started tentatively and then started to get excited. 'It's only natural that a man should want the best he can afford for his family. I've been thinking about it a lot, lately and I've been looking around, to see what I could find. I've found a nice place but it's in Willenhall.

'That's the only thing I can find wrong with it as it would mean moving away from the friends you've found in Wednesbury. It's not vacant yet, but if you'd like to have a look at it, we could go over on Saturday. It's not available until March, but we could start getting a few things together, if you like it, that is. We might even be able to push them into letting us have it earlier. They might be pleased to start getting the rent in sooner.'

He's done it at last! God bless him! Maybe he's not such a stick in the mud, after all! Elsie found herself asking questions about the house that would be their new home. Dan's enthusiasm was infectious. Now all she had to do was to find the most economical way of travelling to Wednesbury, to collect her rents in.

The young couple travelled the following Saturday to Willenhall to inspect the house. Work to improve the house was still being carried out and the builders would be working there, on and off, until the New Year. The house was quite smart; she could see that, and she was pleased with the results. Although she knew it would be completed on time, Dan didn't, and he was always grumbling about the time they were taking to finish the work. Elsie admonished him for his worrying.

'What are you worrying about, Dan? If it ain't finished 'til May, it'll give us chance to get some furniture before we move in.'

Dan was scowling as he replied, 'It's just that I've had to arrange this lease, and the work won't be completed for some time. The babby will be months older before we move in. There's all sorts of complications you know. I mean to say, how are you going to manage if you can't get to Wednesbury for that little job at Jenkins'? You'll have to get a job at Willenhall if you want some pin money. I mean; I don't mind you working but don't get ideas beyond your station, you know. I'm the master in my own house. You're just a housewife and you've no right to think you are anything else!'

Dan was getting aggressive; Elsie could see that. He had borrowed the money from Mary for the rent on the house that she had bought, and all of a sudden he was master in his own house! She'd bide her time and show him when she was ready!

Elsie hardly spoke after that, and Dan knew why but didn't care. He would brook no usurping of his male traditional authority as head of the household. Elsie spoke to Luke about her impending move and he said there was a possibility of a move to the Willenhall office but she didn't really want to do that as all the tenants from whom she collected lived in Wednesbury. She recalled what Mary had said about the possibility of a pony and trap. That was the answer to her problem.

Mister Jenkins supplied part of the solution. He sent for her after hearing that she was in the middle of arrangements for moving. It was not often that he asked to see her and she was a little apprehensive as she entered his office.

'Good morning, Elsie. How are you?' Mister Jenkins waited for her answer then went on. 'I understand you are thinking of moving?'

Elsie answered him as best she could, explaining her reasons and ambitions. As she talked, she observed him and the way he paid complete attention to what she was saying. She always felt that no one else ever paid as much attention to her and what she had to say. It gave her encouragement to open her mind to him. When she had finished, he smiled at her.

'Thank you for being so frank with me, Elsie,' he said, softening his tone. 'That's one of the things I've always admired about you, right from the first day that we ever spoke about your hopes for the future.' He coughed and shuffled his papers in front of him. 'I do have a concern about your plans and that is; where do we fit in? By we I mean Jenkins and Co.

'You've been a part of our planning for some time now, but what about the future? I would like to think that there is going to be an association between us for the rest of your working life, even if, in the end, we only provide advice for you. Are you planning to continue with your collections for us, after you move to Willenhall?

'If so; how do you propose to travel, and how do you think you will be able to do that, with a child to take care of? If you can be frank; so can I? My first concern is the well being of the firm; you must realise that.'

Mister Jenkins's face, usually so passive, became animated as he revealed that he too, had a driving loyalty to the firm that he had built up. As much as he thought of her, he would discard her and make other plans as soon as she revealed her lack of interest in the firm. Elsie knew she had to reassure him.

'Mister Jenkins, I've developed a very satisfying bond with the firm and I have no intentions of leaving. My problem, after my husband and I move to Willenhall, is simply one of travel, transport if you like.

'My husband has rented a house in Willenhall, that I am going to buy with help from Mary Bowyer, and he now feels that he has to be the head of the household, so I have to be careful how I show my independence in case I annoy him. I can't let him know that it's my house that he has rented for his family. I know it sounds a bit comical but it's just worked out that way.'

Was that a small smile at the corner of his mouth? Elsie didn't want to respond to it so she put the priority where it had started; on the problem of transport. Elsie decided to bring it up again.

'Mister Jenkins, you may not know, but there's a stable for a pony and trap at the house. I'm sure I could afford to run one; it's just the problem of doing the work and getting in on time, and getting Dan's agreement to it.'

Her employer did smile this time as he questioned her. 'Would it help if the firm supplied the pony, Mrs Barr? You could then, if you wished, do a little collecting in Willenhall and either bring it with you to Wednesbury, or pay it into the bank at Willenhall.

'The firm could buy a pony, with the use of it as your annual bonus. I don't really know what we would do about supplying a trap. It might mean too much of an outlay to be practicable.' He sat there, obviously giving the problem some serious thought. 'Perhaps we may find an answer to the dilemma when we've slept on it. We'll see. You move in during the spring, don't you, Mrs Barr? Good. That means we've still got plenty of time to resolve the issue. If anything crops up, I will see you again.'

He was bringing an end to the interview.

'Thank you, Mister Jenkins. If I hear of anything, I shall consult you immediately.'

The problem still hadn't been solved but at least she had had the offer of a pony. Who knows what might follow from that? Elsie hurried home; her collecting started at nine o'clock in the morning and she had to get the house into good condition for Dan to come home to.

Sam Jenkins sat at his desk, smiling. He knew Elsie would find a way to implement her plans. Her husband had no idea what sort of woman he had married! Dan would soon see the other side of Elsie if he tried to rule her with a rod of iron. He recalled when he had tried to rule his own wife, before they left the Valleys. She had put him right. Elsie seemed to have become more mature since the boy, Tom, had been born.

Luke had been listening to the interview and was intrigued by the problem. Was there anything he could do to help the young woman? He would have to keep his ear to the ground to hear if there were any light vehicles going for a bargain price. There was an auction coming off in a day or two, and if there was anything worth having, he would soon hear about it. He would make enquiries.

It was not often he was tempted to do favours for anyone, but this young woman filled him with an unconscious need to help with anything she wanted to do. He was not yet in a position to analyse his feelings; what would happen when he did?

Chapter 13

Dan's Accident
1907

Elsie was worrying about the fact that she had deceived her husband. She felt that she was rubbing his nose in it, to let him pay rent to her, for him to provide a home for his family. It was a strange situation. She had a business address at Jenkins' so anything to do with her property enterprise was delivered there. In the end she decided to say nothing. It was her insurance. If Dan ever became aggressive with her she could just have him evicted for some reason, even if it meant waiting until the current lease expired. She had no reason to think Dan would become aggressive; it was just a feeling that she might need a defence.

Christmas was now approaching; it was November and the weather was getting colder. The nights were foggy and Tom was getting difficult to cope with. Elsie carried on rent collecting as if it was easy but she knew she was feeling the strain. Luke sometimes accompanied her, carrying Tom as if he was the fond father. When the fog was at its worst, Mary started minding Tom and he quickly became fond of her.

Elsie's mind wandered again. It was funny how she'd always considered that Dan's opinion of things was the right one. He was well-read, though. Perhaps that's where he is now, she thought; in the library. It seemed unlikely; there was a good incentive for getting home on a night like this. He was better read than Mary and that was saying something! The thought of Mary made her wonder how she was.

If Dan hasn't come in soon, I'll pop in to see Mary for five minutes, she thought. Her eyes looked up as the clock struck eight o'clock. She could see great flakes of snow falling past the window. Where is he? Elsie felt herself panic for a moment. Dan's never been this late before; what can have happened?

Elsie stood and placed a few pieces of coal on the fire then protected it with the large, mesh fire guard, to save coals falling on the rug. She wrapped a large scarf around her neck and threw on her heaviest coat. She opened the door and stepped out. The snow had eased now, and it was easier to see where she was going. She intended to go to Mary's house but something seemed to draw her up the slope towards the High Bullen at the top of Upper High Street.

I'll just walk as far as the High Bullen and then I'll come back, Elsie told herself. Her steps seemed dangerous, each one slipping almost out of control. She had loved slipping and sliding about in the snow when she was young, but somehow tonight seemed to be more dangerous. She stepped out as smartly as she could in the snowy conditions.

Suddenly her attention was brought to a heap in the snow. She moved forward hesitantly and saw that it was a man; it was Dan!

'Dan, Oh Dan! What are you doing here? Oh, God! What's the matter with you? Can you get up? What's happened?'

Elsie tried to pick her husband up but he couldn't seem to move properly. She bent down and heard him trying to say something.

'What did you say... your ankle?'

She bent, looking, and saw that Dan's ankle was swollen and realised that he must have fallen from his bicycle. There was a lump on his head too. The machine was lying on the ground, a few feet away. Elsie bent to him again. Her husband's face seemed very pale.

'I'm going to see if Fred's still in the forge. Hold on a minute!'

Elsie stood and sped across the snow as quickly as she could. It was only a minute later when she was at the door to the forge. There was a light shining inside. She banged on the door as loudly as she could, and a moment later there was a scraping as the large door was pulled back.

'Who the hell's that?'

Elsie didn't recognise the figure silhouetted there. It wasn't Fred. Then she saw that it was Ruth's husband.

'Oh, Mister Mallory, I didn't recognise you. Dan's fallen from his bike; he can't get up and I can't lift him. He's too heavy! Help me please!'

Jack Mallory took a quick look at her, recognising who she was instantly. He turned on his heel and shouted into the darkness of the forge.

'Fred! Fred! Elsie Barr's here. Dan's lying hurt in the snow and she can't get him up. Come and give us an 'and, quick!'

Fred appeared out of the darkness of the forge, took in the situation and they trotted cautiously along the snow-covered Upper High Street towards the fallen figure, Jack Mallory following quickly. Between them, they picked Dan up into a sitting position. It was obvious that he could not walk easily so they placed his arms around the shoulders of the men. Elsie stood the bicycle up and wheeled it behind them.

Dan was improving as he was helped, almost being able to walk unassisted by the time they arrived at the front door. They placed him on the settee in the house and placed a cushion under his injured limb. Elsie knew though, that he would have died in the snow, with no one to render him any first aid. He must have been knocked silly by the fall, she thought.

Addressing the two men, she said, 'You'll never know how grateful I am for your help, Fred, and you, Mister Mallory. If I hadn't spotted him in the snow, I feel sure he would have died of exposure before long. It was only because he was so late that I went to look for him.' As she was speaking, Elsie was making tea for the four of them. She handed one to each of them. 'I've just got to pop across the yard. I'll be back in two shakes of a lamb's tail.'

Elsie disappeared through the door and strode across the yard to Ruth Mallory's house. She went straight in, as had become her habit since the affair of the arrears. As soon as she was in, she started speaking.

'Hello, Ruth. I just thought I'd better tell you; Jack's in our house. He's been helping Fred to carry Dan down from the High Bullen. He's fell off his bike and twisted his ankle. I suppose it means that Dan'll have to lose time from work. That won't please him, I'm sure. I'll get back now, to see what I can do for him. I don't think Jack'll be long. They'd more or less finished work at the forge; I was lucky there was anybody there.'

Elsie turned to go when Ruth reached for her shoulder.

'It goes to show; what you send out comes back. That good turn you did me with Mister Bryant has come back to you. If you hadn't done that good turn, neither Jack nor me would be living here now, and who would you have been able to turn to, then?'

'Yes, Ruth; you're right in what you say. Anyway, I believe in helping where you can, don't you?'

Elsie left Ruth before her friend had chance to answer. There was still a lot to do. How was she going to get Dan to work in the morning? Would he be able to work if she got him there? Would he want to go, anyway? There was a lot to think about. She didn't really want him under her feet, tomorrow.

Elsie had a lot of rents to collect in from local traders. Mister Jenkins had heard from the Adjutant of the South Wales Borderers that Henry Brown, who had been employed as a collector for Jenkins had 'died in the line of duty' in South Africa. Elsie had taken his position in the firm; now she had to cope with it.

Somehow, hearing of all the imperfections of humankind seemed to make Elsie determined to put herself into a position that was financially unassailable. The only sticking point, in her opinion was that she wanted to do it on her own, and not be answerable to a husband, or to any man. So far, Dan had no idea how much wealth she had accumulated since she had started working for Sam Jenkins, and she was concerned that if he did find out, he would want to get his hands upon it. She made up her mind to consult Mister Jenkins when she got the chance.

Elsie returned to her own home and found that Fred had gone but Jack was still there. They were discussing the possibility of exchanging jobs.

'Look, Dan, I could soon learn to file a lock an' I'm sure you could learn to swing an 'ammer.'

Dan looked up at him as if he were a child. 'You listen to me, Jack. You might think that you could soon learn the trade of a locksmith but it's not as simple as that. You have to have served an apprenticeship and when you've passed out from that, you have to present a lock to your employer to show the quality of your work. No, I'll stay at my own trade, thanks for the idea. If you're not happy where you are, tell Fred. Perhaps he'd be able to find some other work to give you some sort of variety, so to speak. Just tell him how you feel. He's always been reasonable with you, hasn't he?'

The point hit home. Jack knew he had been lucky to get taken on, with his drinking habits at the time. Elsie was trying to listen without seeming to do so. Her main problem was to get Dan back to work as quickly as possible. Tomorrow, she would ask to see Mister Jenkins about her financial position.

Elsie interrupted the men's conversation. 'Jack, I've been round to tell Ruth that you'll be late because you and Fred were helping Dan to get home.' Elsie turned her head to her husband. 'Dan, I've had a look at your bike. It seems to be all right. How are you now? Did you get much of a bang to your head?' She leaned over him and gently pulled his head to her so that she could see it better. 'It's not so bad; it's not as swollen, now. Do you think you'll be going to work in the morning?'

Elsie knew he would sooner go to work than hang around the house. Dan held his foot up; it was still swollen but not as badly as when they'd brought him home. Jack Mallory was looking at her as if she was trying to force her husband to do something beyond his ability.

Elsie explained, 'You don't know Dan, Jack. He won't lose time from work if he can possibly help it. I've seen him get up from a sick bed and go to work, so don't think he's being bullied, he's not.'

'Oh no, Mrs Barr, I just hope he gets on all right. I'd better get back to Ruth and the kids now.'

He got up to go but Dan restrained him.

'Elsie's telling you the truth, Jack. I will get to work if I possibly can. I'd like to say that I appreciate your help, tonight - and Fred's.'

Jack mumbled as if he was embarrassed and moved to walk out of the door, but as he got to the door, he turned and said, 'You just lie back now, Dan. I can see that you've had a nasty tumble. I've heard that if you can apply something cold to a swelling, it'll help to get rid of it. What I should do, if I were you, is to protect the settee with something that's waterproof and go outside and get some snow to put on your leg. It's worth a try, ain't it?' He disappeared out of the door.

Elsie smiled at Dan. She had heard of the treatment before. Dan smiled back at her, weakly.

'Anything's worth a try, Elsie, if it will get rid of the pain. If you tuck my mac' under my leg, it'll protect the settee. You can put snow and ice inside it then.'

Dan lay back and waited for the cold of the snow to come. Elsie took his old raincoat down from the hook where she had hung it, and lifted his leg. As she did so, she rolled his trousers up and exposed his leg. It was looking better already. She pushed the coat under and spread it round the settee then picked up a bucket and coal shovel. In a matter of minutes she was standing at his side with a bucket full of snow.

Elsie lifted his leg again and placed a lump of snow under his ankle, then put snow around the ankle joint. She heard him wince but carried on; this job had to be completed. It was soon done and she brought another cloth to soak and wipe the snow that had started to melt. Dan lay still as she carried out her task. It was getting better but the cold was getting into his bones.

'Hang on a minute Elsie, love. The cold is too much. I shall be getting gangrene or something.' He moved to make himself more comfortable. 'Let my ankle thaw out a bit, then it'll feel the benefit of the cold.'

Elsie moved away from him and handed him a hot, refreshing cup of Oxo tea.

'I made this for you earlier. I thought you might like a hot drink of beef tea. Get it down your throat; you'll soon be up on your feet!'

Dan picked the cup up and tasted the contents. 'This is lovely, love. It's almost worth falling off a bike for!' He drank the remainder as quickly as he could and subsided into a heap on the settee. 'You say the bike's all right? The way my ankle is improving, I should be able to ride it in the morning.' He sat up as Elsie was mopping the rags from around his leg and pulled her down to him. 'I appreciate what you're doing for me, you know.'

He kissed her lustily on the lips and slid his hand up her leg. There was a quick knock at the door and Ruth Mallory walked in. Dan pulled himself together but not before Ruth had noticed what was going on.

'Well,' their neighbour said, 'I heard that somebody was lying next to death's door in 'ere, but it can't be 'im, can it? He's far too active to be doin' a die.'

Dan and Elsie both blushed.

'I think he is getting better, Ruth. It's the ice treatment. The cold gets his circulation warm and it heals him! I've got to go and fetch some Witch Hazel to reduce this swelling; could you keep an eye on him, please, Ruth?'

Ruth was still with Dan when she got back. Elsie could hear them giggling like a young couple. Ruth was kneeling down at the side of the settee, towelling his legs. Elsie walked in and Dan had the grace to blush. Not so, Ruth. Elsie spoke to put Ruth in her place.

'Thanks for what you've done, Mrs Mallory. He looks a lot better, doesn't he? I'll see you in the morning then.'

She held the door for Ruth, who took the hint and left. Elsie asked, 'Do you think you'll be able to get up the stairs all right, Dan? I couldn't help you up; you'd have to manage it for yourself.'

Her husband lifted himself up, proudly.

'Of course I can get up the stairs. What do you think I am - a cripple?'

He turned and made his way slowly up the stairs, Elsie following.

Morning found the snow melting in a sudden warming up of the weather and Dan started out earlier than usual to allow himself more time for the journey to Willenhall. Elsie started earlier, too. She wanted to get finished as soon as possible so that she could visit Mary. She had collected all her rents and done the accounts when Luke called across the office to her.

'Go on, Elsie, there's nothing to be done now, and I know you want to go and see Mary.'

The look on her face thanked him and she slipped her coat on. It was cold as she moved up the hill and round the corner to Mary's house, where the little woman was waiting for her with a cup of hot tea.

Elsie was explaining what her transport difficulties would be if they moved to Willenhall when Mary interrupted her.

'Why don't you just ask Dan? What have you got to lose, Elsie? If he says no, you're no worse off than you are now. If so, you will know how much you can rely on his support in the years to come. If he says yes, you will know that he is a generous man who is willing to put himself out for his wife.'

Elsie thought it over and later that night she put it to him. He was cleaning his boots as she asked, thinking that he was in a mild sort of humour. The boot just missed her head as he flew into a temper.

'What do you think I'm made of, woman? Money? I've been working all the hours that God sends in order to afford this bloody house you wanted. Another word from you and I'll wash my hands of the plan altogether, and you can have your posh friends down at Jenkins' to keep you! No, I won't help you to buy a bloody pony and trap. That's the end of that.'

Elsie picked up the boot he had thrown at her and opened

the front door. She had had enough of that kind of talk!

'Here's your boot then, Dan Barr. When you want to throw it again, you can go and get it out of the yard! Any time you want to throw your weight about, with me on the end of your temper, you just try it, and I can soon get somebody to throw your weight about for you, you bastard!'

Elsie coiled her arm back and let the boot go as far as she could throw it. She walked out and entered the washhouse. Her washing stick was leaning against the window sill. Her anger filled her as she picked it up and stalked back in. The stick raised, she advanced towards him.

'Get out of my sight, you bloody bully. Nobody bullies me, I can tell you that. I'll get my own back on you if I have to wait 'til you're fast asleep. As a matter of fact, I wouldn't go to sleep tonight if I were you; you might just get this washing stick wrapped round your head!'

Dan backed off from her, his face paling at the sight. He had never seen his wife in such a mood. He tried to reconcile her to him.

'I'm sorry, Elsie. I've just had a lot on my mind and the extra expense was the straw that broke the camel's back. How do you think I could bloody well afford a horse and trap, just so you can ride around collecting rents?'

Dan suddenly realised that he was shouting and the last thing he wanted was to let the neighbours hear about Elsie's job. He quietened his words.

'Look Elsie, how do you seriously think I can afford a pony and trap? Just tell me; that's all I want to know.'

He closed his mouth, still seeming shocked at the way his wife had attacked him. Elsie stopped and put down the washing stick, her breathing becoming less hasty. She thought of his words. All of a sudden she seemed to relax. She spoke forcefully but more quietly, as if she was talking to a child.

'You listen to me, Dan. All I wanted from you was some

help towards a trap. I've already had the promise of the use of a horse or pony, whenever I want it. Mister Jenkins has already made me that offer so that I can come from Willenhall to collect his precious rents. All I wanted from you was the loan of a few pounds so that I could bid for a trap at the auction, next week. I didn't want anything from you, only a loan. Now I don't want it; I can get a loan from somewhere else. Just remember, someday you might want a loan from me! Yes, you never know!'

The anger came back into Dan's voice as he replied. 'Well, that's all very well, but who's going to clean out your precious pony; that's what I would like to know? I suppose you know how to drive it, don't you?'

Dan was getting desperate; every time he tried to hold his rightful authority and power over her, she thwarted him. He knew she could control a pony; he had seen her. How could he show her who was boss? He made one last stabbing remark. 'Another thing; I suppose the landlord will want extra rent for stabling. You know what they are, don't you?'

Elsie responded immediately. 'If there's any more to pay, Dan, I'll pay it; how's that?'

'Where will you get the extra cash from, then?'

'Not from you, anyway, but I'll find a way, even if it means renting the rig out when I don't need it!'

The thought hadn't occurred to either of them before but it was a valid answer to the objection, they knew. Elsie could see the potential of a small increase in her income; Dan could see Elsie getting a small increase without feeling the benefit himself. The advantage was again going to Elsie and he felt frustrated. Dan sometimes felt that she moved in a circle of knowledge that he was not part of and it made him angry. They each fell silent as they took in the idea that she had put forward as a rebuttal to his objection. He could see no further objections except to put forward the idea that he was the head of the household, and that had not worked.

He decided to give in. 'Well perhaps the extra money might come in handy to buy things for the house, if we decide to stay here.'

Dan was including an almost hidden threat in his words; the threat that if it didn't work out to his satisfaction he would decide to give up the house. Elsie smiled silently; as if he could make her give up her own house! She had plans for the rent that he would be paying her!

The energy of quarrelling left them both drained and they were silent for the rest of the evening. Tom was crying; needing feeding. He was growing fast and starting to move around on his feet, holding onto the settee.

Mary was almost indispensable to Elsie now, looking after the infant when she felt she was needed. Christmas came and they had little time to celebrate, having to get ready for the move to Willenhall. Dan was still surly about the move although he was the one who had made the enquiries without consulting Elsie. He had made the decision, he felt, and should therefore be in charge; after all, he was the man!

Elsie asked him what he intended about the furniture they already had. He had paid for most of it. She just wondered how he would react. Dan didn't want to let it go. He had bought it out of the extra money that Mary had lent him. Elsie had looked around at what was available in Willenhall and liked it. She wanted the old furniture to be left for the next tenant in their house in Wednesbury and she had talked it over with Mary, who had agreed to give her a good price for it. Elsie broached the subject with her husband.

'Dan, do you think the landlord might want the furniture? You might get a good price for it and then you wouldn't have to pay to transport it. You might do better like that.'

Here she was again with her ideas! She was always coming up with something. Perhaps she was right. There was always that possibility. She seemed to be right a lot of the time. He decided to go along with her, this time. He had nothing to lose.

'Yes, all right then, Elsie; I'll leave it to you to make enquiries and then tell me what you find out?'

He looked at her as if to say 'it was your idea; now get on with it'. He made one further comment.

'If we can make a profit out of the situation, why shouldn't we?'

Oh, she thought. He's using his head. That's a change. I'd better go along with that or I shall get the blame if anything goes wrong.

'All right, Dan. I'll see what I can find out.'

She resumed her feeding of Tom. Things were quietening down between them. Perhaps Dan was getting mellower. They passed the rest of the evening in quiet conversation, talking about the way they should have their new curtains, and how they would stable the pony, if and when they got it.

Luke had been to see her about that. Mister Jenkins had bought a pony in preparation for their move and Luke was going to bid for a trap on her behalf. There was an auction between Christmas and New Year, and Luke would bid up to twenty pounds for her if he found a suitable vehicle. Dan would have a fit if he knew, Elsie thought.

Dan had two days off for Christmas and nothing off for New Year. Elsie always preferred New Year, feeling that it was the start of something new, whereas Christmas always felt as if it were already old. January the second came and with it came Stephen.

'Happy New Year.'

He was standing in the door. Dan was at work and Elsie felt alone and vulnerable.

'Happy New Year.' She paused; it seemed like a long pause. 'What are you doing here?'

'I had to see you.' He paused for a long time. 'I had to wish you Happy New Year and bring you this.'

He stood back. 'This' was Mister Jenkins' pony, pulling a newly painted trap. Stephen pulled out a piece of paper that looked official. It was a bill of sale from a Mister Fred Smith, auctioneer, acknowledging the receipt of fifteen guineas for one trap, as seen. Stephen spoke again, nervously.

'Mary Bowyer asked me if I would like to deliver it for Mister Jenkins. Here it is. If you are not moving yet, I can stable it at the factory for now, and you can pick it up when you move in. When are you moving in?'

Elsie and Dan had decided to move in at the weekend but now she could, if she had the use of the pony and trap, do some of the sorting out and travel back and forth each day. The young woman moved past Stephen and walked around the pony. He was a beautiful grey Welsh Cob who looked alert and ready to do her bidding. She smiled and looked across to Stephen to see he was smiling too. Elsie walked round the trap again. It had been painted a rich green except for a gold coloured line running around it, parallel to the edges. It looked easy to handle and the pony looked as if he had been born with a bit in his mouth. There was room for two at the front and another two in the back. Elsie replied to Stephen's question.

'I don't know. We planned on Saturday now the repairs are done and I think we still shall, but now I shall be able to move some things in, ready, before we go.'

Elsie became conscious that she kept saying 'we', as if she wished, somehow, to separate and deny herself from any sort of relationship with Stephen. He was standing on the doorstep still. She found herself opening the door wider.

'Come in. It must be cold outside.'

Stephen walked in, still smiling. Tom was moving round,

at the end of the settee. They looked at each other, father and son, and liked what they saw.

'Hello, son.'

Stephen had stopped smiling, the first time ever, she thought. What was going to happen now? He took hold of Elsie by her shoulders and pulled her to him. She was tempted to pull away but the temptation to stay there was too great. She settled her head on his chest and lay there, content.

There was something moving round her feet. She pulled away and looked down. It was Tom, looking up at the pair of them.

'It's a wise child.' Said Stephen, his smile reappearing as he spoke softly and slowly. 'That's a true saying. Look at him; he's the image of us.'

They settled against each other and relaxed. It was as if they were one, she thought. The thought must have occurred to Stephen as well because his hand moved from around her shoulder to her breast. She flinched and made to move away but he held onto her more tightly and she decided that her breast's position, against his hand, was a good enough position for it to be in.

Elsie turned her face up; it was a natural seeming thing to do, and either he kissed her or she kissed him. Either way, things seemed to get warmer then. She pulled him down to her, on the settee and put her hand on his leg, feeling for him and finding him. Stephen moved closer and she found her clothes being pulled up around her waist. He was inside her now, moving in heat and dampness. Moving around her, his hands on her breasts, he moved her dress to one side so that he could kiss her. Her body started moving as if in response to a switch, convulsing up and down, feeling, kissing and whispering words of love.

The heat was too much now; she could feel him getting

hotter and hotter inside her until she could contain her emotions no longer.

'Stephen!' She shouted. 'Stephen! I want you, forever!'

Elsie could hear him shouting too, telling her all the mad crazy things that a man tells a woman. There was a blinding moment; a moment she had never experienced before. Then it went quiet. She could not recall afterwards whether she fainted or whether she just went to the top of the pile, as she thought about it later. It just seemed to last forever.

Tom was crying again and didn't seem likely to stop until he had been fed. The young woman stood and picked him up; her reflexes making her do their bidding. Stephen reached out his arms to Tom and Tom started crying louder. Elsie smiled; a relationship had to be earned, it seemed.

Stephen put his arm round her again. It was a sort of signal, in advance of saying goodbye. He moved to the door. The everlasting moment was over. She moved with him and, as she opened it, Ruth Mallory was walking across the court. She looked at Stephen as if he were alien.

'Are you all right, Mrs Barr? Is there anything I can do for you?' She turned to Stephen but spoke to Elsie. 'You shouldn't be interrupted when you are looking after a young 'un!'

Ruth glared at Stephen, as if asking him who he was. Elsie felt the need to put her right. She thought for a moment.

'Thank you, Mister Stone, for showing me the pony and trap. They'll certainly be useful. If you would stable them for me in Willenhall, I'd be grateful. I'll look after them when we get there.'

Stephen took her cue and touched his hand to his head, as if he had a cap to touch.

'Thank you very much then, Mrs Barr. I shall more than likely see you in Willenhall. Good day to you, madam.'

He turned his back on the two women and climbed up

onto the seat of the trap then picked up the reins. 'Walk on, walk on.'

The pony went to walk on but Elsie put a hand out to stop the pony. 'Please, what's his name?'

The pony stopped to feel the tender touch. 'Chalky.'

The pony moved on. Ruth was standing, staring at her. She seemed to be wondering about something. Elsie looked at Ruth.

'What are you looking so gormless about? I've got more to do than stand around all day, farting about with ponies. I've got to get ready to move home.'

'Yes,' said Ruth. 'I can see that you've got more to do than stand around; not that I blame you; he's a nicely built man if I ever saw one, and I've seen a few. I've 'ad some fun, you know, down in Bromyard, while I was doing some hop picking.'

Ruth turned round and walked away towards her own house. Elsie looked after her for a moment and then closed the door on the court. Tom was calling her. She undid her bodice and sat him on her lap. He pulled himself to her, eagerly. Always hungry, he was, always hungry. She felt satisfied and frustrated, at the same time.

It was obvious to her that Stephen had recognised himself in her child. Was it as obvious to everyone else? It couldn't be; no one else had mentioned a likeness, if indeed, there was one. Maybe it would become more obvious if the three of them were seen together more often.

The memory of their encounter was still with her, almost making her want to own up to the whole thing and let the world know what her feelings were. It would suit her character, she thought, truthful and honest. The situation within the Stone family inhibited her and made her angry. It was all about money and the acquisition of more power for their family within the lock industry. Her little affair with

Stephen had no priority with Albert Stone. If the affair was revealed she would be made to go away, one way or another. She might even lose her friendship with Mary. She wouldn't like to test it.

Tom was content now, smiling up at her; like his father. The thought and her acceptance of it frightened her. She had to decide! What should she do? Should she accept Stephen's restraints and find occasional happiness, if that was what it was, within the restraints, or should she make a clean break from him and try to forget the feeling they had? It was like an ever turning roundabout and she knew that wherever she got off would be the wrong place, leaving her falling and spinning with the dizziness of it all.

Elsie recalled what Stephen had said about the situation and the expression on his face as he had spoken. He always tried to smile and he had told her that he could not face life without knowing that they were part of each other's life, so they might as well smile, whatever the outcome. Anything else was just words.

Dan would be home soon, looking for his dinner; she was doing stew today. She had better get on with the potatoes. Once they were boiled they would keep for a time. What had Ruth said about the hop yards? Elsie knew that a lot of the women travelled to Worcester and Hereford to help to pick the crops. Perhaps what she had meant was that she had found men friends down there. It was an easy way to get away from the rules of normal society without committing a sin too openly. The thought intrigued her, as if some part of her mind was taking it in and storing it for future use.

Elsie placed Tom in his small cot, asleep, and started cleaning the potatoes, thinking as she did so. Should she tell Dan about the pony and trap? Her mind wandered as she scraped and peeled. The rig couldn't just turn up out of the blue. She would have to say Aunt Mary had sent a man round with it and she had sent him away with it until they were ready for it. There was a noise; it was Dan, home for his dinner. How would he get on with Chalky?

Chapter 14

Moving in
1908

It was Saturday and the move was well under way. Dan had agreed to sell the furniture to their landlord who had made him an offer that ensured that he would not make a loss, especially when he found that he might get a discount on any new furniture he might buy. Fred had agreed to lend them the flat wagon and most of what they were taking was loaded, not taking more than half of the load space. The work had all been carried out on the house so they were gaining months on their original expectation.

Elsie had told Dan about the pony and trap but he did not seem to have taken much notice. He hadn't seen it yet. It would be in their stable now, eating hay, she thought. She had fallen in love with the cob, his greyness seeming silver to her. He seemed to be very intelligent and had handled well as Stephen had driven him away. Elsie had not paid for it yet, assuming the auctioneer would send her a bill. She pulled out the bill and saw that there was nothing exceptional about it; it was just an ordinary bill. Then she noticed that it said Paid in Full at the bottom, and there was the signature of Fred Smith, the auctioneer. Mary must have paid the bill!

Elsie walked across the court to say goodbye to Ruth Mallory. It was not a real goodbye because she would be seeing her next week to collect her rent. Dan was in Ruth's house, saying goodbye. Elsie had not known that he knew her that well. He shouldn't be seeing her again. There was something about the way the pair of them were standing that made her curious; had there been something going on there? She put the thought out of her mind and hugged Ruth.

'I shall miss you, Ruth. We've become good friends, ain't we? It's not often you can say that about anybody. I'll be seeing you, of course, and you can tell me all about Bromyard and the hop-picking. I might go myself if the chance comes up.'

Dan seriously shook hands with Ruth and thanked her for the help she had given. Ruth was crying as they disappeared into Union Street. Elsie had kept the key, Ruth noticed. Who was going to live there? She had enjoyed the friendship of Elsie and Dan. He was a nice man when he wasn't being too serious; when he was being playful.

It took them two hours to get to Willenhall. They stopped near the market to water the great Shire horse. He seemed quite at home, nodding to other horses as if they were old friends. He was the biggest; a mountain of black muscle moving in a stately way, pulling the cart as if it was nothing. He neighed loudly as they approached their new home and was answered by a shrill neigh from the back of the house. Someone had installed Chalky in the stable! Dan looked at Elsie.

'What's this, then? Whose is that cob in our back garden?' He looked as if it had been put there without his consent. 'Is this the cob you told me about?'

Dan sat on the cart, waiting for an answer, his face livid, as if he was annoyed about the whole thing. The cob neighed again, as if to welcome them home, and somehow that made Elsie wonder again who had paid for him. The Shire drew up alongside the cob and the two animals greeted each other, nuzzling each other's noses. Elsie and Dan jumped down and walked round the pony, inspecting him.

'What do you think, Dan? Don't you think it was kind of Mister Jenkins to supply us with a pony and trap? The neighbours will think we're really something.'

Dan seemed amazed that he had the use of a pony. He had never dreamed that it might be possible. The anger left him abruptly.

'He's a lovely thing, ain't he, Elsie? Have you had a go yet?'

'No, not yet, I suppose we could go to church in the trap on Sundays. You'd be able to drive him, wouldn't you, Dan? In the meantime we'd better get the cart unloaded and put the house right.'

Elsie picked up a bucket from the back of the cart and started filling it with cleaning items, speaking to her husband at the same time.

'Have you got the keys, Dan?' She started marching up the path. 'Come on, man; there's work to be done. For all we know we'll be having visitors and I wouldn't want them to see the place untidy.'

Dan fell into step beside her and they carried the articles for the house between them. The new furniture was coming later. She looked along the road and saw that a man was walking towards them. He waved to her and she hung back to see what he wanted.

'Hello,' he shouted, coming closer. 'Mister Stone has asked me to give you an 'and, for this afternoon.' He stopped and Elsie could see that he had recognised Dan. 'Hyah Dan! Are you on this lark as well? It's another half a day's pay!'

The man suddenly recognised Elsie and realised that he was making a fool of himself. 'I'm sorry, Elsie; Mrs Barr. I didn't recognise you. It's been some time since you worked in Stones' ain't it? We could do with you back now. The young un's ain't half as fast as you.'

He smiled. Elsie had known him when she had worked

with him; he was a cheery type of man and she could not take offence at his familiarity.

'Hello, Harry. Thank you, and whoever sent you for the help. Are you any good with horses? I don't know who brought Chalky here and we've only just got here ourselves. If you know what you are doing you can see what needs doing in the stable. Chalky seems friendly enough but be careful, won't you?'

'Don't you worry Missus. I'll soon get that sorted out. It'll tek me 'til cup o' tea time and that shouldn't be long, should it, Dan?'

It was obvious that he knew Dan well. He grinned at him as if he was expecting Dan to make the tea. Dan didn't seem to know what to do. Elsie was taking charge and it didn't seem right for her to do that. It seemed as if he was pulled between changing the orders that Elsie had just given, or just accepting them. In the end he followed Elsie into the house and started to check round to see that all the work had been done.

A small carpet had been laid in the living room, and there were armchairs on the cart for the kitchen. The fire was not laid so Dan laid it with folded paper and there was soon a comforting glow in the fireplace. Elsie sat there with Tom on her lap and Dan just asked what was to be done next. Inside an hour, the house was warming and the kitchen range was getting hot. Elsie had sliced some bread ready for toasting; with a basin of dripping ready to spread on it and pepper for the taste of it.

Dan came into the kitchen, sweat on his brow. He threw his jacket onto the back of a chair, picked up a long fork and stuck it into a thick slice of bread.

'That's that, Mrs Barr. It's all done. It'll be nice now we have more than one room to live in. We should manage all right here, don't you think?'

Elsie looked round. There was a small entrance to the top of the cellar steps and to the right of that there was a door that led to the lavatory. There was also a door that hid the stairs that led up to the three bedrooms. It was not large but it had more room than they were used to. The fire was casting heat and fast-moving shadows that livened up the room.

'The furniture we ordered should be coming in the morning, Dan. It'll be nice to have the house furnished but there's no hurry after all. We're here for some time. Mister Jenkins has given me Monday off, for the move, but I'm bound to be wanted on Tuesday. I'll have to take little Tom to work with me. Aunt Mary's told me she'll look after him while I'm working.'

Dan was looking down the stairs into the cellar space. Just like him, she thought. He wasn't listening; he is wondering what is down there.

'Go on, then. I can see you're dying to go down and explore, just like a kid, you are. Here's a lamp to see with.'

Elsie grinned and handed the oil lamp to him and he trod carefully as he disappeared down the steps. She peered down the steps as he disappeared in the shadows cast by the lamp. There was a pause as she heard him moving around. Then he called, 'There's plenty of room for coal down 'ere, Elsie. In fact, there's already enough to last us a month. It's a wonder it ain't been pinched.'

Dan's old-time way of expressing himself made her think that he must have been exposed to it at an early part of his life, but he was right, as he usually was about such things. She buckled to and within the hour had finished the moving of furniture, which was delivered as they were standing talking. She made tea and they sat to discuss the house. Dan set the agenda.

'First, the horse; what are your intentions regarding him?'

Dan laid himself back in his new chair. He had liked the look of the chair but now he had it, he didn't like the feel of it against his back. Elsie soon changed his mind for him.

'You'll soon get used to it, Dan, and it'll grow to the shape of your back. It suits you, somehow. Straight-backed and not too easy to sit on, but strong and ready to take on any weight.'

Dan didn't seem too displeased at the way she described his character. She answered his question next.

'The horse stays here, Dan. He'll cost us the hay, that's all. I may be able to get Mister Jenkins to put in to that cost. He'll pay the vet's fees, as well. What Chalky will give in return is carriage for me and Tom, to Wednesbury, whenever I have to go, to perform my duties for Mister Jenkins. He'll take us to church on Sundays, and to see Aunt Mary afterwards. If she's at church, she'll be given passage home as well. If there's a journey you want to make for yourself, you have the use of the trap.

'I shall have to start out a little earlier to get to Wednesbury but I should be home earlier because of the speed at which I shall get round my clients. Mary'll look after Tom when necessary. We've got a horse and trap that'll carry at least four people, and at no cost to ourselves. That's not such a bad situation for us to find ourselves in, is it?'

It was not often that Elsie spoke as quickly or for such a long time. She sat and composed herself, awaiting his answer.

'I can't fault what you say, Elsie; you seem to have covered everything. As you say, it's a good deal. We'll have to see how it works out. Have you got the paperwork, you know, the bill of sale and anything else?'

'Of course I haven't. It's in Mister Jenkins's safe, I expect. It's his horse.'

Tom was crying again as he was hungry. It was time all of them ate so Elsie bustled into the small space that was called the kitchen. It was really the landing at the top of the cellar steps. She soon had thick cheese sandwiches made and put in front of them and sat nursing young Tom while she ate bread and cheese herself. They had finished with work for the day. The new bed would come from the furniture shop, this afternoon and the delivery men would place it. Harry had finished in the stable and gone, after a cup of tea.

'Would you like to go to church tomorrow, Dan? We could wash ourselves and go in the trap.' She saw his eyes glisten with interest and pressed her point. 'It would be nice for us to arrive as a family, don't you think?'

'Yes, we'll do that. It'll let people know we are moving up in the world, even if our kitchen is at the top of the cellar steps.'

Elsie smiled at him. She was finding the layout quite useful. You only had to turn round with the food from the kitchen shelves, and it was on the living room table, ready for cooking on the fire. They continued their discussion next morning while they got ready for church and then drove to Wednesbury. Surprisingly, the journey was uneventful. Dan had driven before and showed her how to handle the pony in the turns and how to alter speed.

As usual, on the way, he had comments to make about the performance of the Government.

'Now they're going to raise another Army. It was in the paper; a hundred and sixty thousand men! That'll lower the unemployment figures, I bet. That's what they call an Expeditionary Force. That should be enough to beat any o' them natives.'

The journey became a pattern in their lives for some time. They enjoyed the trips and the visits to Aunt Mary when they came out of church. Sometimes Fred Stone was there and Elsie enjoyed his company, even when he teased her about how he first met. Elsie was becoming more elegant in style as she matured, and becoming more well-known around the small town.

Sometimes Luke accompanied her to teach her the finer points of driving, and how to use the long whip that had come with the trap. She was surprised how she soon learned to use it.

'You never know,' Luke said, 'you may have to defend yourself some day and it's best if you can use it.'

Elsie's discussions with Aunt Mary led her to make larger investments in property and her income became greater than Dan's but she would not discuss her investments with him as she felt that he might take advantage of her and try to take a superior position with regard to her ownership.

All in all they lived together with a little love showing now and then, like many other couples. The Black Country people were not noted for the romance of their inhabitants, more for their ability to survive successfully as marital teams.

The summer came and passed and Elsie noticed that Aunt Mary was losing weight. Autumn was cold and she had to wrap up early on the trap, to keep the wind out. Elsie, for the first time, felt completely in control of her life as she completed the journey to Wednesbury each day to collect her rents for Mister Jenkins. Tom was beginning to talk now and she held childish conversations with him as she drove along the way. Occasionally she visited Ruth Mallory apart from collecting rent from her, and Ruth told her stories of her amorous adventures in Herefordshire. The life of the hop-pickers was hard but provided such a contrast from their normal life that the rules of normal living were often forgotten. Elsie determined to try it out for herself and spoke to Dan about it.

'You can please yourself what you do so long as you make sure that I have my meals while you are away,' was his response. 'Just make sure you look after the babby and be ready for me if I decide to visit you while you are down there.'

What would he say, she thought, if he knew of the things Ruth had done? She felt a thrill of guilt in advance, knowing she could never really indulge in the sort of behaviour that Ruth had told her about – could she?

Chapter 15

To Bromyard
1909

Aunt Mary improved as the spring of 1909 passed and Elsie told her what she was thinking of doing for a little time off in the summer. Mary was all for it.

'The experience of living and working with Black Country people will do you good,' she said. 'I used to go when I was younger and I must say I really enjoyed it.

'The people from the area are really rough in manner sometimes, but they have warm hearts and in character they are pure salt. You go my dear and enjoy yourself. Dan'll survive without you for a few weeks and I am sure that Luke will be able to cope with your work. He's done it before, and he may ask you to cover for him one of these days, eh?'

So, Elsie prepared a hop box with all the things she was advised by Ruth to take with her, long gloves and leggings and something to wear if it was raining. The season started on the first day of September and she decided to go by train, the way that the majority did, and leave her trap for Luke to use. He was delighted and told her that he would make full use of Chalky, collecting her rents in.

Tom was her problem but she was told that many pickers took young children with them. He was growing fast, now and getting quite bossy. When their friends spoke about it, they said it was because he was a chip off the old block. It always made her feel the guilt of his actual parentage.

Stephen often passed near her route to Wednesbury and he waved to her each time he saw her. He occasionally called at the house on the pretext that he was looking for Dan, to ask for some information about a particular job at work. Both of them knew that that was not the real reason, and they had succumbed to their passionate feelings on a number of occasions. Each time, Elsie had felt guilt for days afterwards but gradually she became more philosophical and took the view that she should take love where she could find it.

She told him her plans a week before she was due to travel and he was excited about it.

'I'll see you down there if you'll let me have the address where you are staying.' He looked at her with passion shining from his eyes. 'I can't let the chance go by, can I, love? I must see you when I can. It's pity that Mabel can't come with you. All she thinks about is her little business.'

Mabel, his wife, had opened up a dress shop at the front of the factory and it was doing well, by all accounts. All her goods were sold for cash, as advocated by Samuel Smiles, and, although her customers were complaining about having to pay for the goods before they were allowed to take them out of the shop, they did not boycott her goods, knowing them to be of superior value and quality.

Stephen was gradually being groomed to take over the management of the company and he was proving an enthusiastic pupil. He had improved on the design of three of their locks and found ways to speed the production of them without losing quality.

The first of September came, and Dan saw Elsie and Tom off on the special train. He seemed sad to let her go and she was glad to see him that way as she had begun to doubt his feelings for her.

'Off you go then, the pair of you. I shall miss you for

everything you supply me with, and you, young un'.' He smiled at Tom. 'You look after your mother: you're the man o' the house down there, you know.'

Dan backed away from the carriage window and stood looking around as if he didn't know what to do. There was the sound of slamming doors and steam whistles and the engine began its slow starting sound that gave it the nickname of chuff, chuff. Elsie suddenly panicked and caught at Dan's sleeve.

'Look after yourself, love. I'm going to miss you; I'm missing you already. I'll write and tell you how we're getting on. Tara, love.'

Elsie could see his lips move into a sad smile but the great engine suddenly blew its whistle, drowning all other sounds. She clutched Tom tightly against her breast in the illusion of giving and receiving security. Her hand went up and she waved through the window to the rather sad man she was leaving on the platform. He slowly disappeared from view as the train sped away. She felt a tear drop from her eye and, turning, stepped into the first compartment in the carriage. There were two other people; an elderly man and a young woman.

Elsie sat down and placed Tom on the seat next to her. He looked up at the man and smiled. The man smiled back and patted him on his head.

'Hello, young man; what's your name?' He looked at Elsie. 'He looks a bright young thing; is he as bright as he looks?'

Elsie returned his look.

'Yes,' she said, 'he follows his dad.'

The man smiled back at her.

'Yes,' he said. 'I can see that!'

They both started to laugh at the turns the conversation had taken and they suddenly felt comfortable with each other. It was nice, being able to talk without having to weigh the words before you spit them out. Neither of them had anything to win or lose from the chat.

Elsie had little experience of talking to strangers but there seemed little harm in it so they spoke about this and that, and then Elsie spoke to the young woman sitting at the side of her.

'It's a nice day for travelling, anyway, isn't it? How far have we to go now? Do you know?'

Elsie peered at the young woman. She looked nondescript at first glance but her shoes were of good quality and her skirt was a well-sewn one. Her face was what Aunt Mary called well-travelled, with lines of care showing under her young eyes. There was something about her that indicated to the observant that she had been through some emotional trauma quite recently. She turned slowly to Elsie and nodded in agreement.

'Yes, it is a nice day. As far as I know, we've got about twenty minutes before we get to Bromyard. I've only been twice and that was many years ago. I'm not used to travelling much; my mother died recently and this is my first journey since then. I have to find work of one sort or another and this was suggested to me by a friend.'

Elsie could see that the woman was waiting to be drawn out so asked her another probing question.

'I've never been here before either, so if you want somebody to share things with, I don't mind.'

Elsie let the words hang in the air so that the woman could pick them up or drop them without being offensive. The woman seemed to deliberate with herself over the idea, then she visibly relaxed.

'My name's Betty, Betty Thurston,' she said 'What's yours?'

That was the moment when they each found a friend in

the other. It was apparent that they would be working and living together. Tom soon got used to Betty and sat on her lap for a few minutes until they came into Bromyard. He was delighted when the engine sounded its great whistle again.

There was a wagon awaiting them, outside the station. It was drizzling with rain and Elsie wondered how they were going to manage. The driver, seeing her discomfiture smiled and shouted to her.

'Here y'are girl, if you're going to Home Farm. There's a tarpaulin folded on the bed o' the wagon. It's a good job you're late. If you'd been on the earlier train you wouldn't have been able to get under it; there was too many!'

There were only six people going to Home Farm and they were soon installed on the back of the wagon. Three of them were old hands and they soon started singing with 'Down at the Old Bull and Bush'. The atmosphere was jolly and little Tom perked up, looking round at the people singing in the rain. When a raindrop landed on his head, he pulled the tarpaulin over him to shelter. It was a great game to him and he laughed for five minutes. It was a good day's end for him too and he was asleep in half an hour. The rain stopped shortly after that, and the hedges glistened with raindrops, while the fields started steaming as the wagon trundled past.

It's like a foreign country, Elsie thought. The accents were familiar though; the rough accents of Wednesbury mixing well with those of Darlaston, Dudley and Quarry Bank, pronounced Quarry Bonk. The old hands soon made them feel at home as they encouraged the two new hands to join in with them.

The driver was a friendly young man; in fact Elsie thought he was too friendly when he asked her to sit by him on the seat of the flat wagon. Somehow she didn't trust him.

It was as if there was a sexual aspect to his friendly invitation and she didn't want to get into anything like that. She had enough problems to contend with, what with Dan suggesting he might come down to the farm to see them, and Stephen having said that he might drive down for a visit!

The rain was starting again and this time Tom was not amused. He was trying to sleep and the rain kept waking him up. Betty had him lying with his head in her lap and Tom seemed to accept that arrangement, while looking up at his mother. After half an hour, one of the old hands spoke to Elsie.

'Where am you from, cock? We'm from Hill Top, on the way to West Bromwich. Do you know it?'

'Yes, I know it. I walked over it when me and my Dad walked from Birmingham to Wednesbury some years ago. We were looking for work at the time.'

Elsie went on to tell Rita, the girl, how she and her father had tried to find work and how Mary Bowyer had offered them food and shelter, and had been helpful in finding them work. The revelation that she had worked at Stone's Locks seemed to surprise one of the girls.

'I know the place,' she said. 'I used to work there. The old man, Albert Stone gave me the sack. His son, what was his name, Stephen, I think, made a pass at me and, like a fool I let him do the thing that you shouldn't let blokes do. I told him I was pregnant but he must have told his dad. The Old Man had me in his office and put a few sovereigns in my hand and told me to clear off!' She looked at the astonished faces of the two listeners. 'I can't blame him, I suppose. I was just trying it on and he knew it.'

Elsie listened with interest to what the girl, Annie, was saying. She wasn't surprised at Albert's attitude. After all, she had been effectively shut out herself because Stephen had been planned as Mabel's husband.

Elsie looked at the changing scenery; they were almost there and they could hear ducks and geese and the lowing of cattle. It made her think of Bible stories. Everything seemed slower. There were so many new smells in the air. Betty was looking at her; her nose wrinkled in disgust. They were turning in now, the wagon scraping on the sides of the massive five-barred gate. They were there.

The wagon became suddenly silent and they noticed the absence of the squeaking. Other noises took their place. There were the bird and animal noises and voices of the people who worked there.

'Come on! It's time to get down from the wagon.' The driver leaned across to the tarpaulin and gave Tom a playful push. 'Come on, young Tom, come and look at the baa-lambs.'

Tom stood and looked around, the strange sights gradually becoming clear to him. He jumped as a cow coming in to be milked from the next field, mooed loudly and he stood and laughed at the sight. The rest of the passengers jumped down from the wagon and waited to be told where to go.

'I suppose you're all starving, aren't you?'

Elsie turned at the sound of the voice. A young countrywoman stood surveying them from the doorway that led into the kitchen of the farmhouse.

'If you all get your gear stowed away upstairs in the barn,' she pointed to the steps that led upward into the barn. 'there'll be time for you get yourselves a meal.'

'Come on, Elsie.' It was Betty calling from the wagon. 'I'll bring what I can if you can carry a bit.'

Betty picked up Elsie's case with her clothes in, and started to climb the stairs. Elsie, feeling a little bewildered, picked up the remaining small bag which held her money and small private things and started up the steps after her.

As she entered the building, it suddenly became so much cooler that she shivered for a second. The feeling was quite pleasant though and she stood and looked around.

The roof of the barn was about thirty feet long and twenty feet wide. Half of it was floored and the other half was open up to the thatch. There was a line of milking stations along the wall opposite the large wooden doors that led into the barn. As she looked, the first of the cows was being led in for the evening milking. Tom clung tightly to her at the sight.

'It's a cow, just a cow, Tom. Moo.' She imitated the sound again and smiled at him. 'Moo, moo!'

He turned and looked again.

'Moo, moo, Mommy.'

'That's it, Tom, moo.'

He seemed delighted now, stretching his neck to see the sights below. The smell of the animals suddenly hit them and he screwed up his nose.

'Moo, poo!'

Elsie laughed and Betty and the others, who had been watching, joined in, all making cow noises to amuse him. The cattle looked up, uninterestedly, and moved to their favourite biers. Elsie had been advised to bring bacon with her so she put Tom down and put reins on him so that he couldn't fall over the edge of the floor. She reached for her bag and picked a loaf out of it. Betty was tidying her particulars and preparing for her evening meal.

Elsie lifted Tom under one arm and stepped gingerly down the steps. At the covered end of the barn there were wrought iron devils for cooking on so she put a few sticks under one of them and paper under that, then lit it with a match. The wooden kindling soon flared up and she put her frying pan on top of the devil to heat. The fire was spreading a little now, so she put her kettle alongside the pan. In a few minutes the tea was made and the bacon was crackling.

'Come on, Betty,' she called. 'There's a bit o' peck here if you want it. It'll be going cold if you don't move your arse!'

There was the sound of the girl tripping down the steps and then there she was, her face flushed from the guilt of having no food. Elsie noticed but decided not to notice.

'Here you are. Get that down your throat. There's no need to starve you know. There's plenty more where that came from. You can get a sub off the farmer if you feel the need, and if you've done enough work.'

Elsie noticed that she was absorbing the accents of the people around her; she had noticed that before, as if she was a chameleon. She had sounded like a business person when she was collecting rents; now she sounded like an 'op-picker!

Betty sat down on an empty barrel and picked up a sandwich. She was obviously starving but trying to eat in a ladylike manner. She came up for air.

'This is bloody marvellous. Can I have another sixteen, please? I'm really hungry.' The joking little confession seemed to open her mind and mouth at the same time. 'I really am,' she said, 'and I bet you are as well.'

Her face dropped and she picked up a handkerchief. 'I've got to tell you, Elsie, I don't have a very wonderful life, living with Dad. He's very feeling if you know what I mean.' She looked at Elsie to see what sort of reaction she would get. Elsie nodded; she had the situation in her mind.

'He loves me, if you know what I mean, but I think he misses Mom lot. He needs…and I have to…'

Betty stopped talking. She did not need to say anything else. Elsie's look told her that she understood. Elsie was shocked. Her own experience of life, similar to Betty's in some ways was entirely without the horrific practices to which Betty had been forced to submit. Her father had exemplified all the ways an ideal father would act. Betty carried on talking as if she needed the release from the fears in her mind.

'Mom died from stoppage of the bowels; she was dead in a week,' Betty said. 'It was only a few months ago. You miss your Mom, don't you? I know I do. My life has been a misery since she's gone.'

The afternoon sun gradually lowered in the sky as the women exchanged confidences and memories and the exchanges forged a bond between them. They would be starting work in the morning and they had no idea what they would have to do, or what they could do to prepare for it but they each had a friend to do it with.

The two young women looked round at the noisy crowd who were billeted with them. The pickers, mostly women, were all talking to each other in just the way they had been on the wagon. Elsie made up her mind to ask, to find out what she didn't know. She moved over a little, to be standing near one of the other pickers.

'We've never been picking before. Can you put us right about the best way to go about it?'

Elsie tried to act innocent and mild, to get the best answer to her question. The woman, a chubby blonde, darted a glance at her.

'I know you, don't I? I've seen you walking round Wednesbury, shopping. Yes, we'll put you right; you'll soon get the 'ang of the picking. Your 'ands'll get black from it and you'll have hundreds of little cuts all over 'em.

'You come and work with we in the morning and we'll show you what to do. We start at about seven o'clock if the weather's right for it, and so we tek a bit o' lunch wrapped in paper. If you can find a bottle, fill it with cold tea; it'll save the walk back, and you'll earn a bit more; that's what it's all about, ain't it?'

The other women had stopped talking and were noticing

the newcomers. In a few minutes they had all introduced themselves as Daisy, Gert and Florrie. Two were experienced hands and promised to share their knowledge of the hop picking with the novices.

The time went by more slowly now and the fire cast shadows on their faces as they sat telling stories of past years and the times they had had with the gypsies and the locals. Two of them had gone home pregnant some years ago, but had managed to persuade their husbands that the new offspring were theirs. The stories were told amidst the giggling that showed the excitement that the recalling brought forth.

Each of the women had a turn to hold young Tom and he was passed round, a sleeping parcel, from hand to hand. After a while, he awoke and started to cry as he found himself in unfamiliar arms.

The woman laughed. 'That's the last time he'll grumble about finding 'imself on a strange pair o' tits!'

Gert cuddled him to her and he seemed to perceive that he was safe and dropped back to sleep in a few minutes. Gert passed him back to Elsie as the women stood and made their way to their mattresses of straw and hop pockets. It was getting dark and they were all tired but looking forward to the first day of work, tomorrow.

Betty had made her sleeping bag next to Elsie and as she lay down she turned to her and kissed her gently on the cheek.

'Thank you for what you've done for me today.'

The kiss was a surprise to Elsie. What other new surprises would she find?

Chapter 16

Starting Work
The Attack
1909

The morning came with sunshine, a slightly unseasonable event but welcome. Elsie lifted her head from the pillow and looked round. Betty was lying next to her, her clothes spread around her, looking perfectly asleep and relaxed.

This was to be an exciting day, Elsie felt. She looked at her watch; it was six o'clock. There were noises coming from below as the herdsmen shoved the grumbling cattle out of the barn. One of them looked up at her and winked, making her aware that she was in very light clothing. She blushed and turned her head away but felt pleased that a man had noticed her, if only for her body.

She recalled the conversation she had had, with Ruth telling her of the male friends she had made while hop picking. The thought of feeling another body against hers was making her feel what she called 'broody'; a nice feeling but disturbing at the same time. Does Betty have such feelings, she thought? Was that why she had volunteered the goodnight kiss?

Betty awoke then but there was no playfulness in her eyes. Instead, her eyes looked slightly bloodshot and the lines on her face seemed just that little bit deeper, as if something was troubling her. Elsie had never heard a confession like she had from her the night before. Somehow she had to lift the young woman from her depression.

'Good morning, Betty. Today's the day we start work. You'd better wake up.'

Elsie stood and threw on her working clothes and picked up what she called her grocery bag. Another movement brought her, her wash bag. She tripped down the steps to the yard as she looked round for a pump. There were three other women standing there so she joined them.

'Good morning, ladies,' she said, and placed herself ready to pump the water into her bucket. 'Lovely day for the picking.'

'Mornin,' 'ow bin yer? It's all right for some,' one of the women grumbled. 'I've got to cook for four this morning. My daughter-in-law won't stir herself; idle sod! She's the same at home; does nothing till she 'as to.'

'Well, that's your own fault,' said Elsie. 'If I had the chance to lie back and wait for others to wait on me, I would. As it is, I have to be responsible for myself, so that's what you should do; make her responsible for herself. If you don't, you only have yourself to blame.'

Elsie bent and lifted the pump handle and pressed downward. The pump lowered and the water came flooding out of the nozzle, filling her bucket in three pumping motions. She bent and lifted the bucket and as she turned her back on the women she heard one of them mutter, 'stuck up bitch!' and was about to turn back when she heard one of the others speak.

'The trouble is, Martha, you don't take any notice of good advice when you get it. You would sooner moan 'an do anything about it.'

Elsie smiled to herself. At least one of the women agreed with what she had advised. Betty was lighting the kindling when she got back to where they were going to eat breakfast under the overhang of the barn. The girl took the bucket from Elsie and hung it on the tripod. The kindling was ablaze now and larger pieces of wood were put on the fire. They sat in silence for a few minutes, and then Betty said, 'This is a lovely life, you know, Elsie. I could live all of my life like this.'

She turned away and put more wood on the fire. The water was getting warm, now and Elsie put two teaspoonfuls of tea into her billycan. She looked across at Betty. She was just sitting there, holding a large cup, ready for Elsie to fill it. She had an odd look on her face, as if she were recalling events.

'I'll just go and get half a dozen eggs. I'll be back in a minute. Will you get the frying pan ready, Betty?'

Elsie stood again and made her way across the muddy yard. There were three others waiting outside the farmhouse door. One of them was Martha, the one who had been grumbling.

'I've left her, the daughter-in-law, cooking the breakfast. I just thought I'd try what you said. It seems to 'ave worked, anyway. I don't see why she should get away with it all the time.'

Martha turned as the farmer's wife opened the door, smiling.

'Yes, young lady,' she asked; 'have you got everything you need? Eggs? Bacon? My name's Jenny, Jenny Walker, by the way.'

In a few minutes they had all been served, either for cash if the picker had got it, or in exchange for a signature putting them in debt against the week's wages, to be repaid on pay day.

'You can sign for what you want at the farmhouse.' She announced the news to Betty who was frying sausages when she got back. Elsie looked at them in surprise. 'I thought you were skint, Betty. You're a dark horse.'

Betty was looking pleased with herself. 'I just wanted to

know what sort of a person you were. If you hadn't have offered, I would have cooked myself some sausages last night. Now I know what you are like, I can share with you. Don't you think that was a good idea?'

Elsie laughed. 'What about if I had treated you the same way? Neither of us would have eaten at all last night.'

Elsie sat down and Betty started cracking eggs into the pan. In a few minutes they both had plates full of breakfast and tin mugs of tea. Life was very pleasant.

There was the sound of women's talk around them. There were very few men; they were either in bed or had already started earlier. Either way they would be arriving for their breakfasts soon. Martha shouted across to the two learners.

'Yo' can work with us, if you like. The daughter-in-law wants to work on her own.'

That would mean four of them working into a crib. It might work out. If not they could always move. Elsie looked at Betty and by mutual consent they nodded across to Martha and her friend Gert. That was settled then. They were a team. They stood up and each started to tidy their own area; cups and plates were quickly cleaned and put away.

'Come on then,' Gert shouted. 'We want to get a good crib before everybody else wanders across.'

The four of them crossed the yard into the first hop garden. Ned, the busheller, nodded.

'Nice to see somebody who's keen.'

He pointed to where the hops stood in tall stately rows, eighteen feet high. They made their way there and Elsie was immediately struck by the silence as they moved into the shadow of the hops. She felt surrounded by them and surrounded by the peculiar smell in the air. At least it was better than the cows, she thought.

Gert nodded to her. Elsie hadn't really taken much notice of the Black Country girl. She was tall and angular, but with large breasts that seemed to jut out; quite a figure of a woman. She seemed to be looking at the busheller, Ned, as she worked, stripping the bines and putting the hops into the cradle.

The day warmed and their speed increased as they gained expertise and momentum. The day seemed to pass quickly. Every time Elsie looked at her watch an hour seemed to have passed. She realised she was the only one with a watch. Everybody else relied on the church chimes. Her hands were getting sore but she was determined to carry on as long as she could.

At length, Ned gave them a shout. 'Have a break, girls. You won't be able to carry on at that pace all day!'

They stopped thankfully and sank onto the grass at the side of the hop poles. A pony and trap was working its way along the bines, bringing tea and water to the pickers. Mrs Walker, the farmer's wife, was driving it. The pony was a Welsh Cob, just like Chalky, and Elsie couldn't help a tear falling down her cheek. She stood and waited for the pony to come abreast of them. As she did so, her hand automatically went to stroke his head.

'Hello, my beauty; you're looking in good fettle.'

Her hand caressed the pony in the special way that Chalky loved. The way she did it must have signalled to the countrywoman. Mrs Walker looked at her in surprise.

'I didn't know we had a driver with us! You seem to know what you're doing, my dear.'

Elsie stared at her then realised that she had let the cat out of the bag. What should she do? She held Mrs Walker's hand for a moment.

'Listen, Mrs Walker; I've got a Welsh Cob, very much like this one. He's named Chalky and I use him for getting about on, for my work at home. I've got a trap that's a bit like this as well but it's more like a governess cart, you know, where you get in the back. It's handy for Tom, my son. I love him, Chalky I mean. I love my son, Tom as well of course. I'm getting mixed up now. I'm sorry. I'm missing Chalky.'

Mrs Walker stepped down from the trap. 'Here you are, my dear, you can have a go and if you look like you're any good at it, you can take over this job. We can work out what I should pay you when it becomes necessary. Is that all right?' She waited for Elsie to nod her answer then went on. 'Right, the first thing you can do is give me a ride along the bines, so I can hand out the Billy-cans to the pickers. Then we'll have a little chat, I think. There's more to you than meets the eye, my girl. Come on, climb aboard!'

Elsie climbed up onto the bench seat at the front of the trap and took hold of the traces. She clicked her teeth and spoke gently to the pony.

'Come on; walk on.' The pony walked slowly along the line of pickers and Elsie turned to Jenny Walker. 'What's his name?'

'George.'

They drove on silently and Elsie was getting used to George. He was very well behaved, she thought. Some of the pickers had children with them and they came up to the pony and stroked his nose, enjoying his friendliness. Elsie suddenly remembered Tom and turned the trap round.

'I've left my little Tom back there. I've got to pick him up!'

Jenny Walker said nothing but sat there smiling. She had seen how excited Elsie was to be driving the pony, to the extent of forgetting her son! As they came to the end of the line, Betty came out with Tom in her arms.

'Here's your little one, Elsie. Don't forget him, will you?'

She smiled, accusingly, then lifted him up and placed him in Elsie's lap where he snuggled down beside her and looked at the scenery as they drove past it.

'Thanks, Betty,' Elsie shouted, as they drove past her.

They were coming down the slight hill now and nearing the farmhouse. Albert Walker was standing outside the farmhouse. He looked slightly severe, as he strode towards them. He stood and waited by the farmyard gate as they approached.

'I don't know what I'm going to do about that new labourer, Henry Wilkins I mean. I saw him lying in the field, with his hands behind his head, just taking it nice and easy if you please! I ought to sack him but I've only just taken him on and I feel that I should give him a chance to show us what he is made of.'

'I wouldn't!' Elsie couldn't help the exclamation leaving her lips. 'If I were you I'd find someone else and start them on. If a man can't be found to be working on his first day, when can he?' She gathered her thoughts and let them out. 'Put it like this; if you'd just started a new job, would you be lying down on the job, or trying to impress your new gaffer about what a good worker you are? I'm sorry; I know it's nothing to do with me but I can't help getting annoyed at people like that, people who don't appreciate a good employer. Send him on his way. I would!'

Albert and Jenny Walker, both in their twenties, looked at her and burst out laughing. 'You sound like my old granddad,' said Jenny. 'He was always a hard man when it came to new people. Anyway, I think Elsie's right, don't you, Albert? If you can't look after a new job, you won't look after an old one. He'll just get worse.'

Albert Walker stood, taking aboard the opinions of his wife and this new, upstart young woman. He examined her critically. She was of medium build but well built with plenty of shape showing under her blouse. He wouldn't mind getting her in the hay for half an hour! He coughed to take his mind off the thought. She seemed to have a sense of humour as well; she had made them laugh straightaway. She seemed to be a cut above the rest of the pickers.

Jenny had noticed as well, or she wouldn't have given the girl the charge of George. She was getting down from the Cob, now, and showing a very nice ankle as she did so. Her backside was nicely plump as well.

He liked a well shaped girl. Occasionally, he was able to have his way with one of the pickers; it brought a bit of variety to his life, not that he had any complaints about Jenny. She was a passionate woman, a very desirable trait in a farmer's wife! He looked again at the young picker. Her blue eyes were set wide apart on her face and her lips were well shaped. Her hair was long, almost below her shoulders. He'd like to run his fingers through it. He brought his mind back from contemplating Elsie.

'Yes. I'll do that, I think. He'll have to find some other farmer to rob of his wages.'

He turned on his heel and stalked off towards the bottom field. When he got there, Wilkins was still sitting with his head lying back on his hands, his hands resting on a small mound of grass. He stared as Albert marched towards him.

'I was just having a little blow, gaffer. I've only been here two minutes.' Wilkins stood and brushed himself down with respect. 'Everybody's entitled to a little blow from time to time, ain't they, gaffer?'

Albert didn't speak for a moment or two; he was too angry.

'Well, Henry, you're obviously a better liar than a worker. I saw you sitting here half an hour ago and you haven't moved since. The best thing you can do is to come down to the house with me and I'll give you your wages, such as they are. Just be off my land before the hour is out!'

Albert Walker turned round and marched off towards the house. There was a sound behind him and he half turned to see what it was. Before he could complete his turn he felt a sharp crack on the back of his head and he stumbled, to fall in a heap on the meadow grass. At the top end of the meadow, Elsie and Jenny observed the blow and watched the result. Wilkins was about to hit the farmer while he was lying on the grass.

Elsie shouted. 'Come on, Jenny!' Elsie held out her hand to the farmer's wife, pulled her up onto the step of the dog cart and placed Tom in her arms. Instantly she cracked the whip and, startled, George bounded forward to a gallop, moving swiftly towards the prostrate farmer. The labourer, Henry Wilkins, saw them approaching at the last minute and tried to get away but Elsie cracked her whip, the tip hitting him on the cheek, causing him to fall, cursing as he did so. She leaned from the cart and stood over him, her voice taking on an air of severe authority.

'Yes, you'd better lie there, you murderous bastard! Don't even think of trying to move. I can take your eye out with this whip and it wouldn't trouble me to do it either.'

The man sat there holding his hand to his face, a look of hate and fear mixed. There was a trickle of blood from his cheek, giving credence to the threat that Elsie had made. Two of the bushellers had seen part of the event and came running up to the scene.

'What the hell's going on, Missus Walker? What's the matter, Henry?' asked one of them. Jenny Walker explained in a moment what had happened, telling of Elsie's courage and skill with the whip.

'She was just like one of these circus performers. I've never seen anybody handle a whip like that.' She turned to Elsie. 'How did you ever learn to handle the whip like that, my dear?'

Elsie had to explain. 'I was told that because I'm a woman, somebody'd try it on, so I decided to put myself in a position where I could look after myself. I got a friend to show me how to use a whip; it seems to have paid off, doesn't it?'

The four men and Jenny all looked at Elsie as if they had never met anyone like her, before. The culprit, still sitting on the ground, decided that he wasn't going to get anywhere near this strange young woman.

Albert Walker once again noted the sexual qualities that seemed to radiate from her that caused his body to respond with such vigour; Jenny did, too, as she noticed her husband's reaction – and her own as she observed the body postures of the young woman, the deep breathing in response to the stress of the last few minutes, the reddened cheeks and wider open eyes as she fought to regain her normal body functions. The other two men just stared; the whole experience was too far outside their experience for them to feel that they had any part to play in judging her. Albert Walker gradually recovered his composure. He gingerly got up, recovering from the blow to his head.

He turned to the bushellers. 'Take him to the gate and send him on his way. Don't be too gentle with him. I don't want him to think he has any right to come back here, for anything.' His eyes took in the sight of the man on the ground. 'Here's a sovereign; it's more than you deserve. Now be off with you! I don't ever want to see your face on this farm or any other near here. You're lucky I don't have you put in custody. Get out!' He turned to his wife as the bushellers pulled Henry Wilkins to his feet and led him off. 'Come on, Jenny, my dear. You still have the rest of the Billy-cans to hand out to the pickers. We don't want them complaining, do we?'

Albert Walker stood and watched for a moment as Wilkins was half-led, half-dragged in the direction of the lane that led to Bromyard. Then he climbed aboard the dog cart. They'd all had enough to put up with so far, today! What could follow that?

Chapter 17

The Man from the past
1909

Elsie gradually returned to normal. It had been a shock to her. She knew that she had made an impression on the Walkers and the bushellers and she wondered how they would react. Henry Wilkins didn't matter; he'd gone, forever she hoped. Would they be shocked at her control of the situation and want her to leave? She sat quietly, allowing her body and mind to become calm again.

In a way she was quite pleased; she had managed to save Albert Walker from a horrific beating, she felt. Who knows how far Wilkins would have gone in his anger? On the other hand, she had shown herself up, she felt, when all she wanted was to merge with the rest of the pickers and just get on with having this little working holiday. Jenny was still holding Tom who seemed happy to have held on during his exciting ride in Jenny's arms.

Wilkins was quite a big man and she had no doubt that if he had been able to seize the whip from her, he would soon have made short work of her and Mister Walker. Elsie held out her arms to Tom and he moved across the trap to her.

'He did well, didn't he?' Elsie cuddled him close to her as Jenny said, 'He could have been really hurt, you know. You shouldn't have taken such risks. Really, I've never seen anything like it.'

Jenny's face softened as she smiled to show that she was not seriously admonishing Elsie, who was still disturbed by the idea that she might get a degree of fame from the incident.

'I would rather that nothing was said about this, if you don't mind, Mrs Walker. I don't like a lot of fuss. It's not my way. Shall we get on with putting out the Billy-cans?'

Mrs Walker smiled in reply and Elsie felt that she would not say anything, though the bushellers, who had seen the whole incident, would almost certainly spread the story around. They spent the next hour handing out tea as the pickers gathered round to see what was to be had. Most of them had been to the farm before and knew the way things were done; others followed their lead. The morning passed quickly and the job was soon completed.

'Right, now is the time for you to go back to what you were doing,' said Jenny to Elsie. 'You can give out the cans tomorrow morning, if you like. I've got plenty to do myself, so it will be good to have some help. This afternoon you can collect them in and wash them, all right?'

Oh well, thought Elsie, so much for fame. It's nice to be back in the rut. She took Tom from Jenny and sat him on the seat of the trap.

'Keep still, now, there's a good boy.'

The journey round the pickers to collect the cans was uneventful and the last one was in the trap within the hour. Elsie arranged that she would meet Betty after work and they would eat together. On the way back to the farmhouse she crossed the path where they had had the trouble earlier. There was a Welsh Cob standing near the gate. It seemed to be waiting for her. She took a second look at it and shouted.

'Chalky! Chalky!' Elsie pulled on the traces to let George know she wanted him to go faster and he broke into a canter, moving over the grass easily. 'Come on, George, move yourself! Fancy, Dan actually taking the trouble to drive all the way down here from Willenhall!'

Elsie took another look at the pony in the distance. It was

Chalky but it wasn't Dan on the trap. It was Stephen! Elsie was suddenly excited, wanting to hold him and all the rest of it. Anything as long as it was with him. She was close now, and she was suddenly and unaccountably shy. George slowed down and then it hit her that Stephen didn't know that it was she who was approaching. For fun, she pulled her hat over her face to hide her identity as long as she could then, when she was just a few feet from him, shouted his name. He looked up in shock.

'Elsie! I didn't recognise you. I thought I'd have to wait all day to see you. I was going to go up to the farmhouse to enquire for you but I thought it might embarrass you, especially if Dan came down as well.'

Stephen jumped down from the trap and seemed to leap towards her, pulling her down from her dogcart and folding his arms around her, he kissed her lips, making it obvious what he had in mind. He pulled her down to the grass at the side of an old oak tree and pressed his body against her. She pushed him away vigorously.

'Stephen! You can't just come down and immediately seduce me, you daft thing. Let me up!' For all his strength, she was still able to free herself. 'Look what you're doing to my clothes. I shall never live this down. Haven't you got any sense?' Elsie stood and brushed herself down again, her face red with anger. 'I've just been fighting with a man who was trying to kill Mister Walker. Now I have to fight off a rapist! Is there no way a girl can get any peace? I came down here to get a bit of relief from everything and then I find life is harder here than it is in Willenhall!'

Elsie stood glaring at him and then he started laughing, as he usually did, she thought. Whatever happens, you can rely on him to laugh about it. It was the most endearing and annoying quality she found in him; she had seen him in all sorts of situations and he had always laughed. Perhaps there was a release from the stress of the situation if he laughed, and maybe it also gave him a few seconds grace to think things over before he decided how to react.

The young woman found herself laughing with him, and their laughter blended in the air as she found herself drawn into it, the blending bringing them together in a closer bond. There was a special closeness between them that seemed to rise above any feelings for another person that she had ever known before. The laughter was part of it but there were other aspects of her feelings, too. His presence alone induced a special atmosphere and she felt that she had the same effect upon him. Then she realised that she was supposed to be doing a job.

She looked round at Chalky. He was standing at the side of the other trap, his face up against the other pony. They were enjoying each other's company. She turned back to Stephen.

'Look, I'm in the middle of something I've got to get done in the next few minutes. I'll see you after work, if you like?'

He replied quickly. 'I'll wait all night for you, Elsie; just tell me where!'

They agreed to meet at the top of the lane at seven o'clock and Stephen turned the cart round and trotted off into the afternoon. For Elsie the next few minutes were engaged in catching up with the afternoon's work. No one seemed to have missed her, but Tom was hungry, and so was she. She trotted up the steps and made sandwiches for them both. Tom would have to make do with water for a drink.

She took the Billy-cans to the farmhouse and washed them all out carefully with Tom getting more miserable now. He was getting tired so she put him over her hip and took him back to where Betty was picking hops. Tom was pleased to see her and went from his mother willingly. Somehow Elsie felt displeased that he would be so happy to leave her.

Betty soon put things back into balance. 'It's all right, young man, for you to be given all this attention but we've got hops to pick. Lie yourself down on this bit of grass, here and close your eyes while me and your Mommy chat to each other.'

Betty lay him down and although he cried for a minute or two, he soon closed his eyes and dropped off to sleep. Elsie and Betty then got on with the serious business of picking the hops. Elsie's hands were soon black from handling the bines and her back started to ache but she felt that she could not really moan because she had not been picking for half the length of time that Betty had. Betty looked at her over the top of her glasses.

'You were gone a long time, Elsie. What else did you get up to?'

The young picker had heard about her friend's adventure with Henry Wilkins but knew nothing about her meeting with Stephen and Elsie decided to take her friend into her confidence and tell her the story of her relationship with him. Without asking a question, Betty listened to her story; how they had met when she was younger, how they had fallen in love and met in the market, how they had made love in the country; how Steve had been forced by family obligation to marry Mabel, how later Tom had been conceived, making him and Elsie forego what would have been the normal route for a lover's relationship to take. Then, how Steve had come down to the farm to meet her – with her pony and trap!

'That was a bit foolish, wasn't it?' Betty asked. 'You would have thought he would have come down with a rented pony, wouldn't you? It's as if he really wants to be found out. A lot of people do things like that. It's as if the secret life they're living becomes too much to bear and they just want to own up and pay the price in an honourable way.'

Elsie thought about it for a minute, thinking through what Betty was saying before replying. 'I know what you mean but the price, as you call it, can sometimes be too high for a man or a woman to pay. They have to snatch bits of love here and there and try to be content with that. It's all very well to say that love conquers all, and all that stuff that's written about it in romantic books but many a man – and a woman would have to give up a lot to try to conquer all!' Elsie paused for a moment to put her thoughts in order again. 'What would you do if you were me? No, I can't really ask you that question because you don't know what sort of life I have in Willenhall. My husband does his best for me and Tom; I know he does. For all I know, he suspects that he is not Tom's father, but he never mentions even the possibility. He just carries on like a perfect husband should do. If I were to let him know the sort of life I live he would be shaken to his foundations, I think.

'Mind you, I've wondered about him and one of my old neighbours in Wednesbury but I've never had it exactly thrown in my face. Ruth was a good friend and neighbour to me so I've kept my thoughts to myself, and it's worked out all right because we left there to move to Willenhall and now we live in a better house than some of the locksmiths. They live in hovels!

'I've always worked for myself; that's the way I look at it; I never believed that I work for an employer, even if they think so. I think I'll have my own business, one day. When that happens, I may decide that I can be independent of men all together; we'll see.

'There are alternatives, you know. Look at us the other night, all broody. I don't think I'd like to be one of them women who only like sex with women but I think I would like to be free to explore the options that there might be out there.' She spread her hands in an all-embracing gesture.

'Perhaps there are men who feel like that too, but can't do anything about it because of the social circumstances in which they live.

'Look at Prince Albert! They say that he was homosexual, don't they? Eddy they called him and well they might; with him going back and forward with men and women! If he had lived, what do you think he'd have made of his life? He had no more choices than us, really.'

Betty was looking at her friend as if she did not know her.

'How do you find out all these things, Elsie? You really are a dark horse, Elsie. You're full of surprises to me. I never knew those things about the Royal Family. If I'd known, I would probably have felt it was nothing to do with me; the Royal Family have never kept to the same rules as everyone else. You shouldn't talk about them in that way, you know. You might find yourself in a mental hospital until it was 'His Majesty's pleasure' to let you out!'

Ned, the busheller, was walking towards them, along the line of bines. He smiled when he got to them.

'I heard about your escapade earlier, Elsie, and Mrs Walker has told me not to expect too much from you in the way of picking. I think she's got other plans for you.' He turned to Betty. 'What are you doing later Betty? D'you fancy a stroll down the lane with me? There's a nice little pub in Bromyard and we could stop and have a nice quiet drink of lemonade or maybe a cider. D'you fancy that?'

Betty blushed. She'd had no idea that the busheller had any ideas about her but he was quite nice looking and well-mannered. She thought over the conversation she'd just had with Elsie. Why shouldn't she have a bit of fun? It was a risk but life was full of risks, wasn't it?

'Yes, all right, but I want to be in for ten o'clock. I intend doing a lot of work tomorrow. I need the money: I'm saving up.' She turned to Elsie as if seeking consent and saw the slightest nod of assent, then turned back to Ned, 'I'll see you in the yard at about seven, then.'

Betty turned away and started to walk towards the barn where she and Elsie slept. She felt quite pleased that she hadn't let him know what she was saving for.

'Hey, wait a minute!' Ned called to her. 'I have to weigh what you've done today between you. Don't you want to witness the weigh in?'

Betty blushed again but didn't want to look as confused as she really felt.

'Why should I want to witness it? You wouldn't cheat me, would you?'

Betty smiled at him to show how happy and trusting she felt and her face lit up. It was obvious to Elsie that her friend was delighted to have been asked out so early in their stay at the farm. Ned blushed then, to their surprise. It always seemed unlikely that a man would feel shy. They were supposed to be the dominant gender, weren't they?

In fact, Ned was just as shy as the women. He had spent most of his life on farms but had had very little to do with the Black Countrywomen and men who visited the farm for a few weeks each September. They spoke and acted differently and seemed rough compared with his peers. Tonight was going to be an adventure into unmapped territory for him as much as for Betty. Ned still lived with his mother in a small cottage and he knew that if she heard of him indulging in any sort of sexual activity she would take a stick to him regardless of his grown up status. He had never been with a woman and had no real expectations for the evening. What happened; happened!

In Bromyard, Stephen Stone couldn't wait for the evening; he too was going to have an adventure! The sight of Elsie in the fields, handling the trap with such skill had excited him and the mere thought of her caused his body to react with passion. The wind had pressed her skirt and blouse tight against her body and the memory of it aroused him again. She had been excited too, he felt, and her face had been all red, as red as a turkey cock's arse, as his father said. What was she feeling, waiting for him? Did she feel all queer, as he did?

It was time to take the trap back to the hotel. The pony was a good cob, easy to handle and without a temper; he wouldn't mind one for himself. He had borrowed a trap from the firm before now but it would be good to own one of his own. Aunt Mary had made it possible for him to borrow Chalky and it had been an eye-opener to him how the Welsh Cob had travelled the journey down from the Black Country to Herefordshire with no trouble at all, just kept clip-clopping away and covering the distance in half a day.

The only time Chalky had given trouble was when they had passed a farm, with mares standing looking over the fence at them as they had sped past. Chalky had stopped and tasted the air as they had come close. One of the ponies had been in season, standing there; her legs wide to accommodate what? All the small herd of mixed ponies had whinnied loudly as they had approached and had gathered at the fence to watch them.

Stephen turned the cob round and headed for the Hop Pole. He had an evening meal and Elsie to look forward to. He was aware that he had a better life than Dan but gave no thought to it. It was part of life. Some did better than others. Others had a better life than him!

The meal was served to him by the barmaid who had attended to his needs earlier. He felt that there was an opportunity there, too, but Elsie was his first and true love. He couldn't wait to meet and hold her!

Chapter 18

Bromyard by Night

Stephen sat back from his drink and breathed deeply. He was conscious that his breath might smell so he decided to go up to his room at the Hop Pole to wash his mouth out. It was five o'clock; he had two hours to wait before he met with Elsie. He was impatient for the feel of her against his body. The memory of her breasts was strong in his eyes and hands. Elsie was not what he would call a beauty but she had something in her eyes that made a man feel that her thoughts were just for him. Perhaps it was true. He liked to think so and always had since he had first met the little wild-cat that she had been at fifteen, with her father, at Uncle Fred's.

The barmaid had a nice body too, and if he hadn't planned to meet with Elsie, he might have dallied a bit with her. Elsie was different though; always had been. God, why had he let himself get saddled with Mabel? Men were unfortunate creatures, always following the trail of a body-scent, or the smallest view of an ankle or out-of-place blouse. It must be something in their make-up. He was in love with Elsie, married to Mabel, and aroused by an unknown barmaid. What a stupid arrangement!

Stephen nodded to the barmaid and mounted the stairs to his small room at the back of the inn. The water in his ewer seemed stale but was good enough for washing his mouth after cleaning his teeth. He stripped off to his waist and tipped the ewer into the large porcelain bowl. The water was cold to his body but he enjoyed it like that and let it pour down his chest to be caught by a towel on the floor. There was a quiet tap on his door and when he looked round, the barmaid had entered his room with a large bucket of water to fill his ewer.

He felt as if she were appraising him for a sale of bodies; the towel on the floor at his feet was wet.

'I'll get you a clean, dry towel, sir,' she said. 'You need a large towel to dry a body like that. Just a minute and I'll do it for you!' The girl seemed to float out of the room and returned a moment later with a large towel. 'There we are, sir. We'll soon have you dry.'

The barmaid stepped closer to him, lifting the towel around his shoulders then she let it slip down his back as far as his waist. She pulled on it with the effect of bringing their bodies into a closer situation.

The girl lifted her face to his and smiled.

'Do you think I'm a cheeky young hussy, sir? I'm not really; I just like a young man like you to want to be close to me. You do, don't you, sir? Want to be closer, I mean? Is this close enough, do you think, sir?'

Molly pushed herself up against him, her breasts trying to break loose from the confines of her blouse. He responded for a moment, and then broke away from her closeness. He didn't want to offend her but he did not want to give up his male decisiveness, either. He preferred to make his own mind up.

'Listen, I'd love to stay but I have an appointment very shortly. Have a drink ready for me when I come into the bar, later on tonight. I think you're very lovely and any man who gets into your bed is very lucky.'

Stephen pulled away again and started to dress himself, pulling his shirt over his head. Molly, the barmaid, pouted for a moment then let her hands close over the sovereign he'd slipped into her hand. The night was not such a dead loss, after all!

She leaned forward to kiss him good night and felt his hand slip inside her blouse, to take hold of her. He kissed her for a brief moment and then pushed her away with a slap to her buttocks.

'Go on with you, you young hussy! I'll see to you later!'

Stephen smiled at his own forwardness and turned his back on the young woman who gave him another of her appraising looks and then moved silently out of the door. Maybe there would be more fun later!

Stephen loosened his collar and lay on the bed. He wanted to arrive at his meeting with Elsie in as good a condition as he could, not half-spent! The next hour slowly passed as he thought his thoughts and dreamed of the outcome of tonight's meeting.

*

Elsie was ready for the walk to Bromyard, to meet Stephen. Betty and Ned were to accompany her because it was quite dark on the way there. Ned was a very quiet man. It was as if he didn't feel as good as the girls and wanted to walk a few steps behind them. Betty was quite talkative to make up for his taciturn way and soon had a conversation going with Elsie.

The walk, along the paths that lined the fields, was leisurely and they each felt invigorated by it. The relaxation of the walk seemed to put extra energy into their steps. As they walked, the moon slowly rose and climbed into the sky, showing almost a full face that watched them. Betty was very excited by the prospect of a beau, as she called Ned, and she wasn't quite sure what was expected of her. Ned was in a similar situation; he had known no women intimately although he had chatted to some of the hop pickers in the few years he had worked at the Walker's farm. Mrs Walker had introduced him to a few young local women and he had found that they were also as shy.

Elsie was the only one of them who was married and the other two were jealous in a way of her experience and the fact that she had Tom, to show for it. He was with Jenny Walker this evening after making a bit of fuss. Jenny had put his mind at rest by giving him some of her son's old bricks to play and build with.

The small group arrived at the Hop Pole at eight o' clock and sat outside, looking at the clouds scudding across the heavens. The sky was an enormous vista that they had never seen in the same way before. In the industrial Midlands, their view of the sky was usually limited by buildings; in Herefordshire the whole of the sky could be seen.

There were a few locals sitting around when they arrived, mostly farm labourers who had been working all day in the fields. One of them knew Ned. He called out,

'Hello Ned! That's a nice pair you've got, hanging on your every word. How on earth have you managed to attract them? You've never had anything like that before.'

Ned turned round so that he could see who was addressing him.

'Hyah, Jack! I didn't see you sitting there. I just have the looks and the talent, I suppose. That's what it is. I let the talent come out occasionally; the looks speak for themselves, I imagine.'

They all laughed at Ned's attempt at humour and he joined in. There was a crunch on the gravel of the public house yard and a tall, better dressed figure joined them. It was Stephen.

'Hello, lads,' he said, looked around at the company and then looked, smiling directly at Elsie. 'Hello, Elsie Barr. How are you? Could I interest you in a glass of cider that the moon has shone on to make it ready? There, then; that's that settled. How about you, Betty? Would you like to take a sip or two, and you, Ned?'

Stephen didn't wait but stepped back into the bar, returning a few minutes later with a tray and four glasses. He set each one down with a flourish, acting the part of waiter and giving a small compliment each time he did so.

'Here you are, Ned. I know you are Ned because Mister Walker told me when I spoke to him earlier.' He turned to Betty. 'And here you are Betty. Don't you be drinking all that at in one go. It won't go bad if you leave it for a minute or two.'

Stephen didn't explain how he knew their names. It was obvious that he must have spoken to Elsie earlier as she was the only one who knew their names. Stephen sat and joined them for a time, and then he started the splitting of their company.

'Look, Elsie, there's something I need to talk over with you.' He turned to the others and asked, 'Do you mind if I take Elsie away for a few minutes?'

Stephen didn't explain and they didn't seem to want an explanation. It seemed to them that the whole thing had been arranged earlier. They just sat there, nodding. Stephen stood and waited as Elsie finished her drink. She stood and linked his arm, feeling shameless as she did so. He led her round to the front of the inn and then up a narrow path to the gate of a small field.

'They say the view from this field is the best one in Herefordshire. Would you like to see it?' He slipped the rope from over the gate-post and held it open in a courtier-like way. 'Here you are, Miss; the gateway to Paradise!'

Elsie passed through the gate and heard it close behind her, then Stephen was at her side again, his hands attentive. She felt them slide onto her body and turned to him impulsively, the way she had when they had first found release from their passion. He threw his large coat off and placed it carefully on the grass.

'We don't want to be walking too far, do we?'

It wasn't a question. More a sort of command and a suggestion all mixed up in one. His lips bent to hers as she responded and she found her knees feeling weak and she knelt on his coat while he undid hers. Then she lay back and looked up at the sky. It was full of thousands of glinting little lights, making the darkness just a little less deep and providing a soft backdrop as she felt his hands exploring first her blouse and then her skirt. Elsie became aware of his nakedness as his legs seemed to insinuate themselves between hers. Her breathing seemed to match his as she allowed him full access to her body. Then he exclaimed,

'Elsie, I love you!'

Somehow she hadn't expected the words and was not all that impressed by them. If he loved her, why hadn't he married her when he could? As the thought came into her mind, she knew that the question was not a fair one, given his circumstances. She replied without hesitation, her words repeating and replying to his.

'I love you, Stephen!'

The simple words embodied all their feelings, ignoring all the complications. Stephen lived the life he did and she lived her life the way she did!

The stars witnessed their joining silently, as they had witnessed so many unions between men and women, not even feeling the slightest excitement as the scene was played out to them in the deep darkness of the Herefordshire night. The lovers knew they were taking chances and risks but they paid their fee willingly to have a rare taste of love. For either of them to be caught would be a tragedy. How long would they be able to keep their secret?

Chapter 19

Dan's Visit
1909

A fortnight had passed since Stephen Stone had been down to see her. The novelty of his visit had gone, and Elsie was getting used to the monotony of the work. She didn't think about him much now. The young woman was conscious that time was passing and that she would be going home in another three weeks. What would she find when she got there?

Elsie had learned a lot in the three weeks since she had arrived. Her hands were black now, with the constant contact with the hops. She knew more people too, and had made many friends. A number of the pickers at Home Farm were from the Willenhall area and were employed in the lock industry during the rest of the year.

Some of them had unemployed husbands who did other things to make a penny or two. There was a carpenter, and a tinker who specialised in mending buckets and bowls; it was said that if he mended a bucket, it wouldn't leak. There were others who had illegal ways of making a few coppers. There was a burglar who had spent much of his adult life in Winson Green Prison, in Birmingham.

Elsie had never known such a diversity of people and morals. She decided to let Mrs Walker hold onto her pay until it was the day they were going home. In that way, no one would be able to rob her. Mrs Walker was quite trustworthy, she felt sure.

Betty did the same thing with her wages, just leaving it with Jenny and taking about three shillings each week to cover her small expenses. They had not been out since the three of them had sat at the Hop Pole and had been joined by Stephen. Earlier on this particular night, Ned and Betty had suggested to Elsie that they go there again. Elsie thought about it and decided to accept.

She was deciding what to wear, not that she had much choice. It was the skirt and white blouse or the red dress. She decided for the black and white.

'What are you wearing, Betty?'she asked. 'I'm wearing this – again!'

Elsie smiled and picked up the blouse. It had seen a lot of wearing and she was thinking about buying a new one. She had resisted the idea because she wanted to show a bit of a profit at the end of her sojourn in Herefordshire. She knew there would be an addition to her balance at Jenkins' the solicitor from the investments she had made there, but she did not want to break into it.

There was no time to buy a new one now, anyway. Elsie put the blouse on and noticed that it fitted her much easier than it had three weeks ago. It must be the extra work, she thought. It had taken away the fat she had had at Willenhall. She stood and appraised herself in the small handbag mirror. She didn't look too bad! She knew she had good posture and was conscious that she held herself erect. Her mother had taught her that when Elsie had been small, and the lesson had stayed with her. Now it was time to go.

It was a strange feeling, to go out with a couple. There was always the sense that you were there as some sort of chaperone, she thought. She had never done it before. It had been either Stephen or Dan, no one else. Where were they now? She wouldn't mind if either of them turned up – but not both! She laughed to herself. That eventuality was unlikely.

She trotted down the steps and found Ned waiting in the yard. He took off his bowler hat and bent a knee to her.

'Good evening, Miss. It's very balmy, just the night for a stroll along the promenade.'

Ned laughed at his own little joke and she responded in kind.

'Just you mind you don't fall in the sea at the end of the pier then, Ned.'

'What's all this about falling in the sea, then, Elsie?' Betty spoke from halfway up the steps. 'I didn't know we were that close to the sea.'

They all laughed together and Ned held his elbows out for both the young women to link him as they strolled. They tip-toed across the farmyard to avoid the worst of the cow pats, and passed into the short path that led along the edge of the field, towards the lane that led into Bromyard. They climbed the hill and stood at the top to regain their breath. As they did so, Elsie saw the familiar sight of a pony and trap in the lane.

'It's Chalky,' she said excitedly. 'It's my pony. I didn't expect to see Stephen again!' She stood and shaded her eyes against the setting sun. Who was that? 'It's not Stephen; it's Dan!' Elsie shouted loudly, 'Dan!'

Elsie started to trot up the hill and saw him start as he saw her. The pony saw her at the same time and didn't need encouragement to break into a trot. Dan fell back into the trap and it was only with difficulty that he regained his composure. He immediately whipped up the pony and waved to her as he attempted to control the excited young stallion.

'Elsie!' He shouted as they drew up alongside her. He dropped the reins and jumped down. 'I've been looking for the farm. I wanted to surprise you!'

His face was flushed with excitement as though looking

for his wife had been some sort of undercover activity.

'Well you've certainly done that,' said Elsie, 'but it's lovely to see you. I'd begun to think you wouldn't come down.' She paused for breath and noticed that his eyes were taking in her friends who were approaching them. 'We were just on the way to have a glass of lemonade.' She blushed, herself, as she felt slightly guilty at taking time off. 'We can still do that. Chalky can take the four of us, can't he?' She let her hand move to scratch Chalky behind his ears. She moved to let him have a better view of her friends. 'This is my husband, Dan.' She turned round. 'This is my friend Betty who I work with, and her friend Ned. Tom is with Mrs Walker, the owner of the farm. He likes her.'

Betty and Ned smiled and mumbled a greeting to Dan who nodded back to them. He doesn't seem all that pleased to see me going out for a drink, she thought. She knew he was old-fashioned in his ideas of what a married woman could or could not do, in the absence of her husband.

'This is only the second night I've been away from the farm,' she said, trying to explain. 'I've been working twelve hours a day ever since I arrived three weeks ago and I thought it was about time I relaxed for a night. Don't you think I am entitled to, then?' The look on his face made her think he was going to criticise her and she did not feel like appeasing him. 'Have you been working hard, Dan? Have you missed me?'

Her questions made Dan realise why he was there.

'Of course I've missed you.' He nodded at the cob. 'He drives well, don't he? I've enjoyed bringing him down here. I wanted to see young Tom as well. I'm going to stay overnight if I can find somewhere to get my head down. Do you know of anywhere?'

'Of course I do, you silly!' Elsie laughed. 'You can sleep with me, in the roof of the barn. We can put up a bit of sacking to give us a bit of privacy and cuddle up together. When have you got to get back? Well, anyway, Chalky can be with the horses, in the field. He'll like that. You never know; he might make a friend! If you like, we can go and have a little drink, with Chalky to take us and bring us back. Then, I can go and see Mrs Walker; she's expecting me anyway, to collect young Tom. He'll be delighted to see his Dad. We can sleep together, then. How does that suit you?'

Dan was silent for a moment and she suddenly realised that he was shy in strange company. Then his face suddenly lit up.

'Well, this looks like being a better night than I thought it was going to be.' He turned to Betty and Ned. 'Come on, you two; climb aboard the good ship HMS Chalky and we'll soon get you there.'

The young couple coming with them let out a cheer for the lift and climbed into the seat of the trap. Dan seemed to relax as he spoke to Chalky, 'Walk on, Chalky, walk on.'

Dan coaxed the pony who, having travelled forty-five miles that day, soon got moving again and got them to Bromyard in a quarter of an hour. They all made a fuss of the pony and found a patch of grass for him to graze on.

The evening passed quickly but not without looks from the barmaid, who had seen Elsie with Stephen two weeks before, and was trying to work something out. Elsie felt intimidated at first but decided that if the barmaid was going to start trouble, she would just retreat for the evening and then sort things out with the girl later. She did not speak about Stephen at all, perhaps deciding that it would be better to keep silent on the subject.

Elsie kept to lemonade but Dan seemed like a man who had spent too much time in a desert. He drank twice as quickly as Ned and was at the bar, waiting for the next round of ale before the rest of them had started on their drinks.

The drive back to Home Farm was uneventful. Betty and Ned blushed as they left Elsie and Dan on their own. They were on their own, too! After they had put Chalky into the paddock, Dan went with Elsie to see Mrs Walker when they called to collect Tom, who was excited to see his father. Mister Walker offered Dan a job at the hop-picking which he politely refused, offering the fact that he had to be back at his workbench at eight o'clock on Monday morning as an excuse.

Tom lay asleep in Elsie's arms as she walked through the farmyard. It was time to go to bed then and they walked as quietly as they could through the yard and up the steps onto the first floor of the barn. Elsie turned round and Dan was already lying down. For all his quiet advances to her during the evening, he was in a deep sleep almost as soon as she slid in beside him. He opened his eyes for a moment and whispered.

'I'm really glad to see you, Elsie. I was lonely without you. That Ruth at Wednesbury wanted to give me my dinners but I thought you might not want me to go along with that.'

Dan turned on his side and started snoring almost immediately. Elsie felt shocked. It was obvious that Dan had seen Ruth Mallory but under what circumstances? Elsie recalled the day when she had seen him in Ruth's house. Perhaps there had been something going on. There was nothing she could do about it tonight, but she would find out what she could, when she got home. She was not going to let things go! A moment later her own guilty conscience caught up with her. What right had she to judge him, when her own behaviour had not been exemplary? Anyway, she had bared her soul to Ruth.

Where were her thoughts going to take her now? It seemed that there were two sides to every problem, her side and the other. Could she never win? Dan was a good man;

there was no doubt about that but he had still committed a degree of infidelity, if infidelity could be measured in degrees! How dare he, when she'd been eating her heart out for her lover, and working hard to avoid him?

Elsie thought for a few minutes longer and then the comical side of the situation came to her and she started to giggle to herself. She started to imagine Dan and Ruth Mallory making love while Dan had his leg in splints. The mental picture was too much for her and she laughed out loud. The laughter suddenly reminded her of Stephen, who was always laughing, regardless of the problems he faced. Dan rolled over and she thought he had awoken and would be asking her awkward questions but he suddenly rolled back and it was obvious from his face that he was fast asleep.

Gradually the tensions of the day left her and she fell asleep across the body of her husband and was then woken by Betty moving into her place at her side. Dan put out his arm and it caught Betty round the shoulder and he pulled her down to him. Betty was about to scream but Elsie held a finger to her lips. Betty blushed but looked prepared to scream anyway as Dan put his hand on her breast. He squeezed and started to move as if to mount her but she pushed him away, energetically.

Tom sat and looked at the little scene in front of him.

'Daddy likes Auntie Betty!'

He spoke loudly, and both of the women started laughing again.

'Go to sleep, Tommy.' Betty hissed the words at him and he snuggled quickly down in the bosom of his mother. 'Don't let me hear you whisper again tonight!'

The dominance in her voice seemed to convince him that he should do as he was told and he immediately fell asleep. Betty looked across the two bodies at Elsie and lifted her hand to squeeze Elsie's.

Morning came with a speed that left Elsie surprised. She sat up and looked at the barn floor around her. She must be the first one to wake up, she thought. Dan was still snoring, his hand across Betty. Tom was fast asleep, unmoving. There were other bodies sleeping noisily. A few of them had been at the Hop Pole last night and it looked as if some of them would regret it. There was a faint smell of vomit in the air but smells didn't seem to bother her now. There were so many new smells in the farm area that they no longer disturbed her.

It was getting light now; time to start getting ready for work. First, the breakfast had to be sorted out. She slithered out of the blankets and moved silently across the floor. There was a small sound and she looked back. Ned was lying on the floor, just a few inches from Betty! Oh, well; they'd better sort it out, themselves. Perhaps they had been closer than she realised. Changing her mind and getting back under the blanket, she dozed off again.

Later, Betty opened her eyes and stumbled her way down the stairs to light the fire under the wrought-iron devil that they cooked on. A few minutes later the frying pan was crackling to the music of fat from the sausage. As they played their way, she cracked the eggs into the pan, causing a loud hiss from the frying pan. She felt as if she was the orchestra leader, making new noises to merge and mingle and make a more melodious sound.

The fire was still slow in warming the water for the tea but she knew the bucket was getting hot now and the water would be boiling in a few minutes. There was a footfall at the edge of the barn canopy and when she looked up, Jenny Walker was looking at her.

'Good morning, Betty. You must be the first one up. It was Elsie Barr I wanted really. She was going to prepare the tea for the pickers. I didn't tell her what time she had to get ready and it's early yet. It's about twenty past five.' She looked at the expression of surprise on Betty's face. 'What time did you think it was then?'

Betty was amazed at the time. She had thought it was late.

'Seven o'clock,' she confessed. 'I wondered why nobody else was moving.'

Betty giggled and Jenny joined in and they stood there, giggling like young girls who had been caught in the act of breaking a minor rule. A sound from above made them lift their faces upward; it was Elsie, dressing herself quickly.

'What time do you make it, Betty?' She suddenly caught sight of Jenny Walker. 'Oh, good morning, Mrs Walker. What time do you want me, this morning? You didn't tell me yesterday.'

'Come down here, Elsie. I can't talk to you with my head stuck in the sky, now can I?'

Jenny turned her back and walked to the edge of the canopy that protected people who were working on the ground floor. Elsie trotted down the steps and stood with her hands behind her back, as if she were a schoolgirl about to be admonished by a headmaster. Jenny smiled at her.

'It's no good looking the innocent with me. I know there's a lot more to you than meets the eye. You don't deceive me at all. Anyway, what I want you to do is to start making the tea and pouring it into the Billy-cans as soon as you like. They'll keep hot for a long time in the cupboard at the back of the dog cart. Then muck out the stable and feed George. He'll want plenty of water as well, of course. I know you know how to do that job because I've seen how expertly he was handled.' Jenny didn't move as Elsie lifted her eyebrows at the thought of mucking out the horse. 'Everything you need is in the tack-room. He'll need grooming when you get back from the tea trip. Do you still want this job?'

Jenny's look was a challenge to Elsie who responded immediately.

'Of course I do! I'm quite used to mucking out, or anything else that needs doing. Just let me have a bit of breakfast and I'll be ready to start. Is that all right?'

Jenny smiled as she turned her back on the young woman. It was easy to get her going! She wondered about Elsie as she turned to her own tasks, preparing breakfast for her husband and herself.

Once, she would have employed staff to do these things for her but it all used money and money didn't grow in the fields like the other crops! She thought again about Elsie. She felt that there was a lot about the young woman that was kept hidden, and Jenny didn't like her workers to be a mystery to her. Still, there was plenty of time yet, to find out all about her. She returned to her work in the farmhouse, concentrating on the jam-making she had been trying to find time for.

Her mind kept returning to the young Black Countrywoman who was such a mystery to her. Elsie was definitely a cut above the average, even if she was prepared to get her hands dirty. What mysteries lay behind her?

Chapter 20

Leaving for Home

It was Saturday again; the last one. There was something about Saturdays, especially in the country. Saturday was for excitement. Sunday was kept sacrosanct for quiet and religious thoughts. In Willenhall, Saturday was a time for rowdy young men to get drunk in their local pubs and throw their weight about, often ending up as part of a brawl.

In the country there was the darkness and that in itself was a thrill. You never knew what was going to suddenly appear in the country. In the last few weeks Elsie had been surprised by both her husband and her lover. She had also seen Betty surprised by Ned, and wondered if Ned had been able to have his way with her.

This Saturday had been different. It was the last Saturday before she returned to her other life, in Willenhall. Elsie was glad and sorry at the same time.

She knew that the life she had in The Black Country was one that no one suspected. She was part owner of a number of local properties and no one knew of this except Aunt Mary and Mister Jenkins. Everyone else, including her husband, thought she just had a spare time occupation working for property owners. She knew it wasn't wise to let people have knowledge that could enable them to rob her.

If Dan knew of her assets, he would rob her, even if the robbing was unintentional. Many men took the view that any money that passed over their threshold, should pass into their pockets. Dan would just regard the properties she had worked and planned so hard to gain, as his assets and use their income as his.

They were supposed to be catching the Sunday train, at about ten o'clock, tomorrow morning. What would happen if they caught an earlier train? Perhaps it would be nice to surprise Dan or Stephen! Stephen would probably be at home with his wife and children; Dan should be reading his Sunday newspaper; perhaps he would be, as well!

It was time she said her goodbyes to Jenny Walker, the countrywoman who had taken Elsie to her heart. Elsie made up her mind and marched to the farmhouse. Jenny was in the kitchen, washing the Billy-cans and putting them away for the next season. She looked up as Elsie walked in.

'Good morning, Elsie. Come to say goodbye and pick up your wages? You look as if you're ready to go now; are you? You are, aren't you? I never thought you would be anxious to go home from here. I know you washed the Billy-cans; I'm just boiling them out as I put them away for a few months.' Elsie looked a bit sad, she thought. What was the matter with her? She decided to press her. 'What's ailing you, girl?'

Elsie let her emotions out. 'It's been so lovely; Jenny, that's what's ailing me! I keep trying to think how glad I shall be to get home, even trying to think how nice it will be to surprise Dan when I get there, but I still feel as if I've been somewhere wonderful, and I don't want to leave it. I feel as if I've been free for the first time, here, and I don't want to put myself back into bondage.'

Jenny's reply surprised her.

'Well, that's what it is like every time anyone goes away. I've seen lots of young girls crying like you. I've a feeling you are one of the lucky ones, one of the rare ones who can live more than one life at the same time.' Jenny smiled at Elsie. 'Yes, I've seen and heard about you and although most of it may be untrue, I do suspect that you have hidden depths that not even those close to you would suspect.'

Elsie blushed and then reminded herself that Jenny Walker would soon just be someone she once knew, when she got home. She replied with vigour.

'You may be right and you may be wrong, Jenny, but that's for me to know, and others to guess at, isn't it?'

Elsie didn't feel like a poor innocent girl now; she was a woman, full grown and she would hold her head high wherever she went. She didn't want to put Jenny in her place but she did want to let her know that Elsie Barr wasn't going to feel inferior to anyone. To her surprise, Jenny smiled at her, obviously not feeling put out at Elsie's rejoinder.

'You tell 'em, my girl! You're as good as any ten of 'em. I like to see somebody like you, flowering from the growing up that you've done. One day I might invite you to join my little group of women. They all have one thing in common; they think things out for themselves. You never know, you might want to come and spend more time here. I want you to know you'll always be welcome. I've a feeling that your family will spend time here.'

Jenny swept towards Elsie and took her in her arms in a huge hug. When Elsie was able to see, she saw that Jenny's face was red and damp with tears. She wiped her face on her apron and smiled into Elsie's face.

How had she known? Elsie was always being surprised by this little woman from Herefordshire. She seemed like a gypsy sometimes, able, by some instinctive gift, to dig deep into a person's psyche and expose aspects of their life that were hidden to others. Immediately, Elsie felt she had to cry out.

'Well, talk about me having hidden depths; you should listen to yourself! You sometimes seem to know everything. If you're so clever, tell me what I should do! Tell me how I should live my life. There seems to be so many commitments and twists and turns in my life at the moment that I don't know which direction to take.'

Jenny returned the challenging look that Elsie was giving her.

'Well, first of all, a girl has to look after her own interests. The law's not always on her side, you know, and she is reliant on a man for her living. It'll change over the years I'm sure, but in the meantime you have to think about what I'm telling you. You need a husband, to provide you with the basics of life; a roof over your head, clothes to wear and decent food to eat. The other things you need; intellectual stimulation, bodily stimulation and the stimulation of being surrounded by a loving and dutiful family all have to be planned for, worked for and enjoyed when they come!

'So off you go. May my love go with you! You must plan for the things you want, and remember, 'an it harm none, do what thou wilt'. That's all I have to say about life. You must be two people, giving, as He said, that of Caesar to Caesar and giving that of Elsie, to Elsie.'

Jenny moved across the room and stood looking out of the window at the other young men and women getting ready for tomorrow's journey. Suddenly, as if someone had called her, she slipped out of the back door and moved over to a group of women. She stood there talking to them, her back to the window out of which Elsie was viewing the whole procedure.

I'd better get ready, Elsie thought to herself. I wonder if Betty is ready yet. They had agreed to travel back together. It seemed to be fitting, as they had arrived together. Betty would be looking after Tom, making sure he was ready. It was amazing how they had taken to each other. Whenever Tom needed comforting there was always someone to do it, and it was usually Betty. She was a naturally maternal woman and revelled in the fact. Elsie turned the corner to the steps that led up to the first floor of the barn, where most of their gang slept. Betty was carrying Tom over her shoulder, up the steps.

'Mommy! I want my Mommy!' He was shouting at the top of his voice. 'I want to go for a ride on a chuffer train. Mommy said I could. I want my Mommy!'

He buried his head into Betty's breast and started sobbing and then he saw Elsie. He opened his mouth again.

'Mommy! I want you, Mommy. I want to go for a ride on the train, Mommy. You said we could.'

Elsie made up her mind; she had to get his agreement to whatever she wanted him to do.

'Hello, Tommy. You know I wouldn't let you go on the train without me, don't you, Tommy? I wouldn't let you go on the train with nothing to eat, would I, Tom? The chuffer train won't be ready 'til the morning, He has to have a good night's sleep first, don't he?'

Elsie waited for the nod of his head that sufficed for his answer. As they were talking she was shepherding them, past the kitchen door, towards the heavy wagon that was going to take them to the railway station in the morning. I think about things and do something about it. That's where I'm different. I'll soon learn; you have to take risks if you want to get everything you want but I'll soon learn to cover my tracks and if I can't, live with it. There now; that's the entire world's wisdom in a few sentences. Remember the creed that Jenny had quoted, 'an it harm none; do what thou wilt'.

Elsie found herself outside in the late sunshine again, two steps from the shadowy world within which Jenny moved back and forth. Everything looked the same. She could hear Tom playing with Betty. Where would she have been without Betty? Where would Betty have been without her?

Elsie intended getting a good night's sleep so she climbed up the steps to where Betty was waiting, Tom on her lap. The pair of them looked as if they would like to go to bed, she thought.

Wasn't Betty going to go out with Ned, just for a walk on the last day?

'Not going out, Betty? You don't have to stay in for me, you know. I'll be quite happy, just getting a decent sleep. We seem to have done everything except sleep, the last few weeks, don't we?' She turned her gaze to Tom.

'Come on, Tom. It's time for bye-byes. We're going on the train in the morning. Won't that be nice? Jenny Walker has sent you a lovely cake to eat on the train. We have to wrap it up so the flies can't get it. We wouldn't want flies all over it, would we, Tommy?'

He shook his head again.

'Right then, are you going to make me do it all on my own or are you going to be big and help me to do it? Good; come on then, we'll soon get it done between us, won't we? Your Daddy'll be very pleased with you. If he was here he would do it himself but he isn't here so you can do the Daddy's work and I'll do the Mommy's work. That's fair isn't it, Tom?'

He nodded and waited to be lowered from Betty's breast. Betty was looking at Elsie with a slightly surprised look on her face.

'I thought I could look after little ones but you're an expert, the way you have him eating out of your hand. How do you do it?'

Elsie didn't answer straightaway but stood as if she was thinking about it.

'It's not hard. I just think he wants to please me most of the time.'

She took her son into her arms, remembering what Jenny

had said about having a loving family around her. Her legs felt weak as she knelt to tuck him in and lie herself down.

When she looked up, Betty was kneeling at the side of her.

'I think I'll have an early night as well, when I get home. It's cool so it might be nice to have a warm body close, to keep me warm.'

Elsie hadn't noticed before, not really, what lovely breasts Betty had, nor how magnetic they were. They seemed to attract your hands. She lay down and dropped off to sleep later, hardly knowing whether it was evening or midnight.

The morning came again with the rain, as it did sometimes in Herefordshire in September. It was still early but Elsie had lost the wish to catch an earlier train. She was quite willing to return to her hay-filled bed for ever but she knew it could not be, so eventually, she got up. It was eight o'clock. Tom and Betty were still asleep. Other people were bustling round, packing their clothes and hopping gear.

She bent to whisper in Betty's ear.

'How's your hopping gear? Mine's ready if yours is!'

That must be what they mean by a double entendre, she thought. The thought came to her that Betty was another one with secrets. She would have to probe her in a gentle sort of way to see if she could find out more. Betty stirred again and Elsie whispered.

'What a lovely time this has been for Tom. It's unpleasant to be disliked by parents. If I can make Tom feel good about doing things for me, he'll grow up into a helpful type of man. I hope so, anyway. It doesn't always work; sometimes he has a bad temper for no real reason and then I ignore him 'til he comes out of his mood. Most of the time we get on all right, the same as me and his Dad. Elsie stretched and made a face. 'Eight o'clock? I'm going to be late! Come on you; it's time to move your arse!' She seemed to relax again for a

207

moment. She smiled across at Betty. 'How will you get on at home now, Betty? What will you do about your problems?'

Elsie saw her friend's face collapse into tears, as if she had been waiting for the question to be asked, to release her inner turmoil.

'Oh, Elsie, I've been waiting to tell you! You see, until Mom died, I lived with my Mom and Dad and as far as everybody knows, we were an ordinary Black Country family, Elsie. We all went to chapel every Sunday and put as much as anyone else into the plate when it came round. It was at night, when Mom went to work at the pub, that trouble started.

'Dad wanted to start playing games, all sorts of games but most of them involve playing at somebody else, like me as a patient and him as a doctor. It always ended with him trying to do, well, you know what. I tried to stop him but he made out it was all part of the game. I know I shouldn't say things like that. He said he'll kill me if I ever tell on him, and I think he means it. I think he loves me; it's just that he has such strong needs, and there is no one for him to satisfy himself with.

'When Mom went out, at about seven o'clock, he would sit there reading for a while and then sort of smile at me and I'd know he's been thinking about what he would like to do to me. It was written on his face and it was as if the smile was a signal to start. He would move over and crowd me into a corner and then start tickling me. I didn't mind that part. He's always tickled me but I never realised that it was a cover for what he really wanted to do. As he tickled me, he got all out of breath with the sort of excitement of it all, and then he started picking my skirt up, higher and higher until he slid it over my head.

"Come on, young madam," he would say, "how can I examine you and find out what is the matter with you if you don't let me look at you, like a doctor likes to look at somebody with something that has to be made better?" Then he goes on to say we can change places and I can be the doctor and look at him and do something to make him better. "You'd make a good doctor," he tells me. "Just pretend there's something the matter with me and that you have to touch me all over, just like a doctor does, and then I'll be better."

'Sometimes he took his shirt off to have a wash and then turned and caught me and held me ever so tight and I was frightened to stop him taking my clothes off. He made out that I needed a good wash and he'd tell Mom if I daren't let him do what he wanted to do. The last time, he took my knickers off and put his finger into me, down there.'

Betty was visibly distressed by the things she was telling Elsie; things that had been her most private secrets until then. After a short rest, she continued. 'I stopped him putting his finger into me by biting him. He said he'd kill me but I stopped him. He's a new game, now, acting the part of a madman who attacks young women, only he's not acting the part; if truth be told he is a madman!'

Betty stopped again for a moment, to try to recover her composure. They moved down the stairs with their burdens. She was sobbing as she told the story she had never told before.

'It all got worse after Mom died. I begged him to stop and he did, but I don't know how long it will be before he manages to really do it to me. What shall I do if I fall for a babby? Nobody will believe it was him that did it to me. They'll all say I've bin a fallen woman and let some stranger do these disgusting things to me. He'll never get the blame!'

By this time they were on the wagon with Tom looking round at all the new sights that he hadn't noticed when they came down, five weeks before. They tried to keep a little

209

separate from the others so that Betty could continue her story without being overheard. Elsie found herself getting angrier with Betty's father who she had never met.

Elsie pushed Betty to the side of the tailgate and they sat there, looking as if they were both just idly taking in the view. She knew she had to help this courageous, frightened young woman somehow, without seeming to; she didn't want to whip the man; it wasn't her style really, but she did want to hurt him and make sure that he left his daughter alone for ever.

'Look, Betty, I don't even know your address so would you write it down for me so that I can contact you if I ever need to?'

Elsie pulled out a pencil; and a small pad and listened as Betty gave her the information. Betty had stopped crying now. It was as if the act of telling someone all her dark secrets had released her tensions. She reached out her hand and the touch spoke of the love she had for her friend.

'It's been lovely just knowing you, Elsie. I think you're the nicest person I've ever met. Just to be able to tell my little troubles to somebody is, I don't know, something I can't describe, but to tell you is better than telling a priest 'cos I feel that although you're as young as me, you can understand my feelings.'

Betty fell silent; she very rarely spoke for as long as that. I will help her! How could she not? Elsie swore an oath to herself. Men seem able to get away with most things but there has to be a limit somewhere. She knew that there was very little she could do immediately but when she got back she would make her own enquiries.

That was one advantage of her experience in working for Mister Jenkins; she had become aware of some of the seamier sides of life and how it was manipulated. Elsie knew that Luke, Mister Jenkins' Chief Clerk, was able to make enquiries and if he couldn't get the results he wanted by himself, he was able to employ private enquiry agents. In the meantime she would keep her own eyes open for opportunities.

There was one other string to her bow, she thought. She had at her disposal, the expertise and wisdom of Mary Bowyer. Mary was sure to know things that probably she would never think of without a prod from her.

That was all the thinking she could do for today. Now she would relax and enjoy the journey home. Little Tom had quietened down and was beginning to sleep on her shoulder and she was feeling the effect of the gentle motion of the giant Shire horse as he pulled the wagon along the bumpy lanes. For a time it seemed that the journey would take forever. Then she noticed the distant shrill whistle of the trains as they passed across country lanes on their way to Bromyard and Worcester.

They were getting closer now; she could sense that there were gradually more cottages and occasional people. Then they were there, moving carefully down the gentle slope that led to the station. The train was standing there, as if it had been there waiting for them, for the whole five weeks. Stiffly they lifted their backs from the tailboard, allowing the driver to take the pins out that held the tailboard in place. Down it fell with a bang that woke Tom out of his doze.

'Look, Mommy, there's a train. Can we go for a ride on it, Mommy?' Tom was excited again with the new stimuli; looking at everything about the train. The engine driver, the fireman, the ticket collector at the gate and the guard were all asked questions.

'Can I come on your train, Mister Driver? Can I put some coal on the fire? Where do you put the tickets when Mommy gives them to you? Is it time to go yet?'

The engineers stopped and answered his questions as if Tom was grown up, then they walked along the platform, admiring the garden, tended by the staff of the station to show their pride, and then it was time to board. They climbed up the steep steps into the corridor and then into a compartment. Tom sat alone, near the window, and as soon as the train started he was back into his doze. The time and the journey passed quickly as they chugged northward, past Bromsgrove and Birmingham, into the Black Country.

'Blower's Green!'

It was the guard shouting to let them know it was time to get off. It was time to say goodbye to her friend.

'I'll see you soon, Betty. I'll miss you too much to not want to see you. Now that I know where you live, I'll be calling round on you, don't you worry. Now I must go. I think Dan might meet us at the station with Chalky and the trap.'

'Daddy! Daddy! There he is, Mommy, down there, Mommy!'

Elsie looked down the short platform and there, amid the smoke and noise, was Dan. He looked towards her and grinned as if he had a secret to tell her but was keeping it to himself. It was just because he had taken the trouble, trouble indeed to hitch up Chalky and come to meet them at the station. Still, it was good of him. He could have gone to the pub instead.

Elsie grinned back at him; he never seemed to change. He got on her nerves, sometime, with his slightly mean ways but he did his best and that was all you could ask of anyone. Tommy was practically standing on her shoulders, shouting.

'Daddy! Here we are, Daddy!'

Elsie turned to look at Betty who was looking at her. Suddenly their moment of parting seemed painful. Elsie felt as if she had everything and Betty had nothing. There wasn't even a chance to offer Betty a lift in the trap as she was going in a different direction. Betty looked as if she was trying to be brave but her bottom lip seemed to be trembling. She looked at Elsie and managed to speak,

'Tara, Elsie. I hope you have a wonderful homecoming.'

The young woman turned and was gone, even before Elsie could open her mouth to answer her. Elsie stood looking after her for a moment or two. Somehow she would make a difference to the younger woman's life. Then she turned; Dan was waiting for her and she had her own life to sort out. There were plenty of things for her to do.

It didn't take long for them to get home. Dan had obviously been using Chalky a lot; he had got used to handling him now. Nevertheless, Chalky was pleased to see her and Tommy, standing with pleasure as they stroked his muzzle.

Dan stopped at the entrance to their front garden and they walked up the short path as Dan led Chalky to his stable. The room seemed cool after the warmth of the afternoon. There was a scent in the air; nothing she could put her finger on and recognise but it was there, all the same. She was still sniffing the air when Dan came in, and he saw her and smiled again.

'You're just like a woman, wondering who or what has been going on while you have been away.'

I hadn't been wondering anything of the sort, she thought, and wondered why he had made the remark. Why? The thought left her mind and she turned to him.

'Would you take these things upstairs for me, please, Dan?' She pointed to her small case with her hopping clothes in. 'I'll have to wash them as soon as I get chance; to get them ready for next year.'

Dan's face turned slightly pink as he answered, 'What do you mean, next year? I should hope you've got the hops out of your system by then. You've got better things to do than go traipsing off to Herefordshire. If you want a holiday, you can go away with your husband!'

Swiftly she replied

'Oh Dan; thank you, my love. I never thought you'd want to pay for a proper holiday. Where do you have in mind? They say Llandudno is nice, or Blackpool. Anywhere else'd be too far to go for our budget.'

Dan looked at her, nonplussed. He hadn't actually offered to pay for their next holiday but the way that Elsie had put it, he had! She had learned too much, he thought, while she had been away. She was nevertheless attractive, with her hair piled high, making him want to pull it down so that it framed her face. He was never quite sure of her; perhaps that was her attraction. Elsie always seemed to have a sort of sideways view of things, and he was sure she earned a lot more than she let on.

Dan could be sure she wouldn't be handing her hop earnings over to him any more than he would be handing over what he had earned. He had had a good time with that. Oh well; it was time they both returned to normal, like other couples. Perhaps she'd brought him a treat, though there was no sign of it up to now.

It had been nice renewing acquaintance with Ruth Mallory and he felt sure she had enjoyed their trips out with Chalky. It couldn't last, they both knew, but a change was as good as a rest. Elsie had been close with Ruth, so in a way it was surprising that Ruth had been as willing for a bit of dalliance, but there it was; you took your chances where you could.

Perhaps Elsie had seen another side of life, away from him. He hoped not; he'd kill the bastard, whoever he was. Dan grinned at his own form of justice, and then quietened down. It was time for bed and he'd missed Elsie more than he'd have cared to admit to Ruth Mallory!

Come to think of it, wasn't it Ruth who'd encouraged

Elsie to go away for her holiday? That had led to their days out. Women were devious, the way they worked things out to suit themselves, and you never realised it 'til it was all over. He had no regrets anyway, but what would the future hold for him now? Would he have to kerb his appetites or would he be able to see Ruth occasionally? Would she want to see him?

Life always seemed to have questions and the answer to one seemed to lead to more questions, like a big circle. Still, it was interesting.

Chapter 21

Back to Normal!

The dull Willenhall morning was slow in waking the sleeping woman. Elsie stirred, slowly at first and then suddenly realised it was six o'clock and almost fell out of bed. There was something familiar about her surroundings when she awoke, but it was also strange, dark and much smaller than she remembered. The air had a different quality from that of Bromyard, as if it was made of smoke. She peered round the bedroom curtains, saw the street, covered in refuse, and felt slightly sick.

She crept down the stairs and lit the fire, ready to start the breakfast. There were a few eggs and bacon on the stone shelf in the larder but she put some fresh in the frying pan, ready for Dan as soon as he stirred. At least he had taken the trouble to stock up on a few essentials. Of course he had had full control of his own wages. He probably thought he was going to get control of hers. We'll see, she thought. The bacon was crackling now; it was time to get Dan moving. She crept back up the stairs and shouted, 'Dan! Are you getting up? You're going to be late if you don't hurry!'

Elsie pulled back the blanket from him and Dan moved. Slowly he sat up.

'Your breakfast is just making its way out o' the pan onto the plate. If you hurry, you'll catch it before it gets away!'

Elsie turned and started down the stairs. There was a bump behind her and her husband was looking over her shoulder.

'I'm always ready for a bit o' bacon. Is it on the plate yet, woman?'

She sped down the stairs and picked up the pan. In a second the bacon was there, flanked by two sausages and an egg.

'I brought these back from Bromyard, especially for this breakfast, so don't let 'em go to waste. You won't get any more without paying for them.'

Elsie smiled back at him; she had promised herself that she wouldn't comment on his meanness. Oh well; no one was perfect. She waited for his word of thanks and when it did not come she made her way back up the stairs. Tom wasn't used to these stairs; she didn't want him falling down. It was dark and he might not notice the first step, and the next one would be at the foot!

Her son was lying asleep, his thumb in his mouth and she sighed a sigh of relief as she bundled him up in her arms, suddenly frightened for what could have happened. She'd have to be more careful with him. He was growing quickly, in every sense, but it was still possible to hurt yourself if you were in unfamiliar surroundings. She was missing Betty, she realised, and she had made herself a promise to alter the girl's life for the better.

Tom stirred and she was suddenly stuck by his resemblance to Stephen Stone. Would anyone else notice? Children were often noted for their likeness to other people, outside the family. It was all in her mind. Nobody else would see what she saw. Tom stirred in her arms and Elsie sat at the table with him on her lap as he slowly woke up. He looked round at his surroundings.

'Daddy. Hello, Daddy.'

Dan looked at him and smiled.

'Hello, son. Good morning.' He turned to his plate, cut a small piece of egg and put it on a slice of bread. 'Here you are, son; a bit of Daddy's breakfast.' He lifted it up and placed it in Tom's mouth. 'There you are, ain't that nice?'

Dan turned round to Elsie. He wasn't looking too happy. All the welcome from the night before had faded from his eyes. He pushed the breakfast away and stood.

'Some of us have to work for a living, not just go sitting around in pubs in the country.'

Elsie said nothing. She would be amazed if it turned out that he hadn't had a drink while she had been away. She picked up his plate and threw what was on the plate into the small tin she used for rubbish. She didn't usually get leftovers. She couldn't, wouldn't allow herself the luxury. He'd been spoiling for a quarrel. She was glad she hadn't given him the satisfaction.

The young woman took Tom into the small kitchen on top of the cellar steps and wiped his face over with the flannel she kept for the purpose. A moment later he was dressed.

Elsie bent over the sink and lowered her head, lifting water onto her face. She felt better, like she had in Bromyard, under the pump in the yard. She towelled her hands and face until she felt invigorated, picked Tom up and carried him on her hip, up the stairs, to get dressed. The bed was tidied in a moment.

There was something different about today, not just because she was at home, not just because Dan was in a mood but there was something depressing, almost evil about the day.

'Tara! I'm off to work!'

Dan didn't really want to speak to her; he just wanted to slam out with an atmosphere that said everything was her fault, including his mood, which she had caused. There was a bang; it was the door closing. He had gone. That told her where she stood with him. Nowhere!

For a moment, Elsie felt the tears sting her eyes. Then she stretched and pulled herself together. She would not let his mood affect hers. It was a lovely day.

She was going to have a lovely day. She would be seeing Aunt Mary and Luke, from work. He was always nice to her. She would be taking Chalky to Wednesbury to carry her round to the tenants she had to collect rent from. It would be nice to see Ruth Mallory again. Elsie smiled as she recalled how she had thought of Ruth and Dan when she had last called on her. What had started that thought?

Elsie sat down and ate her breakfast of toast and butter. She had a few things left to unpack from her hop box. There were apples and pears from Bromyard. She could make a few pies from them, when she got the time. Tom was looking at her, wanting some of her toast, and grinning, reminding her of Stephen. She was suddenly conscious of how alone she was. The comparison with Bromyard made her feel like crying again.

In Bromyard she had never been alone for more than a minute or two. There had always been the sound of chattering Black Country voices. In her home there was only silence and the remnants of the atmosphere that Dan had created. What had been the matter with him, anyway? Sometimes he went into a bad temper for no apparent reason at all.

Stephen came into her mind. Elsie knew that she should try not to think of him. There was no point, really, no future, but she couldn't help seeing his laughing face in front of hers. The thought came to her that if she never saw Stephen again, it would be as if he had died, and the feeling of grief came to her, overwhelming her with its depth. She sat down for a moment or two, allowing herself the luxury of the heartache. .

Tom called to her and she pulled herself out of her

depression and got herself ready for work. She was going to take Tom to Aunt Mary's, to let her look after him while she conducted her own small business affairs. She put her son onto her hip and walked out of the front door, then turned into the small area that they called the stable.

It was much cooler here, even though it was only thirty miles further north. Chalky whinnied as she approached. He was pleased to see her. It was good that someone was pleased. She was feeling sorry for herself. She put her hand into her pocket and, pulling out an apple, gave it to Chalky. He stood while she stroked his muzzle, receiving the caress with pleasure. It would be nice if she were on the receiving end of a caress. Stop it, she thought, self- pity isn't really part of your nature.

As she cleaned out the stable and fed hay to Chalky, Elsie thought about her situation. She was married, and that gave her a certain status, even if she wasn't madly in love with her husband. He did his best, in his own way, even if he did like the drink a bit more than he should. Hundreds of men were bullying drunks; at least she was better off than their wives. Certainly, as a couple, they were financially better off than the average.

Elsie continued with her assessment of her circumstances. She had a lover occasionally, a lover to whom she was desperately attached but with whom she was unable to make the relationship a visible one. She had to live with that, she knew, because of Stephen's circumstances. Circumstances! She was fed up of his circumstances! She wondered how Dan felt about their situation. Was he happy? Was Stephen happy? Was anyone happy? Suddenly she felt lucky when she compared her situation with other women she knew.

Betty was desperately unhappy. Ruth Mallory was the only woman she knew who seemed in any way happy.

Perhaps she too had her problems, making her life less than perfect. Elsie smiled to herself as she recalled her moment of suspicion when she had thought Dan and Ruth were too familiar. Had they met while she and Tom had been down in Bromyard?

I'd better watch myself, she thought. I don't want to lose Dan to a friend. Although a wife was, in some eyes, seen as a possession; it worked the other way round, too. There were advantages to her situation that she was unwilling to give up.

Elsie straightened herself and backed the pony into the shafts of the little cart. Tom was sitting in the cart as if he were driving. He had not been in the cart since yesterday and he was thrilled by the feeling it gave him. Elsie climbed up, steered Chalky out onto the road and started the journey.

Elsie was looking forward to seeing Aunt Mary more than anyone else. She had missed the older woman. There must be so much news waiting for her return. There was always something happening in Wednesbury. Mister Jenkins was always driving a bargain with someone who thought they were clever enough to hoodwink him.

Luke would have things to tell her. He had been collecting her rents for her. Maybe she had another house in her partially-owned portfolio of properties, as Luke called it. He would be able to tell her about Ruth Mallory and how she was paying her rent. She had had her last chance. Her husband had climbed aboard the wagon and Ruth was proud of him. He no longer got drunk three times a week and he was looking smarter in appearance, too.

Elsie wanted to talk to Luke about Betty and her problems. Perhaps he knew of somewhere the girl could stay, safe from the hands of her child-loving father. The thought of Betty made her click her tongue to Chalky, urging him on at a slightly faster rate. He loved cantering along the road. It was as if he was aware of how neat and dapper he looked, pulling the little trap. People often stopped and watched him go by, especially the local gypsies.

There were many gypsies around the Black Country, all finding work in various ways. The women canvassed the local shops, selling small charms to bring the purchaser luck. Often they sold home-made pegs too, using a sharp knife to whittle bits of soft wood to their traditional dolly shape and nailing the tops together with a small length of pliable tin-plate. When they found a friendly purchaser of their wares, they chalked a gypsy sign on the premises to inform anyone who followed in their path.

The journey was going beneath the feet of the little Welsh Cob and within the hour they were clattering down Upper High Street in Wednesbury. Elsie regarded the little town with affection. It was to here that she had walked with her father from Birmingham, looking for work. Mary Bowyer had taken them both in until she had introduced them to the Stone family.

They had really fallen on their feet in Wednesbury. Instead of going down to the offices of Mister Jenkins, she turned right down Union Street, and then into the court where Aunt Mary lived. There was barely room for the trap to get through but she was used to handling him now and she pulled up outside the small house that looked no different to the others. A small boy came over and she offered him a penny to look after Chalky and make sure he got some water from the trough. Elsie walked straight into Mary's house.

'Mary! I'm home, Mary.'

Elsie pushed through the door and into the room beyond. There was no one there. Oh well, Mary had the right to go out after all. She had had no warning that Elsie might come to see her today. She was probably out shopping. Elsie turned and walked back out of the door. The small boy was still stroking Chalky.

'D'you know where Mrs Bowyer is, son?'

He looked up at her, a small boy, serious in his dealings with grown-ups. He was obviously a little jealous of Tom who was still sat in the trap, looking round, wondering where he was.

'She went up the hill this morning. I don't know where she is now. Shall I carry on looking after the horse?'

'He's not a horse; he's a pony. Yes, you can carry on looking after him. Where do you live? I'll ask your Mom if it's all right.'

He pointed and she crossed the court to the small house. She gave the door a push and peered inside. It was like many of them; small and neat, with evidence that someone cared how they lived.

'Hello, is there anybody in?'

There was the sound of movement from upstairs and a clatter as a small woman came down them. Elsie explained what she had asked the small boy to do, and the woman looked pleased.

'Yes, it'll be all right. Young Albert's a good boy. If he says he'll look after the pony, he will. I've seen you before, haven't I? Yes, it's a little time ago but didn't you stay with Mary Bowyer for a time with your father?'

Elsie felt pleased that the woman remembered her father. Perhaps she knew how Ruth was. The woman replied to Elsie's unasked question.

'Yes, Ruth is all right. She's got a job, now, as well as her husband. They are coming on well in the world. Not every man likes his wife working but it seems to make them better off, don't it? Would you like a cup o' tea while you are waiting for Mary? I was just going to have one, anyway; it's up to you.'

The day was hot and Elsie was too, so she walked into the woman's front room and sat down at her invitation. She sat and listened as the woman, Martha, made the tea. They sat without speaking for a minute or two then Martha questioned Elsie.

'I seem to remember that you were pretty well hard up when you came to Wednesbury; you look a lot better off, now! Did you come into some money?'

Elsie laughed and explained that she had got on mainly through her own efforts and the pony and trap belonged to her employers, Jenkins, the solicitors in Lower High Street. She worked for them in a part-time job, calling on their tenants if there was any trouble. She kept it to herself that she collected rent for them. Martha knew Mary Bowyer quite well.

'A lovely woman, always willing to do you a good turn, if she can, is Mary.' Martha poured another cup of tea and went on to say that Mary had lent her five pounds when her husband died, to pay for the funeral. She'd been paying her back ever since, whenever she could afford a copper or two.

Elsie thanked Martha for the cup of tea and stepped out of the house again, into the small court. Mary was just walking across the court. She was walking smartly as if she were in a hurry. What could be the matter? Was something seriously wrong?

Chapter 22

Mary Bowyer

'Mary! Mary!' Elsie broke into a trot and Mary turned to see Elsie, her face lighting up as she saw her young friend. There was a moment when Elsie saw something other than gladness upon her friend's face and then Mary held out her arms and enveloped Elsie. The pleasure of the meeting showed in her words.

'Elsie, it's so good to see you, my dear, dear girl. How are you? Stand back and let me have a good look at you. You do look beautifully tanned, like a proper country girl. I almost wish I could have come with you. Come into the house. We seem to have half the population of Wednesbury watching us.'

Elsie laughed. 'Oh, I am very grateful to half the population of Wednesbury, well, not half of them, Martha gave me a cup of tea while I waited for you to come home.'

'Oh, good,' said Mary. 'I know Martha's a good woman and would do you no harm, but you've never felt unable to go into my house. You could have gone in and made yourself a cup of tea.'

In a way, it seemed to Elsie that she was being admonished mildly, but she knew it was true; she could have gone into the house without needing permission. Then Mary spotted Tom, sitting quietly in the trap. She moved swiftly to him and held out her arms to him.

'Hello, Tom. My goodness; you've grown a lot while you've been away – and it's only been a few weeks as well!'

Tommy loved his Aunt Mary and quickly responded to her, standing on the back of the trap, ready to jump into her arms. She moved to him and folded her arms around him. She held him for a moment and then moved to the pony.

'Hello, Chalky. I think you'd better have a drink.' She turned to Elsie. There's a trough down the bottom of Union Street where he can help himself. Come on; it'll only take a minute or two for us to walk him down there, and he'll feel that much better for it.'

They slowly turned the trap round and moved out of the court, to find a drink for the Welsh Cob. When they got there, he put his head into it and took a long draught of the cooling liquid. Mary sat on the long bench alongside the trough and patted the seat beside her.

'Come on, let's have a chat. You can tell me about all the adventures you and Tom have had while you were away from me. I bet you've been up to all sorts of things, haven't you?'

Elsie sat down beside her. She knew she wasn't going to reveal all she had been up to, as Mary had put it. That would have been too much! Slowly, she took Mary through the events that had occurred while she had been away, telling of how the bines had blackened her hands, giving her calluses; how the man had tried to attack Mister Walker and how she had fought him off, thanks to the skill she had learned from Luke on how to protect herself with a whip.

The young woman described how she had made friends with her workmates and how Betty had helped her with looking after Tom. Gently, without being too explicit, she described Betty's difficulties with her father and the determination she felt, herself, to help Betty to find a better life than she was living with her father. Mary was horrified to learn of the ordeal that Betty had had to go through, every night of her life, trying to ward off the predatory sexual attentions of her father.

The older woman was pleased to learn that Dan had come down to see Elsie and Tom in Bromyard, and the way he had joined in with their drinking, when they had gone out for a change, and she laughed when Elsie told her of how Dan had mistaken Betty for Elsie, in bed.

Mary told Elsie that she knew that Stephen Stone had been down to see her, and the fuss his family had made about it, and the way he had laughed in their faces. He had told her about it, himself.

'Stephen has never been a dishonest person. He's always told me the truth, even when he was a very young man and first met you, Elsie. He told me how he felt about you, years ago, and that he would marry you if he could. Well, now we all know that he can't, but he'll do the next best thing. What do you think about that?

'Mabel is a lovely person and she really doesn't deserve to be hurt by all you pair's shenanigans. I love you very much, Elsie, but I don't know how you will square the circle, I'm sure.

'You're not the only one who has fallen in love with the wrong man, you know. At one time the man would just join the Army or the Navy and say goodbye, hoping to find a better life elsewhere. I knew a young man, once; he's in South Africa now. I very rarely hear from him but I know he's married to a very nice woman who went with him. That wasn't an easy thing to do. He was promoted due to his courage and military skill and they have a good life together, now. He is a Major. I am an old widow woman. There are all kinds of courage and loyalty, aren't there?'

Mary suddenly looked older and let her hand drop into Elsie's. What a life she must have had! Elsie made up her mind, that moment, to get everything out of life that she could, whenever the opportunity came to her. She would lie and steal, but she would live! She looked at her aunt and her determination must have showed.

'Ah yes, I can see that you will have a different sort approach to life, altogether to me. What can I say? I just wish you luck. What I will say is; don't trust your husband with any knowledge of your financial assets. As soon as you do, he'll disappear. Just live quietly, not above your usual station and keeping your own council. When you are older, maybe even after you've lost him, you'll be able to live the life you deserve.'

That was all very deep, thought Elsie, but it did make sense to keep your own council, letting no one know everything about your business. Mary had always seemed to have secrets tucked up her sleeve. Perhaps she was in a mood to reveal a few. Elsie sat down again. She had been ready to go to work. Young Tom was getting restless. He never could sit still for long. Her thought popped into her mouth.

'I think I'll just pop into the baker's and get us a tanner's worth o' cakes to go with the cup o' tea I know you're going to make.' She turned to Tom. 'Come on, son. Let's go and get a cake for Auntie Mary.'

Elsie leaned towards Mary and gave her a peck on the cheek and then took Tom's hand and led him out. Chalky was all right so she left him; the attention of two small boys pleasing him. She made up her mind to bring them a cake, too. Union Street was busy, not as busy as market day but with quite a few people shopping.

The baker's shop was only a few doors away and she stood among others, awaiting the baker. He was one of her people, as she called them, one of the people from whom she collected rent for Mister Jenkins. He caught her eye.

'Good morning, Mrs Barr. You look very well, if you don't mind me saying.'

He smiled as she gave a small blush. The traders were all the same, she thought always willing to give a bit of attention to the women in a sort of false flirtation, just for the purpose of brightening the day up. It was a way of breaking out from the social mores they had to keep, she realised.

'Good morning, yourself, Mister Henshaw. I think I'll have a half-dozen of those egg custards. Oh, and a farmhouse loaf please. That'll be all, thank you.'

She smiled at him; she didn't want to be too friendly to him and waited as he bagged her custards carefully, and paid him with a florin. He gave her change and then she left, turning back the way they had come.

The teapot was on the table when they returned and a plate was ready at the side of each of the two cups. Mary always used her china tea-set when she had visitors. Elsie recalled how she and her father had been given two large mugs the first time they had entered her house, dirty, tired and hungry. It had seemed like a little miracle when Mary had put them up overnight and introduced them to her brother, who had given them work until they found something more permanent at Willenhall.

Elsie smiled affectionately at Mary. She felt the greatest love for the little Black Countrywoman and on impulse, she showed it, enveloping her in loving arms. Mary returned the hug and they stood back from each other, surveying what they saw. Both of them had been changed by the years since they had first met but whereas Elsie had taken on the mature beauty of a young married woman, Mary seemed to have shrunk. She still had the twinkle of intelligence in her eyes, though, and her back was as straight as a soldier's.

There was something else too, Elsie thought, she has a sort of confidence, the sort of confidence that allowed her to make generous gestures like she had with Elsie and her father, years ago. She didn't seem worried or concerned when she did these things. She just did what she thought was right and lived with the consequences. What had given her this confidence? Was it the confidence of wealth? It could be, Elsie realised. Wealthy people could usually buy their way out of trouble and buy their way into opportunities for increasing their wealth. How wealthy would you have to be, to have that sort of aura, she wondered.

On impulse, she decided to ask. She remembered how she had discussed Samuel Smiles' philosophy in his book, 'Self Help', with Albert Stone, when she had first met him. He had seemed impressed by her interest.

'Do you remember how Mister Stone talked about Samuel Smiles and his book, when we first went there?' She waited for her aunt's nod of assent and then went on. 'Do you think the book works, really works? It seems a lot to expect that just by showing a bit of determination; you can achieve the ownership of lots of money.'

Elsie was aware that she sounded a bit naïve; she intended to. She did not want to sound as if she knew everything. She had a few pounds herself, as she knew her aunt knew. What she wanted was a way to increase her small fortune to a point where she was beholden to no other person, even her husband. As she was talking, Mary was pouring the tea but listening with interest. She passed the cup to Elsie and sat down. She looked quite serious when she turned to Elsie to reply.

'Look, my girl. I know you are not doing too badly with your small investments. I know you only let your husband know about half of your income, maybe not even that. You also have a pocketful of earnings that you have brought back from the hop-picking. You make me smile when you act so simple. You're doing all right. Just keep doing what you are doing and you'll soon be one of the wealthiest women in Wednesbury - and no one will know it but you! You've many friends here, now. Mister Jenkins, Luke and myself of course. Of course, you live in Willenhall but your money is being made in Wednesbury. You might like to reflect on that, and whether it is right to make your money here and spend it somewhere else!

'You should return some of it to the pot that you took it from. What I mean is that when you make a big purchase, you should let the traders of this small town get some of the benefit. There are also the poor people of this town as well. They've helped you by paying rent to you and this has helped to keep you in work and supplied you with the capital to make investments. I made an investment, if you like, when I helped you and your father. That investment has paid for itself a hundred times. It is not only money that multiplies, you know; it's love as well.'

Mary became silent and sipped her tea delicately without looking at Elsie. It was obvious to Elsie that Mary was a little embarrassed by the amount of feeling she was revealing and it suddenly came to her that Mary was an exceptional human being, strong but compassionate, shrewd but generous. There was no other person she knew who had these admirable qualities to the same extent as Mary Bowyer. Mary seemed to steady herself and gave her protégée a strong smile.

'I'm sorry. I don't often reveal how I'm feeling; it doesn't pay, I've found. You're different of course. You are my Elsie, the daughter I never had. If there has to be someone to whom I can tell how I feel, it has to be you. If I can teach you what I know as wisdom, such as it is, I'll do so. You can read books like Sam Smiles' book on wisdom and getting rich until the cows come home but it's what you see and observe and absorb from experience that really forms your character for good or evil, for stupidity or brightness.

'You were lucky in a way, to have a good mother and father, even if they did die younger than they should. They each taught you the basics of a good-living life. You also found out from your own experiences that there always has to be compromises. The wisdom comes from knowing which compromises to accept, and which ones to reject.

'I've tried to teach you by example the right way to live in this hard society. Many people die young because of the conditions in which Black Country people work. I've tried to protect you from the worst of that. Now you are your own person and I'll be just a memory sooner or later. That's the way of the world. All I can say about that is, try to be a good teacher to your children. Yes, you will have another, I am sure. Perhaps the next one will be Dan's.'

Elsie looked at her in amazement but Mary just kept on talking, as if she had locked up all the words she had wanted to say, and they were all coming out at once.

'That, I believe, is the biggest responsibility we have; to be good teachers to our children. There is no greater triumph than the achievements of your children. It is a kind of immortality; the best kind.' She paused. 'Tommy becomes more like Stephen every day. There's just that something about him. He will probably laugh a lot, as he gets older! Never mind; I'm sure you'll solve all your problems in life as you grow older. Let's have another cup o' tea.'

They sat there for a few minutes in the friendly silence that followed Mary's deluge of words. Elsie was waiting to see whether Mary had anything else to say and she was not disappointed.

'You know, Elsie, we Black Country women have a hard life but we are the salt of the earth. Our men have to risk their lives in the mines, in the foundries, in the forges, everywhere there is industry. They die by the hundred because of the terrible conditions they have to work in.

'So, they get drunk. They have to do something to get rid of the fear that they have to live with all the time. We, the Black Country women I mean, have to sustain them through it all, and help to earn a living as well. There can't be many people who have a harder life, can there?'

This time it did seem that she had said all she wanted to.. Elsie smiled to herself. What an amazing woman Mary was. If only she could be like that. She was determined to follow in Mary's footsteps. Her appreciation showed in the way she answered her aunt.

'Aunt Mary, I can't tell you how much I admire the principles that you live by. I'm going to adopt them for my own. I'd sooner be like you than anyone else on earth.'

This time they both fell silent, drawn into a new togetherness by the confidences they had shared. There was a cry from the floor and they started. It was Tom, playing with the fire-tongs. They each laughed and bent to give him the attention he wanted. Mary bent to him.

'Hello, little Tom; come here and let me tickle your tummy!'

She lifted him up and sat him on her lap where he sat quite happily. The moment seemed right for Elsie to mention Betty.

'He goes to other women quite well. It seems that he feels safe wherever he is. He was just the same down in Bromyard with Betty. I just wish there was something I could do for her.'

She finished, looking at Mary expectantly, as if she could give the answer to her problem, just off her cuff. Mary sat silently for a moment, as if thinking it over.

'I'm sorry. I don't think there is anything I can do. Sometimes, a woman has to make her own move, not just stay there, suffering.' She changed the subject abruptly. 'When are you going back to work? Mister Jenkins was asking me about you, the other day. Luke's been collecting in the rents that you are responsible for but it's a lot of extra work, as I'm sure you can appreciate.'

Elsie answered,

'I planned to go in today, to see what's happening, and to start back tomorrow. Do you think that'll be the right thing to do, Aunt Mary?'

'Yes, I should think that'll do. You might find though, that he may not look with favour on a similar type of holiday, next year.'

Silence fell again, to be broken by Tom, calling for his comforter and Elsie smiled.

'Oh, well, there's no peace, is there?'

Elsie started getting ready to go and reached out to give Mary a kiss on the cheek. Mary was looking at her in a peculiar way. She stayed Elsie with a touch of her hand.

'Elsie, would you please leave me Betty's address? I'm making no promises but I will make a few enquiries. That's the best I can offer. Bye bye then, Elsie. I'll see you when I see you.'

Mary stood as Elsie scribbled the address on a slip of paper and allowed her to pass on the way to the door. They nodded to each other and the light from the sun streamed into the front room as if the sun were inside.

Elsie walked out into the sun and placed Tom on the seat of the trap. She opened the back door of the trap, climbed in and turned Chalky round, to enter Union Street. They turned up the slight incline towards Upper High Street and then down to Jenkins' office.

As she walked in, Elsie felt that she had returned to the time she had first applied for a position. She still had the same sense of anxiety as she mounted the dark staircase. Would Mister Jenkins still want her to work for him, after being away for so long? Elsie walked along the narrow corridor that led to the office where she had been given a desk of her own. The door opened easily and she walked in. She looked relaxed but she did feel uneasy.

Luke was sitting at his desk and at her entrance he looked

up. He stood immediately and reached out his arms to her.

'Welcome home, Elsie. It's wonderful to see you. I'll be able to have a bit of a rest now.'

He pushed her away to arms' length and inspected her. His eyes gave away his feelings for her. Elsie had never thought of him as anything but a very good friend and the look on his face caught her unawares. She laughed nervously to conceal her feelings. He seemed so tall and handsome; she had never noticed before. His eyes smiled as he spoke.

'Well you look like a peasant, you are so brown, and look at the state of your hands; black as the ace of spades!'

Elsie looked down and realised that he was mocking her. She had taken a lot of trouble to retain the look of her hands. He hadn't changed!

'How are you, Luke? It's nice to see you too. You look well. How's Mister Jenkins? Is he well? What am I to do? It seems like months since I was here and I don't know whether I'm welcome or not.'

Elsie felt like a little girl standing in line to see the Headmaster for some crime. There was a cough behind her.

'Hello, Mrs Barr. When you've finished saying hello to Luke, perhaps you could spare me five minutes.'

Jenkins turned on his heel, like a soldier on parade, his back vertical as he turned. As far as she knew, he had never been a member of the military. She turned back to Luke who just stood and lifted his eyebrows. What was this all about? She turned on her heel and followed Mister Jenkins into his office. He sat and waved her to the seat opposite himself. As she sat, he was sorting out papers in front of him. Was he going to dismiss her? Eventually he looked up at her and extended his hand.

'Firstly, Mrs Barr, I'd like to say what a pleasant day this has become, now that you're back with us. I believe you have a pony of ours in your custody.'

He sometimes forgot that he was not having a legal conversation. She nodded, pleading guilty to the offence. His face lifted slightly as he smiled.

'You also have a trap to go with the pony, but the trap is not ours; it's a gift from us to you. It's to give you an idea of how this firm values what you do for us.'

He always spoke in the plural as if he were fifty strong, when he was talking for himself but didn't want to be seen to be having any sort of pleasure from the experience. His next words surprised her.

'It wasn't just from me, you understand. I shared that pleasure with Mister Stephen Stone as a token of his gratitude for the way you have looked after his tenants.'

Elsie went to stand but sat at his wave.

'I didn't know he had any tenants with us – and I certainly didn't know that I was responsible for collecting their rents. This is a shock to me. I don't know what my husband will say when I tell him.'

Mister Jenkins smiled his thin smile that he used when he was getting the better of someone.

'Mrs Barr, if I were you, I should just say that the trap and the pony have been supplied to help you with your work. You need not tell any lies at all. Your husband won't mind if you have the use of the vehicle, will he? He hasn't minded up till now. He was often seen out with it while you were away.'

Having got her welcome out of the way, and the ownership of Chalky and the trap, he went on.

'There's one other thing I want to discuss with you and that is the state of your own investments. This is how they stand at the moment.'

Sam Jenkins passed the large sheet of paper over to her. It was covered with figures. When she came to the end of the sheet, she was shocked to see that her worth was now well over two hundred pounds. She'd never thought that it might be possible that she could be so prosperous. She could now make some life-changing decisions but did she want to? This would take some thinking about. How could she have the benefit of the extra income without giving away her source?

Dan would be a nasty problem if he found out. She recalled what Mary had said about the conditions that Black Country men lived and worked in and sympathised with the point of view that Dan would have, but that was no good to her. She had to survive, herself.

What was the best way to put this new knowledge to her best advantage?

Chapter 23

The Nature of Mercy
1909

Luke listened carefully to what Mary was saying. He knew the man well and had never liked him, but now liked him even less. There was nothing worse, in his opinion, than a man who abused his defenceless daughter. The punishment must be carefully carried out. It must be carefully done, with no possibility of any blame to come in his or Mary's direction.

More important than punishment was the task of ensuring that he would never commit this particular offence again. He would have to be warned in no uncertain way. Then she heard of a girl, a virgin of thirteen, who had been made pregnant by her father, against her will. He had brutally beaten her to get his own way.

The anger within her made Mary change her mind about the nature of the punishment. She decided that a good beating up was the most suitable way of protecting a young girl against the danger of becoming pregnant at the hands of such a cruel paedophile and determined that the molester of Betty would be paid in a suitable coin.

When she saw Luke, a few days after listening to Elsie's story, she explained what she wanted done, and her reasons. Luke listened as Mary outlined what had happened and he too was overwhelmed by feelings of anger. He agreed that what she proposed was the best punishment and it would effectively prevent the man from carrying out the same crime again.

As chief clerk to Mister Jenkins, Luke often inhabited a strange, shadowy world, where the righteous mixed with the criminal to their mutual advantage when the ass of law could find no solution to their problems. Luke probably knew more criminals in Wednesbury than the police. The town had had a bloody past since the Vikings invaded England and, rumour had it, raped and pillaged as far West as Wednesbury, giving the town its name, after Woden, the great god of the North.

One of the unwritten laws of the criminal was, and still is, that child molesters do not get away with it. Rightly or wrongly they are not accepted in prison and if found out, they have very difficult lives.

Luke made his way to the Lamp public house towards the end of Upper High Street and bought a half pint of mild. A few minutes later he was joined by a mild-looking man. They spoke quietly for a few minutes and then parted. The transaction had taken place, along with its justification and payment. Luke walked quietly out of the public house and went home to a good night's sleep.

The nights were dark around Wednesbury. No public lighting had yet been installed and the darkness and silence, at three o'clock in the morning, was so intense that to see your own hand was an effort of sight.

A few nights later, Jack Thurston had a message that he was to meet a man who would pay him half in advance for a certain job, and the balance when the job had been done. He was to meet someone to learn the details and get the first instalment of his pay. Thurston walked along the canal bank towards the rendezvous he had arranged. He was not disturbed by either the time of night or the meeting place. It was quite common to arrange a seemingly strange spot for a meeting. There were bushes in the distance and he was considering whether to place himself behind them to be in position when the other party to their meeting arrived.

Thurston moved behind the bushes and, as he did so, he felt a dull thump on the side of his head. There was a sound and feeling of terrible impact in his leg. His last thought before he lost consciousness was that he had been tricked but he did not know why. Their victim lay still, his face pale and his pulse very irregular. Neither of the two men knew why they had been allocated this job. It was not their usual pattern of work.

They left; each man making off in a different direction. They were close to a bridge so as soon as they climbed up, they parted with a quick nod, as of a job well done, and disappeared into the night's gloom. No one followed them or saw them as they went, one tall with a limp, and the other of medium height, with a swift walking action that showed his fitness.

The next morning, a coal barge carrying coals to West Bromwich halted. The bargee looked at the Shire horse pulling them and jumped to the bank. Something had disturbed the horse. It might be to his advantage to look. Inside, his wife was putting the kettle on the coal stove to make tea, to be drunk after they had finished breakfast.

'Ivy!' There was a short pause. 'Ivy! Come here!'

Ivy didn't want trouble. She knew what he was like if he called and she didn't jump. She climbed the three steps and looked round.

'What's the matter, Joseph?'

'Never mind what's the matter. There's a man 'ere who's got a lot o' blood comin' from 'is 'ead, that's what's the matter. I suppose we'd better tell somebody. I've never seen so much blood in my life!'

Ivy scrambled to fasten the horse securely to the bush. The horse wouldn't pull away from that. She knew that tied meant fastened till untied. Joseph was fastening the stern end. He climbed up to the road that crossed the canal and waited until a horse came into sight. He stepped into the road.

'Excuse me, young man. There's a chap lying on the bank, with blood all over him. He's not dead yet but he will be if 'e's left for long. Can you tell a copper, or a doctor, please?'

The man listened and then pulled the reins on the horse sharply, urging it into a gallop. The word was out. Within five minutes a constable was at the scene. He grumbled as he lowered himself down the steep slope that led to the canal. He looked at the bargee, deep suspicion in his mind. He was a deeply suspicious type of man.

'Right, what's the story then?'

The constable tried to browbeat the bargee, but his wife jumped to defend him.

'I knew it'd do no good to tell coppers. All they think about is getting you in the nick.' Ivy rounded on the constable. 'Well, my man's committed no crime. All 'e 'as done is try to save 'is life.' She indicated the prone figure lying on the towpath where they had left him. 'Look at him; covered in blood all over 'is private parts. It's either a shame for 'im or somebody 'as got their own back for what 'e as done to somebody. You see if I ain't right, sir. I ain't got nothin' else to say.' Ivy moved away to stand by Joseph then she picked up his hands and inspected them. 'See what I mean? 'E ain't got any blood under 'is fingernails and there's no sign that my Joseph's been in a struggle, is there?'

The constable was writing everything down on his notebook, but he was taking it in as well. It was true; the crime could not really be tied or traced to the bargee. He turned to Joseph.

'What's your name? Address? What are you doing here anyway? How did you come to find him?'

The constable was asking questions and writing the answers down all at the same time it seemed. Eventually he turned to Ivy and repeated his barrage of questions. He found out that the couple were not married but had been living together for four years. Just as he was running out of questions a trap pulled up and after a clatter of boots, a figure came hurrying down the slope with a small bag. He looked at the constable as the first one probably able to give him any facts about the unconscious man. The man was Doctor Maskell who lived nearby. He lifted his eyebrows in enquiry.

'Good evening, constable. What's the story then? What are these people doing here? Let me see the rabbit. Yes, he's had a bad time. He's been thoroughly beat up. Well, well, well. It's a long time since I came across one as bad as this. There's not a lot I can do for him. He'll either live or he won't. I wonder why this was done. Looks like a bit of local, unofficial justice, to me. I wonder what he's been up to. What do you think, constable?'

The constable was not going to reveal what he thought, which was little. He was more interested in trying to think what he should do next. He coughed in the dark, smoky air. There was no crowd because of the lateness of the hour. Somebody had to think of something and it turned out to be the doctor.

'Do you think we can rig up some sort of stretcher for this poor chap?' he asked Joseph.

'Well, I've got a plank on the boat, Doctor. We can get him up the slope on that and then into your trap, to take him to where they can do him a bit o' good.'

The constable assisted them in getting the form up the slope to the waiting trap. It took the four of them to lift him into the trap, with a narrow rivulet of blood following their path. The doctor got busy immediately, tying bandages and padding round the man's head and leg. Thurston was starting to recover consciousness, now and was groaning in pain.

The doctor started off to the hospital and the constable, after having a last look around and giving permission to Joseph and Ivy to leave, left himself, to report the incident to his inspector. The small amount of noise that had been raised by the incident died down to a silence that was normal for the area and time of night.

The next day, there was a write up of the incident and much comment. Sam Jenkins spoke to Luke about it over a cup of tea in the office. They were expecting Elsie back from her work and were enjoying a little conversation before she arrived.

'It's terrible, the things that are happening in Wednesbury, Luke. Have you seen this report? There was this poor man who was attacked by thugs on the towpath last night. Apparently he was covered in blood. He had been stabbed a couple of times, too. Thank God it doesn't happen all that often.'

He passed the newspaper across the desk to Luke who, after looking at it briefly passed it back, along with his comment. 'There's no sign of who the poor man was. Perhaps he was a stranger to the area and he was robbed just as a speculative robbery, to see what he had in his pockets.'

There was a clip-clop up the stairs and they both knew it was Elsie climbing them. She was back! Both of the men had missed her cheery company and were looking forward to speaking with her. As a last comment on the newspaper report, Mister Jenkins spoke. 'It's quite possible that no one will ever be brought to book for this crime. I wonder what the motive was.'

He looked across at Luke but Luke was deeply involved in adding up a column of figures and did not reply. Sam

Jenkins sighed and went out of the office just as Elsie was entering.

'Good morning, Mrs Barr. Nice to see you back working, so soon after your holiday.'

He went to raise his hat and realised that he did not have it on. Elsie took a small hold of his sleeve as he was leaving her.

'Mister Jenkins, I'd like to have the opportunity of a short meeting with you. I have my earnings from my time in Bromyard, and I want them to be included with my investments rather than fritter them away on little luxuries for the home. I would be grateful if you'd tell me when we can meet.'

It seemed to Elsie that Mister Jenkins seemed to blush when he replied, as if he were guilty of some small crime. Perhaps he was not looking forward to the meeting with her.

'Well,' he started, and Elsie noticed that when the correct words were awkward to come by, he always started his sentences with 'Well.' 'Well, I think it would be a good idea to meet up after you have finished collecting your rents in, tomorrow. Would that suit you?'

'That'll suit me fine, Mister Jenkins. I'll look forward to it.'

Elsie turned and went into the rent office where Luke was sitting. She picked up the small collecting books she used to carry around with her in the trap. She had fitted a small cupboard where she was able to lock things. Luke looked up at her. 'Hello, Elsie. It must seem strange, to be back at the collecting job. I suppose you'll soon get used to it. Have a pleasant day. By the way, your friend Ruth Mallory is up to date with everything, now. She seems to have taken the lesson to heart that you gave her.'

'I certainly hope so, Luke, but it wasn't all her fault, you know. Her husband was too fond of the drink. He must be one of the few men who've been able to give it up. I'll see you later on, when I come back to pay the rents in. Bye, Luke.'

Elsie walked out of the door of the office. Luke was giving her strange looks. Was he in love with her, from afar? Elsie romanticised about it and decided that it was unlikely. He was far too dry and dour. Perhaps he had been able to do something about Betty's situation. Time will tell, she thought. She tucked her bag under her arm and stepped out smartly. The town was coming awake; all the shops were now open and there was a nip in the air.

Winter was on the way. Elsie made her way up the High Street, calling in at the shops that were the property of Jenkins and Co. Before the afternoon was gone, she had collected all the rents that were due and the sovereigns were weighing heavy from those who paid by cash. Some paid by cheque, which in a way, was much more convenient, as if she was robbed, the thief would not be able to make use of them.

Elsie was thinking of Mary as she walked along and before long had decided to call in to see her. It was surprising, she thought, how fast the day went when she was busy. She had left Tom with Mary and she knew he would be well-cared for. He loved Mary and she loved him. She was always giving him some little treat.

Elsie took the money back to the office and left the cash with Luke to be locked in the safe. She still had a lot to do and time was passing. She carried on collecting until she considered that she had collected enough for the day and then she made her way back to Mary's house. As she passed through the court, she saw Ruth, standing at the side of Chalky. She was stroking his muzzle and speaking tenderly.

'Just you stay here, eh, Chalky. You've waited here a time or two, ain't you, my beauty?'

Ruth stood back, looking him up and down. Elsie immediately turned and walked out of the court, quietly. She turned left up Union Street, walked to the corner and then walked back down again, noisily. As soon as she saw Ruth by the pony she shouted.

'Ruth! Hello Ruth!'

At the sound of her call, Ruth turned and saw Elsie just entering the court and she brightened her face and smiled. Elsie could see that Ruth was under some sort of stress so she trotted the last few feet and flung her arms round her friend.

'Oh it's lovely to see you, Ruth. I've really missed you while I've been gone. How are you? How's Jack? Is he still on the wagon? You do look well. Are you going to make we a cup o' tea?'

Elsie took Ruth's arm in such a show of open friendship that Ruth could not deny her. Indeed, Elsie was keen to talk to her old friend. How had she become so familiar with Chalky? The pony had seemed to be enjoying the attention as if he and Ruth were old friends. There was no point in starting a dispute, she thought. Let's see what comes out.

They walked into Ruth's house. Tom could wait a little longer for her. He was used to being with other women. Perhaps she would find out more about Ruth; perhaps she wouldn't. It didn't matter all that much. In a few minutes they were chatting over a cup of tea, each asking and answering questions.

'Yes, Jack's still at the forge. He's quite an expert now, and Fred Stone knows it. He's getting on now and Jack's tekking over a lot o' the things 'e used to do. The only trouble is 'e's there all the time an' I don't see much of 'im now.'

Ruth voiced her feelings to Elsie who replied immediately. 'Well, why doesn't Jack do what Fred did, take on a helper? It wouldn't cost too much and it would continue the way of working that Fred used. After all, that was part of the reason that Fred took him on, to build a sort of continuity into the running of the place. I know it's only a small forge, but if anything happened to Fred, Jack might be out of work.'

Albert Stone would probably take over the management of it, Elsie thought, but he wouldn't work all the hours that God sends. He would just give the job to someone he knows. It might be a good idea if Jack tried to expand his activities in different ways from just working by the sweat of his brow. She put her thoughts to Ruth.

'My Dad explained a lot to me. He said that when a man is young, he works with his body, using his head to learn more about his work. As he gets older, he uses his head more and his body less. If he uses his head properly, he ends up just using his head, paying other men for the use of their bodies.'

The memory of her father saying the words made Elsie feel choked for a moment and she fell silent. After a moment, Ruth answered.

'Sounds to me that your old man had his head screwed on properly. It makes sense, don't it, that a young man seems to take more pleasure in the accomplishments of 'is body but an older man, having gained a bit o' common sense, what you might call wisdom, is able to make use of what experience he's picked up while he's been working 'is guts out.' She too, sat silent for a minute or two, and then went on. 'I think I'll 'ave a word with him about what you've been saying. He might see the sense of it. There's more to you than meets the eye, ain't there?'

Elsie sat for a second and then spoke.

'Another cup o' tea? Good, then I'll have to go and see Mary Bowyer. She's looking after little Tom for me, today. It helps me to get my work done.'

Ruth poured the tea. Elsie had had no need to remind Ruth that she worked for Sam Jenkins, Ruth's landlord, but it didn't do any harm to put the fact in front of her face, occasionally. Perhaps she would be more careful to keep her hands off her husband! Perhaps it was just a coincidence that Ruth was so friendly with Chalky. She made up her mind to mention it in passing.

'Have you always been so fond of animals, Ruth? I could see as I came down into the court that Chalky was fond of you.'

Elsie let the question hang in the air as Ruth absorbed it. Ruth sat as if in a small state of shock. She hadn't thought that an innocent stroke on the pony's muzzle might reveal her guilt.

'Ah, well, your husband, Mister Barr, sometimes brought the pony when he came to see Mrs Bowyer, and 'e left the pony standing outside. I couldn't help giving him an apple or a lump o' sugar; 'e loved it. You do see a lot with those pretty blue eyes, don't you?'

The way that she gave a detailed reason for her attention to the pony, convinced Elsie that she was covering up some sort of relationship with Dan. As Luke sometimes remarked, motivation and convenience sometimes go hand in hand, each a result of the other. Relationships were like cobwebs, starting with just a single thread of contact, and then developing into something that could not be reversed. Anyway, who am I to condemn?

The tea finished, Elsie helped put the crocks away and put on her coat.

'I must go and see Mary now, and pick up Tom. She'll wonder where I've got to. I've got to get home for Dan's dinner, as well. He's most particular about his dinner. I wouldn't want him to get dissatisfied with the way I look after him, not that he is. We have a very good marriage, something like you, Ruth, but you have to be there to make it work, and I was away far too long, I think.' She stood and turned to leave, then turned back and gave Ruth a hug. 'I value you as a friend, you know, Ruth. I should hate anything to come between us.'

Elsie left Ruth staring after her, silently.

Mary was sitting with Tom on her lap when Elsie entered the small house. Elsie recalled how she had thought the small back-to-back dwelling was crowded, when she had entered for the first time. Now she was more observant, she noticed how cleverly everything was put together to give the most convenience in the small space. After all, there were many families that raised five children or more, in the same amount of space. Though it was full, everything there was of a good quality.

Mary had never been ostentatious. She just liked to get the most out of every square foot, she said. She did not go along with the current fashion of acting as if the loss of Queen Victoria had been a personal loss, with evidence of mourning everywhere; she had to continue with her life. They had a few minutes together and then it was time to go.

'Come on, Tom,' Elsie said excitedly. 'Daddy will be home before us if we're not careful, and then he'll be angry and hungry. Daddy wants his dinner.'

She held out her arms to him and he came running across the room. She swept him up in her arms. 'Say 'bye bye' to Auntie Mary.'

Mary leaned across and gave him a quick kiss on the cheek, knowing that Elsie had to move swiftly to get back to Willenhall before Dan got home, or he might get annoyed and be in a bad mood. She kissed Elsie who whispered, 'I'll see you when I can.'

It really was time to go. She stepped outside. The little boy from the court had fed and watered Chalky. She put her hand into her purse and took out a penny.

'Here you are, son.'

The boy slipped it into his pocket and ran but as he turned the corner he shouted, 'I usually get tuppence!' and ran on.

Elsie smiled to herself and filed the remark away. When would he have got tuppence? Was he mixing her up with someone else? Was it all coincidence? She turned to look at Mary but she was just closing the door.

Chapter 24

Feelings and Frustrations

WEDNESBURY MAN ATTACKED ON TOW PATH! There was a billboard leaning on the wall with large letters on the headlines. The journey up to the High Bullen seemed slow as she assimilated the things that had happened during the day. As she passed the newspaper man on the corner, Elsie leaned over and took one from him.

The sight of the headlines made her feel faint and she could hardly hold the traces as they re-started. The incident was on the front page with continuation on the third. She allowed Chalky to resume his normal walk and then she let herself read the item

'Yesterday evening a Wednesbury man, John Thurston, 55, was found by Joseph Smith, 44, bargee, and his wife Ivy, 38 as they were moving a load of coal to Wednesbury. The boatman told our reporter, 'The horse gave me the first warning. We were making good time when all of a sudden he stopped, and wouldn't go another step. I got Ivy to hold the boat while I jumped off to see what the matter was. There was a man lying there. He looked as if he had suffered a terrible attack. There was blood all over him, I can tell you. I went up to the road and stopped a man on a horse and asked him to tell the police and a doctor as soon as he could, and he galloped away. He must have told somebody 'cos a policeman came inside ten minutes and said the man had been beat up. The doctor came soon after and we got the man up to the doctor's trap on a plank I got from my barge. The policeman asked me some questions and then 'e went away. I never seen so much blood. His leg looked broke as well. I hope the poor chap gets over it, though I can't see how he can, really.'

No explanation has been found for the crime, though the suggestion that it was an act of revenge for some act by the man, has been put forward. There are no suspects but the police say their investigations are making progress.

Elsie leaned over the side of the trap, desperately trying to prevent herself from vomiting. Although she had thought calmly about the possibility of this happening, she had never dreamed that she would feel like this. She felt mainly the guilt of starting the course of actions that had terminated in the terrible event. How could she have even considered it?

Then Elsie recalled how she had felt when Betty had told her how her father had sexually assaulted her – raped her, in fact, time and time again. At least that will not happen again, she thought. She started to calm down and think whether there could be any link that led back to her. The first thing she had to do was to make certain that the person injured was Betty's father, then she had to deny it – even to Betty.

Betty could easily drop a word out accidentally that would implicate Elsie's little circle, and they didn't deserve that any more than Betty had deserved what had happened to her. Elsie thought again: he had deserved it and she had better learn to live with the results. He was a bastard and he had got rough justice and if she had the chance, she would arrange it all over again!

Her feelings seemed to go from one extreme to another and back again, all in a few minutes. She took a grip on her emotions. There was nothing she could do about what had happened. It was history now. She determined to put it out of her mind as much as she could. The road from Wednesbury soon passed and before she knew where she was, she was leading Chalky out of his traces and into his stable.

As she drew up outside the stable, she saw that Dan was already home. She had dropped the newspaper on the road, determined that she would do nothing that made what she was doing out of the ordinary. She stepped into the small living room and as she did so, compared it with Mary Bowyer's little back-to-back dwelling. So much had happened today. He greeted her.

'You're late, tonight, Elsie. Have you had trouble?'

Elsie looked him straight in the face and replied, 'Yes, the collecting took longer than I thought. Mary sends her regards, as does Ruth Mallory.' Dan frowned as though he was trying to recall Ruth. 'You remember Ruth Mallory who lives by Aunt Mary?'

'Oh yes, I remember her. Doesn't her husband drink? Is that the one?'

Elsie moved to start getting their evening meal ready and he joined her as they moved into the kitchen. He pulled her close to him fiercely, putting his hand onto her breast. She turned to face him, feeling the moment, as she did at these times. Dan was very impulsive, taking his needs as and where he felt like it. Sometimes she enjoyed the encounter and sometimes she wanted to walk away, never to return.

He slid his hands up the back of her legs and lifted her up, moving her skirt out of the way as if it were nothing, until he was able to enter her. Then he moved into her body, his organ throbbing until he could not contain his passion. She felt him explode inside her and she broke away, feeling dirty and used.

'Well, you're a great lover aren't you?' Elsie exploded the

words in the same way that he had exploded inside her. 'Do you think you're the only one here, or would you rather you were by yourself - or perhaps with somebody else?'

Her words got through to him; she could see that. He denied it vehemently.

'I'm sorry, my love. I want you to have as much pleasure as me but the feeling is just too much for me. If I could hold back, I would, but I feel it would make less of you in some way.'

Dan turned and walked away, slamming the door of the house behind him as he went and somehow she felt that he was sincere, though it was no consolation to her frustrated self. She leaned on the door of the tiny kitchen and cried, the sobs accompanying her tears sounding a dirge of sadness.

At length, she settled a little and attempted to carry on with her chores, her hands and eyes reddening as she peeled the potatoes for her small family. Tom was crying for her and she could not bring herself to go to him until she had calmed down to a point where her appearance would not upset him. She moved to his side and picked him up tenderly.

'Oh, Tom,' she said. 'I do hope you have a better life than this.'

Elsie knew she wanted love and only rarely got it; not the way she defined love. The kind of love she wanted was a closeness of two people. She wanted a kindness, a laughing, a sharing kind of love, with more than a portion of passion and even disagreement, to show that each of the pair had some personality of their own. That had to come from a shared vitality and viewpoints. Sometimes, she thought she would never get her kind of love. The nearest she got to it was when she shared bodies and laughter with Stephen. Nothing else came near it.

Gradually her anger and frustration reduced itself until she could think of other aspects of her life. What had happened to Betty's father? How had it all been arranged? She knew that Luke had links with the so-called underworld of the Black Country. Had it been him that had, on her behalf, as a favour to her, arranged the loss of manhood for that poor unfortunate man? Why the hell should she care? He had certainly earned the punishment that had been meted out to him.

Elsie's heart hardened. Would Betty approve of what had been done? She wanted to know but she didn't want to be seen making enquiries. There had to be some way she could find out. Perhaps if she kept reading the reports there would be something in there. That was what she would do, unless something else came to mind.

What was the next problem? Was Dan having what they called an affair with Ruth? There was an easy way for her to get the answer to that question. She would ask Mary to keep an eye open for her. How could she ask Mary to do that? She knew that Mary respected Dan and if he were innocent, she didn't want to slander him by making a false accusation. How could she do it? She didn't want to ask another favour of Luke; she felt she had asked enough of him.

Life seemed full of problems and questions; was it always going to be like this? She was not really in a position to accuse Dan of anything. It would be hypocritical, in light of the way she felt about Stephen. Still, after today's performance, she couldn't be blamed for wanting something that any red-blooded woman wanted!

Next problem! How was she supposed to act with Dan when he came back from the pub? That was bound to be where he had gone. She'd be better occupied getting the evening meal. The potatoes were all scraped now so she put them in a saucepan with a little salt and put them in the hanging cauldron to boil. She'd had some lamb chops from the butcher in Wednesbury so she put them in the fireplace oven. They would soon roast in there, and if he didn't like it, he could do what he wished. She was fed up of hoping for a more kindly, loving relationship from Dan.

There was nothing to hang her hat on, to say why she was dissatisfied with him. Dan was no better and certainly no worse than thousands of other Black Country working men. Most of them did what they considered was their best for their families, working long arduous hours in dreadful conditions. There was no obvious way out of the vicious circle of work and sleep, with too much of the one and not enough of the other.

The skills the men had to learn were the skills involving hand and brain coordination, filing, chiselling, and handling hot and sharp pieces of metal, all to be accomplished with as little damage to the hands as possible. It was difficult to avoid all accidents so it was not uncommon to see men with the loss or use of various parts of the body; a finger, hand, or an eye, through the damage caused by hot and sharp slivers of iron, steel or brass.

Elsie suddenly felt that, although she hadn't grown much older, she had gained about ten years in the last few months, facing problems that many didn't face in a lifetime. Tom was three years old now, and getting brighter and fuller of energy every day. The world had passed her by; she had been so full of what she had been doing that she had not paid much attention to what had happened in the wide world just beyond her own immediate access. Dan usually kept her informed but she had not been home from Bromyard long enough for any of what he told her, to sink in.

It was time to be getting ready for bed and he was not home yet. He would be drunk when he did. She picked Tom up.

'Come on, son. Let's get you to bed before your father gets home and decides to let his temper out on you.'

Elsie knew that Dan had a temper and the force of it made many men back down before it. Although he attended church occasionally, he still liked to spend a couple of nights a week, drinking at the local pub. He sometimes found himself in the centre of a drunken brawl and he had the reputation of being a good exponent of the art of fisticuffs. For that reason she was very wary of him when he came home the worse for alcohol. She made her way up the narrow stairs and put Tom down into the bottom of the bed where he usually lay.

'There you are, little Tom. I love you more than any man I know. You ain't been spoilt by drink or work. I'll try to see that you ain't spoilt, either. You have to grow up big and strong like your father. I'll make sure you do! Goodnight son. See you in the morning.'

He was wrapped up safely in the big blanket. The blanket had been almost a gift from one of her tenants on the High Street. There were not many who had blankets of such quality. Elsie was learning to be a bit more careful how she accepted these 'gifts', knowing that they were a way of getting some sort of favour from her. What they usually wanted was a little of her time in the back room of their shop!

Tom looked up at his mother, the one who always cared for him, and developed just a little further, the unique bond that would develop into love. The blanket was warm and enveloped the child with its slightly luxurious caress. His eyes gradually closed as he drifted off into an innocent sleep. Dan didn't seem to realise the benefits that accrued from her little part-time job for Mister Jenkins! She laid her head on the pillow and dreamed and thought of the things that had happened recently. She had been through a lot – and without the help of her husband. He was too busy looking after his own affairs!

Like Tom, she was worn out with the tribulations of the day. She lay back and hoped that Dan wouldn't be in too difficult a mood when he returned. She went down stairs and laid out the evening meal and picked at her own. Tom had had a small snack of yesterday's stew which he always enjoyed. She made her way back upstairs. Dan's dinner was in the fire oven, keeping warm. It was eleven o'clock before she heard his unsteady feet on the stairs. She could have picked out the sound of his footfall from a thousand others.

There was a bustling movement beside her as he got into bed. His arm went across her body to tell her that everything was all right with them. A moment later he was asleep, his breath getting louder and louder as he gradually cast off what ever had made him lose his temper earlier on. The moon shone on Elsie as she lay in its light, gradually losing consciousness as she conjured up other scenarios where she would be the most important character in a cast of two!

Chapter 25

Betty and Ruth
1910

The next morning, Elsie tried to appear as if what had happened the day before had been wiped clean from her memory. She got up at six o'clock and prepared the breakfast for Dan and herself without saying a bad word. Tom was, as usual, the centre of attention for both of them, laughing, as he did, at most things. Like his father, she supposed.

Dan went out at his usual time and Elsie immediately started getting ready for her trip to Wednesbury. She needed to see Aunt Mary, to ask for her help in regard to Ruth Mallory and her relationship with Dan. She also wanted to see Luke to find out what she should do with regard to Betty and her father's attack. There would be plenty of people talking about the assault and some of the traders might know where Betty and John Thurston lived.

The weather was so stormy that Elsie had to wrap up in her oilskins to prevent both of them becoming drenched but Chalky took it all in his stride. She thought about him; he was a wonderful animal, always reliable regardless of weather or terrain. They drew up in the court where Mary lived and she let the pony's traces dangle as she lifted her son down.

'You're early this morning, love. Is there something the matter?' Elsie turned and Mary was standing in the doorway, smiling. 'Come and have a cup o' tea with we. You can tell me all about it then.'

Her smile made Elsie seem better and she could not refuse her an acknowledgement.

'You always seem to know when there is something wrong, Mary. I do have things on my mind so I might as well tell you about them, and then you can lay them to rest.'

She fastened Chalky to the pump in the middle of the yard and followed Mary into her house. There was a teapot full of tea on the cast-iron hob and Mary bent to lift it, her back obviously aching from the effort of bending. Elsie noted it but said nothing, just watching as Mary poured the tea and, sitting back into her armchair, looked pointedly at Elsie.

'Now, my girl, tell me all your troubles. I've encountered most things in a lifetime and I've always found that if you can find someone you trust to share them with, an answer will present itself. Let me guess: is it anything to do with Dan?' Elsie stared. 'No, it's nothing clever to guess at the husband when there's trouble. Most women have stresses and strains that way. I did, and you are not so much different to me.' She waited a moment. 'So; what is it, then Elsie?'

Which problem should she put forward first for advice? Elsie almost tried to put the two together.

'It's Dan; it's not having any love, you know what I mean. He only tries to please himself and I come nowhere. I need love as well. I'm not the only woman who likes to love, am I? He don't seem to think I might have feelings as well as him. It's not fair!'

Elsie broke down, showing for the first time the extent of her feelings. For a moment, Mary stayed where she was and then pulled the younger woman to her arms, lovingly.

'There; there. It'll all come out in the wash. Your man just needs more practice; more, and more often. The other thing of course is that you might see Stephen again. He might not be any better as a lover than Dan, but at least, between them, you would be having a better time, wouldn't you?'

Mary laughed. She reminded Elsie of her nephew; always laughing.

'Love doesn't have to be grim, you know. You can make it a bright and pleasant time of experience in the happier side of life, whatever the church and their rules might say. What I say is, if you're going to have to wait 'til the next life before you are going to be punished, enjoy the life you are living. My brother always says it's better to die living than to live dying. There, that's that problem solved. Now, what's the next one? Come on, let's hear it.'

Again she fell silent and Elsie found that in the face of the advice she was being given, she was having difficulty in running her husband down – and was having difficulty running her friend Ruth down. She had to try to make her friend an evil, anonymous woman, and she couldn't so she made a fictitious character seduce Dan.

When she had finished, Mary smiled again.

'There you are again, worrying about so little. The more time he spends with her, whoever she is, the more he will be under control when he is with you. There's just one thing. Just because I've advised you to go to Stephen for a bit of love, it doesn't mean that you have to give your rights away! I'll certainly keep my eyes open and let you know if I find anything out. When I do, I'll let you know what to do about it. Right, that's that! Is there anything else? Surely not! There is! I can see it in your eyes. What is it then? Spit it out.'

Elsie looked her in such a mournful way that Mary burst out laughing.

'What is it now?'

Elsie whispered the name that kept coming to her lips. She wanted to say Ruth's name but didn't want to pronounce it. Mary leaned forward in order to hear her more clearly and in the end she heard. She drew in her breath sharply and sat immoveable, it seemed. She seemed to be thinking.

'Ruth. Did I hear you say Ruth?'

Elsie nodded her head, obviously in profound misery. Mary leaned back and laughed.

'Do you think she'd clutter life up with the likes of your Dan? Compared to Ruth, he's just a boy! She's got too much to think about, what with her kids and her husband. Don't you realise how much you've helped that woman? She owes you her very home, don't she? If it wasn't for what you've done for her, she'd be homeless, her kids'd be in the workhouse and her husband would probably be lying dead in some pauper's grave.'

Elsie looked up at her aunt and friend. Could it be that her most serious worry was about to go flying away? It was true that she had given a helping hand to the woman but she had not thought much more about it. Nothing in her experience had taught her that people who had been helped would show any sort of gratitude. She felt the sides of her mouth start to curl up and a feeling of something like happiness came over her.

'Why do I think she might be playing around with my Dan then, Mary?'

'God only knows, our Elsie. Sometimes we almost bring about the thing that we fear most. Maybe that's what you've done. Anyway, you'd be all right, even if he was knocking it off with her. I know there's somebody who would look after you; you wouldn't have to worry, so why worry?' She sat back for a moment, and then continued, her face becoming more serious. 'Next problem? What other worries have you to put before me, Elsie? Let's have 'em all together, shall we?'

There was one, deadly serious problem left at the end of her list. Elsie sat for nearly a minute then blurted it out.

'Mary, I think I might have been the cause of a poor man getting beat up!'

Elsie tried to explain how she thought she had been involved in the incident on the tow-path. She knew she did not have to go into great detail for Mary to understand. Mary read the newspaper each evening and would certainly have seen the report of Jack Thurston's attack.

Elsie had not gone far before Mary shut her up.

'Wait a minute, Elsie. Instead of letting it all come out, let me ask you questions. In that way, you will not have to let too much out of the bag, if you understand what I mean. Now, is it anything to do with any of the people we have been talking about? No? Then it must be to do with somebody else, yes? Good. Now we are getting somewhere.' She stopped again and looked at Elsie's pale face. It was ashen and her hands were hanging at her sides. She was in no real condition to answer questions but Mary asked her, all the same.

'Has somebody been hurt, Elsie? Is that it?' She seemed to have an instant of prophecy. 'Who is it that has been hurt?' She had stopped asking indirect questions now and was firing them direct. 'Who is it? Is it anyone I know?' She looked again as Elsie shook her head. A thought seemed to cross her mind.

'Is it that man who was attacked on the tow-path, him that was in the newspaper?' She could see from Elsie's expression that she had hit the target. She moved to another approach. 'Do you know why he was attacked? Oh, no; it's your friend from the hop-picking isn't it?'

Mary saw the despairing look on her young friend's face. At last the secret was out. It was the abusing father of Elsie's friend who had been attacked! How could she best help and support Elsie? She had heard about the incident as she often did, from her own sources, but she hadn't linked it with Elsie's worries.

Mary had no sympathy for Thurston. No one did, really; at least he would never carry out the same sort of attack in the future. That was why she supported hanging for murder; they never did it again. Maybe there was an occasional miscarriage of justice when an innocent man was sent to the gallows. It was terrible that that happened but better that way than a man – or woman, who had got used to the pleasures of murder, got away with the crime and continued at their leisure.

Mary thought about the sort of life that the girl, Betty, had been forced to live. The thought made her shudder. How Betty had put up with it, heaven knows. The man was still in hospital. They would have to nurse Thurston through the healing process, and then let him out into the world again. There would be attempts by the police, to get him to confess to something, anything that would give them a sort of clue to the perpetrator – perpetrator of what had been described as a horrendous crime.

The two women were sitting quite still, the older one trying to find a way to put the younger one's mind at rest; the younger one glad the incident had happened but not knowing whether her view of the crime would meet with much sympathy. At last, Elsie expressed her opinion.

'Aunt Mary, I know it was a terrible thing that happened to Mister Thurston but I can't find any real pity for him in my heart. If you'd heard Betty pour out her story to me, you'd have felt the same. Whenever he felt like it, often when he'd had a drink, he used to sneak into her room and just take her, like an animal! She cried her heart out when she told me, and I cried my heart out too, just from listening to it, never mind feeling what she had had to feel! I hope he rots in hospital 'til the day he dies!'

Elsie sat there, her hands in her lap, wondering if she should feel ashamed of her feelings, but not feeling any sort of second-hand remorse for the fiend. At the end of all her thoughts she had no regrets for the condition of the man.

Mary leaned across and placed her hand on Elsie's cheek, in an attempt to soften the deeply etched lines that had appeared there since her discovery of the crime.

'Listen Elsie, sometimes, just sometimes, we're able to influence the course of unofficial justice and arrange a punishment that somehow seems appropriate. When that happens, you shouldn't feel guilty, you should feel proud. After all, it wasn't a woman who actually carried out the punishment, was it? It was a man. Now just stop feeling guilty about the evil bastard! It would have been no good just threatening the man, after all, would it? He wouldn't have given up his pleasures, would he?

'What we have to do is make sure that no suspicion falls on us or any associate of ours. What you have to do is to say nothing, and I mean nothing!' She emphasised the point she was making with a sweep of her hand. 'If anybody says anything to you, you just say what a terrible thing it was for a man to be attacked like that. There's no reason at all why you have to keep away from Betty. After all, you were friends in Bromyard, weren't you? What you must not do, in any circumstances, is to admit anything, or take any credit for what happened. Betty may think what she likes but she must be discouraged from thinking you were instrumental in getting Thurston beat up. If you should happen to meet the man, give him all the sympathy you feel able to. Do you understand the position you're in? You and I know what happened, and that, with the other people you haven't mentioned, is enough.

'We women have enough troubles without looking for more. Look what they've done to that woman in Winston Green. They're going to have an enquiry about it.' Elsie looked blank. 'Winson Green is a prison in Birmingham. A woman, Laura Ainsworth, I think, was serving a fortnight's sentence for 'obstructing the police' when Lloyd George went to visit Birmingham. She went on hunger strike like a lot o' women are doing now, and they actually force-fed the poor woman! They clamped her mouth open and put a cork gag in, to keep it that way and then they put a two-foot tube into her. I don't think it'll happen again once the board of enquiry hears of the offensive way those men went about things.' She looked across at Elsie who was staring at her as if she did not know her. 'Right, any more problems? All right, you'd better get on with your work then. Come on, Tom; let's have a look at Mommy driving Chalky down the court.'

Mary led the way out of the house to where the pony and trap were standing. Chalky lifted his head to her in greeting and Elsie climbed the step into the driving seat and spoke to Chalky.

'Walk on.'

The pony turned in his traces and headed for the bustle of Union Street. She turned right to let him have a draught of water from the trough at the bottom of the street and then started on her usual round, meeting men and women she knew, passing the time of day. The day seemed somehow surreal; as if reality was made up from the things she had read about while what happened in front of her eyes was nothing more than a magic lantern show. Elsie had the feeling that Mary had only told her a tiny amount of what she knew about Betty and her father.

The day passed slowly as she got down to the serious business of the day, the rent for the investors in Jenkins and Co. Elsie was one of them herself, so she ought to do her duty to herself, she thought. She walked down the High Street and it was then that she saw Betty. She was obviously shopping and she hadn't seen Elsie yet. A moment later she had, though, and she crossed the street, dodging the horse traffic on the cobbles. It was still raining gently and that, perhaps, was what made her slip. Down she went and Elsie dashed through the people to help her back to her feet. Betty looked at her and then recognised her.

It was as if the two things were separate activities, the look and then the recognition.

'Elsie!' Betty spoke the word as if it was a prayer. She climbed to her feet and looked Elsie full in the face. 'I thought I'd never see you again. I always knew you were brave from when I saw you save Mister Walker when that man tried to kill him, down at the farm, but I never thought you'd do for my Dad!'

Elsie was astonished. Betty thought she had had her father beat up! She did not have a chance to reply, as Betty continued, 'The police have been to see me three times and have asked me loads of questions, but I never even mentioned your name. They seem to think it might have been some bloke who he owes money to. Dad has recovered a bit, and I'm expecting him to be coming out of hospital soon. One good thing has come out of it; he's not likely to visit me in the night again for a long time, is he?' Betty giggled and then changed the direction of her conversation. 'How are you getting on, Elsie? I can't tell you how grateful I am to you for changing my life for me.'

Betty stopped to get her breath and Elsie took the opportunity to speak.

'Listen, Betty. I guessed what you might think but I had nothing to do with what happened to your father. I've worried myself sick about what I could do to help you but I couldn't think of anything I could do. For goodness sake, don't be so grateful. I've done nothing to deserve it!'

She stood, denying the crime as strongly as she could.

'Of course you haven't, Elsie. I'm not that daft. I knew you'd say that. I've got to go now. I'm helping to work one of the stalls on the market, the big rattler in the middle. You know, the one who throws his crocks up in the air, the rattler.

If you ever need anything doing, or a new tea-set, a proper china one, mind you, just come and see me. I've had a brand new set for myself for half a crown, including all the dinner stuff as well. Thanks for helping me up. I'd have gone arse over tip if you hadn't. It really is nice to see you. Tara, Missus Barr.'

Before Elsie could say anything, Betty had disappeared into the crowd and Elsie did not feel inclined to follow her. It was obvious that the woman really thought that she had played a part in meting out punishment to Thurston. It had changed her, too. She seemed more confident now, as if life was more precious and meaningful to her.

As Elsie moved through the crowds, dropping into a shop here and there to collect rent from the proprietors, the thought suddenly hit her. She had been instrumental in the incident! She had to face the fact that she had asked Luke to help and give her advice and look what had happened since! What was he likely to say when she saw him in the office? It was obvious, really; he would deny any knowledge of the affair. He would take the same attitude with her as she had with Betty, and that had been on the advice of her Auntie Mary. There was no point in even mentioning it to him.

Elsie was getting everything into perspective, now, and was beginning to understand that she had a lot of power in her hands if she wanted to use it. It was quite frightening. Her investments were beginning to pay off and if she looked into the future, she could see that she might be a powerful person in the town. Did she want it? Yes, of course she did! It was always useful to be able to get your own way when it suited but it was nicer still to be able to do something in the background, to melt into the general view of things, to be just a housewife, out shopping like hundreds of others. That was what she would do in future. She would be a Nobody!

Chapter 26

Losses
1910 – 1911

It was October; her twenty-first birthday was approaching, next month. Elsie was to get a few extra privileges then but she didn't feel it would make much difference to her life. Luke had intimated to her that that she could soon become a director in her own firm but she was content to let Aunt Mary carry on looking after her affairs until she achieved her majority; that was the best strategy.

The year had been a different one, with the King dying earlier in the year and his funeral on the twentieth of May. Elsie recalled how she had felt on the day she heard of his death. Although he was ruler of the greatest empire in history and thus had great responsibilities, he had not forgotten how to enjoy his life, and most of the world knew it. She felt a strong loyalty and closeness to him and it made her wonder if she should emulate him, living her life with as much participation as possible. It also made her realise that some beings were missed more than others when they died, and it was nothing to do with their status. She was going to miss the news of his latest escapade; he was a loss to the country.

I would sooner die living than live dying, she said to herself, and it became, if not her motto, her creed, as it had been for Fred Stone. Surely, if the king can have fun without being pilloried, I can have the little of love I can find?

November the sixteenth, her twenty-first birthday, came and went. Dan bought her a new scarf. The day was otherwise brightened by Aunt Mary giving her a copy of Samuel Smiles, 'Self Help'. The next day, a card came from the Stone family, wishing her all the best for her life as an adult. She felt sure that Stephen had been party to it, and the cryptic message it contained.

As Christmas approached, Aunt Mary became ill and was admitted to hospital. Visiting was not allowed because of the infectious nature of her disease. It was New Year before Elsie could visit her and then only for a few minutes. The sight that Mary presented to her was shocking. She had lost a lot of her body weight and her body was weak. Her breathing was laboured and she seemed to have lost her sparkle.

Slowly Mary recovered and in February was allowed home. Elsie visited her constantly, keeping the small house in the way Mary wanted it. She took a temporary lease on a small house in the same court as Mary, at a reduced rent, much to Dan's annoyance. Each day, after Elsie saw Dan off to work on his bicycle, she would carry out her tasks for the firm of solicitors. Then, she would go to Mary and sit with her, talking of Mary's youth, and the way she had started to be an investor.

'I was something like you when I was a young girl,' Mary told her protégée, 'always wanting to do the right thing in life, always wanting to be popular and hard-working at the same time. Then my parents became ill and died. There was nothing I could have done about the way they were. I was sixteen; I had a house to keep and the rent to pay. Somehow I did, and got wind of a job where hard work and attention to detail paid well. It was with my uncle! I went to see him, Mister Jenkins Senior; he's dead now, God bless him. He gave me a job and allowed me to keep living in the house that Mom had raised me in. He showed me how to save money and gave me a copy of the book that I gave you.' Mary coughed and the cough seemed to rock her feeble frame. 'Hand me that glass of water, please, Elsie. Thank you. As I was saying, he gave me a job and taught me a thing or two, the same as Luke is showing you. You just pay attention, my girl, to what he tells you. There is more to investing than meets the eye.'

The elderly woman lay back on her pillow and closed her eyes. Just sitting up and talking seemed to be too much for her, lately. Elsie was suddenly frightened for the future. What would she do if she lost her Aunt Mary? The year suddenly seemed a sad one. She lay back against the wing of the armchair and rested her eyes. When she opened them again, Mary was tapping her arm with her stick.

'Elsie, Elsie, it's five o'clock. You'd better get home, soon. You've been asleep for three hours!'

The older woman seems to be more awake than me, thought Elsie. Which one was supposed to be ill? Dan would be home at half past six, and would expect his dinner to be ready for him. He had no idea what work Elsie put in during the course of a day. She stood up and bent over her Aunt.

'Thank you for waking me, Mary. I shall be in to see you tomorrow.'

She banked up the fire with small coals to keep it going for the night. The winter seemed to come right into the house. She kissed her Aunt and stepped outside. There had been a small fall of snow. She stepped into it and made her way to her own house. There was a lot to be done. As she stepped across the court to her house she heard a cough from somewhere. It was Ruth Mallory.

'Hello, Elsie. How's your Aunt? You're keeping some hours just lately.'

'She seems to be gradually improving, thank you Mrs Mallory. Thank you for asking.' They looked at each other, almost formally and then Elsie spoke. 'How are you, anyway? I see things have looked up for you, now. I'm so glad they have. I was really worried for you that time when I had to see you with Mister Bryant.'

'Yes, thanks to you, things are much better now. Jack has stopped drinking, and he's been regular since Mister Stone took him on at the forge. I owe you a lot an' I'll never forget it.'

They looked at each other, two women with feelings and a man in common, and each knew they were linked by more than just casual friendship; it was almost as if they were family.

They separated and made their way home to carry on with the work of the day. There was much to do for each of them. It was dark and the middle of winter but their tasks would not wait. Elsie peeled potatoes and prepared a stew. There was nothing Dan liked better than a stew when he got home. When she had put the stew into the large cooking pot that hung over the fire, she went into the scullery and chopped kindling wood for the fire. Her back ached; there was so much to do lately.

Dan would be late tonight, in the snow. The bicycle would be hard to control, and he would have a job to see where he was going in the swirling wind. This year's weather seemed to be no better than the last. He'd had one accident; she didn't want him to have another.

Life seemed to be hard. How Mary managed, she could not see. She had been surprised to learn of the older woman's earlier difficulties in life. She had been a spinster or a widow for most her life and had learned to carry out all the tasks that a husband would have been expected to perform.

Had Mary ever found a man friend, Elsie wondered? She had always been a very attractive woman, with a vivacious nature. Surely men would have been drawn to her like moths to a flame. Old Albert Stone always paid her a lot of attention when they visited the family at Willenhall! Elsie speculated on the possibilities of the relationship, and then gave it up. There had never been a hint of anything there.

Elsie was ready for Dan now. He would be home soon. She looked at the clock; it was seven o'clock. He was late. She put an Oxo into a cup and stirred hot water into it to make a revitalising drink. On impulse she reached for a large mug and crumbled another of the small beef stock cubes into it. Perhaps Dan would appreciate a hot drink when he came in.

Elsie recalled the last time Dan had been late. Had he hurt himself again? The thought came to her that he might have had to work late. He did, occasionally, although not for some weeks. Whatever the cause of his lateness, he still remained at the front of her mind. He might have done this; he might have done that; you never knew with men; he might be working his eyeballs out or he might be drunk in some pub on the way back from Willenhall.

Dan had decided to move back to Wednesbury with her when she had moved into the small house to be near Mary. Elsie couldn't keep away from her Auntie Mary and Dan couldn't keep away from Elsie either! It was just that it was further for him to travel. Another thought came to her. Was he with some woman? Could it be Ruth? The thought came with a rush of air into her lungs, making her gasp. Surely he wouldn't be unfaithful to her now.

She decided to go to call on Ruth, to try to ascertain whether he was there. It was only a few steps across the yard and into the small house. She could hear children talking as she passed over the threshold, but no men's voices. Where was Jack? She turned and made her way out again and then turned and knocked the door. She pushed it and spoke as loudly as she could without shouting.

'Ruth! Hello, Ruth!'

There was the sound of movement from the back room and Ruth came through the adjoining door. Her face was welcoming.

'Hello, Elsie, come on in. We're just waiting for Jack to come 'ome. He's late tonight. I wonder where he's got to.' There was a questioning look on her face. 'Do you know something I don't know, Elsie? You must be here for some reason.'

Elsie didn't know how to answer her. The woman was innocent and her husband was missing too!

'I'm just looking for Dan, hoping you might have heard something. He's late home from work as well and you know what happened before. He fell off his bike in the snow, remember? We thought he'd broken his ankle!'

Elsie sat down by the fire and wondered where the two men were. It was now almost nine o' clock. They should both have been home hours ago. Where were they? Ruth picked up the heavy kettle from the hook over the fire and poured boiling water into the teapot. She turned to her sons.

'Come on, you two, you should be in bed now. I've told you twice!'

Her voice carried when she raised it.

'Goodnight, Mrs Barr. Goodnight Mom.'

They spoke in unison and disappeared, laughing their way up the stairs into the darkness. The two women picked up their cups and sipped at the tea. They sat in silence for a few minutes, each thinking thoughts about their men. There was a sound of the front door opening. Jack's voice came through, loud and clear.

'Hello, love. Pour me a cup o' tea. I'm parched.'

'That's a relief anyway. It's just wonderful to know he ain't been drinking.'

Ruth smiled at Elsie, who suddenly felt unwanted now.

'I'm going now. Wait a minute. Perhaps Jack knows where Dan is. Perhaps they've been together.'

Elsie walked through into the front room.

'Hello, Jack. How are you? You look well considering the weather. How's Fred?'

Jack Mallory looked at her strangely and then answered.

'Well, I'm fine, Elsie. I've just seen your old man going into your house. He's all right, if you've been wondering about him.'

There was something about the way he spoke that prevented her asking further questions. She ought to be normal.

'Oh well, I'll be off then, Jack.' She raised her voice. 'Goodnight Ruth. I expect I'll see you in the morning.'

Elsie pushed past him and went into the darkness without a backward glance. It was only a few yards across the court to her little house. She marched in. Dan was sitting by the fire looking into the flames. He looked up as she entered.

'Hello, Elsie. I wondered where you were. What have we got for dinner?'

Just like him, she thought. Not a word about where he'd been until this time. Why can't he think? He'd soon complain if she wasn't in. He'd only to look in the pot to see what was for dinner. She turned on him.

'The last time you were this late, you'd fallen off your bike. D'you remember? I was looking for you. I've just been over to Ruth. Jack has just come in late as well. I suppose you've been somewhere together. Is it a secret?'

There was a sort of defiant bravado in his voice as Dan replied.

'No; it's not a secret. We've been finding out about the Territorial Army. You get paid for going for a few nights' training you know. We could do with a few bob more, couldn't we?'

Not a thought for her day; all he had been thinking about was how to get a few bob more for his drinking. There was no likelihood that she was going to get the benefit of it if he did decide to enrol, enlist or whatever they did to join. It would just suit Dan; it would take him away from the house and he'd get the chance to exert his forceful way over the others in his section or whatever else they called it.

They had been advertising for men to join the Staffordshire Regiment as part-timers, Elsie knew. He always went on about wanting to be a foreman at Stones' but the nearest he'd got to it was to be made an unpaid charge-hand. Perhaps this would be an opportunity for him to advance himself, as he called it.

'How did you come to make up your mind to do that, Dan? You've never said anything about it before.'

She'd better try not to sound too discouraging otherwise he might take it out on her. When he didn't answer her, she asked him another question.

'Did you meet Jack Mallory then? I can just see you two in uniform! Mind you, you would look real good in khaki. Have you made up your mind, then?'

'No, I haven't really. I just saw Jack and we got talking about the sign telling you all about it. We went to see what was going on but there were only one or two there and it hardly seemed worthwhile. Perhaps if there was a war on the way I might consider it. I'll think about it – whatever you think about the way I look in khaki!' Dan smiled at her across the little room. 'I've got too much to do here to think about gallivanting about with Jack Mallory. Mind you, he don't drink now.

'He's a changed man since he went to work for Fred Stone. He practically runs that place now, so I've heard. How's Mary? The last time I spoke to you about her, she was low in health. Is she any better now?'

They spoke about Mary for some time and Elsie was relieved in a way that Dan was not immediately joining up in the Army.

*

The nurse who had been employed on a temporary basis answered the door as Elsie pushed it. She was very experienced and had come highly recommended.

'Mrs Bowyer is pretty low,' she said. 'The doctor's not long gone and he doesn't seem to be very happy about her. That pneumonia she had has brought her down, you know. Go on up. You know where she is, I dare say.'

The spring had come without seeing much of an improvement in Mary and Elsie immediately felt the anxiety she always felt if there was a downturn in Mary's condition. She flew up the stairs to where Mary was lying in bed, her face pale and drawn. It was obvious that she was very ill. Elsie looked round to see if there was anything that needed doing or buying. Everything was in order.

'Oh Mary, I've only just heard you're poorly again. What's the matter?' All of a sudden, it became too much for her and she knelt at the side of the bed and held her hands together. 'Dear Jesus, please protect this woman from illness. She has the same name as your Mother, surely that entitles her to a bit of help.'

Elsie remained on her knees as the events of the day caught up with her. First Dan and now Mary! What a night! Her sobs disturbed Mary who opened her eyes and looked at Elsie.

'Whatever's the matter, Elsie? I've only just been able to get a bit of rest. The doctor gave me some Linctus for my cough. I was coughing all night, last night. Mrs Jones, Martha, fetched the doctor in this afternoon and I've started to get a bit better since I've been taking the Linctus.'

Elsie admired Mary's courage as she lay, trying to comfort her! Mary had become such an important figure in her life that she seemed to be another mother to her. How long could she hold out, Elsie wondered. She tried to change the tone of the conversation, telling Mary of Dan's idea about joining the Army. Mary paid attention to what she was saying, and then she interrupted.

'Listen, Elsie, I've been thinking about Dan. Life is going to be very difficult for him soon, and I want him to feel good about me. I know you've always kept secrets from him so I shall make a gift to him. No, don't interrupt. I know you want your own independence, but so does Dan, so I've made sure that he'll always be reliant on the Stones' to give him work. I'll leave him a certain sum of money that only he will know about and receiving that should leave him less curious about your affairs.' Mary lay back on her pillow. 'I'd like to get some sleep now if you don't mind, Elsie. Marjory, the nurse, has agreed to stay the night with me. I'll see you tomorrow after you have finished your work for Mister Bowyer.'

Elsie bent over her recumbent form and kissed her gently on the forehead.

'Goodnight then, Aunt, if I must go. I'll see you as soon as I finish work tomorrow. God bless you. Thank you, God, for what you are doing. Let me know if you need anything.'

Elsie hurried back to her own house where Ruth was supposed to be playing with Tom. She turned to Elsie. 'He ain't half coming on, Elsie. He'll be going to school soon, I shouldn't wonder. I've put him up, now. See you tomorrow.'

Elsie crept up the stairs to the attic and looked in at Tom. He was fast asleep at the bottom of his bed.

She went back down again to lie by Dan. The night seemed to get warmer as the snow melted in the early hours. At six o'clock she awoke naturally. It was still dark. She looked to see how Dan was and saw that he was no longer in bed. She went quietly down the stairs, peered round the dark room and saw him, He was cutting slices of bread; getting ready for work.

'Morning, Dan,' she whispered. 'How are you feeling?'

It was unusual for him to be preparing his lunch at six o'clock! He turned and looked at her.

'I'm all right you know. I just think I've got a bit of a cold. I'll soon be on the way to work.'

Elsie pulled back the corner of the curtain and looked out. It was raining.

'You can't go out to cycle all the way to Willenhall in this weather. I'll get Chalky out to take us. Tom and I'll go home and when you finish work you can come home in the trap and I'll have dinner with you and that will be that. I'll look in on Aunt Mary during the day, to make sure she doesn't need anything.'

It was the perfect answer. It was extra miles for Chalky but he could do it. If not, he would be close to a stable where he could rest for a while. She mounted the stairs and woke Tom. He was quite sleepy so she wrapped a blanket round him and carried him down the stairs with his day clothes over her arm. Elsie threw her coat on and prepared to go and fetch him from his stable in the High Street. She spoke to Tom, 'Stay with your father for a little while,' she said, 'and then we can go for a drive with Chalky.'

Elsie gave her son a smile and left the house. It was cold but at least it was warmer than it had been for the last few days. In a few minutes she was back, the pony steaming from the sudden exposure to the elements. Tom was getting heavy now, she noticed. It wouldn't be long before she would be able to get him to do one or two little jobs around the house; she had no intention of bringing him up idle.

Dan wobbled for a minute as he came out of the little house and then he seemed to gather strength. It was as if he knew he wouldn't be able to spend the day sitting around so he might as well show willing. Elsie smiled at her own thoughts. For all she knew he might not be thinking that way at all! He might really want to go to work!

The journey through the snow took them about an hour. When they got to Willenhall, Dan gave both of them a quick kiss and then he was off to work a ten hour day. She had meant to go into their own house but she felt that Aunt Mary would need her so she immediately turned the trap back towards Wednesbury and drove at a fast pace. The roads were thawing out now so there was no danger, just the chance of getting wet from the spray coming from other vehicles.

At half past eight they were back in the court off Union Street. It was time to start work. She lifted Tom down and carried him into Mary's house. She was sitting by the fire, drinking a cup of tea, as usual. Her face was a little flushed, it seemed to Elsie, but apart from that she seemed to be better than the night before.

'Are you sure you're all right, Aunt?' Elsie asked. 'You do seem a bit red round the cheeks to me. I hope you're not spinning me stories, you know. And another thing; what's all this about giving money to Dan? He's done nothing to earn it and he will probably send it splashing up the wall!' She stopped, realising the sort of language she was using to her aunt. 'I'm sorry, Aunt Mary, but it just gets me mad to see what you have worked and invested for going to waste!'

Mary chuckled and held out her hands to Elsie.

'Listen, my girl, I know you believe in the fair distribution of wealth and that those who work the hardest should get the most but it doesn't always work out like that. Sometimes those who play a supporting role have to be rewarded for their contribution. Dan has supported you and your child to the best of his ability – and that is without the possibility that he is supporting the bastard child of his employer! He should be rewarded for that, don't you think?'

Elsie just sat there, taking in what Mary was telling her. She was right! The feeling of guilt came back to her. What have I done? Dan should have what he was entitled to. There was one advantage about Mary's plan; if Mary did what she was suggesting, Dan would never know that his wife was becoming a rich woman by the use of her brain and her physical strength. She would be safe from his suspicion for years, maybe forever. He wouldn't want to discuss money questions because she might want to ask questions too!

The young woman nodded to show Mary that she understood the thoughts behind her words. With a bit of luck Dan wouldn't get to inherit for many years yet, hopefully never.

'I have to go now, Mary,' she said. 'I've a lot of work to do, today. Are you sure you'll be all right with young Tom? I'll be finished as soon as I can. Is Ruth still popping in to see you at night?'

'Yes, she never misses; she seems to think a lot of you, for some reason. Perhaps she still has fantasies about Dan!' She chuckled at the change of expression on Elsie's face. 'Seriously, Ruth calls in and makes sure I'm comfortable, as she puts it. She really is a nice woman and I'm sure you have nothing to worry about as far as Ruth and your husband is concerned.' She turned to Tom. 'Come here, young man. Come and sit on Mary's lap and watch Mommy through the window. You just get off with you, Elsie. If you've got a lot to do, you'd better make a start at it, hadn't you?'

Elsie conceded. Mary was not going to give up no matter how badly she felt. The snow had nearly all gone when she got outside so she was able to make a good start with her work. The day passed quickly; the traders all seemed pleased to see her for a change. People were now getting used to a woman performing what used to be the sole right of men to accomplish.

Women were the real heroines, nowadays, she thought. Look at Mary and the way she just carries on with whatever she has put her mind to. Look at Florence Nightingale. She had been buried with all honours a few weeks ago. Even Alexandra, the Queen Mother, had sent her a floral tribute, along with the survivors of the charge of the Light Brigade. Perhaps soon, women would be admitted as equal partners of the country, with equal responsibilities recognised, to be given places in the House of Parliament!

The day passed and she picked up Tom from Mary, not able to stop because of the need to get back to Willenhall to prepare Dan's dinner. He was much better when he came home, and in a better mood but concerned about the extra miles that Chalky had been obliged to cover that day.

'That poor pony has the spirit of a Trojan; nothing ever beats him. I'll stay here tomorrow so he only has to go there and back once. How's Mary, anyway?'

Dan was asking because the reason they had stayed in Wednesbury was to look after Mary as much as possible. Elsie tried to tell him about her fears for Mary. She too was a Trojan and they ought to appreciate her as much as she appreciated them, she told him. Dan didn't seem to agree.

'Well I don't think she's done much for us, you know. All she's done is a bit of child-minding. Still it was good of her to volunteer for that, I suppose. My cold feels much better now, so I shan't have to lose any time. The gaffer asked me what was the matter with me, this morning. He don't often bother. When I told him, he was quite encouraging, said he could do with more men like me! I hope he wasn't taking the piss.' He changed the subject. 'Have you got to go to work, tomorrow? It'd be nice for you have a day off without having to worry about rents and Auntie Mary. If you have a day off, I will.'

Elsie immediately lost her temper, rounding on him.

'Don't you come that with me, Danny Boy. You must think I'm still green! I have to go to work because we need the money. You have to go to work for the same reason. My Auntie Mary as you mockingly call her has worked for longer than you've been alive so forget using me as an excuse to knock one off. I don't suppose it'd fool your boss, anyway. He's seen it all and knows all the skiving tricks. Just you try and impress him with the way you go to work under the difficulties of a bit of a cold!'

Elsie then got on with the business of keeping house and preparing the meal for the evening. Dan was quiet throughout the meal and scarcely looked at her. He was obviously displeased with her opinion of things.

'I'm going out for a drink with the lads; perhaps I shan't be told off for doing my best!'

He slammed out of the door. This was becoming a pattern lately, she thought. Who does he think he is? I work all day, then come home and start again while he goes out and gets drunk. The day will come when I'll no longer be beholden to him and when that day comes, I'll walk out of the door, never to come back, and I don't care if Stephen comes to me or not. I'll be my own boss that day!

She angrily put Tom to bed crying and she couldn't bring herself to be sympathetic to him although she knew that the constant bickering between herself and Dan was in part the cause.

'Just you get to sleep, young man! I've got too much to do to be looking in at you all night.'

Elsie finally finished at half past nine when she got herself ready for bed. Dan hadn't arrived home at half past ten so she took herself up the stairs. She had too much to do the next day to be staying up all night!

The following morning Dan was up and ready for work before she arose. There was too much of a silent quarrel between them so she merely grunted when he waved across the room as he left. Ten minutes later she was on the roadway and was met by Ruth Mallory as she entered the court.

'I'll look after the little one today. Mary's in bed. Mister Jenkins came round. I don't know how he found out she was ill. He said to call in and see him, early.' She leaned across the trap to Tom. 'Come on, young Tom. Come with your Auntie Ruth today. Aunt Mary is too poorly to look after a big boy like you.'

Elsie helped him across to her, her feelings too numb to think properly.

'Thank you, Ruth. I shan't forget this good turn.'

She turned and trotted across the court to Mary's home. The door was open and when she got up the stairs the nurse was sitting at the side of her aunt.

'Hello, my dear; I was told you'd be coming in to see her. She's too ill to say much and I don't want to risk your health and your son's by allowing you to stay more than a minute or two. Mister Jenkins is paying me to look after her for a time, and the doctor is calling in twice a day.'

Mary looked very wan, lying almost unconscious in the bed and Elsie could see that no good would be done by staying. She turned to the nurse.

'I'm going to see Mister Jenkins. He's asked to see me so I'd better get it over with. I'll call back later, er, what's your name?'

'Marjory, Marjory Sullivan. I've been nursing about twelve years now, and she'll be properly looked after, I can assure you.'

She gave Elsie a smile that raised her hope that Aunt Mary would be fine. You never know, she thought, anything might happen. She made her way out of the court; Ruth had taken Tom into her house. Stepping up into the trap, she cracked her whip and Chalky responded immediately. In less than three minutes she was getting down again outside the offices of her employer.

Luke was waiting for her and he ushered her into Mister Jenkins' office as soon as she entered. Mister Jenkins was waiting for her and waved her to a seat opposite him. She wondered if she had done something wrong.

'Sit down, my dear. No, you haven't done anything wrong; quite to the contrary, everything you do is as perfect as it can get. You've heard about Mary Bowyer's illness I suppose?' Mister Jenkins didn't know that she had just come from there but he saw the look of dismay on her face and he placed his hand over her hand to comfort her as he continued. 'No, the worst hasn't yet happened. I saw her doctor this morning though and from what he says, it is most likely that Mary will have passed on before the end of the day.' Elsie felt suddenly weak and he guided her to a closer seat and called for a cup of tea. 'She's not really recovered from the pneumonia that she had a couple of months ago, and this is really going to be too much for her. She's always been a tough old stick, as they say, and we expected her to last forever. You know as well as anyone that that doesn't happen. If you want to take the rest of the day off, I will understand.'

Elsie could barely recall what she did in the next half hour. She remembered leaving Chalky to stand outside the office and running up the street to the court. She made her way up the stairs again. Marjory, the Nurse, was expecting her it seemed, and waved her in to see Mary who was lying, breathing shallowly. As Elsie entered the darkened room, Mary's breath, as she breathed out, seemed to be taking minutes before she started inhaling again. Mary felt that she was only partly conscious and wondered if the doctor had given her laudanum to ease her pain and to ease her into the next world. She felt like protesting but knew that whatever had been done had been done out of love and kindness.

Elsie sat down at the side of Mary and tried to compose herself. She knew instinctively that the end was not far away; Mary's eyes seemed to flicker open occasionally and then close for two or three minutes. Elsie felt that she wanted to hurry the process but couldn't face the loss that the end would bring. She watched in a sort of anticipation for each shallow breath to begin. She felt a hand on her shoulder; it was Marjory.

'A cup of tea for you; it'll help you to relax. It's not easy on the loved ones. In a way it's easier for Mary than it is for you. She hardly knows anything about it, but you're aware of every instant, and each breath will be imprinted on your mind for the rest of your life so try to relax if you can. The end will come shortly, I can see.'

Elsie took the tea almost mechanically and took a sip. It was obvious that there was some sort of alcohol in it. As she put the cup down, Mary leaned forward slightly and the breath she was taking just stopped; her eyes became glazed, her life obviously gone. Marjory reached and took the cup from Elsie, her hand a steadying influence for the duration of the never-ending seconds when Mary's spirit passed on.

Suddenly Elsie found herself keening a low wail that seemed to express the loss she was feeling. She turned and found herself in Marjory's arms, both of them expressing, in their own way, their loss. They stayed that way for a few minutes and then Elsie felt the nurse withdrawing from her, needing to be doing the practical things that she had to do for Mary. The moment had passed.

She sat looking on as Marjory lovingly prepared Mary's body for her final journey, and then nodding to her, left the house to bring Tom to pay his last respects to the woman he had loved as a grandmother. Ruth was expecting her, having heard her cries of distress across the court.

'Come and see Granny Bowyer, Tom. She'd like you to have seen her before she goes to Heaven.'

Elsie took him by the hand and led him across the court. The neighbours, rough Black Country folk, were standing outside their own front doors around the court in silent respect. She could hear one or two strangled sobs as she passed.

The next few minutes passed and she could never remember them. Marjory seemed to take charge of everything. How would she cope with the loss of the person who had played such an important part in her life?

This seemed to her to be the last loss she could accept this year. Everything seemed to have changed. The loss of Mary, her staff when she needed one, was too painful to accept; she had to get on with her work. This too, was part of life, she thought. This was part of the living life with greater participation that she had decided she wanted. How would she manage without Mary's wisdom?

Chapter 27

Gains
1912

Mrs Elsie Barr, as her husband called her in public, knocked on the door of Mister Jenkins's office. She had taken a day off from work for the funeral. She was glad it was all over. There had been a wake at the King's Head on the corner of Union Street and Upper High Street and it had seemed that half the business people in Wednesbury had attended.

Elsie had been called for again by Luke simply telling her that Mister Jenkins wanted to see her. She heard him shuffling his papers, as she had heard him do many a time, before calling a client in, to give them his advice. She knew that he had handled Mary Bowyer's affairs for years and that she was likely to be included in the list of beneficiaries. She wondered what she was going to be given. She also knew from talking to Mary that she had had the intention of leaving something to Dan, 'to stop him enquiring into what she had received', she had said.

'Come in.'

Jenkins had a dry voice and he was beginning to look his age although his silver- grey hair seemed to suit his height and bearing. As Elsie entered he looked up and smiled at her, putting her at ease. She moved over to the seat at the side of him, as she had grown used to doing as she became friends with him. He indicated the sheaf of papers in front of him.

'This is Mary's will, Elsie.' She looked and saw the grief

in his eyes. 'I have the duty of telling you what your part in it is. Mary had a great deal of liking for you: love is, I suppose, the more appropriate word. You knew of course that you are a beneficiary?' He waited for her nod of assent and went on. 'It is not my duty to inform you of the rest of the will and how your family might benefit from it. In other words I cannot tell you of her wishes regarding Mister Dan Barr. Nor shall I be telling him of her wishes regarding you.

'So, having got that out of the way, I have to tell you that Mrs Bowyer has left a hundred pounds to Master Thomas Barr, to be given to him on his twenty-first birthday.' He rustled and shuffled his papers again. 'There is a sum to be left to your husband, of course. He has been left a sum that he should think equalises him with you.'

Get on with it, Mister Jenkins, she thought. Why does he always go on like this? Perhaps he's frightened that the amount I've been left will be so small after all the expenses have been paid, that there'll be nothing left! There was a cough from the older man.

'Now we come to you, Mrs Barr. Mary has left her shares in our jointly owned property venture to you, and a hundred pounds in cash, to show your husband. She hoped you would continue with our venture, to our mutual success.'

Elsie sat there nonplussed. It seemed fair to her; a hundred to Tom and a hundred to her. Wait a minute; what had Mister Jenkins said about shares and continuing with a venture? She sat there, knowing that Mister Jenkins would tell her in his own time, then the elderly man said, 'The shares I spoke about are probably worth about five thousand pounds and have been used to buy up property in the area in the same way that the money you invested has been used. You are probably one of the richest women in Wednesbury now. If I can read from the will that she wrote in my presence, 'I would hope, Elsie, that you have sufficient business acumen to know that the money I have left you in the form of shares makes you quite well off.

'I have left Dan a sum to make him think he is as well off as you but he must never know how much you are really worth. If you do tell him, he will try to take it from you. It's his nature, believe me. You must keep your wealth a secret from him and everyone else, so that you can be independent of him and all men.' She meant every word of that. I know she did. Do you understand, my dear?'

Elsie sat stunned for a moment and then realised that she had a great deal of power in her hands. How would she use it? It would take a lot of thought and she would need advice from Mister Jenkins, she felt sure. A thought crossed her mind. Would Mister Jenkins give her the best advice or would he try to manipulate her to his best advantage? No, he had always guided her well and she felt he would continue to do so. He was looking at her, waiting for an answer.

'Yes, I understand, Mister Jenkins. Do you want me to tell Dan that you want to see him?'

'No, Elsie. I shall write to him, informing him that there is a bequest from Mary to him, and that he has to come here to hear the details. He must not, at any time, think that you know anything about the bequest to him. What you tell him about your bequest is your business but I certainly think you should heed Mary's advice.' Mister Jenkins was standing, leading her towards the door. 'If you have any questions about any part of the use of your shares, you only have to ask and I will advise you to the best of my ability. Good morning, my dear. I'm sure you have a lot to do today, and a lot to think about.'

Suddenly Elsie was on the outside of his office door, feeling that she had been told very little. She must think about it all. Who could she trust? She knew she could trust

Luke. He had helped her to learn about the profession she had taken up, and he knew a lot about Jenkins's business, as well. She would ask him about her bequest, after she had thought things through as far as she could on her own.

Luke Bryant was sitting in the small office, looking through the window, when she walked in. He looked hurt. That was the only way she could describe it. He had known Mary for many years and had admired her greatly, Elsie knew. It was obvious that he was feeling the loss as much as she did. He had attended the funeral but had then gone back to work.

'Hello, Luke. It's terrible, isn't it?' She saw him pull himself together, almost physically and try to smile at her. 'I know how you feel. She is such a loss, such an important person. I know she's not considered to be important, but I think she was - an important person in this town.'

Elsie felt her emotions come to the surface and suddenly she was in Luke's arms and they were crying, with their arms round each other for the first time. Suddenly she felt comfort as she had not felt comfortable for months, and she relaxed within the circle of his arms. A few minutes passed and she decided that that was enough. She could not stay like that; Mister Jenkins could walk in at any moment.

Elsie released herself and looked out of the window, her favourite viewpoint. The street looked quite busy. People had been carrying on with their usual occupations while she had been enjoying herself in Luke's arms. She turned and he was looking at her a little strangely. Perhaps he had been feeling the same, just enjoying himself. Elsie hadn't really noticed him as a man before. He had always been her mentor and advisor, never a man. She thought of him as a man now though, and saw him in a different light. He was a gain and a loss all at once.

Perhaps he wasn't a loss. Time would tell. He was

certainly a gain. He had never discussed his home life. Elsie knew he lived with his mother and never had much to do with girls; he was always too busy, he said. He was still looking sad.

On impulse she walked and pulled him to her, lowering her head onto his chest, trying to relive the moment of a moment ago but it had gone forever. The feeling she had now was not that of comforting a deprived friend but more like the caress of a lover – and it would not do!

She lifted her head to pull away but this time he resisted her attempt, lifting her face to be kissed. For a moment she continued to pull but something made her want to stay with the kiss. She pulled him to her, pressing her body against his; feeling his body against hers, feeling the mounting sense of urgency of his body as it seemed to almost penetrate hers.

This couldn't carry on! She pulled away sharply and tried to compose herself. Luke was standing, breathing deeply. There was a very different look on his face now. The look of sadness had gone. She had to take control, before he did!

'No, never again, Luke!' She snatched her body away from him. 'This must never, never happen again. It's far too disturbing and it would interfere with our lives to the extent that it would ruin us. I like you a lot but I'm married and my husband loves me. He'd kill you if he thought there was anything going on between us.'

Elsie was breathless, she knew, but the realisation that if she were not careful she would have two lovers made her take immediate effective action. What would Stephen think if he ever found out? She was not far removed from a whore! How did this balance with her wish to live her life with as much participation as possible? Luke too, was breathing heavily, but at least he was a single man, with no commitments to be faithful or unfaithful to. He was pale as he said, 'I am sorry, Elsie. I've admired you from afar for too long and now I know what it's like to admire you from close up. I'll try to forget that today happened, in deference to your wishes but I'm not sure I'll succeed!'

He smiled, turned away and buried his head in his ledgers. The episode was over.

Elsie found herself trembling. Yesterday had seemed strange, right from the funeral in the church on the hill. She had attended there many times with Aunt Mary, as she still thought of her but she had never really felt that feeling of faith that she had longed for so badly. Mary had had the same misgivings but had attended because 'she was working towards faith'. Perhaps she would do the same. She stood up and took her coat from the hook at the side of the door. There was a lot to be done.

*

She tried to vary her route each day. Today, Tom was at school in Willenhall. At least that gave her time to get to Wednesbury, get her collections done and get back to Willenhall. Before Mary's death, she had looked after Tom. Now it wasn't necessary. Chalky was waiting outside. She had mostly commercial rents to collect today. Her housing rents were picked up by herself on Friday, after the men had been paid. If she was late, the rent would be spent, and she would have to wait for the next week's collection before she could credit the amount to the ledger.

Today she would drive Chalky to the top of the street, by the High Bullen, and then walk down, collecting rents as she went. Chalky would stroll along beside her. He was a very intelligent pony and often he would be given carrots and other small treats by the shop owners as she went past.

As she walked down the long slope, people were stopping, commiserating with her, giving her sympathy for her loss. She found comfort in the respect that the local business community paid to Mary. She stopped at the local bakery and picked up a loaf and a few cakes to eat while she had a cup of tea with Ruth Mallory, a small treat that they both looked forward to. Ruth was waiting when Elsie arrived.

'You're late today, Elsie. I suppose it's been a busy day for you?'

Ruth sounded sympathetic so Elsie told her everything except about the fortune she had just come into and the 'episode' with Luke. She still couldn't bring herself to completely trust Ruth in the same way that she had trusted Mary. It was while she was comparing the people she knew that her mind went back to Betty and her problems with her father. It's about time I looked her up, she thought. She had deliberately tried to keep the woman from her mind; she had been too closely involved to keep an innocent face.

Elsie made her excuses to Ruth so she could complete her work and pay in the money by three o'clock. It was raining again. She walked Chalky as fast as was possible and was finished by four o'clock. Instead of stabling him, she set off to find Betty and was soon knocking on the door of what she hoped was her house.

'Who's there?' called Betty and Elsie was delighted to hear her voice and know she had found the right place.

'It's Elsie, Betty; Elsie Barr.'

There was a pause and then she heard footsteps along the hallway, the sliding sound of a bolt, and then Betty was in front of her. Her face was welcoming, the smile as friendly as ever but there was a slightly wary look on her face.

'Hello, Elsie. What a lovely surprise. It seems years since we saw one another, in town. You'd better come in. My father's not in. He's trying to find work; he's a lot better now since he came out of hospital.'

Elsie couldn't bring herself to pretend that she didn't know what Betty was talking about. That would have been just too hypocritical, so she just nodded as if they were discussing the weather. They walked through into the living room. It was a very large house compared to Elsie's, more than adequate for the two people who lived there. She looked through the window at the cemetery opposite and then turned to her friend.

'How are things between you and your father? I should think they must have improved.'

Betty replied quietly, 'Well, they have in one way; he no longer pesters me in the way that he did before he was attacked, but it's obvious he blames me for the injuries he suffered. He still limps with the leg, you know. I'm sure he sometimes thinks that I arranged it! I probably would have done if I'd been able to but I can tell you, Elsie, that it was nothing to do with me.' She paused for a moment. 'Have a cup of tea. I know it's not as nice as you make. I used to long for a cup of your tea. It's funny how one person makes it differently to another, even though they've followed the same instructions; do you know what I mean?' Betty didn't seem to be able to stop talking. It was as if all her conversations had been bottled and now she was taking the top off. 'Do you know, I even wondered if you had something to do with Dad's injuries?'

The young woman stopped for a moment and Elsie laughed lightly as she answered.

'Oh yes, I remember you telling me! I knew where he was likely to be! I sneaked out so that Dan wouldn't know I'd gone out and then I attacked your six-foot father and took a sledge-hammer to him, hurting him so badly he had to go to hospital. I read all about it in the paper and was frightened to death to come anywhere near, to tell the truth. There seemed to be so many police put on the case that I thought that if I merely asked how you were, I would be put in prison just for that. I've had to pluck up my courage just to come to see how you are.'

She laughed again. She sounded better now, she thought. The atmosphere seemed to lighten and they talked for about an hour.

'Well, I've got to go now, Betty. Dan'll be wondering where I am.'

Elsie stood and was just about to leave when there was the sound of the front door opening. She sat back down and tried to look as demure as she could. The door opened and Thurston walked in. He smelled of whisky and looked as if he had spent the last night drinking it. He looked at Elsie and laughed.

'Well, who's this then? A nice little bird, waiting to be plucked, I see. Perhaps it's not plucking she wants but fucking. I can't oblige you, my dear. I wouldn't be quick enough on this leg. What do you think about that then?'

Thurston flung himself on the settee and was immediately asleep. Elsie glanced at her friend. 'Will you be all right, Betty?'

Elsie was expressing the concern she felt for her.

'Yes, don't worry about him. He don't know who attacked him. As far as he's concerned it was something to do with the way he abused me! Now he thinks it might happen again, but this time his life would be forfeit, not just a little part of him! Yes, I'll be all right, Elsie. I can see it couldn't have been you. I remember thinking how brave you were when you rescued Mister Walker from that brute of a man. It must have been a once-only sort of act.'

Betty seemed to be genuinely pleased that Elsie was going but disappointed at the thought that Elsie had not been involved with her father's assault. Elsie herself was relieved that the incident was safely out of the way.

'I'm glad you weren't involved, really', Betty said. 'He's such an evil bastard, even if he is my own father! He's already told me that if he finds I had anything to do with his injuries, he'll kill me! He might not be able to rape me, now, but he can still hurt me. I dread to think what he'd do if he thought you were involved in any way.'

Elsie sighed to herself. She would have to be careful how she handled this situation.

'Well, I had nothing to do with it so there's nothing to worry about, is there? Just you concentrate on finding a home for that money you kept to yourself at the end of the picking season. I hope you didn't waste it,' she said, speaking the words with a mock-serious expression on her face. 'I've got to go now, Betty. I hope your life improves and that you find the happiness you deserve.'

Elsie leaned forward and gave her friend a kiss, and then an idea occurred to her.

'Why don't you come and have a piece of cake and a cup of tea after Evensong with us on Sunday? Dan is quite particular about that. He won't have visitors before church in case it might make us late. I'll look forward to it then.'

Betty didn't refuse. She seemed quite pleased to be invited to meet Dan again. What Elsie wanted now was to invite Luke as well so that he and Betty could size each other up. She felt a little guilty about the arrangement but managed to speak to Dan about her plan. He didn't comment but she sensed that he found the idea amusing. He had never met Luke but she had spoken of him so he was quite pleased to be entertaining a guest of a slightly higher social class.

*

Elsie thought her plan seemed a bit obvious as she stood looking out of the front window waiting for her guests on the following Sunday. She was trying to solve two problems at the same time. Would it work out? All she could do was to throw her bread on the waters and see what happened. She smiled to herself at the thought of the possibilities and then gave a sigh as she saw Betty walking down the path.

'Here she is, Dan,' she said. 'Try to make her feel at home. You managed to do that for Ruth!'

He didn't comment, just smiled at her and walked across and opened the door.

'Come in, my dear. You must be Betty, Betty Thurston. I've heard so much about you – all good of course. Here you are, come and sit on this chair. How long did it take you to get here?'

Elsie felt relieved again and very hopeful that the evening would go smoothly. If only Luke would act how he was supposed to act. Where was he?

Dan was still being attentive to Betty, offering her a cup of tea. She had never seen him so hospitable. It was as if the simple act of inviting two people to tea had turned him into a practised host. She knew he was ambitious so perhaps this event, small as it was, was providing him with the chance to behave as he saw his 'betters' act. There was a knock on the door. It was Luke in his best suit and tie. It looked as if it was going to go as she had planned.

Elsie had spoken to Luke before the weekend started and he had been quite pleased to be invited. She had explained who Betty was and the attitude of her father and he hadn't seemed worried at all. Dan was just as attentive to Luke as he had been to Betty, sitting near him so that he would be able to converse with him easily.

'Here you are, young man. We shall be able to talk about

something important now, and we won't have to listen to what the ladies are saying about us. Ha! Ha! '

The evening passed with the two men having the bulk of the conversation. There was nothing that Dan liked better than displaying his political acumen. Tonight it was Germany's turn.

'I can't stand them, to tell the truth but they certainly seem to be good at organising things, I'll give you that.'

Chapter 28

The fighter
1913

Luke was about to answer when there was a loud banging on the door. Dan stood and moved faster than Elsie had ever seen him move. He stood back from the door and reached to pull it open. Jack Thurston stood there, his anger showing in his face and eyes as he spoke.

'Where's that whoring daughter of mine? Where is she? I'm going to take a belt to her, coming to a place like this. Stand aside and let me get at her!'

Dan hardly seemed to move but raised his fist and gave such a blow to Thurston's jaw that he fell flat on his back. Dan then pulled him into a sitting position, leaning against the wall and slapped him across the face with the back of his hand. Thurston moved immediately, the slap bringing him round. He started to get to his feet but Dan kicked his feet from under him. He sat back and looked up belligerently.

Dan spoke quietly to him, 'Listen mate, I don't know or care who you are but I do know this. There are two ladies in my house, as well as another guest of mine. Nobody gets away with your kind of manners, d'you hear? No one! The words you used to describe a working man's home ain't good enough. If you don't like it, you can call the police and I'll tell them that you started trying to force your way into my home! Who are you anyway?'

Elsie suddenly realised that Dan was the only one of them who didn't know the intruder.

'Thurston. I'm Jack Thurston. That's who I am, and you're stupid if you think you can get away with assaulting me.'

Dan laughed. 'Well, I have got away with it! And you don't look as if you're going to do much about it.. You'd better shove off before you do yourself an injury.'

Dan grasped hold of Thurston and lifted him up until he was on his feet and then led him down the path, his arm up behind his back until they got to the gate, and then he gave him a mighty push. Thurston landed in a pool of dirty water, face down.

'Just one more thing, Thurston, if I hear you've been bullying this young woman again, I shan't be responsible for what happens to you. Now piss off!'

Dan turned and walked back to the house. The two women and the young man stared at Dan in amazement. Elsie hadn't known that he had the sort of ability that he had displayed that evening. Neither did she know he had heard about the attack on Thurston. He was very adept, that was for sure, and dangerous when roused. He didn't seem to have raised a sweat, just took it all in his stride. Dan closed the door and turned to Elsie. She was trembling.

'Now, perhaps you could tell me what that was all about,' said Dan, looking at her expectantly. It was obvious that he thought she knew all about the man.

Before she could answer, Betty spoke up, 'I think I might be in a better position than Elsie to give an explanation. After all, he is my father.'

Dan still looked dangerous and she was shaking. He tried to put her mind at ease. Elsie was beginning to see for the first time, how, by his behaviour, he was more attractive to women than she had thought.

'Sit down, lass, and tell me all about it then. Don't worry about him, even if he is your father. I like to know what I'm up against.'

Betty sat and gathered her thoughts and then she explained the circumstances starting with the way she had been abused by her father. As she continued with her story, explaining that her father had been attacked by an unknown assailant, she seemed to let go of the history of her life, allowing herself, for the first time, to tell all of it. Elsie already knew some of it as did Luke, but he had heard only part of it and that had been second-hand. The two men's face grew grim as they heard of the abuse and pain that Thurston had put his daughter through.

Dan stood up at the end of the tale and looked out of the window; Thurston had gone. Dan spoke his mind, 'I remember reading about this in the paper and wondering about it. If I ever get chance to cause 'im an accident I'll take it; that's for sure.' He paused for a moment and then seemed to relax. 'Let's forget it now. There's no need to let him spoil this lovely evening. I must say, I haven't enjoyed a night so much for years, even the little tussle with your father.'

They started talking again, relieved of the stress of the events they had been discussing for the earlier part of the evening. Dan came into his own when they spoke of Government Affairs, and the International Situation. He was of the opinion that they would be at war with Germany within the next year or two.

'Kaiser Bill wants to spread the size of his empire,' Dan stated. 'He's frightened to death that England and France will surround him and reduce his importance. The time'll come, I think, when there'll be a call up of Reservists and I believe we should be ready for that. I'm going to join the Territorial Army to do my bit. Everybody'll have to join eventually so it'll be best to join early, to have the fastest chance of promotion. If a war is declared, I'll transfer to a Regular Unit. I've been to see the South Staffordshire Regiment Recruiting Sergeant and he reckons I'm just the sort of man they are looking for. I could be a Sergeant myself in a few months!'

Elsie sat back. Dan was full of surprises lately. She had known for a long time that he was interested in fighting and boxing but she had never known that he had carried his interest this far. She was not the only one with secrets!

He carried on talking to Luke and Betty with enthusiasm.

'The South Staffordshire Regiment is one of the most famous regiments in the British Army. The First Battalion fought in South Africa and even the militia battalions went out there. I could do that!' He looked round the company as if he were making sure of an audience. 'If you join the Territorial Army, you can transfer to the Regulars. That gives you an even better chance to get promoted. England will be looking for men to defend her shores soon, you see if I'm not right.'

It was obvious that Dan had been making serious enquiries as he seemed to know all about it. Luke looked at him with trepidation wondering if he could be called upon to fight. If Dan was right, then a possible conflict would affect thousands of other young men. Without them, local industry could grind to a halt. There would be a demand for the skills of all of them, locksmiths and rent collectors. Women with children would be exempt of course. Tom would be safe. Would Elsie be expected to contribute to the national coffers in some way?

It might never happen, of course, Elsie thought. It might just be Dan justifying his interest in fighting. Perhaps it was his way of getting some power. Elsie didn't really care about his motives and she knew she would not try to stop him. Let him go if he wanted to, for King and Country. She would stay at home and keep things going. Suddenly, she felt freedom move inside her. Perhaps it would not happen but if it did she would live every minute of every day.

Would Stephen and Luke go? All these things were in the

future. She had no idea of how their lives would be affected. Perhaps they would all be called up in the same military unit and be killed in some mad charge, like the Light Brigade. It was a horrific thought but it could happen. The thought of Stephen being killed suddenly made her weak and she gasped and sat down.

Dan saw her and exclaimed, 'What on earth is the matter, Elsie? You look as if you've seen a ghost!'

They all turned to look at her and she explained, 'It's just the possibility of you both getting killed. It gives me the creeps. I can't stand it. It's all very well talking about glory but tell that to Thomas when he's got no food in his belly and a German in charge of food distribution!'

After listening to her words, they all sat there for a moment or two, absorbing the possibility. Dan was the first to recover.

'Don't you worry, my darling. We'll soon repulse them terrible Huns and throw them back into the sea. As for young Tom, he'll be proud of his father, in his best uniform, showing off his medals, marching down the High Street.'

He suddenly became silent as if he realised how naïve he sounded. Perhaps it wouldn't all be glory and medals! They each decided to change the subject as much as possible. Elsie spoke up,

'The Hun's not the only enemy, you know. We women have been fighting for a decent voice for years and it's about time women had a voice in the House of Commons. What makes men so special that they are the only ones who are brainy enough to speak for their constituents? Women are having to solve problems of shortages every day and are performing deeds of bravery all the time. Look at that American lady last year, flying across the English Channel. This year, Norwegian women have won the right to vote in their Government. Are English women less able?'

'Another thing,' Betty said, deciding to put her opinion

forward, 'a woman has been made a professor in London. Her name's Caroline Spurgeon. She's a professor of English Literature. Women are getting qualified all the time and will be in Government before you know it!'

Betty suddenly went red and sat back down on the seat, only belatedly noticing that she was standing in a militant pose. Dan began to laugh easing the tension of their small gathering. Luke joined in but his laughter seemed different, as if he was laughing with the women, not at them.

The women joined in too and they all seemed friendlier now, chummier than they had before. The only bitter taste was Elsie's. She knew that Dan had kept his trip to the Recruiting Centre a secret, not telling her until there had been others round to bolster his stupid male ego.

Elsie suddenly realised that they were each living their own lives, getting in their own way the bits of life that were important to them. How could she blame Dan for something that, in her own way, she was doing herself? Elsie made up her mind then that she too would get all she could out of life, whether what she did was approved of or not, starting now! She stood and spoke, 'I've got to get these crocks washed. Dan, would you like to crack a bottle or two with Luke while I'm doing it? Perhaps Betty would like a milk stout.'

Betty blushed. She knew the local saying about stout; 'a babby in every bottle'. Neither of the men showed that they had noticed and they all got on with arranging the room to their own comfort. Each had a corner or side of the table to themselves to show they were not crowding any one. Elsie speedily cleared the crockery they had used, and put it away. Dan pulled out a pack of cards and started to deal seven of them to each of the others.

'What would you like to play?' he asked Luke. 'Is Rummy all right?'

At a nod they each fanned out the cards in their hands

and placed them in order, ready to lay them down in the order to suit their strategy. The evening passed swiftly, each concentrating on the best play they could muster with the cards they held. At eleven o'clock Dan looked up.

'This'll have to be the last hand, I'm afraid. I have to be at work at eight o'clock in the morning. Thank you for the pleasure you've given us, Luke. As I said earlier, I haven't enjoyed myself so much for years.'

Luke agreed. He seemed very happy as he replied.

'I'm sure we've all enjoyed this evening, Mister Barr. The only one who didn't was Mister Thurston. He came to throw his weight about but it turned out that it was his weight that got thrown about. I'm sorry, Betty, but it did seem a bit comical after all; don't you agree?' He looked at Betty and saw that she was not offended at the comments he was making about her father. He continued, 'I think I'm going to take Betty home and make sure she comes to no harm. I couldn't possibly let her walk home in this darkness.' He turned to Dan. 'Thank you for a really enjoyable evening, Mister Barr. I shan't forget it. Goodnight, Mrs Barr. I may see you in the morning.' He turned again. 'Come along, Betty. You'll be safe with me!'

Betty waved her hand at Elsie as she was led out of the house and Elsie tried to wave back. It was out of her control now. Whatever happened; happened! She stood with Dan and watched them disappear down the path into the darkness. She still had things to do. What a year this had been; a year of losses and gains, and it hadn't ended yet. She was going to lose Dan shortly, maybe forever. She ought to show her gratitude, she thought, for all he had done for her. He was more prosperous now. The money from Aunt Mary had made him that way. She had managed to stop him from drinking it all and it had grown. She too had accumulated wealth, although Dan knew nothing of it.

Elsie now owned the freehold on five business properties and a number of residential properties for which she now had the right to ask for the weekly rents, some of which she collected and some of which were collected by Luke. He had never tried to repeat the 'episode' as she called the incident in the office. It was just as well. She had enjoyed it too much to try and stop him, although he didn't know it.

Elsie hadn't seen Stephen for some time. He was probably busy trying to keep up with the orders they were getting from the Government. Stones was one of the lucky firms. A lot of men were suffering from unemployment. Perhaps it would change when the country geared itself up to a war arrangement. Most of the young men would be in the Forces then, and they would need the women to fill the spaces and gaps, and there would be plenty of them.

Elsie felt Dan's arm around her shoulders in the chill doorway. Would there be a similar situation in Germany. She had no quarrel with young German women as they were trying to cope, in the same way that the English were. Who had a quarrel?

It must be the Governments. They fell out with each other and sent their subjects to sort it out while they rode around on their horses. The thought struck her; would Chalky be requisitioned by the Army? The thought left her feeling a dread threat from somewhere, as if it was the Government who was the enemy, not Germany. She hadn't better let Dan, or anyone else, know how she felt.

Who was going to plough the fields and pick the hops while the men were away? It would be the schoolboys and girls and the old men and women – and the young women! She was feeling quite morose now with all this wondering. She moved into the house and pushed the door to. There was too much of a chill in the air tonight.

Elsie knew she would never forgive Thurston and would

do anything she could to mete out punishment to him. She had heard of men who slept with their daughters but she had never met one.

She thought back to the relationship she had had with her father. He had been everything a father should be, loving and caring; willing to admonish when necessary but always with a sense of humour. She remembered when he had heard her swearing and the way he had told her off. He had always worked as hard as he could, to provide for her and her mother. A tear left her eye and trickled down her cheek.

'Come on, love. I know it's a shame for the girl but you can't solve everybody's problems for them. You know that.'

It was Dan, doing his best to comfort her as usual. He reached up and slid the bolts across the door and she wondered what thoughts and feelings had made him do that. Perhaps it was Jack Thurston, the dirty bastard. She felt a rush of affection for him and turned, offering herself to him. Somehow she felt he knew that he wasn't the love of her life but he was grateful for what she gave him.

'Come on; it's time we were in bed.'

There was something cheerful about the way she said it. He would be lucky tonight!

Elsie was up early the next morning. She wanted to see Dan off to work before she got busy with her chores. She had a lot to do today. There was a family in arrears to be counselled, for the last time, before she had to put them out. She always remembered how she had managed to save Ruth Mallory and her family from eviction. Perhaps she could do it again.

As soon as Dan had gone, Elsie set about her washing. She could afford a woman to do it for her now, but she thought it best to do it herself. Dan would complain about her expenditure and want to know how she could afford it, and she didn't want to tell him.

Chalky was ready for a day out. He loved their days in Wednesbury together. Elsie often wondered if he had a particular mare there, as a special friend. As soon as she had seen the non-paying tenant and given her the benefit of her advice, she started collecting her rents in the middle of the town.

As she walked down Upper High Street, she could see that there was some sort of meeting going on. It was not market day so she carried on working her way down towards the small crowd who were gathered there. She went into the butcher's shop to collect her rent.

'Good morning, butcher,' she said. 'What's all the fuss about? We haven't had a decent circus for some time now.'

Elsie laughed at her own little joke but the butcher didn't. He seemed quite serious.

'It's not a circus, Mrs Barr. They're recruiting for men, for the Staffies. They were here last week as well. Quite a few of our young men have joined either the Territorial branch or the Regulars. If we go to war it'll be useful, I suppose, but the trouble is that these young men only think of whom they will be killing. They don't think that the enemy are thinking in exactly the same way, and they're all looking for glory and the name of a hero! It's a shame, it is.'

The look the butcher had on his face told her eloquently how he was feeling and she wondered if he had lost a son already. She thanked him for the rent and left the shop feeling sad about the whole day. As she walked along, she could see the smart uniforms of the Staffordshire Regiment. They were very impressive, she thought. The sound of the drums made her look up. Dan was standing in front of the platform! Ruth Mallory was standing next to him, not close enough to be linking his arm exactly, but close enough. It was obvious that they were together.

Dan marched to the end of the platform and walked up

the steps onto it. The crowd cheered and they acknowledged him as a local hero. He bent and signed something and the Recruiting Sergeant ceremoniously placed a shilling in his hand. A small queue formed at the foot of the steps and slowly they moved up, accepting the King's shilling when they got to the top.

Elsie moved forward, her loss becoming deeply apparent to her. Her husband was deserting her! She heard herself scream and Dan's head came up. .Suddenly she found herself on the ground, looking up into his eyes again. She had been unconscious; she didn't know for how long. She knew now that she had lost him twice; once to the Army and again to Ruth, her friend. Why had she fainted? She knew she didn't faint for nothing, like a Victorian heroine.

The thought came to her, I must be pregnant! It was so obvious, really. If she was, it was Dan's this time. It would be a half brother or sister to Tom. Dan must never know! Maybe it would be a girl! She could see a face behind Dan. It was Ruth. Elsie didn't want to see her or anyone else now. They could all go away as far she was concerned!

Chapter 29

Confessions
1914

An hour later, they were home, in Willenhall. Elsie was sitting in her favourite chair with a cup of tea close by. She could see that Dan was trying in his own way to make up for things. What exactly was her situation? She felt as if she might be pregnant so she probably was. She wasn't one of those who imagined pregnancies. If so, it was Dan's, a fact that filled her with no joy at all.

Elsie needed time on her own to work things out. How did Ruth feel now? The woman must be suffering, she knew. Serves her right! She picked her cup of tea up and went to sip it. Then she changed her mind and threw it at Dan, but not very hard and it missed him. His reflexes were far superior to hers.

Dan picked the cup up and spoke.

'Would you like another cup of tea, Elsie?' He looked at her in his own quiet way, not taking offence by the cup being thrown at him. 'I'm sorry, love. I know I'm not perfect and she was – available.' It was obvious that he accepted that she had found him out. 'I know she admires you greatly and she loves Jack and her kids. I don't know how these things happen, do you?'

Dan's tacit admission of guilt coupled with his question surprisingly filled her with admiration. Hadn't she been in the same situation with his gaffer? How would she expect him to react if he found out about Stephen – and Tom? She knew he wouldn't regard her with admiration; it would be an affront to his male ego. She replied to his remarks with a little bitterness in her tone.

'What about you, Dan? Do you love me? You're rich now. You've probably got enough money to buy a dozen houses and yet that's not good enough for you. You still want more of everything.'

Elsie felt she had the superior argument as he answered, 'I know you're right, Elsie. I know you are. The trouble is, sometimes we don't see much of each other and I happen to see Ruth, and Jack works all the hours that God sends. I suppose I should respect him for it but I see it as a weakness in him, not looking after his wife. You wouldn't even leave Chalky alone, would you? You'd at least make sure he didn't get pinched!'

Yes, thought Elsie. You're leaving me on my own, while I get on with earning enough for us to live on and looking after my son. She smiled at him.

'What are you going to do now then, Dan Barr? Are you going to look after us better than a horse, or are you going to spend your time with the one woman who I thought would never betray me?'

That was a question he could not answer, she knew. Whatever he said was going to be the wrong thing to say. His answer didn't shock her but it was a surprise, nevertheless.

'I'm glad you asked me that question, Elsie. The only thing I can think of to do is to join the Army! You know I was thinking about it; I told you I was. I think I shall have to go eventually, the same as thousands of others. The way I see it is if I join up now I may have the chance to get promoted.

'I'll send you an allotment out of my pay, every week. I'll come home to you and our son every chance I get. There, I've said it now. I'm going to go. I can't help it. I've got to do it! I'll be doing my duty. That's what every Englishman should be doing at this time. I suppose if I were honest, I would admit that it would give us both time to get over the shock of – this!'

Elsie sat there and considered what he was saying. She would miss him for his security, even though she was wealthier than him. The kind of security he gave her was a physical one, like when he had taken Jack Thurston on and defeated him easily. She also felt like making love to him whenever he felt like making love to her. It wasn't exactly love but it filled a need.

She would miss him but his place would be taken in part by Stephen when the opportunity arose. She would almost certainly feel that she was betraying Dan but she would live with it. Now she wanted all the details of his leaving. She wanted to know everything that could be known.

'Well, when are you going then? Where do you have to report to? When do I get my allotment? I suppose you'll be going with enough money for your own needs! I suppose you think I'll earn enough money to keep your children!'

Dan suddenly cocked his head up. He had suddenly realised what she had said.

'What do you mean, my children? What do you mean, Elsie?'

She answered instantly.

'You know what I mean, Dan Barr! Your children! That's what I mean. You've put a bun in the oven again! I don't know how far gone I am but I'm certainly gone, that's for sure.'

The soldier in him retreated and the lover advanced. He crept to her side like a mischief-making pup, awaiting her forgiveness and she almost burst into laughter at the sight of his pathetic face trying to get approval for something – anything.

313

'Oh, Elsie, why didn't you tell me before?'

'Why? I'll tell you why! Because I only found out myself when I saw you with your fancy piece! I could see you'd betrayed me and you were likely to betray me again. I knew when I came round after that stupid faint I had. I'm not the sort to faint for nothing, am I? I've told you as soon as I could! That's your question answered straightaway now. When will you answer mine?'

Elsie's knew she was looking quite aggressive but she didn't feel like that. She felt like being a woman and having somebody take matters out of her hands to arrange things in a nice, neat way, so that everything was organised.

Elsie sat and started crying, her body heaving with the emotions she was feeling. How could he do this to her? She suddenly thought of Stephen and how he would react to this situation, and she started to smile to herself. That was exactly what he would do, the silly ass! He wasn't silly, though; he was very bright. He would soon put things in perspective for her. She felt a sudden need to see him. She would see him tomorrow, but first things first.

'When are you reporting for duty then?' Elsie shot her words out like bullets. Appropriate, she thought. 'Have you made arrangements to cover your responsibilities then? Have you spent your King's shilling then? Are you going to tell Jack Mallory that you've been bedding his wife? Are any of her kids yours?'

She felt like crying again, and then like laughing. Dan looked upset; he had been found out, the bastard.

'I'm reporting the day after tomorrow. I'll make all the arrangements for you that I can. I'm sorry things have turned out like this. I love you so much.' He turned as he was about to go out of the door. 'I do love you, you know. I hope you can find a way to forgive me. You can have the bed. I'll sleep on the settee.'

Dan strode out of the door and down the path. He would come home drunk again. She wouldn't mind getting drunk herself! She went to bed early to make sure she got enough sleep. Halfway through the night, Dan came in and she heard him treading the stairs. He got into bed and pulled her to him and she couldn't help the urge that always came over her and she clung to him as he satisfied first himself and then her. Elsie dropped off in his arms wondering what the morning would bring them.

*

There was a crowd of men at the Recruiting Office and a number of them were accompanied by their women; mothers, sisters, sweethearts or wives. Tom was excited at the prospect of his father becoming a soldier. There seemed to be a cheerful feeling about the occasion, as if they thought that those few were going to settle the coming conflict with no help from any others, as if they all regarded themselves as invincible and immortal.

When Dan went into the office, Elsie saw Ruth Mallory waiting as well. Why was she there? She walked over and spoke to her best friend.

'Hello, Ruth. Is Jack going then? I didn't see him yesterday.'

Ruth turned to her, the stress of the occasion showing in her eyes.

'Oh, Elsie, I saw you yesterday when you fainted. I know I've been found out. I just hope you never get found out! It'll never be through me, I can tell you.'

Elsie stared at her friend in consternation. How had Ruth plumbed her secret? She raised her eyebrows, trying to act the innocent but Ruth was not to be fooled.

'I saw you and Stephen Stone yesterday. It was obvious

to me. You don't have to draw me a picture, you know!' She shrugged her shoulders. 'It looks to me as if we're in the same boat. Jack's decided it's his duty to fight for the Country and his King. To me it's a load o' bullshit but there's many who're falling for it.

'Regardless of what's gone on in our families, it's the women who have to keep the next generation safe while the men go and get themselves killed and lie with the Frenchwomen when they get the chance!' She turned and faced Elsie, her eyes resolute. 'You and I can make enemies of each other or we can help each other. The choice is ours. I put my hand on my heart when I say I would sooner be your friend than your enemy. What do you say, Elsie?'

Ruth reached out her hand, her face showing the courage it took to ask the question. Elsie reached out too and the women enveloped each other, taking responsibility for the future of the two families.

When Dan came marching out of the office, he had Jack with him. They both saw the two women in each other's arms at the same time and the inscrutable look that passed between them. Then Dan came to Elsie's side and put his arm round her. He looked down at Tom and spoke.

'Well, I'm going to be a soldier now, lad. What do you think about that then, young Tom?'

Tom smiled but couldn't find the words to say what he thought. Elsie had never seen the young boy looking so serious. Elsie took hold of his hand.

'Come on, Tom. Can't you tell your Daddy what you think about him going to be a soldier? Stand up and tell him then.'

The eight year old boy looked up at both his parents and burst into tears, then he spoke up to his father.

'I don't want you to die yet, Daddy. I don't want you to die until you're an old man. I don't want you to be shot and come home with no arm so you can't file locks and keys. If you do, I'll have to file them for you!'

'Out of the mouths of babes,' said Elsie. 'I sometimes think he can see clearer than grown ups. You'll just have to be very careful and shoot better and straighter than the Germans, that's all I can say.'

Elsie's face collapsed again and she turned to Ruth and the two women wrapped their arms round each other, trying to get the most comfort they could out of the situation. The two men just stood and looked foolish. This time it was Jack who recovered first.

'You women don't understand,' he said. 'It's not all for glory and to show off, you know. If no one goes, we'll lose our Empire to foreigners. Our Empire's had to be bought at the expense of hundreds of lives. The Empire is the important thing now, not the King. The Empire is the place where we sell our goods, our locks in our case. If we let them, the Kaiser's men will take over our markets and our people will be out of work forever! We can't let 'em do that, can we? I'm just sorry I'm not going with them! I've been turned down because of flat feet. If they start conscription, I'll probably be called up but for now they just want the fittest.'

Dan looked at Jack in surprise. He'd always been such a quiet man. Now he was standing up and seemed to be taking responsibility for the whole situation. Ruth put her arm through his.

'My Jack knows what's important you know. It's just that he keeps his own counsel about things most of the time but he knows – he knows!'

Elsie was stunned. Jack Mallory had always seemed so fit. Now her husband was off without him. Jack really looked as if he meant every word he said, too. The others stood, taking in his opinion. It was true that regardless of what actually started the series of events, trade was going to take an important part in it.

Dan said, 'I think we'd better get home, don't you, love? I don't suppose I'll need a lot of clothes after tomorrow. I'll be getting a new suit. I still have a lot of things I want to do before then.' On impulse he bent and kissed Ruth then turned to Jack. 'I'll see you in the morning then, Jack. I hope you'll come and see us off.'

Everyone seems to be changing and looking at things in a new way, Elsie thought. It looks as if all our little secrets are all for nothing compared with the big things that are going on in the world. She looked down. Even little Tom seemed to have an opinion of his own that was as good as anyone else's. She pulled at his hand to let him know that she hadn't forgotten him.

'Come on, Tom. Chalky will be waiting for us at the livery. Let's give him a bit of a run, eh?'

That must have been the right thing to say, she thought, as the little lad sped off in front, along Union Street. Chalky heard him as he approached, and whinnied. The boy and the horse had built up a relationship that was like a friendship. She turned and smiled at Dan.

'If only the world was as clever as our son, making friends everywhere. Just you make sure you come back. That's the most important thing of all. It's all for nothing if you don't, regardless of all the fancy language.'

Elsie linked his arm, pulling it towards her breast. She knew that a little move like that was an aphrodisiac to him. Dan pulled her closer in response, and they climbed aboard the little trap to begin their journey.

Elsie shouted, 'Come on, Chalky! Let's be having you! We need to get home before dark!'

The rest of the day was spent in enjoying each other's company. When would they have the opportunity again?

Chapter 30

Off they go!
1914

It was August 1914, and the clouds of steam were rising from the funnels at the station. The pressures inside Europe were rising too. Tom, eight years old, was watching the parade; his eyes wide open in observation. His father was in the parade, a Sergeant with three stripes on his arm, in contrast with the plain khaki uniform that the other soldiers wore. Dan had told Tom that the Sergeants ran the Army; they were more important, he had said, than the Lieutenants who had just been commissioned. Without the Sergeants, the Army would come to a standstill.

There was a hoot from the engine and another cloud rose from the funnel. Elsie looked around, taking it all in. The soldiers were all volunteers. They were off to do some training before going to France to beat the Huns. Dan did look smart. He was standing in front of a squad of privates who were standing to attention. She could hear him giving orders in his Black Country voice, then the last order he would have to give for some time.

'Squad, faaall out!'

The men turned and stamped their feet, and then looked around for their loved ones; their wives, mothers, mistresses and sisters. Dan knew where she was. He had seen her out of the corner of his eye. He tucked his baton under his arm and marched to them. She smiled and looked up at him as did Tom.

'A well-turned out parade, Sergeant!' Elsie was trying to sound as light-hearted as she could to avoid the tears that were on the brink of pouring down her cheek. She continued in a light-hearted voice. 'You look very smart yourself, Sergeant Barr.'

'Yes, my dear.' Dan was being formal now, as befitted his rank. 'A well-turned out squad, as you say.'

What a foolish lot they are, she thought, all willing to die for King and Country. The time will come when they will all see through the sham of seeing one country as being superior to another. The whole of Europe was caught up in the myth. She turned to Dan again.

'What's going to happen now? Are you all going to travel to France as quickly as possible so you can all get your share of the glory?'

Dan looked at her in a bleak way that showed that he was unwilling to compromise his views.

'You know what I think about such opinions, Elsie. They are defeatist and as such should be shut up! I rely on you as the Regiment relies on all its wives, to uphold the cause by loyalty.'

'Well it's only a few days since you were a locksmith, Dan Barr,' Elsie replied, 'and you were upholding the traditions and loyalties of your trade. You seemed to be willing to trade in your loyalty to your wife for another woman! Ever since you put Jack Thurston on his back, you've been willing to show off by using your bullying methods. You even used them by taking me last night. I hope you were satisfied.'

A smile crept across her husband's face. It was obvious that she had said the right thing.

'Yes, as a matter of fact I was – completely satisfied. Now you know what you've got to look forward to!'

Elsie looked at him disgustedly. She could not now

imagine herself wanting this man. He was not the father of her eldest son she knew, but did he? For Tom's sake she had had to continue the invention. Dan was not really a sexy sort of person, she mused. He was more interested in power. How had he lost his attraction since last night?

A Corporal was standing at the edge of the little group. He was trying to attract Dan's attention. Elsie took Dan's arm and indicated the Corporal, pointedly. He was instantly alert.

'Yes, what is it, Bradley? Can't you see I'm trying to say goodbye to my wife?'

'Yes, sorry Sergeant. Major Horrocks has asked me to remind you that the train leaves in five minutes and he wants the two platoons to be aboard before then. Shall I start to get them aboard, now, Sergeant?'

Elsie smiled to herself. Dan had obviously frightened all the self-assurance out of the young man.

'Of course get them aboard. Do you have to be told everything? God All Mighty, move yourself, man!'

All the young man had needed to do was to tell Dan that he was loading the men and that would have done the trick, Elsie thought, as the Corporal went scampering away like a young terrier. Dan turned back to Elsie.

'Well, I'm going now, Elsie, to make sure everything goes smoothly. Horrocks likes everything to move along, even if he has to delegate most of it. I'll write to you as soon as I can. Goodbye, young Tom!'

He reached and put his arms around Elsie and for a second she felt the rush that always accompanied the action. He kissed her and crushed her against him then held her away, looking past her eyes. She wondered if it was to impress the soldiers standing on the platform. A lot of them were on their own, just standing, not even talking to their comrades. It was probably the first time they had been away from home and they were ignorant of the way to behave. The whistle blew again and the conductors started to wave their flags. Dan moved away from her, now looking into her eyes.

'I love you, Elsie,' he said, speaking more loudly now, as he moved further away. 'I'll be thinking of you.'

He turned and mounted the first step. The train gave what sounded like a huge sigh, as if letting go of a great emotion, then moved forward an inch or two. There was another sigh and the wheels seemed to skid for a second, then the whole train started to move. Elsie felt a tear in her eye for all the young men who might never return.

Dan moved inside the corridor quickly; he had been showing off, but to whom? Elsie looked round at the young women clustering closely as the train gradually picked up speed. He waved out of the window but she was not at all sure to whom he was waving. As the train disappeared round the broad bend in the track, Elsie had a last look round and saw Ruth. She hadn't seen her since yesterday. Ruth made as if to walk out without acknowledging Elsie but she was forestalled as Elsie almost jumped in front of her.

'Hello, Ruth. I didn't know you were seeing anyone off today?'

There was a tear in the corner of Ruth's eye, as if she had just seen her husband off, and she hadn't, because he was still at work, working for Fred Stone. Fred was just about ready to retire but he felt that he should keep going as long as he could to help the war effort. Jack Mallory was running the place now. He wouldn't be called up due to his foot trouble. He had been graded quite low when he had tried to volunteer. Ruth tried to think of something to tell Elsie who smiled as if to make out that there was nothing to cry about.

'It was all the young men, Elsie.' Ruth spoke quietly. 'We

might never see any of them again. I'm sorry, I know your husband's gone but it's not just him that's gone. It was a hundred of them, today, an' it'll be another hundred tomorrow.'

Ruth looked into Elsie's eyes and couldn't pull her own away. There was just something about Elsie. The woman seemed to be able to see what you were thinking. Elsie had been her best friend and she had repaid her by having an affair with her husband!

The sadness in Ruth's eyes made her feelings quite transparent to Elsie but she hesitated to accuse her friend. She waited and finally Ruth broke down in tears. Her face seemed to melt and collapse under the strain of the feelings she had held back for so long.

'I knew you knew, when Dan hurt his foot. He looked at me an' I felt as if he was the most wonderful, powerful man on earth. I love Jack and I always will but there is something about Dan – Mister Barr that just turns me into jelly. I can't expect you to understand. I owe you so much and I know the way I feel is wrong but I can't help it.'

Ruth stopped, crying, and Elsie seemed to stand and just observe her, trying to see the similarity between Ruth's feelings for Dan, and her own feelings for Stephen Stone. How should she handle the situation? The last thing she wanted to do was to confess her own feelings. That would put power into Ruth's hands. She decided what to do. She put her arms round Ruth and pulled her close.

'I know just how you feel, Ruth, and I shan't tell Jack. I know you can't help it. We women are weak in some ways and we have to live with it. You and I've always been friends and this isn't going to change that. I can't forget how you and Jack helped Dan when he hurt his ankle. Come on, let's go and have a cup of tea somewhere.'

Ruth took Elsie's arm and they wended their way

between the other women who had seen their men off. They had more in common than Ruth suspected, thought Elsie. She now had to face the problems of surviving without Dan's wage each week. She knew she could do it because the house was paid for; it was her own house! Her transport was paid for; Chalky was hers and didn't cost much to run. She just had to find the time to keep the house clean and tidy and to run her small business.

The main problem was Tom. He was growing quickly now and had taken a keen interest in the soldiers. He had to be educated somehow. He was doing all right at school but there was a gap between the time she finished work and the time Tom came out of school at the end of the day. Still, hundreds of mothers had the same problem; she would find a way. One thing, she mused, she might get a chance to see Stephen more often! What was he going to do about the war?

The two women found their way into the ladies waiting room and Elsie managed to get tea for them both. She placed them carefully on the table in front of them. Now was the time to make the best of her time – and Ruth could help her.

'Listen, Ruth, I've got a pair of problems and you might just be able to help me with them. You'd get paid of course. Are you interested?'

This was just the beginning, she knew. Ruth would want to know what she was expected to do. She was looking at her as if she had just been saved from drowning.

'Well of course I'll do anything I can to help you, Elsie, but what is it you'd expect me to do? You are a one, Elsie, always playing your cards next to your chest.'

Ruth was looking expectantly at Elsie. Elsie for her part was more interested in looking at Ruth to try to gauge her response to her suggestions.

'Well, I'm going to try to do some war work and I'll need someone to look after Tom for me, while I do.' She waved her hand to let Ruth know she hadn't finished laying the job on the line. 'He has to be taken to school each day; the house has to be kept tidy and clean and there's shopping to be done. I don't know if I'll be allowed to keep Chalky. They'll need all the horses they can get, for the war, so I'll move back into Wednesbury, into my old house if it becomes vacant, so we might become neighbours again. If so, I may let the house in Willenhall to bring a few coppers in. That'll give me enough to pay my way.'

'Blimey Elsie, that's a lot of things to tell, all at once! I don't know how you keep it all in your head. How much of that do you want me to handle? I do have kids o' my own, you know – an' a husband to look after.'

Ruth stopped, realising that she could put her foot in it and Elsie smiled to herself. Ruth had managed to do quite a lot before Dan had gone away but she didn't feel inclined to point it out to her. Ruth obviously knew that that was a course not to be followed. Elsie was beginning to realise that she was more mature and sensible than a lot of people around her, even if it did lead her into some strange situations. She continued explaining her plans to her neighbour.

'Well, I've still got a lot to do, today. I can't let Tom come out of school and find me out of the house. I'll come over to see you later in the week, Ruth, with some ideas. If you agree to them, we can go ahead as soon as you like.'

Elsie stood up and nodding at Ruth, just turned and walked out of the waiting room. She still had to collect as many rents in as she could. The sooner she started the better. She had a secret world that she had created for herself, that had to be coped with. It was too soon to be expecting Stephen but she wanted him as soon as it was possible. He'd take advantage of Dan's absence to see her, she knew. It was just a question of when.

Dan had taken her, last night, roughly as usual. That was his way. Perhaps that was why Ruth loved him. Loved? She hadn't really thought about it that deeply. Perhaps Ruth felt the same emotions for Dan that she herself felt for Stephen. Dan wasn't sensitive; he just wanted to scatter his seed around before he marched off to glory. Perhaps Ruth had been given a little of his seed, too. What would happen if she showed the same attitude, picking up seed from here and there? The thought made her think of Stephen again. It seemed to have been a long time! On impulse she strode out of the station and climbed up onto the trap.

'Come on, Chalky, let's get it done.'

The pony was chewing a carrot. Elsie smiled, people often left him something. The cob started off as if he was glad to be travelling. Standing still for long periods didn't suit him, she'd noticed. She looked down and on the floor of the trap; there was a small posy of flowers. It had to be from Stephen, a carrot for the pony and flowers for her! She looked around but there was no sign of him. He'd probably gone off on business. He wouldn't stay around a train full of troops going off to battle as it'd be embarrassing for him. He'd be back, though; she knew that.

Suddenly the sadness of saying goodbye to Dan was submerged beneath the knowledge that the future could hold possibilities for her. Perhaps Dan wouldn't be away for long – who knows – but she'd grab with both hands any chance of happiness that presented itself.

Elsie looked up and saw that she was close to Fred Stone's smithy. Stephen was standing outside. He caught her eye and a beaming smile crept across his face as he lifted his hat to her.

'Good morning, madam. It's a lovely day for it, whatever you've got to do. Can I help you down?'

With all the dignity she could muster she climbed down

and moved into the doorway of the smithy and into the arms of the only man she had ever really loved. There would be difficulties ahead but for now, now was all the time she needed and wanted. In a few weeks, her condition would become obvious. What would Ruth and the men think about that? Ruth would probably think it was Dan's child inside, and she was right! That'd give her something to think about!

Elsie felt that she was entering a period when her life would open up for her now that she was free from Dan's bullying manner, and closing as her second child grew inside her to give fresh responsibilities. She meant to participate fully in life, making it as exciting as possible while Dan was away

Ruth Mallory walked out of the station and began the long walk home. Elsie had left her to find her own way home. That was unusual. She felt that normally Elsie would have offered her a ride in the trap. As she passed the smithy at the top the High Bullen, she glanced that way hoping that she might get a glimpse of Jack. Dan might have gone away but she still had her husband, and he was a good one now his drinking had been curtailed.

There was Chalky outside the smithy; what was Elsie doing there? She stood and watched for a few minutes and then saw Stephen Stone come through the door. In a moment of intuition she guessed why Elsie was there. Swiftly she walked down the street, wondering how she could use this bit of information. The smart little madam wasn't as clever as she thought! This could change her life for the better. Perhaps Elsie Barr wouldn't have life all her own way!

*

Dan Barr sat back in the carriage and sucked on the cigarette that the young recruit had offered him. Dan had been sad to see the women disappearing into the distance as the train with its shipment of young men had departed from the station. It had caught at him for a moment but they were gone now. He was leaving into an unsure future, in charge of a platoon of ignorant young men who would rely on him to save their miserable lives for them. He was in charge. He was in charge! If he played his cards right and he could get that stupid Sergeant Major killed off early he would certainly be the obvious replacement for the position.

*

Stephen Stone stood looking as Elsie drove off, the pony looking as if he were enjoying it. Danny Barr was out of the way now and Elsie had come looking for him! The future was going to be a wonderful time. He had often regretted the necessity of marrying Mabel but she had been a good wife and they had been a good team in the way their family had prospered. That had all been due to the shrewdness of their parents. The trouble was that no woman had ever made him feel like Elsie did and it was unlikely that any ever would.

Stephen had to live with the consequences and just keep smiling. No one had ever been able to knock that out of him, and he had managed to live moderately happily, with the occasional rapturous interweaving of his life with Elsie's, as a major component. Life was looking good and the future was unfolding in ways that he had not visualised before. The war was going to be good to some people and terrible to others. He intended to make the most of life.

From now on, he and Elsie would take every day as an extra payment of happiness, whatever others thought. Life was for living and he intended that the two of them should live it to the full. The extraordinary thing was that Elsie was so unpredictable, making the next moment and the one after that a delightful surprise. He smiled, as he watched Elsie moving away up the High Street.

*

Elsie was thinking; she seemed to be doing a lot of thinking, today. She recalled her resolutions, to live life to the full, to die, if she had to but if she did, to die living; never to live dying. She'd love Stephen regardless of his circumstances, and she would raise Tom to be a good man; that was her greatest responsibility.

'Come on, Chalky. Let's get on with it!'

She picked up the reins and drove off, a Blackcountrywoman about her business.